The Thing About Clare

ALSO BY IMOGEN CLARK

Postcards from a Stranger

The Thing About Clare

IMOGEN
CLARK

Text copyright © 2018 by Imogen Clark

Published by Lake Union Publishing, Seattle

www.apub.com

Amazon, the Amazon logo, and Lake Union Publishing are trademarks of Amazon.com, Inc., or its affiliates.

ISBN-13: 9781503904965
ISBN-10: 1503904962

Cover design by Emma Rogers

Printed in the United States of America

For Tabitha, Jemima, Alexa and Seth.

ANNA – 2015

I

It was far too sunny for a funeral. It had been crazily warm all month, with the newspapers building themselves up into a frenzy. The headlines were now threatening death and disaster as water levels dropped. The fact that it had been the wettest spring since records began suddenly seemed to count for nothing.

Anna cast a furtive glance at her fellow mourners as they stood around the open grave. Everyone seemed to have faced a similar dilemma. Dark clothing appeared, by its very nature almost, to be thick. Heavy overcoats, sombre suits, dingy hats – that was what one wore to a funeral by rights, and the weather should be accommodating them by raining, or drizzling at the very least. A blazing sun did not create an appropriately morbid mood.

Anna had had to go last-minute shopping to buy a suitable outfit. That had seemed all wrong too. Shopping should be a treat, a pleasure to be savoured, not a chore. Buying clothes for a funeral took all the fun out of it. Anna had no black in her wardrobe at all. It made her look like death warmed up, her mother had told her during her brief but intense Goth phase. Once she had decided that in this matter, as in all things, her mother had been correct, she had stopped buying herself anything dark.

So, with a heavy heart, she'd wandered into town in search of a black dress. She had started in the cheap budget shops. After all, she was never going to wear this dress again unless someone else decided to shuffle off in the middle of a heatwave. As she stood amongst the tightly packed racks of badly finished garments, she could hear her mother chiding her.

'You can't be wearing something as cheap as that to a funeral, Anna. Have you no respect for the dead? They'll turn in their grave when they see those hems, and the yoke is set all wrong. Put it back.'

So she had, and headed up the High Street to where the clothing, although no doubt still produced in the same unsavoury sweatshops, spoke quietly of class. There wasn't much choice. The dresses all seemed to be floaty and bohemian, in zingy oranges and reds, or Mother-of-the-Bride-fitted in muted pastels. Anna thought about suggesting that the funeral go with a bright-colours theme but such new-fangled ideas had no place amongst the older generation and especially not those from traditional, rural Ireland.

Anna tugged at the pleats of the shirtwaister that she had eventually found stuffed at the back of a rail behind the shoes. It didn't really fit her and kept riding up at the hip but needs must. She had briefly considered leaving the label on its plastic string hanging itchily down her back all day and then returning it to the shop after the funeral. Her mother's loud internal tutting had put paid to that and it was with reluctance that she had wrenched the tag from the dress. This, to add insult to injury, had made a tiny little hole in the fabric, which, though small, would be impossible to repair and would grow like a cancer throughout the day until the dress was no longer fit for purpose. Perhaps it was a punishment for being so mean-spirited?

The other mourners seemed to have made a better stab at looking funereal in the heat. It was easy for the men. Everyone had a dark suit, and if it was more woolly than the weather necessitated, one could always take one's jacket off at the wake. The priest looked a bit hot.

Anna wondered whether he had summer-weight robes. Maybe they wore the same summer and winter but had more layers on when the weather got a bit chilly? Had she ever noticed priests looking more rotund in the cooler months? It must cost a fortune in dry-cleaning bills, being a member of the clergy. Could you claim for robe-cleaning as expenses? Did priests even get expenses or was it all just part of the cost of worshipping the Lord? Anna almost giggled but she caught herself. That would never do, laughing at a funeral. She would be struck down there and then and topple headlong into the grave, hideous black dress and all.

'We now commend the soul of our dearly departed sister Dorothy to the ground,' said the priest. The pall-bearers began lowering the coffin slowly into the hole. The sides had been cut sharply, and Anna could see the patterns made by the various strata of soil: grey at the top but then meandering through oranges and browns, a bright-yellow stripe of clay halfway down. She tried to identify each layer, to calculate how long they had lain there just out of sight. Mr Monkhouse, her erstwhile geography teacher, would be proud of her. At least it would be cool down there in the hole. A droplet of sweat trickled down her upper back before being absorbed by the tight binding of her bra, also black but with more of a chance of further use.

They had reached the part when the chief mourners throw soil down on to the coffin. The stars of the funeral show had tossed what was really just dust as there had been no rain to reconstitute it for weeks. Anna watched as one by one the family members grabbed at a handful of earth and then dropped it into the hole on to the shiny brass plate. The soil seemed almost to float down, containing no water to give it solid form, and it landed gently on the coffin top with a little patter, like tiny raindrops at the beginning of a storm. Sebastian, youngest child and only son of the deceased, went to wipe his dusty hand down his trousers and then thought better of it. Perhaps he could also hear the ever-present voice of his mother in his ear, even at her graveside.

Anna noticed that he was crying, not with the emotional heaviness of the others but small, unselfconscious tears that just trickled down his cheeks. He made no effort to wipe them away. Maybe tears would soon be the only form of moisture on the earth, Anna thought. Each tear would become so precious that it would have to be captured and then desalinated. The world would have to become inconceivably sad in order to generate enough tears. Fines would be imposed for laughing, unless it was so hard that precious tears were induced. Only extremes of emotion would be acceptable. There would be no mediocre middle ground, no room for merely feeling fine. How would the tears be saved, Anna wondered? They would surely evaporate if you caught them one at a time. There would need to be an awful lot of crying.

There were plenty of tears here now, if anyone was looking for some free moisture. Anna seemed to be surrounded by shaking shoulders and sniffing noses. Grief, it seemed, was contagious. Somewhere someone was wailing. Not here, surely? Dorothy Bliss had been old, and at the end of a highly satisfactory life. Sad, maybe, but not enough to induce something as soul-shattering as a wail. Anna and a couple of the other less grief-stricken mourners looked up to trace the sound. It was coming from another party over in a different part of the cemetery. Was that right? Two funerals at once? One would have thought that whoever took the bookings would ensure that there was only ever one group mourning at a time, to avoid confusion if nothing else. It would never do to grieve at the wrong graveside. Perhaps there'd been so many deaths in this heat that it wasn't feasible to space the funerals out? Maybe the doom-and-gloom merchants of the national press were right after all. People must be dropping like flies.

As the second, impostor, coffin made its slow procession along the gravel path to its final resting place, Anna saw the gaudy flowers arranged skilfully into letters and balanced on the tiny lid. 'Benny'. A child? That would probably explain the wailing. Was the death of a child, with so much ahead of them, so much sadder that wailing was permissible, whereas at her own little gathering it would be thought of as over the top? How many dead old people were the equivalent of one dead child?

Anna pulled her attention back to her funeral, so to speak. It was working, all this random distracting thought. She was still holding it together. There'd been no weeping and wailing from her. Barely any tears, to be fair. She needed to hold fast, for if she lost control of her emotions she was not sure how she might pull herself back. Not long to go now. The priest was wrapping up with prayers and what have you. Not before time. The sun was punishingly hot, hurling its heat at anyone unfortunate enough not to be hiding in the shade. Some of the older mourners looked as if they might keel over at any moment. The priest seemed to be praying faster. Was he needed at the other funeral? No. That had already started. It must be a two-hander. How many clergy could they rota in at any given time? Was two the maximum? More than two funerals and it would begin to feel like a party and that would never do.

The priest had finished. He lowered his arms and backed slowly from the graveside. The mourners raised their heads, looking slightly relieved. A few were blowing their noses. Anna saw a man she half-recognised draw a mobile phone from his inside pocket and check its screen. No messages. He was apparently more dispensable than he had believed. He popped the phone back into his pocket and shrugged apologetically at no one in particular.

Slowly, the common-or-garden mourners withdrew until there were just the four of them left. Nobody spoke. They just stared down into the shady hole.

'Well, that's that,' said Clare eventually. She smoothed down her tatty dress with an air of finality. 'We better get back to the cars or the rest of them will be there before us.'

'It's not like a wedding,' snapped Miriam. 'There's no need for a receiving line. We'll get there when we're good and ready. Are you okay,

Sebastian?' she asked tenderly, taking her brother's arm and giving it an awkward squeeze. Sebastian looked up. He must have wiped away the tears with a dusty hand as there was a streak of dirt running from his nose to his jaw.

'Yes,' he said quietly. 'Clare's right. We should go. There's no reason to hang around. It's not like Mum's really here. Come on.' He held out his hands to his sisters. Miriam took one in both of hers and Clare the other.

'Anna?' he said. There were no more hands left but he raised his elbow towards her anyway. Anna fell in beside Clare and, when prompted by a sharp tap on the thigh, took her sister's hand. Walking in a line, the four of them turned their backs on their mother's grave and headed off in the blistering sun towards the car.

II

By the time they got to the golf club the wake was well under way. Someone had declared the buffet open, and a snaking queue had formed. The bar was busy too.

'Do you think we should have started a tab?' asked Sebastian as he looked at their friends and relations standing three deep waiting for service.

'No,' said Clare, shaking her head like this was a disastrous idea. 'There's plenty of tea and coffee on offer. If they want something else, then they can put their hands in their pockets.'

'Seems a bit miserly. She was Irish, after all.'

'She wasn't a drinker, though, was she? And there's only Uncle Stephen from over the water and he's only here in case there's something for him to inherit.'

'He'll be disappointed, then,' said Anna under her breath.

'It's fine, Seb,' said Miriam, taking charge. 'There's plenty of food. If people want to booze they can buy their own.' She cast a glance around the room. 'We're going to have to circulate a bit. Chat to people.'

'In that case I'm going to the bar,' said Sebastian. 'Anyone else want one?'

'I'll have a double whisky, no water,' said Anna.

'Really?' asked Sebastian, eyebrows shooting up towards his blond curls.

'No. Not really, I suppose, although that's what I'd like to help me get through this. I'll have a gin and tonic, steady on the tonic. Want a hand?'

Anna looked at Sebastian in what she hoped was a meaningful way but he wilfully refused to grasp her meaning.

'No. I'm fine. You go and circulate and I'll come and find you.'

'I'll have a gin too, please,' said Miriam. 'Clare?'

The word was uttered lightly, in a throwaway tone, but all of them were focused in on the response. Clare didn't meet anybody's gaze.

'I'm fine with tea,' she said, and headed off to where a small gaggle of mourners was gathering and looking out across the eighteenth hole.

Anna watched her go.

'Is she okay, do you think? She seems sober enough.'

'I think so,' replied Miriam. 'We'll just have to watch her like a hawk. I can't cope with her kicking off on top of everything else.' She fanned herself ineffectually with her hand. 'God, it's hot in here. Can someone not open those patio doors?'

Miriam strode off purposefully and was soon throwing open the doors to allow such breeze as could be found to enter. The hot air rushed in. No respite was forthcoming.

Anna turned to speak to Sebastian but he had already turned his back on her and was waiting his turn in the queue. Miriam was right. Clare was as volatile as nitroglycerine on an ordinary day. Lord only knew what might happen if someone pushed her buttons here.

Anna's mind strayed back to their mother and her eyes began to brim with uninvited tears. Their mother had always tried so hard with Clare, never giving up on her even when she'd tested Dorothy's patience beyond what she could possibly endure. Parenting the rest of them had been a walk in the park by comparison. Of course, they'd each had their moments, but no one had courted catastrophe quite like Clare. She had crashed from disaster to disaster without anyone ever being really sure what drove her on.

Maybe the answers to the questions about Clare would be in that letter. Guilt pricked at Anna's conscience as she remembered her mother's very clear instructions. Retrieve the will and the letter from the house without telling the others and burn them both. Anna had taken the documents as instructed but, rather than destroy them, they were still hidden under a pile of magazines in her kitchen. She wasn't sure why she hadn't yet done as her mother had asked her. Was it mere curiosity or the feeling that the letter might contain something important that shouldn't be lost? Anna wasn't sure, but the one thing she did feel very strongly was that she shouldn't confess what she'd done to her siblings. This was her mother's secret and she was its guardian.

She looked around the room, taking in its contents. There were perhaps sixty people there, mainly their friends with their partners. The four Bliss children had not done very well on that score. Only Miriam had managed to find a spouse and hang on to him, which wasn't entirely surprising. Miriam's girls were there, looking like they were going to a party and not a funeral in their short black figure-hugging dresses and their towering heels. They stood together, slightly apart from everyone else, Rosie nibbling on a sausage roll. Miriam's husband, Richard, was fending off two of her mother's friends from church who seemed intent on smothering him with attention. He was smiling and nodding his head as he tackled a piece of anaemic-looking quiche.

Anna scanned the room for River, Clare's son, but wasn't really surprised that she couldn't see him. None of them had expected him to turn up. Anna had had a soft spot for her nephew as a boy, deciding that, despite outward appearances, he was good at heart. His prickly persona was just a front built in the interests of self-preservation to protect him from the chaotic world that Clare had created around them both. Or so Anna had thought. It was hard to hold on to that good opinion of him now that he was a grown man. As an adult he had distanced himself from them all, and even from Clare, as if he somehow blamed them for the cards that life had dealt him. This felt harsh to Anna, given the endless offers of help that the Bliss family had made to Clare and her son over the years, but she couldn't change things. It was a shame but there it was. It might have been nice for Clare if he'd bothered to show his face here, though.

Anna spotted Clare having what looked like a spat with Uncle Stephen but it could just have been the way Clare had arranged her features. An argument was never very far away from her sister. Even when they were kids, Clare could start a row in an empty room. It was funny how they'd all just grown up into older versions of their childhood selves. Miriam, the eldest and in charge. Clare, trouble-magnet. Sebastian, loveable and indulged. And her? Well, she was the favourite. Everyone knew that. Or at least she had been whilst their parents were alive. Their mother had always denied it but they had all known the truth. Anna was the favourite and Clare was the black sheep.

She needed something to do with her hands. Where was Sebastian with that drink? She considered the buffet but she was too on edge to eat and the sandwiches were curling in the heat already. She would have to go and talk to someone.

'She was such a lovely woman, you know,' a gravelly voice said somewhere to her left. 'Couldn't do enough for you. She helped with the flowers at church right up until she went into that home. It was a shame, that.' The voice dropped to a stage whisper. 'I mean, you'd think with four children that one of them would have taken her in. It's the least you'd expect, isn't it? After Frank died, I mean. But to shove her off into a care home when she'd got family close by. You know me, I'd never judge anyone, but I thought it was a disgrace. Poor Dorothy. Not that she complained, mind you. She wouldn't hear a word against those children. Not one word even though they abandoned her to die in a strange bed without her loved ones.'

Anna knew who was speaking without having to look. Marjorie Connors and her son Malcolm had lived next door to their mother for as long as she could remember. Anna spun round on her heel and took two quick steps until she was standing at Marjorie's elbow. The sharp smell of mothballs mingled with stale sweat came off the old woman. Marjorie's cheeks were pink and drops of perspiration were sitting on the down above her upper lip.

'Marjorie,' said Anna sharply. 'So kind of you to come. It must be difficult for you to get out these days. No Malcolm? Oh, yes. There he is. Never that far away, is he? Still no life of his own? Such a pity. I'm surprised he hasn't been swept off his feet by someone from that chess club of his. Well, must be getting on. So many people to talk to, you know.'

Anna walked away, leaving Marjorie floundering like a fish out of water, her mouth opening and closing.

'Well! Did you ever . . .?' she heard Marjorie say to her neighbour.

Sebastian was making his way across the room with her drink, carrying the glass above his head to protect it from the sea of people. He was making slow progress, nodding his thanks to those offering their condolences as he passed by. Finally, he reached Anna and handed her the drink.

'I think the ice has all melted. Soz, sis. How are you doing?'

'Not bad. I wish it was over,' said Anna, taking a deep slurp of her gin. 'Are you holding up okay?'

Sebastian nodded decisively. 'Can't say I've been relishing the prospect of today but I think it gets a bit easier after the funer—' He stopped mid-word, closed his eyes, bit his lip and breathed in deeply. Anna reached out and touched him gently on his arm. She didn't speak. What was there to say?

'Anyway,' he continued brightly a moment later, 'at least we can stop paying those exorbitant care home fees now, so every cloud and all that.' He smiled but it didn't reach his eyes. Anna thought about telling him what she had overheard Marjorie Connors say about them but what would be the point. People could think what they liked.

'We'll need to meet up,' she said, 'and make some decisions about the house. I suppose we'll have to clear all the stuff out at some point. I'm not looking forward to that. Fifty years' worth of junk.' Anna smiled. 'Can you imagine what we'll find? Did you know that Miriam came across over a hundred toilet rolls piled up in that cupboard in the eaves? Lord only knows what she thought she'd need them for. And rolls of cling film. Those huge catering-size ones? Honestly. Why?'

'They must have been a bargain,' laughed Sebastian. 'Waste not, want not. There'll be a will somewhere too, I suppose.'

It was a throwaway comment but Anna felt her spine stiffen. She looked at her glass, hoping that Sebastian couldn't see her face. If he did, he'd know she was hiding something straight away.

'She never mentioned a will but if there is one no doubt we'll find it,' she said quickly. It felt like a huge neon arrow was pointing down at her from above. 'Liar' written in flashing red letters floating over her head. Surely Sebastian could see it? It must be visible to the entire room, she thought, but no one was looking. She finished her drink in one gulp.

'That went down quick,' she said, nodding at her empty glass as the neon sign disappeared. 'Fancy another?'

'Do you think we should?' Sebastian asked. 'I mean, is it politic, what with Clare and everything? I notice that River isn't here.'

'Did you really think he would be?'

'Well, she was his grandmother. It would have been nice to show up if only for his mum's sake.'

'I think he's washed his hands of us,' said Anna. 'And to be honest, I don't care whether having another drink is politic or not. I want one. What our sister does is up to her and, let's face it, that's the thing about Clare. She'll do exactly as she pleases no matter what we do. Shall I get one for you?'

Sebastian lifted his glass, which was still three quarters full.

'You go ahead,' he said. 'I'll stick with this one. Someone ought to go and talk to Uncle Stephen before he gets too blotto to remember where he is and starts singing "Danny Boy".' He stood up. 'Catch you later.'

Anna watched her brother weave his way over to their uncle. The room was now oppressively hot and the smell of stale food and warm bodies was making her feel nauseous. She would get her drink and then take it outside. Miriam had been cornered by some women Anna didn't recognise. She should probably go and help her but bugger that for a game of soldiers. It was Miriam's job. Miriam was the eldest, she was good with responsibility and she could do small talk. She'd be fine.

Anna ordered her drink and then stepped out through the French doors on to the patio outside. A group of three men in gaudy polo shirts were just putting at the eighteenth, two of them laughing heartily at the third as he missed his shot, collapsing under the pressure to perform at this hole, right outside the clubhouse, like anyone was even watching or could care less.

She quickly headed towards a small copse before anyone could catch her, and when she reached the trees, she skirted round until she was out of sight of the clubhouse. As she slumped to the ground, she heard the seams of her funeral dress give. She wouldn't be able to take it back now, with or without its label. The last two weeks had passed in a kind of fug. Since she had taken the phone call from Miriam telling her about her mother, everything seemed to have been moving in slow motion and here, in the dappled shade and for the first time, Anna finally let her guard drop and wept.

DOROTHY – 1961

I

If this baby, her firstborn, the light of her life, the precious fruit of her womb, did not stop crying soon then Dorothy Bernadette Bliss (née McBride) could not, in all conscience, be held responsible for her actions. She lifted the child up at arm's length and examined its hot little face, as red as a cardinal's cassock and twisted all out of shape. It was barely recognisable as the beautiful cherub in the Bounty Baby pictures that Frank had convinced her to pose for in the early days of motherhood, back before she decided that her child was a test sent to her by the Devil himself. Indignation radiated from the baby's every pore, as if it could not believe that it had had the misfortune to be born to a woman as incompetent as this one. Mother and child stared at each other with what, to an outsider, might have appeared to be thinly disguised loathing. The baby locked its gaze on to Dorothy's like a heat-seeking missile, paused briefly to fill its lungs with a fresh supply of oxygen, and began to scream again.

How could something so small cause so much wanton destruction, wondered Dorothy. Before the birth of her longed-for offspring her life had been calm and ordered. She had sailed through her days, carrying out her many and varied duties with ease and to a timetable that suited her needs without fear of interruption or contradiction. Now the simplest of tasks could take an eternity to complete. Just getting herself washed and dressed was as an expedition up the north face of the Eiger. Thank the Lord that Frank wasn't here to see her floundering around in the mire of this caricature of her former daily life. Whilst there were times when she cheerfully cursed the bones of him for being gone for days on end, at least she was able to raise her game to having a semblance of control when he came home.

'What is wrong with you, child?' she asked the screaming Miriam, who responded by increasing the volume by a notch or two, thus screwing Dorothy's already over-taut nerves another frantic turn.

Dorothy ran through the checklist of possible causes for this anxiety, helpfully provided by the patronising health visitor when she had first brought the bundle of joy, lungs and voice box that was Miriam home from the maternity hospital. Too hot? Too cold? Too hungry? Too full? Wet nappy? Dirty nappy? Too tired? Wind? Sheer bloody-mindedness designed simply to drive her mother to a point of no return so that Social Services and possibly even the police would need to be called? Dorothy settled on the latter. This child was surely a demon. Dorothy crossed herself as this thought escaped from the darker recesses of her frazzled mind. Her faith in God and the Church might be hanging by the finest of gossamer threads but there was no point tempting fate, now, was there?

As the child couldn't possibly be hungry and had a clean nappy, as far as her bloodhound-like nose could discern, Dorothy decided that the only thing for it was to put distance between her and it. She peered out of the windows, more smeared than they had been before she was thrust into motherhood, to see what the weather gods had sent today. Well, it wasn't raining so that was a blessing, and now that spring was finally creeping in, apologetic for its late arrival, at least the babe wouldn't freeze to death if she left it in the garden.

The Silver Cross pram (top of the range – 'Only the best for my darling Dorothy and the fruit of my loins.') stood abandoned in the hall. Left stranded at a jaunty angle, it hinted at the speed with which Dorothy had extracted Miriam from it on their arrival back from their march around the park some two hours ago. Had this child been screaming since then? Dorothy had lost all sense of the passage of time. She didn't exactly drop the baby into the pram but she would have to admit that she had used more care in the past. Miriam looked slightly shocked at her sudden change of perspective, finding herself all at once prone in her pram. Her arms flung out and she took a couple of short sharp breaths before she regained momentum and began to scream again.

Negotiating her way past the console table and all the while bouncing the pram up and down with such vigour that it was a miracle the child didn't just bounce out and on to the floor, Dorothy manoeuvred it through the front door and into the garden. Dorothy was proud of her front garden – the outward signs to all those that passed by of the order inside the house. Of course, there was not much to see at this time of year. A few snowdrops and the beginnings of some early daffs – but the borders were weed-free and the square patch of lawn was neatly mown and edged, despite the season.

Miriam screamed on, and Dorothy wondered if gags for babies had been invented yet and whether they were legal. She saw a whole new business venture opening up in front of her. Gags in any fabric you could want to match your pram or the child's outfit or the colour of their eyes – in Miriam's case, a dirty grey so far.

The front garden was not much to write home about in terms of size and in five quick strides she had reached the brick wall that marked its perimeter.

'That child's teething,' said a familiar voice. 'You'll be wanting some oil of cloves. That'll do the trick.'

Every part of Dorothy seethed. Slowly she turned round to see Marjorie Connors standing there, her head be-curled, her bosom resting on folded arms. Sometimes Dorothy wished she could take Marjorie Connors and . . .

'Yes, poor little mite,' she said through gritted teeth. 'I can't seem to settle her at all today. I'm sorry if she's disturbed you, Marjorie.'

In fact, right at this moment, Dorothy hoped that Miriam's screaming was acting as some kind of unbearable torture for her neighbour in much the same way as it was for her. If she had to deal with one more smug titbit of wisdom from the thus far childless Marjorie Connors then she may well find herself looking at a stretch for not just one murder but two.

And then a miracle. With one final explosion of wrath at her unacceptable treatment, Miriam closed her puffy little eyes and fell asleep and at once looked like butter would not melt nor even alter its consistency one iota in her tiny rosebud mouth. Dorothy let out a long and heartfelt sigh. She affixed the brakes to the pram, checked the cat net was firmly in place and then tiptoed away, waving apologetically at Marjorie as she backed towards her front door and slid inside. Even as she made her way towards the kitchen to put the kettle on, she was mentally calculating how long she thought she might have before Miriam required her attention again. Surely the child would sleep for an hour now, maybe two. Enough time to mop the floors and make a shepherd's pie for Frank's supper. But first she would have a cup of tea. She deserved that at least. Was it too much to ask for? A cup of tea? Dorothy fell asleep at the kitchen table before she had chance to find out.

II

'Excellent shepherd's pie,' said Frank later as he mopped around his plate with a piece of white sliced so that it shone clean. 'You are a tiny worker of miracles, my darling wife.'

Dorothy felt like a mere worker. Miracles were very far from her grasp these days.

'Did I mention that I have to go away again next week?' asked Frank lightly as he folded his newspaper expertly so that the crossword filled the quadrant that he had in his hand. 'Local trade unions' conference? Blackpool? Four days, three nights?'

Dorothy noticed that he did not look at her as he spoke: a sure sign of guilt if ever there was one. There had certainly been no mention of the conference before now. She would most definitely have remembered if it had come up in conversation. She could just let it go, probably should. Frank had a good job at the newspaper and these conferences came with the territory, but after the few days she had just had dealing with his child (Miriam was only her child when she gurgled playfully on her mat and kicked her little toes in the air), she was feeling angsty.

'No, I don't believe you did mention it,' she said, her lips pursed into a tight little knot. 'Blackpool is only up the road. Could you not come home for one night at least?'

She knew the answer to this question, but still she felt that she owed it to her diminishing sanity to at least ask.

Frank shook his head sorrowfully, as if driving the fifty miles home to see his nearest and dearest was equivalent to one of the labours of Hercules.

'I would, Dottie, you know I would if I could, but we're expected to be there in the evenings. Shake the right hands, pat the right shoulders. That's where the real stories are sniffed out, you know, in the bar.'

She didn't know. She didn't care. If he left her for the best part of a full week then he might find that he returned to a slightly diminished and certainly less noisy family. But she nodded and smiled in a way that she hoped would show him that she understood these things were beyond his control and that he had to attend, under sufferance, even though it meant leaving his exhausted wife and demon child to muddle along as best they could on their own. She feared her smile might miss its mark.

On day two of the 'Important Blackpool Conference', Miriam's tiny little tooth finally erupted through her red-raw gum and a fragile and temporary peace was restored, although as babies have twenty teeth, Dorothy was very far from resting on her laurels. However, any infanticidal tendencies that she might have been displaying melted away with the return of normal volume levels in the house.

Feeling a bit like she could again be seen in public with her offspring without alerting anyone to the risk of imminent death that had been there before, Dorothy pulled a clean dress on and immediately felt more like a woman and less like a mother. Granted, the floral fabric pulled a little tighter over her hips than it had done the last time she'd worn it, but who would notice? She tied a bonnet firmly under Miriam's chin, in full knowledge that it would be off again before she had locked the front door, and set off to her favourite café in search of adult company.

In the few days since Dorothy had last emerged beyond her threshold, the world seemed to have switched seasons. Early damson blossom was pushing its way out of sap-filled branches, an aura of fuzzy pink replacing their dull winter brown. A blackbird whistled cheerfully somewhere nearby and the air around her felt positively lighter. It was almost warm enough to go without a coat but she knew that only a fool would cast a clout before the May tree bloomed. She left the buttons of her woollen jacket open, though, as a nod to the approaching spring. Even Miriam seemed like a new baby, the troublesome tooth having made its appearance, sitting propped up in her pram and pointing at anything that caught her eye as they passed by.

Dorothy kept up a spirited one-sided conversation with her as they walked along. 'Yes, Miriam. That's a dog. And do you know what that dog is called, do you? It's called Tinker. And how do I know that? That's a very good question, Miriam. I know that because it slips its lead at least once a day and I can hear Mr Mason from number twenty-seven calling for it like his life depends on it. Which it may well do, knowing Mrs Mason.'

And so it continued all the way to the café. Jack's Corner Café had few notable features other than the fact that it was on a corner and belonged to a man called Jack. Jack had been a pilot in the war and, by some incredible stroke of luck, had returned from France outwardly unscathed. He had opened a café and slipped seemingly seamlessly into this new phase of his life, the only telltale signs of what had gone before being a slight limp (worse in colder weather) and a tendency to shake. This latter meant that sometimes more of your tea was in the saucer than the cup by the time it arrived at your table, but if the tea lake was particularly bad Jack would pour you a fresh one and leave it on the counter for you to collect yourself.

Dorothy had started visiting the café when she fell pregnant, determined to do as Frank kept instructing her and take things easy. She liked the anonymity of the place. It was far enough from her street not to be filled with her neighbours, and Jack, whilst always polite, was never curious about her life. He seemed interested only in what was before his eyes and never strayed beyond that in his brief conversations with her. Once she started frequenting the café as a duo rather than a plump singleton, Jack simply asked after the health of mother and child. He did not even need to know the child's name so that Dorothy found herself blurting it out anyway because she was so used to having to trot out the same vital statistics to anyone she met.

'This is Miriam. She is X weeks old. She was seven pounds eight ounces. She sleeps well, thank you.'

(This last part was a lie, but Dorothy had discovered that if you confessed to other mothers that your child didn't sleep you either got smug, sympathetic smiles or a list of foolproof and guaranteed-to-work remedies to try.)

Today the café was quiet. Miriam's ten o'clock feed meant that they had missed the breakfast trade but were too early for those requiring lunch. Dorothy parked the pram on the pavement outside, gathered Miriam in her arms and carried her inside. The smell of toast still lingered on air made slightly damp by the water boiler, which hissed and bubbled like a geyser.

'Good morning,' said Jack without turning from the sink where he was washing up, sleeves rolled with Forces precision and arms plunged deep in soapy water. 'With you in a second.'

'Just a cup of tea would be grand,' Dorothy said, trying not to look at the teacakes that were ready split on the counter and just crying out to be toasted and smothered in melted butter. Judging by the snug fit of the dress, she still had a few baby pounds to shift.

'Right you are,' said Jack, wiping his arms on a threadbare towel. 'You sit down and I'll bring it over.'

No post-war shakes today, then.

Dorothy chose a seat by the window, took off her jacket – no mean feat with Miriam under one arm – and then sat down balancing the baby on her lap, her tiny, twig-like spine pushed up tight against her own slightly flabby stomach. She wrapped her arms tightly around Miriam's waist to prevent her from slipping down. Then she looked around to see who else was in. There was a woman she thought she might recognise from one of her now rare appearances in church who was chatting earnestly and sotto voce to another woman who might or might not be married to the sexton. A cursory glance at their body language told Dorothy that some poor soul was having their character assassinated in absentia. This was one of the challenges that Dorothy found with the Church of the Holy Trinity, which had adopted her after her arrival here from Ireland. Its frequenters were the least Christian people she had ever met. She looked away, hoping that the women would be too intent on their gossip to notice her but knowing that that was, sadly, extraordinarily unlikely.

The only other patron today was a man who was sitting, rather awkwardly, directly in her line of sight. He was a similar age to her, maybe a little older: she never had been any good at estimating age. She didn't like to look at him directly but she had the impression of someone who was happy in their own skin and yet self-contained and closed down. He struck quite a contrast to her heart-on-sleeve, loud, confident and open husband and so was immediately intriguing. Dorothy felt her eyes drawn to him until, suddenly embarrassed that he might think her very forward, she switched her focus to Miriam, to the extent that she could with the baby's back to her. Miriam, however, had other ideas. She pointed at the man, waving her arms so wildly in his direction that Dorothy had to tighten her grip for fear of losing her on to the floor. Jack was making his uneven progress across the checked linoleum towards her, her cup of tea holding its own against both limp and tremor. By the time he placed her drink down on the table, only the smallest amount had made the journey from cup to saucer. Jack smiled at this minor achievement and Dorothy was relieved. She always felt awkward when the tea needed to be replaced, not wanting to draw attention to Jack's obvious shortcomings by complaining, but spilled tea never seemed to bother Jack.

By the time she switched her focus from tea back to Miriam, her daughter was fully engaged in a conversation of sorts with the man opposite. He chatted to her, answering what he imagined might be her babbling questions in a voice that suggested a lifetime's experience of communication with infants, and Dorothy was thrown. Whatever qualities she had this man marked down as possessing, child-whispering wasn't amongst them. So intently were he and Miriam absorbed by each other that Dorothy almost felt it would be rude to interrupt. She just sat there, holding Miriam tightly, and smiled as she waited for one or other of them to notice her. The man broke gaze first.

'This child is an absolute delight,' he said. 'And clearly so intelligent. It's in their eyes, you know. That's where the clever ones always give themselves away.'

As he spoke, Dorothy thought she could see a sadness hidden deep in his face, like a clue in a work of art, and she wondered what his story was.

'Thank you,' she said. There didn't seem much else to say.

Securing Miriam with one arm, she lifted her cup to her lips, blowing on the tea and then drinking a healthy mouthful. There was no sipping at a drink when a baby was involved. You drank it fast if you wanted it hot.

Miriam lost interest in the man, turning her attention instead to the fabric of Dorothy's dress. Dorothy, however, found her own gaze still drawn to him as if he were creating his own gravitational pull. Her eyes skimmed over his chest and up, pausing briefly at a small piece of tissue paper attached to a cut on his neck. As her eyes travelled up his face, she was horrified to find that he was watching her too but with what felt like an objective interest, as if she were a model he intended to sketch. His eyes drank in her face, mapping it out in minute precision and with no obvious embarrassment at having been caught staring at her. Dorothy, feeling her cheeks flare, pulled her attention away to Miriam, pointing out the sugar pourer on the table and then instantly regretting it when Miriam wanted to play and expressed her displeasure at having the pourer taken from her with a quick screech. When Dorothy chanced another look, the man was still watching. This time she met his stare, her head raised defiantly. I am a happily married woman, she hoped her expression said, and you are most impertinent to be staring at me in this manner. What she was really thinking was how the concentric circles of grey in his eyes seemed to draw her in, like a hypnotist's watch.

She must stop this. Frank had only just gone and here she was looking closely enough at another man to see the details of his eyes. He was well put together, though: not handsome as such, more . . . attractive than handsome. Was that the word? Attractive? He was certainly attracting both her and Miriam. Dorothy turned in her seat so she could no longer see him and focused her attention entirely on her daughter. She was not in the business of being attracted to strangers in cafés. That was absolutely not her business at all.

III

After that first meeting, Dorothy found that she kept seeing the man all over the place. He wasn't stalking her, she was sure. It was just that having once been raised in her consciousness, she was surprised at how many places they seemed to have in common, and she wondered why she hadn't noticed him before.

The first time was outside the greengrocer's, when Dorothy had popped out to buy cabbage for Frank's tea. She had parked the pram outside the shop whilst she went in, and when she came back the man was in full conversation with a gurgling Miriam. He stepped back sharply when she appeared, as if worried that he might have caused offence. Whilst it was certainly unusual for a man to show an interest in her baby, Dorothy wasn't a bit offended, especially when she saw who it was.

'Hello again,' he said, lifting his hat to her. 'I was just catching up on the news with your delightful daughter.'

'Miriam,' said Dorothy, and then when he looked a little lost she clarified, 'My daughter's name is Miriam. I'm Dorothy. How do you do?'

Dorothy held out her hand formally and the man took it and shook it.

'StJohn,' he said.

'That's an unusual name,' said Dorothy before she could stop herself. She felt her cheeks go a little pink, hoping that he didn't think her impertinent.

'It's a nuisance,' said the man. 'If I say it they can't spell it and if they read it they can't pronounce it. My mother has a lot to answer for.'

He smiled and Dorothy remembered how fascinating she had found his grey eyes the last time they'd met.

'Well, I must be getting on,' she said briskly, cross with herself for letting her gaze linger longer on his eyes than she had meant to. 'Nice to meet you, again.' And she pushed the pram back towards home, wondering if he was watching her but not wanting to turn round just in case.

The next time she saw him, she and Miriam were in the park. The weather was a little warmer now, and Dorothy had taken a blanket and a picnic of sorts. She settled herself on the grass beneath a spreading oak at the far end, away from the main path, where it was quiet. The leaves were just starting to bud and the sunlight was pushing its way through the branches and leaving stripes of light across the tartan. Dorothy enjoyed the feeling of space. Their garden was all well and good but there was no getting away from the passers-by or Marjorie from next door. A picnic held there would quickly become everybody else's business and she didn't want that.

Miriam had reached the stage where she could sit reliably but was still unable to crawl. Dorothy would recognise this as a golden moment with her other children but this first time she was still in blissful ignorance of just how all-consuming a child on the move under its own steam could be. Miriam played happily with a box of bricks, piling them up and knocking them down and each time squealing with delight as if she had no idea what was coming next. It wasn't that exciting for Dorothy but she was happy to snatch moments of calm whenever she could.

Miriam had just knocked her tower down for the umpteenth time when Dorothy heard a voice to her left.

'Good afternoon.'

It was the man from the café, StJohn.

'Hello,' she said, straightening her skirt so that less of her legs was visible.

'Beautiful day,' he added, and Dorothy, judging that this was so apparent that it didn't require comment, just nodded. 'And little Miriam is doing very well with those bricks. How old is she now?'

'Six months,' replied Dorothy proudly. Every one of those months had been a challenge to get through and she wore each of them like a badge of honour.

'And still bright as a button,' he added.

'Well, I can't be saying that for sure,' Dorothy replied modestly.

'They say it's hard, looking after a baby,' the man said. 'Not that I know much about it but I can imagine it might be. One small little being demanding all your attention day and night. I'm sure it's exhausting.'

Dorothy looked up at him gratefully. This stranger had perceived in a matter of seconds what Frank seemed unable to grasp. Having babies was hard. It was boring and monotonous and relentless and there was absolutely no escape from it.

'It is,' she said. 'No one tells you that!' She smiled but he didn't speak, seemingly expecting her to go on. 'I've no family here. My mother is away at home in Ireland. I speak to her on the telephone, you know, but it's not like having someone on the doorstep to help out. And my husband is gone so often. With his work, that is.'

She felt herself blush. She shouldn't do Frank down, not to this stranger, but something about the way he smiled at her made her feel like he was a kindred spirit of sorts. He got it, she could tell. The struggles that she had, how she battled with her concerns that she wasn't actually a very good mother, that she wasn't designed to be one, even.

'I can't begin to imagine how tough it must be,' he said.

'And how about you?' she asked, turning the attention away from herself. 'What do you do?' As she spoke it crossed her mind that she kept seeing him during the day. Maybe he didn't have a job.

'Oh, I keep myself busy,' was his infuriatingly vague reply. 'With gardens, mainly,' he added.

'Would you like to join me?' Dorothy said. 'I have some digestives and there's plenty of tea in the flask.' It was presumptuous of her to ask, forward even, but who was there to see and anyway she so badly needed someone to talk to.

'Well, if you don't mind,' he said. 'I have a moment or two to spare.'

He kneeled down on the blanket, Miriam sitting between them like a chaperone, and Dorothy poured tea into the lid of the flask and passed it to him.

They stayed there, chatting for almost an hour, until Miriam became fractious and wanted a feed. He asked her about her childhood in Ireland and she told him how she had come over to England to work as a secretary and had met Frank at the paper. He listened to her attentively, his grey eyes never really leaving her face, and she enjoyed just sharing. When her story made him laugh she delighted in it and embellished things just to please him, becoming more and more animated as she went along. It was as if the silence of all those months since she'd given up her work were being banished now in one afternoon of chatter.

Finally, he stood up.

'I must go,' he said. 'But I've so enjoyed our conversation. Perhaps we could meet again?'

Without missing a beat Dorothy said, 'I come here most days, if it's not raining.'

That was all right, she thought. It wasn't as if she were making an actual arrangement but if they happened to bump into one another again for a little gentle conversation, who was going to mind?

As StJohn strolled back down the path and Dorothy gathered up Miriam's toys, she thought how much she had enjoyed his conversation. He was such a gentle man, so very different from Frank, and he understood her struggles. And right now that meant more to her than anything else.

MIRIAM – 1977

I

Miriam stood in front of the full-length mirror and twisted her face in fear. Her neck straining at an unnatural angle, she arched her back and stretched out her arms in supplication.

'Please don't,' she pleaded. 'I'll do anything you want but please don't kill me.'

She fell to her knees, closed her eyes and slowly toppled on to her side, her head barely missing the corner of the bed. She lay still for a moment, savouring this moment of death. Then gradually, as if unsure whether or not to break the atmosphere, the crowd began to clap, quietly at first and then the riot of noise filled her head and . . .

'Miriam. What do you think you're doing down there, girl? I was nearly falling on top of you. For all that's holy, stand up and help me with this laundry.'

Miriam came to sitting and smiled broadly at her mother.

'I was practising dying, Mum. Was I good? I was trying to imagine what that woman felt, Patricia Atkinson, the one that got murdered in Bradford. I wish there'd been more on the telly about how she actually died. It would make it loads easier for me to act it.'

'Miriam!' Her mother crossed herself and then gawped at her, horror written all over her face.

That's another one to store in the old memory banks, thought Miriam.

'How can you be thinking such terrible thoughts? And you a good Catholic girl.'

'Come on, Mum. You can't claim that for us? When was the last time we went to Mass? We didn't even go at Christmas last year.'

'I know and I am ashamed to the very bones of me,' said her mother, shaking her head regretfully. 'But once a Catholic, always a Catholic. The good Lord won't be forgetting you now, will he? He'll know what's going on in that fluffy head of yours, make no mistake. And pretending to be dead women is something He won't be liking.'

'I'm not pretending,' said Miriam indignantly. 'Really, Mum. Pretending? It's acting.'

'And what is acting, pray tell, apart from pretending that you're someone that you've no business being?'

Her mother put her hand to the small of her back and puffed out her lips.

'I've no energy today,' she said as she flopped down on Miriam's bed. 'All my get up and go has got up and gone and I've so much to do. I swear, if I sat down and wrote a list of all the things that fell to me in this house, I'd still be writing when hell freezes over. I don't know where your father is. He went out to get some string to fasten up the bunting. That was two hours ago. No sign of him. He thinks I won't notice, what with all the rushing around that I'm doing, but I'll smell it on his breath when he gets back, you see if I don't. He spends more time in that pub every passing year. And Clare's in one of her moods again. I simply asked if she could mop the floor without leaving sticky patches. You'd think I'd asked her to cut her own arm off. The cheek of the girl! Your grandfather would be spinning in his grave if he could hear the way my own children talk to me.'

Miriam wasn't listening. She was watching the way her mother's mouth formed her words, how her eyebrows shot up whenever she felt something stingingly. Store it all up, Miriam. Store it up.

'And there's all the food to think about. Anyone would think that this party's going to organise itself, so they would. Well, I can't be thinking about that yet. I need to get everything straight first. So, will you help me do the ironing? It makes my back ache something chronic, leaning over that board all day long. I don't know what's wrong with me these days. It's like someone came down and stole away all my energy. It must be my age. Or the change.' She shuddered.

'Yes, Mum. Course I'll help.' Miriam was hoping that if she did enough extra, her mother might see her way to contributing to the bus fare to London. It worked to her favour if Clare was in one of her strops. Miriam could play the dutiful-eldest-daughter card. There were few advantages to being the eldest but that was definitely one of them.

'You're a good girl, Miriam.' Her mother levered herself up from the bed slowly and with considerable effort.

'Why don't I make you a nice cup of tea?' Miriam offered, brownie points and bus fares clearly in her sights.

'Oh, you're an angel, but there's no time. I have to get on or we'll never be ready and I can't have that Marjorie Connors thinking that I can't rustle up a few sausage rolls and a trifle or two.' Her mother made her way to the door. 'The ironing board's all set up in the scullery. I don't know why I ever put it down. There's always such a pile, so there is. And your father's work shirts are on the rack.'

Then, with one long puff out of air, she was gone.

'Clare Bliss. I want you out of that bedroom and down those stairs as quick as I can say Jack Robinson. There's work to be done,' she shouted as she made her way along the landing.

Miriam looked again in the mirror and tried to pull a few of the myriad of expressions that she'd just witnessed. They would all come in handy when she got to RADA, and she would be there before she knew it. She had tripped off to the postbox at the end of the road with her application form a week last Wednesday, making sure that no one had seen her. She also had a thank you letter to Uncle Stephen and Auntie

Maggie to post as cover so that no one would suspect that her mission had an ulterior motive. The brochure, which she had hidden safely in her knicker drawer, said that once they had her application form they would be in touch about an audition if appropriate. Miriam was sure that if she could just get in front of them they would have to give her a place. She was born to act. She could feel it in her blood.

She left her room and skipped downstairs, resisting the urge to bang on Clare's door on the way past. The longer Clare sulked the better it would go for her. Clare would always hang herself if you gave her enough rope. She could hear her mother bustling around in the best room, no doubt dusting ornaments that she had dusted only yesterday. There was no sign of her father and Anna was out playing in the snicket at the back of the house. Miriam could hear her shrill voice directing proceedings.

'You. Robbie McKenzie. You need to stand here on guard. No moving, now. Come on, Suzanna. We'll go and see what that Malcolm is doing.'

Anna's voice became fainter as she moved towards the Connors's house next door but Miriam knew that she would still be in charge. Anna was always in charge of her little friends. Miriam was surprised that they didn't rebel and stage a coup but they all seemed happy to be bossed about. More fool them. It wouldn't kill Anna to help out either, but of course her mother would never get her to break off from her games. When Miriam had children she was absolutely, definitely not going to have a favourite.

The ironing board was set up in the scullery as her mother had said. The cord from the iron snaked up to the ceiling. Miriam flicked the switch and went in search of the clothes whilst she waited for it to heat up. The rack that hung from the ceiling was laden, and Miriam took the rope from the cleat and gently lowered it, carefully avoiding the pan of cold fat that always sat on the back ring of the oven. She touched the clothes to test for damp. The shirts at one end were dry, the rest still too wet to iron. She pulled them off one by one and held them into her chest. The cotton smelt vaguely of chips.

Her mother bustled into the kitchen. 'Still no Clare? What does that girl think she's playing at? I swear I shall be hollering for her with my dying breath. CLARE!!'

'No need to shout,' said Clare, who had appeared suddenly at the door.

'Well, about time too,' said their mother, the wind slightly taken out of her sails. 'I need you to pop to the shop. There's a list on the table and there's money in the biscuit tin. Take two pound notes. That should be plenty. And make sure that he doesn't short-change you. There's something shifty about his eyes. I don't trust him as far as I could spit him.'

Clare sloped to the table, picked up the list and gave it a cursory glance.

'Spam? I hate Spam. Why do we have to buy Spam?'

'It's not for you, young lady. There are plenty would be glad of a nice Spam sandwich, and for the numbers that we need to feed beggars can't be choosers. Now hurry before he sells out of cream. There's bound to be a run on it before tomorrow.'

Her mother shooed Clare towards the door with a flick of her duster. Reluctantly, Clare peeled two pound notes from the roll in the battered biscuit tin and slipped them into her jeans pocket. Then she picked up the basket and made for the door. Miriam gave her her sweetest smile as she passed and Clare scowled in return. Miriam mimicked her face to her back and then made a mental note of how her muscles felt. Another one for her armoury.

She licked her finger and then touched it to the sole of the iron. It hissed. Then she began on the first shirt. All her father's work shirts were the same, a pale-blue cotton. There were frays starting on the tips of the collars and she pressed these parts carefully so as not to be accused of making them any worse.

'Mum?' she shouted through to the kitchen. 'Is everyone in tonight? I've got something that I want to talk about at tea.'

Her mother didn't answer but of course they would all be in. They were always all in. Where else was there to go?

II

Miriam finished pressing the last shirt just as Clare returned from the corner shop. She dumped the basket on the table, paying little heed to the safety of its contents. The glass bottles rattled against each other ominously.

'Careful!' said Miriam. 'You'll only have to go back again if you've broken them.'

'No way,' snapped Clare. 'If she wants more shopping she can get it herself. She could do with the exercise anyway. I swear she gets fatter every day.' She picked at a hangnail and then put her finger to her mouth and gnawed at the skin.

'Don't let her hear you talking like that,' warned Miriam. 'She's just got a lot on with the street party and everything. I think she's finally bitten off more than she can chew but she can't lose face over it. Would it kill you to be a bit more cooperative?'

Clare looked at Miriam, cocking her head and raising one eyebrow, but then she relented and smiled.

'Definitely.' She pulled at an imaginary noose around her neck, her eyes rolling into the back of her head and her mouth falling open. Miriam couldn't help but laugh. 'I'm mightily sick of this whole Jubilee thing,' Clare continued. 'Who gives a shit if she's been queen for twenty-five years? What does she do anyway? We should shoot the lot of them and start a revolution like the bloody Russians.'

Miriam looked hastily over her shoulder. If their mother heard Clare swearing there'd be yet another row. 'Keep your voice down,' she hissed, but Clare just shrugged and wandered over to the sink and looked out into the yard where yet more washing flapped idly in the breeze.

'Is Dad back yet?' she asked.

'No. I expect he'll be back in time for tea. I hope so, anyway. I've got something I want to tell you all,' Miriam said, and then immediately wished she hadn't.

'What?' asked Clare flatly, feigning a total lack of interest in anything that Miriam might have to say. 'You're going to be a missionary in Africa? Or a nun. No. Wait. You're up the duff.' She spun round, eyes wide. 'Oh my God, you're not, are you?'

'No!' shrieked Miriam. 'Of course not! It's nothing like that but I have made a decision and I want to discuss it with you all. Not now. Later.'

She folded the ironing board and hung it on the hooks on the back of the scullery door. She wouldn't let Clare put her off. She was bound to be negative about it all but that didn't matter. It wasn't Clare she needed to convince.

The back door flew open and in burst Anna, parting the striped fly curtain with a magisterial sweep of her arm.

'That Louise Chambers is a cow. I'm not playing with her again. She's so bossy. She takes over everything. Where's Mum? What's for tea?'

Miriam and Clare exchanged a sly grin. Anna was incredibly bossy. It was rare that anyone got a word in edgeways.

'Mum's in the front room and it's sausage and chips for tea. Or it will be if I ever get round to peeling the spuds. Give us a hand, Clare?'

'Okay. I just need to go and . . .' said Clare, and left before making it entirely clear what she had to do. Miriam sighed loudly.

'Take these shirts upstairs, Anna, and hang them up. Don't just leave them on the bed. Mum's a bit tired and we all need to help out.' Anna tutted but took the pile of shirts with her.

Miriam got out what was necessary for the task and stood at the sink, peeling the potatoes. As she dunked each potato in the cold water, she marvelled at the clean yellow surface that appeared. No one had ever seen that surface before. She was the only person to whom it had revealed itself, ever. She congratulated herself on her cleverness. No one else in this house would ever have had that thought. They were all philistines. Not one of them was in tune with the world around them like she was. That was why she was going to make a marvellous actress. Whatever was required, she knew she'd be able to pull it out of the bag. She practised again now, pulling her best surprised expression and then judging it in the half-reflection of the window.

'What in the name of all the saints are you doing, girl?' asked her mother, who had appeared at the door, and Miriam stopped pulling faces and looked down at the dirty water.

'Nothing. Shall I make you a cup of tea, Mum? You look done in.'

Her mother lowered herself carefully on to a wooden chair and sighed loudly. 'I'll just have a quick five-minute sit-down and then I'll get on with making the jelly for the trifle,' she said, but having sat down Miriam thought she didn't look as if she would ever get up again.

'You're going to do yourself a mischief if you carry on at this rate. Clare can make the trifle. She is fifteen, you know, and she just pretends that she can't do things so that she doesn't have to. She's made a trifle in Cookery at school. She knows how.'

Miriam looked over to her mother, who had closed her eyes and was breathing deeply. Miriam wondered if she'd fallen asleep there and then but then she spoke.

'Well, that would be grand, Miriam.'

'And Anna can help too.'

'No,' said her mother quickly. 'You leave little Anna to play. There'll be time enough for chores when she gets a bit bigger.'

Miriam bit her tongue. When she was eleven, she'd had two younger sisters to run around after. No one had said she should play instead. Still, there was no point saying anything. Anna was the baby and could, and did, get away with murder. Slowly and methodically she started slicing the shining potatoes into long, thin chips, making sure that each one was as close in size to the last so that they would cook evenly. At least if she cut the chips there were never any hard ones. Or any fat ones. Miriam hated fat chips.

'Is that cup of tea going to make itself?' asked her mother.

'Coming right up,' said Miriam, who had lost the offered cup of tea somewhere in the muddle of her thoughts.

'So,' said her mother, going through her mental list out loud, 'if Clare can do the trifles then the rest of it can wait until the morning. I can't do the sandwiches until then anyway, and the fairy cakes won't take two shakes of a lamb's tail. I'll just get the tea sorted and then I might watch *Crossroads*.'

Miriam looked at her mother. Her greying hair was scraped back from her face and tied in a low ponytail. Tendrils fell loose and were curling around her temples. Her soft brown eyes, usually so sharp and all-seeing, looked tired, and from time to time something flitted across her face as if she had had a fright or was in distress. Miriam made a mental note to practise the expressions when she got a moment alone.

In the hall the front door opened with a creak and then banged shut.

'I'm back. Where is everybody? It's like a morgue in here. Did I miss an alien invasion or have you all run off to join the navy?'

Miriam laughed. 'We're in here, Dad. Well, me and Mum are. The others are upstairs. And there are no aliens!'

Miriam's dad breezed into the kitchen and planted a noisy kiss on his wife's forehead. She smiled weakly at him.

'Tea's not quite ready, Frank,' she said, straightening herself a little in her chair, a hand flitting up to pat her lacklustre hair.

'No worries. No worries,' he said. 'And how are you, Miriam, first-born fruit of my loins?'

'Frank! Really!' said her mother.

Miriam turned from the sink and smiled at her father. 'Fine, Dad. How was your afternoon? Sniff out any good stories?'

'Oh, there's always a story, Miriam, my little sweet pea. Had an illuminating discussion with the junior sports editor about how immeasurably superior Liverpool are to Manchester United. He failed to see the error of his ways but he will, given time.'

'Not letting a little thing like a lost cup final worry you, then, Dad?' teased Miriam with a stagey wink.

'A minor setback, Miriam. A minor setback. We have to throw the underlings the odd titbit of success or they'll all get bored and refuse to play. And may I remind you, not that any reminding should be necessary, that we are the rightfully crowned Champions of Europe? Who needs a poxy cup final when you're holding the crown?'

'No, Dad. I really don't need reminding.' They had heard little else from him since the match.

'The pub was very busy when I walked by.' He threw a little look at her mother to emphasise that he was here and not there. 'It must be everyone avoiding all this street party malarkey.'

'All the men, you mean,' said Clare as she appeared at the doorway. 'When's tea? I'm starving.'

'Forty-five minutes. And you can help by making the trifles,' said Miriam. 'In fact, you could get the jelly going now so it's set.'

Clare looked as if she was going to object but then thought better of it and began filling the kettle.

'Right,' said their father. 'I'll leave you lot to it and go and get washed up ready to eat. Are you all right?' he said to her mother, touching her shoulder tenderly. 'You look exhausted. You need to delegate. Where's our third little helper? Shall I send her down here?'

'No. Leave her to play. There won't be room to turn round in here.'

'And Miriam has an important announcement, apparently,' said Clare. Miriam could hear the sarcastic edge to her voice but let it go.

'How intriguing,' said Frank. 'Are you planning to run away and join the circus?'

'No!' said Miriam, and shot Clare one of her favourite irritated expressions. 'I'll tell you all at teatime.'

The girls bustled about, both doing their own tasks and moving deftly around each other as they worked. Miriam watched Clare pull apart the little red quivering cubes of jelly, surreptitiously slipping one or two into her mouth when she thought no one was looking. Miriam didn't say anything. She needed this unusually jovial mood preserving for as long as possible. She dumped the chips into the hot fat pan at the back of the stove and began frying the sausages whilst simultaneously setting the table. Her mother drank her tea quietly in the middle of all the activity.

'Who's putting up the bunting and all that sh— rubbish?' asked Clare. 'I assume that's a job for the useless men.'

Their mother didn't even rise to this. 'That Mr Williams from number sixteen is coordinating,' she said, as if she had no interest in it whatsoever. 'He'll probably be needing help with blowing up balloons in the morning. And then once the trestle tables have been set up they'll need cloths putting on and laying with plates and cups. It'll be all hands to the pumps tomorrow but we can't be doing any of it tonight. It'll have to wait.'

III

Her father was just wiping away the last smears of brown sauce with a slice of white bread when Miriam decided that the time was right. She needed to hit it perfectly – the exact moment when everyone was relaxed and well fed but before her mother stood and started to clear the plates. She took a deep breath and began.

'I have some news,' she said.

'Ooh. At last. The big announcement. This should be good,' said Clare, showily turning her chair in Miriam's direction and putting her elbows on the table, only to withdraw them again smartly after a warning glance from her mother.

Miriam threw an irritated look at Clare.

'Shut up, Clare,' she hissed. Already she could see that she did not have her mother's complete attention. Whilst she was looking in Miriam's direction, her focus was clearly a long way off.

'And what might that be, my little chickadee?' asked her father. 'Do not keep us in suspenders!'

Under normal circumstances she would have found her father's tendency to make a joke out of any situation entertaining, but this was not normal circumstances. This was a serious business that would affect her entire life and it needed to be treated as such. Miriam sat up straight and held a dramatic pause for as long as she thought she could get away with it, and then made her momentous announcement.

'I am going to be an actress,' she said, enunciating each word with an actress-like precision, and then waited for a reaction.

Clare snorted.

'A noble profession,' said her father in his best mock Shakespearean. 'Although not one without its pecuniary disadvantages.'

'What?' asked Anna, her nose wrinkling in confusion. 'Mum, can you tell Dad to stop using such long words and talk proper English.'

'Whatever has become of education in this country?' joked her father. 'I mean, my smallest child, that acting will not keep the proverbial wolf from the door.'

Anna still looked confused.

'He means you don't get paid much,' explained Clare.

'Oh. Well, why didn't he just say that?' asked Anna.

'Because he's Dad and why use one word when ten will do,' replied Clare.

'Anyway . . .' Miriam almost had to shout over them to regain their attention. 'I have been looking into it very carefully.' She threw a glance at her father to make sure that he had heard. He was always encouraging them to research things that interested them.

'The best drama school in the country is RADA and so I have applied there. I'll have to attend an audition, of course, but once I've been offered a place I shall move down to London as soon as I've finished my A levels. RADA isn't fussy about grades. They are only bothered about talent so it doesn't really matter what grades I get.'

Miriam could sense a change in the atmosphere around the table. Her mother, who had been about to drift off, was looking directly at her with something that might have been concern written across her face, but the greatest shift was in her father. He didn't speak for a moment but when he did all trace of his Shakespearean actor's voice was gone.

'Hmmm,' he said slowly, as if he were choosing his words with great care. 'This is new. I had no idea that you were harbouring thespian aspirations.'

Anna was about to say 'What?!' again but Clare put a hand on her arm.

'Shhh,' Clare mouthed.

'Well, I am. I mean, I have done for a while. Well, for ages, really.' Miriam could hear herself stumble under her father's gaze. 'I didn't say anything, well, because I wanted to learn all the facts first, Dad, like you always tell us to.' She paused to collect her praise but when none was forthcoming she pressed on. 'And now that I've found it all out, I'm ready to work as hard as I possibly can to make my dream come true. You always say that if we want anything badly enough then we have to work hard to achieve it, don't you?'

'Indeed I do,' said her father thoughtfully. 'Indeed I do. What concerns me slightly with this plan of yours, and I do appreciate that you have thought it all through to the best of your abilities and done all your research, but what concerns me . . .' He paused and rubbed his chin. 'What concerns me,' he continued, 'is that acting isn't really a job. It's fine as a hobby. I've got no issues with you spending your spare time treading the boards. But to go to drama school? Well, that's a horse of a different colour. A different colour altogether.'

'I don't really see why,' said Miriam. This was not going the way she had anticipated, had practised in her head. 'You want me to finish school and go to college, so that's what I'm going to do.'

At last her mother spoke. 'I think what your father means is that we were expecting you'd be away to do teaching training or to learn to be a secretary. Qualifications that will lead to a good job at the end of them. But acting? It's not really—'

Her father interrupted. 'It's not at all what we had in mind and you can take it from me that it's not going to happen.' His tone had changed entirely now. 'You will stay on at school next year, study hard and do well with your A levels, and then we can talk about college. But drama school? I think you need to get that idea out of your pretty little head.'

Miriam could feel her breath deepen as her heart beat faster in her chest. She caught sight of Clare, who was smirking. This brought the anger that had been growing deep inside her much closer to the surface. Using almost all her willpower, she ignored Clare and spoke as calmly as she could.

'Well, it's too late,' she said. 'I have already posted my application to RADA and there's nothing you can do about it. And when they write to offer me an audition, and they will, I shall go down to London by myself either with or without your blessing.'

Her father's cheeks blazed red, his fancy words all gone. 'You will do no such thing, young lady. I expressly forbid you to have anything further to do with RADA – or any other drama schools, for that matter. You can put the whole ludicrous idea out of your mind once and for all. There is no way any child of mine, especially one with your brains and potential, is going to flush it all down the toilet—'

'Frank!' her mother said. 'Language, please! Not at the table.'

'. . . is going to flush it down the toilet,' her father continued emphatically, 'by wasting her time at some half-baked drama school for losers and wastrels.'

'But, Dad, it's RADA. The Roy-al Ac-ad-emy,' she said, emphasising each syllable, her frustration making her cheekier than she'd normally be. 'That means that the Queen approves of it. You remember the Queen, that woman that we're all running ourselves ragged to celebrate tomorrow?'

'Miriam!' admonished her mother. 'Don't speak to your father like that.' But Miriam didn't care. It was all going wrong and she could see no way of saving it. In the space of ten minutes her entire life had shattered into a million pieces.

'You're being ridiculous,' she added, but she knew she had gone too far. She saw her father's hand pull back to slap her, although he had no hope of reaching her from where he was sitting.

'Go to your room,' he said slowly through tight lips. 'I will not be spoken to in this manner. This is my house and whilst you are under my roof you will do as you are told. I do not want to discuss this again. The matter is closed.'

Miriam stood up, almost knocking her chair over in her haste, and ran from the room. She chased up the stairs and into her bedroom and threw herself on to the bed, where she lay and sobbed.

After a few minutes the sobbing became too exhausting and she dropped a level to merely sniffing. By the time a little knock came at the door, she was sitting in front of her mirror watching how her mouth twisted itself when she cried.

'Can I come in?' asked a small voice.

'No,' said Miriam, and then, 'Okay.'

Anna's head appeared slowly around the door, followed by the rest of her.

'Are you all right?' she asked.

'No,' said Miriam.

'I thought you were awfully brave standing up to Daddy like that.'

Miriam didn't speak but just looked gratefully at her sister. Anna was okay, really, when she wasn't being bossy.

'It was a bit of a silly idea, though, wasn't it?' Anna continued. 'I mean, if that RADA place is the best in the country like you say, then why on earth would they want you?'

Anna smiled a tight little smile at her, turned on her heel and left.

Miriam stared at the spot where she'd stood, seething but not able to think of a retort fast enough. Sometimes she really hated her sisters. What did Anna know anyway? What did any of them know? Maybe they'd get used to the idea. She could leave it for a couple of days, wait until this whole street party business was out of the way, and then she'd mention it again, casually, like nothing had been settled. They would all have calmed down by then and her father might look at things differently. Yes, that's what she'd do. She'd carry on as if nothing had happened. No point sulking like Clare. She would forget the whole row and then try again in a while. Maybe by then she would have heard from RADA with the date for her audition. They were bound change their minds when she had the actual audition coming up.

She could hear the sounds of washing-up in the kitchen, Anna and Clare fighting about who would dry and who would put away. With her out of the way, her mother must be having to wash the plates. A little shiver of guilt passed over her but then her mother had hardly defended her corner. So what if she had to do the washing-up for once? They shouldn't have sent her to her bedroom if they wanted her to do it.

Later, when the noises from the street were quietening, there was another tap at her door.

'Miriam?' came her mother's voice. 'Can I come in?'

'Yes.'

'Your father's gone to the pub for a quick pint with some of the chaps. You can come downstairs and watch some television with us if you'd like.'

'No, thank you,' said Miriam. Her voice sounded more petulant than she had intended.

Her mother hovered by the door, clearly unsure whether Miriam wanted to talk to her. As Miriam didn't speak, her mother made her way to the bed and carefully lowered herself down on to it. Miriam's attempts to give her the cold shoulder evaporated.

'Are you okay, Mum. Have you hurt your back?'

'I must have overdone it,' she said, rubbing at the hollow of her spine. 'A good night's rest is all I need. I'll be right as rain by morning. I think I'll go to bed, though. It's been a long day, what with one thing and another.' Slowly, she raised herself back up and headed for the door. 'Your father only wants what's best for you, Miriam,' she said, turning back. 'You know that, don't you? And you did rather throw him off guard, so you did. We can talk to him again when he's calmed down but if I were you I'd put all ideas of drama school out of your mind. Perhaps you could teach English instead – and Drama too, maybe. And we can look into seeing who does plays round here that you could join in with. How would that be?'

That would be diabolical, thought Miriam, but she didn't say so.

'Goodnight, Mum,' she said instead.

IV

The first thing Miriam heard when she woke the following morning was the sound of the vacuum cleaner. Groaning, she turned to look at her alarm clock. It was just after six. Why was her mother hoovering? At this time? The party was going to be outside in the street, not in their house. She rolled on to her back and stared up at the ceiling. Judging by the strength of the light filtering through her curtains, it was not going to be a bad day. At least it wouldn't rain.

It might come today, the letter from RADA, although if it did she'd keep it under her hat, at least until after the street party. She was surprised to find that she was looking forward to the party. Clare was refusing to go but then that was Clare all over. She preferred to spend the day under the radar with her friends. By contrast, Anna was quite keen on the idea, no doubt so that she could smile prettily at the neighbours and get them all to say how lovely she was, which they would.

The vacuum cleaner stopped humming downstairs. Any minute now her mother would come and knock on her bedroom door. There was no such thing as a lie-in in the Bliss household. Her mother didn't believe in lazing around wasting time in bed. Miriam heard her mother's slow, heavy tread up the stairs, heard her rapping on first Clare's and then Anna's door, heard the complaining groan from Clare.

'Miriam? Are you up?'

'Yes, Mum,' Miriam lied.

'It'll be all hands to the pumps today and that's the truth of it,' her mother was saying as Miriam walked into the kitchen. 'Clare, I'll be needing you to finish those trifles. Miriam and Anna can be getting on with the sandwiches. We're doing cheese, Spam and jam. Don't bother cutting off the crusts. We need the food to stretch as far as it can. They'll all come crawling out of the woodwork when the stuff's on the table, you see if they don't. There's plenty of white sliced in the pantry but go easy on the cheese. Then when those are done you can go see if you can help Mrs Connors with setting up the tables. We can't be doing that too early, though, or the plates and cups might blow away. She says she's found some fancy ones with Union Jacks on them but I'm not sure there will be enough to go round, so we might have to fill in with those plain red ones that I got in Kwik Save.'

There was no point interrupting. Her mother came at the arrangements like a tornado, picking up and carrying anyone who got in her way. There was something about her enthusiasm that seemed a little forced, though, Miriam thought, and she had uncharacteristically dark circles under her eyes. No one else seemed to have noticed, though. Miriam knew that she was the only one tuned in at this higher level of perception.

'Of course, the most important task of the day falls to me,' said her father with mock self-importance. 'The hanging of the red, white and blue bunting without which no self-respecting Royalist function can proceed.'

'Well, mind you don't fall off that ladder,' said her mother. 'I've enough on without a trip to the hospital.'

'Do not trouble your pretty little head, oh light of my life. I will be the image of prudence as I affix the garlands to the lamp posts. I do need to go now, though' – he wiped the corner of his mouth with his ring finger in an effete gesture which seemed out of place – 'or they will appoint someone else Gaffer. I will see you 'orrible lot later.' He winked at Anna as he left. 'Extra jam in my butties, please!' – and then he was gone.

The girls, working as an unlikely team, got on with clearing the breakfast dishes and then Miriam and Anna set up a sandwich production line whilst Clare whipped cream and decanted custard from pan to quivering jelly and lady's fingers.

'How long do you reckon we have to stay?' asked Clare as she licked custard from the wooden spoon. 'I mean, once it gets going no one's going to notice whether we're there or not.'

'Well, where else are you going to be?' asked Miriam. 'The whole street will be there. The whole country will be having parties. I think it'll be fun. It's like being a part of history.'

Clare scowled. 'Do you think we'll be able to get our hands on any booze?'

Miriam threw a warning glance at Clare, nodding her head in Anna's direction. If Anna had noticed, then she gave a good impression of pretending that she hadn't.

'Probably,' said Miriam quietly. If Anna hadn't noticed before, her ears would definitely be flapping now. 'I think Dad said there are some kegs of Double Diamond and some cider too. You'll just have to be discreet about it but once things get going I doubt very much that anyone will notice. Well, apart from Mum, of course.'

'I'm supposed to be meeting Stuart Kingsley but I might not bother.' Clare was trying to sound as casual as she could but Miriam knew her well enough to recognise the excitement in her voice.

'Isn't he seeing Ruth Dixon?' she asked, simply to cause trouble.

'That's all over. She's a jealous cow. Stuart's well rid of her.' Clare smoothed the whipped cream over the custard.

'Can I put on the sprinkles?' asked Anna, and Clare handed her the tub of hundreds and thousands with a resigned air.

Six hours later and the party was well under way. Everyone seemed to have come out on to the street. A few people had even made an effort with costumes, although most had restricted their patriotic garb to a plastic Union Jack bowler hat. The trestle tables ran the length of the road, each decked with paper cloths and platters of sandwiches, sausage rolls and fairy cakes. Miriam was sitting not far from their own front door with Anna to her left and Malcolm from next door to her right. She was blocking his tedious conversation about the Silver Jubilee First Day Covers by turning away from him and trying to talk to Anna, but he seemed happy to continue the conversation with her back and she didn't have the heart to ignore him completely.

Clare had disappeared shortly after the food had arrived, only to appear not long after with a pint glass which seemed to hold more froth than beer and Stuart Kingsley in tow. Miriam had not seen her father since opening time, which was not surprising, but of more concern was the absence of her mother. Her mother was always centre-stage at this kind of occasion. She would expect to see her bustling around with food, making sure that everyone had what they needed. This task seemed to have fallen to Mrs Connors, Malcolm's mum, whose hostess skills were less well honed. Miriam could see her now, forcing a Spam sandwich on a rather nervous-looking man with a handlebar moustache.

Scraping the remains of her trifle from the waxed paper bowl and popping it into her mouth, Miriam stood up and excused herself. Malcolm was still talking about stamps and Anna had slipped under the table and was now directing play from beneath the tablecloth. Miriam thought she might start her hunt at home. Her mother could have taken herself for a quiet sit-down. It wasn't much like her but then she had done a lot of things that were out of character recently. She walked to their front door and quietly let herself in. The door closed behind her and muffled the sound of the party outside. She stood with her back against it and listened to the laughter. It all seemed to be going really well. Mum would be pleased.

Her attention was caught by a strange noise that she didn't recognise. It was out of kilter with the sounds of the party but she couldn't identify it. The sound stopped and then started up again. It sounded a bit like moaning. Miriam strained to listen but she couldn't tell where it was coming from.

'Mum?' she shouted. 'Are you here?'

There was no reply but then came another moan, louder this time and most definitely from inside the house.

'Mum?!'

Miriam set off up the stairs, taking them two at a time. Just as she reached the landing the moaning changed into something that was nearer a grunt. Miriam flung open the door to her parents' room and there on the bed was her mother. She was lying on her back, her knees drawn up and her skirt serving no function whatsoever. Her knickers were discarded on the floor. They were wet.

'Mum? What's the matter?'

Even as Miriam spoke, she was surveying the scene and piecing together the evidence.

'Miriam. Thank God,' said her mother through gritted teeth. 'You're going to have to help me. I need some hot water and plenty of clean towels.'

Miriam didn't respond. Whilst she could see what was happening, she couldn't quite believe her eyes.

'Miriam. Please,' said her mother through what must have been another contraction. 'I need you to do as I say.'

'I should go and get someone. Dad? Or Mrs Connors? Or an ambulance?'

'It's too late for all that . . . I just need you . . . to get some towels. There's going to be . . . a bit of a mess.'

Miriam was still struggling to comprehend.

'Mum. Are you having . . .?'

'Yes, I'm having a bloody baby, now will you just do as I say. Please.' She added, 'It's not far off now.' And then she closed her eyes and began to pant.

Her mother had just sworn. She never swore. Miriam seemed to be held by some invisible force to the floor. Her mother had just sworn and she was having a baby. The information would not allow itself to be processed. Surely she must have known what was coming? You couldn't just be pregnant and not know, could you? She'd done it three times already, after all. There were signs to recognise, weren't there, or women would be having surprise babies all over the place. And yet there was no denying that her mother appeared to be in labour, not that Miriam had much understanding of what that meant in practice.

Her mother made a muffled screaming sound. She seemed to be biting down on something – a pair of her father's socks? – and Miriam jerked herself into action.

'Hold on, Mum. I'm going to go downstairs and boil the kettle and get some towels and then I'm going to go and find someone to help.'

'No,' came the anguished cry from her mother. 'Stay here. The head . . .'

Her mother seemed unable to speak any more. She was straining as if she were on the loo, and making this grunting sound through her clenched teeth. Miriam reluctantly looked to where she assumed the head would appear. There, between her mother's splayed legs, was a bloodied crown of sticky blond hair. A baby. Her little brother or sister. And it was just there. She could reach out and touch it.

Her mother stopped straining and the head withdrew a little, back into its warm cave.

'It will be born with the next push,' said her mother, sounding totally calm in this small hiatus.

'What do I do, Mum?'

'You catch it and then pass it to me and I'll wrap it up in the sheets to keep it warm. There's the cord and the afterbirth but we'll worry . . .'

Her mother's words trailed off as the contraction built and the grunting noise began again. As her mother strained, Miriam could see the head re-emerging, followed by a tiny pair of shoulders and then the rest of the tiny little life slithered out. Miriam only just had chance to stick out her hands and catch him, for it was a boy. He was slippery, covered in a viscous bloody slime, the purple cord snaking out behind him.

Quickly and without fear she handed him to her mother, who put him to her breast whilst pulling the striped flannel sheet up to cover his tiny body.

'Now,' she said. 'Now go and find Mrs Connors and your father.'

Miriam stood, open-mouthed. She couldn't leave now, not with her mother in disarray and her baby brother still attached to her. But she needed help. She didn't feel qualified to help on her own.

'Will you be all right?' she asked.

'We'll be fine now,' her mother said. 'But I'll need some help with the next bit.'

'There's more?!' asked Miriam. What else could there possibly be?

'I have to deliver the afterbirth and I need someone to check that it's all there. I'm not sure that you can do that.'

'Okay,' said Miriam efficiently, certain that she didn't want any part of delivering anything. 'You stay there. I'll be right back.'

But her mother was no longer listening. She was gazing into the eyes of her newborn son as he sucked contentedly.

Miriam turned and raced down the stairs with gigantic strides, almost catapulting herself into the front door. She hurtled out into the street and was momentarily taken aback by the tables and flags where the cars should be. The street party was still carrying on as if nothing had happened and yet just yards away a miracle had just taken place. She scanned the crowd, searching for the familiar shape of Mrs Connors and found her not far away, decanting squash from a large plastic jug.

'Mrs Connors!' she shouted, but she could not make herself heard over the chatter and laughter. She pushed her way through the groups of women serving food to those seated until she was right next to her.

'Mrs Connors!' she said again, quieter this time but with such urgency in her voice that Mrs Connors immediately stopped pouring, the jug floating in mid-air over the cups.

'What on earth is the matter, Miriam? You look like you've seen a ghost.'

'Something's happened,' said Miriam, being deliberately vague. She didn't want all and sundry knowing before she found her father and Clare and Anna. 'Mum needs some help. Could you come?'

'Well, of course, dear. I'll just finish this jug.' She resumed her pouring.

'No! Now,' urged Miriam, and then, as an afterthought, 'Please.'

'Okay, I'll come right now, although I can't imagine what can possibly have happened to merit all this fuss.'

There was no time to explain.

'Mum's at home. She's upstairs,' said Miriam. 'Just let yourself in and go up. I need to go and find Dad.'

At this Mrs Connors seemed to sense that something was indeed wrong and broke into as quick a walk as her frame would allow.

'I think your dad's gone to The Merry Widow with some of the chaps. I'm not sure the Double Diamond was to their taste,' she couldn't resist adding.

'Thanks. I'll be back as quick as I can. If you see Clare or Anna could you tell them to go home?' she shouted over her shoulder as she headed off in the direction of the pub.

It was hard to see in the gloom of the tap room and Miriam's eyes struggled to adjust. She heard her father before she saw him, sitting at a table between the dartboard and the billiards table holding court.

'So he said, "Well, Frank, my boy, you should have opted for the lemon sole!"' The men all burst into laughter, which her father was absorbing as if it were oxygen. Then he saw her and held his hand up to silence his audience. 'Ah, Miriam,' he said cheerfully. 'It's not all over already, is it?'

'You must go home, Dad. Now. Straight away. Something's happened. To Mum. She needs you now.'

Sensing her urgency, her father stood up at once.

'Well, gents, it looks like there has been some minor domestic drama which requires my attention. I must bid you farewell.'

He picked up his glass, drained the pint in one and followed Miriam.

'What's the emergency?' he asked as they made their way back towards the house.

Miriam looked at him and an enormous smile blossomed across her face.

'You will never guess what!' she began. 'Mum's had a baby!'

Her father stopped stock-still, his brow furrowed, his lips parted, and then, as the significance of what Miriam had just told him sank in, he set off again at a run.

'A baby?' he said as they ran. 'A bloody baby!'

By the time they got back to the house, Clare and Anna were already there. Their mother was sitting up in bed, her hair brushed and with a clean nightdress on. The baby was wearing a pink knitted romper suit which flopped uselessly at the end of each tiny limb.

'I thought you said it was a boy?' her father said.

'It is a boy,' said her mother. 'This is all that we had and I only kept this one because my mother knitted it for Miriam and I couldn't bear to throw it out.'

'Well,' said her father, uncharacteristically momentarily lost for words. 'This is a turn-up for the books.'

'Isn't it just?' said Clare with a smirk.

'I'm not sure I understand,' her father continued.

'Come on, Dad,' said Clare. 'I thought you'd know all about the birds and the bees.'

'Clare!' said her mother. 'It is a bit of a surprise,' she added.

'Did you not know, have no inkling at all?' asked her father. Miriam, who had been wanting to ask the self-same question, looked at her mother enquiringly.

'Honestly I had not a clue. I knew I was carrying a few extra pounds and I was feeling a bit tired and what have you. But when I stopped getting the curse, I just assumed it was the change. I am forty-seven, after all. And there was none of that terrible sickness that I had with you girls.'

'They do say that about boys,' chipped in Mrs Connors, who was busying herself with tidying up. 'I never had a moment's nausea when I was carrying our Malcolm.'

'But a baby . . .' said her father. 'I can't quite take it in.'

'What shall we call him?' asked Anna. 'We can't keep calling him Him.'

'A name!' said her mother. 'I hadn't thought of that. I can't think.'

'I like Zowie,' said Anna. 'Like Zowie Bowie.'

'Don't be ridiculous, Anna,' said Clare dismissively. 'What about Duncan or Paul. Or Woody.'

'Woody's not a real name,' said Miriam.

'We could name him Robert after my father,' said her father. Anna pulled a face.

'I think I shall call him Sebastian,' said her mother. 'I've always loved that name. It's so classy, don't you think?'

'It's a bit girly,' began Clare, but Miriam mouthed at her to be quiet.

'Yes,' said her father. 'Sebastian. Like in *Twelfth Night*.'

'Like in *Belle and Sebastian* on the telly,' said Anna. 'Hello, Sebastian. I'm your big sister.'

Sebastian turned his head in the direction of the sound, his eyes still half-closed from his journey along the birth canal. He had blond hair and red skin and he was very wrinkly. Miriam couldn't help but think that he was really rather ugly. Her mother started yawning widely and Mrs Connors took control.

'Right, you lot. It's all been a bit of a shock, I know, but now your mum needs to get some sleep. Lord knows, it'll be in short enough supply around here for a while. So can I suggest that we all go back to the party and she and your new baby brother . . . Sebastian?' Her mother nodded. 'Sebastian can get some sleep.'

Mrs Connors ushered the girls from the room, leaving her father standing at the bedside shaking his head. As she sloped out, Miriam heard him speaking quietly to her mother.

'Are you all right, Dorothy darling? I can't believe you had to go through all that by yourself.' Miriam saw him lean over to hug his wife and then the door closed behind her.

'A baby!' said Clare as they trooped down the stairs. 'It's disgusting. I can't believe they still do it. Yuk!'

'Do what?' asked Anna.

'Never mind,' said Miriam, and then to Clare, 'I know. I can't believe she didn't know.'

'Well, you heard what she said,' replied Clare. 'It's not the kind of thing you'd cover up. And she looked as surprised as we did.'

'I saw him being born,' said Miriam quietly. 'It was amazing. He just fell out all of a slither. It looked really painful for Mum. I'm not sure I want any children if that's what it's like.'

'No danger of that! You have to do it first, you know, sis,' said Clare snidely.

Miriam smacked her on the arm.

'Do what?' asked Anna.

'Nothing,' replied Miriam quickly, and again pulled a face at Clare.

'I can't wait to tell everyone,' said Anna, and then, 'We can tell people, can't we? I mean, it's not a secret or anything, is it?'

'No,' said Miriam. 'I can't think why it would be and everyone will know soon enough.'

'Well, I'm definitely not keeping him a secret,' said Clare. 'Best bit of gossip that I've heard in ages.'

The three of them stepped out through the front door and into the street. As they did so an enormous cheer went up.

'Hip hip!' shouted Mrs Connors, who must have raced down the stairs and out of the house to spread the news with a haste that Miriam would not have thought her capable of.

'Hurrah!' shouted the crowd.

'A new baby!' shouted someone. 'And on Jubilee Day. That's worth a toast. Let us raise our glasses to the new Baby Bliss. To Baby Bliss.'

'Sebastian!' said Anna proudly.

'To Sebastian,' said someone.

'To Sebastian,' the crowd echoed and then another cheer went up.

Somewhere in the distance, Miriam thought she could hear a baby cry.

V

The first three weeks of life with Sebastian in the family passed in a blur. It was school exam season, and so Miriam had been trying to squeeze her O level revision in around the housework and cooking that she was having to do to help her mother. It wasn't great, to be honest, and she was hoping that someone would write her a note for school explaining how impossible her life had suddenly become.

Her mother did not seem to be adapting well. For the first two weeks she had stayed in bed with Sebastian. Her confinement – that's what Mrs Connors had called it, although that suggested that her mother was trapped up there and Miriam could see no reason why she couldn't just get up. She and her sisters had all tiptoed around, trying not to disturb mother and baby, but as Sebastian quickly seemed capable of making more noise than the rest of them put together, the tiptoeing had very soon fallen by the wayside.

June stretched into July and her mother was still showing barely any inclination to retake her position as the de facto head of the household. She was at least now joining them in the kitchen for meals, with Sebastian in the old Silver Cross carrycot beside the table, but as soon as the plates were cleared her mother would push herself up from the table, gather up the cot and return to her bedroom. Miriam felt that she needed to raise the subject with her father, as things had to get back to normal.

'Dad,' she began one evening when she and her father were taking their turn at washing and drying the dishes.

'Yes,' he replied flatly. Gone were his verbal embellishments. He too seemed totally worn down by the situation.

'Is Mum all right?'

'I believe so,' he said without looking up from the soap-suddy bowl.

'It's just that,' began Miriam, 'I mean, was she like this after we were born?'

'Like what?'

He wasn't making this easy.

'I mean, I know she's tired and all that but she seems to have lost all her spark. Is that what happened when we were babies?'

Her father took his time scrubbing at the edges of a pan that looked perfectly clean to Miriam before he spoke. She continued to dry the plates and waited.

'I think the whole thing has come as a bit of a shock to your mother,' he said eventually. 'Well, to all of us. We thought we were finished with babies. Anna's eleven. We were just moving forward into a new stage of life. Your mother was even talking about going back to work.'

This was news to Miriam. It had never crossed her mind that her mother wouldn't always just be at home waiting for them. It didn't really affect her as she was still planning to go to London after Sixth Form, but the others would be here.

'And with Sebastian being born as he was, you know, just out of the blue, your mum hasn't had any time to get used to the new situation. I think she's still adjusting. It's been a shock.'

'You can say that again!' said Miriam, who still couldn't get the sound of her mother's groaning in pain out of her mind.

'I think we just have to give her time,' he continued. 'And in due course she will get it all straight in her head and then we'll get back to normal, I'm sure we will.'

Miriam nodded although she was already struggling to remember what 'normal' looked like.

'And in the meantime,' he continued, 'we just have to do everything we can to support her so that she doesn't have anything to worry about.'

'Yes,' said Miriam quietly.

This was her moment. She needed to tell him now or she doubted whether she would find the courage again.

'It's just that . . .'

Her father had finished the washing-up and was drying his hands. Miriam began again.

'Do you remember, just before Sebastian was born and there was the street party and all that?'

Her father was heading towards the door, evening paper under his arm.

'Hmmm,' he said, but Miriam could tell that he wasn't listening.

'Oh, never mind,' she said as he opened the door. 'It doesn't matter.'

'Miriam!' her mother's voice shouted down the stairs. 'Could you bring me a bottle and a clean nappy?'

Her father left the room. The moment had passed.

'Yes, Mum. Just coming,' shouted Miriam, but she didn't move. She just stood there. She could feel the folded envelope pressing into her through her jeans pocket.

Clare came in. 'Mum's shouting you,' she said as she got a biscuit from the barrel on the windowsill.

'I know. I heard her.'

'She wants some milk and a nappy.'

'I know. Can't you get it?'

'I'm just going to meet Richie. I haven't got time.'

'What happened to Stuart?' asked Miriam.

'Who, that loser? He's history. Richie's taking me to the flicks.'

'Miriam!' came the cry from upstairs again.

'Coming, Mum,' shouted Miriam.

'It wouldn't kill you to help,' she hissed at Clare. 'It shouldn't be all down to me, you know. I've got a life too.'

Clare just looked at her and laughed. 'I'll be back around ten thirty,' she said, and left through the back door, letting it bang behind her.

Wearily, Miriam put a pan of water on the stove to heat up and dropped a bottle of formula from the fridge into it. Then she pulled down the clothes-airer and whipped off the nappies and liners, folding them into two neat piles. She tested the temperature of the milk by splashing a few drops on the inside of her wrist and then carried the whole lot up the stairs to her mother's room.

Knocking gently on the door first, she pushed her way in. Her mother was sitting in bed. She was propped up with pillows and was wearing her housecoat over a cotton nightdress. Telltale damp circles were blooming over her breasts. Miriam tried not to stare but she was fascinated by them.

Her mother pushed hair that couldn't have seen a brush for a while away from her eyes.

'You'd think now that I've finished feeding him myself that my milk would have dried up but still it flows out of me like a river. Pass me that bottle, Miriam. Or would you like to feed your brother?'

Miriam had revision that she really ought to be getting on with but she reached down into the carrycot and picked Sebastian up. He had grown a lot since he had first slipped into her waiting arms. His face had taken shape, filling out around his cheeks and chin, and he had more hair, blond and with the first twists of curls just starting to form. He smiled now too, a beautiful, engaging smile which was hard to ignore.

'It's not a real smile,' her mother had said the first time he had smiled at her. 'It's just wind.' But Miriam knew that it was real. She could tell.

'How are you feeling today, Mum?' she asked. 'Do you think you'll feel up to getting up tomorrow?'

Her mother patted at her wayward hair, no hope of controlling it with such a feeble gesture.

'I don't know. Maybe. Let's see what kind of a sleep we have. At least he seems to have sorted his days and nights out now,' she added.

'Well, don't worry,' said Miriam. 'We're all coping without you. Clare and I are sharing the cooking and Dad has even done some ironing.'

Her mother reached out and patted the arm that was supporting Sebastian's head.

'You're a good girl, Miriam,' she said, and then let her arm fall back on to the eiderdown as if the mere effort of moving it that far had been exhausting.

Sebastian had fixed his eyes on hers as he sucked rhythmically on the teat. They had been blue when he was born but were now a smudgy grey.

'I think they're going to be brown,' said her mother. 'Imagine that. Brown eyes and blond hair. He's going to be a good-looker. He'll be breaking some hearts, so he will.'

'Mum . . .' began Miriam. When her mother didn't respond, she pressed on. 'Do you remember the day before he was born?'

'The street party,' said her mother absently. 'All that effort and then I didn't even get to go. Was it a good do? I bet it was. I bet they were all talking about me, weren't they? That stupid woman at number twenty-four who's gone and got herself up the duff and hasn't even noticed?'

Miriam would have liked to pursue this line of enquiry further. How her mother could have had a baby without realising was equally fascinating and terrifying. Not that she had any cause for concern herself but she worried about what Clare was getting up to with the string of boys she seemed to be dangling along behind her. However, she avoided the distraction. She needed to get her mother to focus on the other, far more important matter.

'Before then,' she continued. 'The night before the street party. When I told you all that I wanted to go to RADA.'

Her mother's forehead creased as she struggled to recall. Things that had happened before Sebastian seemed to have been locked in a part of her memory that she seemed to be having trouble accessing.

'Yes,' she said after a few moments, her head nodding slowly. 'Vaguely. And your dad said that, well, he said a lot of things but the gist was that you weren't going?' She smiled, pleased that she had recovered the information from wherever it had been hiding. 'Yes,' she continued. 'I do remember that now.'

'Well,' said Miriam slowly, 'they've written back. They want me to go for a chat. It's not like an audition. It's more an open day when you can go and see what it's all about.'

Balancing Sebastian in the crook of her left arm, she snaked her right hand round and retrieved the letter from her back pocket.

'Here,' she said. 'Read it.'

'I don't have my reading specs, Miriam,' her mother said, even though Miriam could see them sitting just next to her on the bedside table.

'Okay. Well, basically it says that they are interested in my application but because I don't have any experience, they want to have a talk to me to tell me what it's all about in case I change my mind when I know all the ins and outs. So . . .' She paused as she lifted Sebastian up on to her shoulder and began to rub his back to make him burp. 'Can I go?'

Her mother was staring out of the window at the telegraph wires and the roofs of the smart semi-detached houses on the opposite side of the street. She didn't speak and Miriam thought she had lost her attention. Then Sebastian let out an enormous, satisfying belch and the noise of it seemed to bring her back.

'Good boy,' said Miriam. 'That's better, isn't it?'

Miriam put Sebastian back in the carrycot, where he could provide no further distraction. He grizzled a little but then began making small contented gurgles.

'Mum?' she tried again. 'What do you think? Could I go? I mean, it's only a chat and nothing might come of it. It wouldn't do any harm to just go and see. I mean, I might hate it when I get there and then we could forget about the whole thing. But if I don't go, if I never know . . .' Her voice drifted off.

Her mother reached out her hand and rested it on Miriam's lap. She held it there for a long time without speaking. Sebastian gurgled. Miriam waited.

'Everything's changed, Miriam,' she said eventually. 'Nothing will ever be the same as it was. Your dad and I have four children to bring up now. All our plans have been thrown out of kilter. All my plans . . .' Miriam had no idea that her mother had had any plans and the idea seemed odd but she kept quiet. 'We're all going to have to work together now,' her mother continued. 'Having a baby in the house is hard work and everyone needs to pull their weight. I know you've all been working hard since he was born but that's just the beginning. As he grows, he's going to need more and more attention. I can't do that all by myself, Miriam. I have the rest of you to look after and I'm not getting any younger. I thought that it was the change coming over me and I was ready for that. But this, a new baby? At my age? It's not something I would ever have dreamed of. Now don't be thinking I don't want him. I love the bones of him now he's here but I don't know how I'll cope. I really don't.' Tears began to run down her face. Her mother never cried and Miriam felt totally lost as she seemed to crumple in front of her.

'Anna's too young to be much help and Clare – well, you know what Clare's like. I'm going to need you, Miriam.'

'Well, I'll help, Mum, all I can. You know I will. I mean, I've got my schoolwork and everything. It's an important time, with my exams and that. But by the time I want to go to RADA he'll be two and all this sleepless-nights and bottle-baby bit will be over and done with.'

Her mother shook her head wearily. 'This baby stage is the easy bit,' she said. She reached out for a handkerchief, almost upsetting a glass of water. It wobbled but did not topple. 'It's after that. The toddler, the terrible twos, playgroup, all of it. I can't face it all again, Miriam. So help me God but I really can't.' She blew her nose and wiped her eyes.

'Don't cry, Mum,' Miriam said anxiously. 'We'll all help. And I'm not going anywhere for ages yet. You'll be feeling better by then. I know you will.'

Her mother was shaking her head, more tears streaming down her face.

'You don't understand, my precious girl. I need you near me. I can't have you all the way down in London. You'll go to college, of course you will. You must. But it'll have to be one nearby so you can live at home.'

The impact of what her mother was saying slowly washed over Miriam. Her life, her plans and her dreams were all to be sacrificed.

'You can't mean that, Mum,' she said. 'I mean, I'm happy to help out and all that but you can't keep me trapped here like a prisoner. None of this is my fault. I didn't ask for Sebastian to be born. It's not fair.' She could hear her voice rising but she tried to keep it in control so that she didn't wake Sebastian, who was now slumbering.

'Well, I can't see any other way through it.' Her mother was no longer crying. 'And your dad already said that you couldn't go to drama school, didn't he?' There was a slightly triumphant tone to her words, as if she had suddenly thought of the killer point in an argument. 'He said that before any of this happened, so he did. So truly, this RADA dream of yours was never going to come true even if there wasn't a baby to consider.' She seemed to relax as she realised that the responsibility for this decision no longer lay with her. 'I think it's best, Miriam, if you put the whole thing to the back of your mind and concentrate on getting good grades.'

Miriam didn't know how to deal with this. Her mother wasn't thinking straight, she couldn't be. She seemed to be suggesting that Miriam gave up her life to look after her brother but that wasn't right, surely? Miriam must have got the wrong end of the stick. She crushed her lips between her teeth and stood up. It was important that she didn't lose her cool. If she just left now, without a row, then no doubt her mum would forget the whole thing. She would try her dad again. She had to. This could not be happening to her.

'You're an angel, Miriam, so you are. I knew you'd understand,' said her mother. And then, as if a weight had suddenly been lifted from her shoulders, she said, 'You know, I might even try getting up for a while tomorrow if it's a nice day. Perhaps we could push him out in the pram, take a turn around the park together?'

Miriam couldn't speak and continue to hold herself together, so she just nodded her head. She walked to the door and was just opening it when her mother called after her.

'Could you be a lamb and just change his nappy for me?'

CLARE – 1979

I

Clare moved the ice cube from the side of her nostril and peered at her nose in the mirror. Her skin had gone a blotchy crimson. Rudolf the bloody Red-Nosed Reindeer, she thought. That was all she needed. She had to look her absolute best tonight. Christmas Eve was pretty much the biggest night out of the year and she was going to turn heads if it killed her. Yup. They'd all be looking at her this year.

She flicked at her nose with her fingernail. It felt numb – well, numb-ish. It would have to do. Without giving herself a second to change her mind, she picked up the safety pin and stabbed it through the side of her nose. There was a disconcerting pop as the point of the pin pierced her flesh.

Shit, that hurt. Her eyes started to water at exactly the same moment as her nose began to bleed. Quickly, she fastened the safety pin into place and grabbed for a tissue. She didn't care about the blood but she had to stop her eyeliner from smudging. She hadn't spent an hour drawing the careful black lines around her eyes for them all to run down her face. At least her mascara was waterproof.

There wasn't as much blood as she'd expected and a few minutes later she had all her bodily fluids back under control. Clare inspected her face in the mirror. The safety pin looked fantastic. She'd known it would. It was actually one of Sebastian's nappy pins and it had a white fastener which made it even more noticeable – not that anyone was likely to miss the massive pin hanging from her nose. Clare gave a little shiver of delight. People were going to be so shocked.

She stepped back to take in her full ensemble and nodded with satisfaction at what she saw. She'd really wanted some tartan bondage trousers but hadn't found anything even vaguely similar in the shops in town. She'd have to hitchhike down to London after Christmas, go to the King's Road and get some. She'd found the tight black jeans at the market and, with a bit of strategic slitting and fraying across the thighs and the knees, they were nearly as good. Maybe she could nick a loo chain or two from school? She'd also cut the sleeves off her T-shirt and slashed it down the front, the raw edges curling up obligingly.

Her new hair was going to take some getting used to, mind you. Until this afternoon, her hair had been a boring kind of fair – not quite blonde but not brunette either. There was no mistaking its colour now. Black. Pure ebony-black and shiny like crow's feathers. She had stuck the fringe up with gel and backcombed it. The rest wasn't quite right yet but she could get it cut after Christmas – or cut it herself. The new colour made her skin look far paler than it was, an effect exacerbated by the dark eyes and panstick foundation. Her lips were ruby-red. And so was her nose.

Clare reached for her concealer and gingerly applied another layer on the area around the safety pin. God, it hurt, but it was all for the greater good. You had to suffer for your art, wasn't that what they said? Well, this wasn't art as such but she was the first punk at school, which made her a trailblazer with her finger on the pulse of the nation. That was definitely worth a bit of pain. She should be in London, really. That's where the scene was, not stuck up here in this godforsaken backwater.

She picked up her money and the front door key and rammed them into her back pocket. Then she took a deep breath and headed downstairs to face the music.

The others were in the lounge. The telly was on, some sitcom or other, and the canned laughter rang though the house. Miriam's teacher training college had broken up for the holidays and so she was back in her other role of Mother Mark II. Clare missed the old Miriam. They had been close, back in the days before Sebastian had arrived and changed everything. Since then Miriam had altered. She was so bloody boring these days. It was like all the fun had been sucked out of her.

Clare thought about just letting herself out of the house without saying goodbye to them all but she couldn't resist trying her new look out on the family. They'd go mental – it was going to be brilliant.

As she approached the lounge door she could hear the conversation going on inside.

'For the love of Mary, what is that child still doing up?' said her mother. 'He should have been away in bed hours back.'

'But it's Christmas Eve,' Anna said. 'You can't make him go to bed early on Christmas Eve.'

'He's two years old. He has no idea what Christmas is yet,' replied her father.

'He does. You do, don't you, Sebastian? You can't wait to see Father Christmas and his reindeer, can you?'

Sebastian said something but as usual only Anna could tell what it was. Clare didn't actually believe that Anna could interpret half of what Sebastian 'said'. She just made stuff up so that she could win arguments.

'Would you put him to bed now, Miriam? There's a good girl.'

Clare heard Miriam sigh.

'Come on, Sebastian,' she said in a fake, sing-songy voice. 'Let's get you to bed, then.'

There were some objecting noises from Sebastian and then Clare judged that this was her moment to make an entrance, before Miriam went upstairs.

She swung open the door and took a couple of steps into the room. No one looked away from the television.

'Care!' said Sebastian, who still couldn't even master her name properly. He pointed his podgy little finger at her and then Miriam, following his gaze, saw her. Her jaw dropped gratifyingly.

'Oh my God,' she mouthed as she took in Clare's new look. Clare just grinned at her. This was exactly the impact she was after.

'Mum!' said Anna. 'Look what Clare's done to her hair!'

Anna always was a little snitch but for once Clare didn't mind.

'And what is that in your nose?' asked Miriam, her voice restored.

Finally, her parents pulled their eyes from the screen and Clare relished the looks of pure horror that passed across their faces.

'Oh dear Lord, bless us and save us,' said her mother. 'What have you done? Your beautiful hair. Oh, Clare, how could you?'

'With a box of dye,' said Clare. 'You know, the way people normally change their hair colour.' She was enjoying this even more than she'd thought she would. And when her parents noticed . . .

'And what the hell is that in your nose?' bellowed her father.

Here we go, thought Clare.

'A safety pin,' she replied, slightly less cocky to her father, who might actually have a go at stopping her from leaving the house.

'It's not,' said Anna. 'It's a nappy pin. A nappy pin!'

Clare threw her a murderous look.

'Through your nose? You stuck a safety pin—'

'Nappy pin,' clarified Anna, with a grin.

'Though your own nose, willingly?' asked her father. 'Of all the imbecilic things.'

'Did you sterilise it?' interrupted her mother. 'You might get blood poisoning. She might get blood poisoning, Frank. Do you think we should take her to Casualty?'

'On Christmas Eve? You have to be joking.'

'And are those the lovely new jeans you bought?' asked her mother, looking forlornly at what was left of them. 'You've totally ruined them. Why did you do that, Clare? They were lovely, so they were.'

Clare, now starting to feel slightly more flustered by their reactions than she had anticipated, decided that this was the time to make her exit.

'Right,' she said as she turned to leave the room. 'I'll be off. I'll be back later.'

'You stay right there, young lady,' her father thundered. 'If you think for one minute that I am going to allow you to go out looking like that then you have another think coming. You can go straight back upstairs, take that thing out of your nose and put some proper clothes on.'

'No,' replied Clare. There was an audible gasp from Miriam. 'It's Christmas Eve and I'm going out with my friends. You can't stop me. I'm seventeen years old. I'm virtually an adult. I can do what I want.'

'Not and live under my roof, you can't. Either you go back upstairs and get changed or you can find somewhere else to live tomorrow.'

'On Christmas Day?' smirked Clare. She'd show them. There was no way they'd kick her out, but they definitely wouldn't kick her out at Christmas. She had played a blinder and she knew it. 'Right,' she said, buoyed up by her killer point. 'I'm off. I'll see you all tomorrow. Merry Christmas.'

And with that she ran for the door, leaving her family staring shell-shocked after her.

II

The Bliss household was no place to be with a hangover. It was always so noisy, people shouting conversations at each other rather than talking, music blaring and that blasted hoover constantly whining day and night. She could hear Anna laughing at something Miriam had said. Why were they all so bloody cheerful? Then Clare remembered. It was Christmas Day.

She groaned and rolled over, knocking the pin in her nose as she did so. The pain was sharp and brought tears to her eyes. Still, it had been worth it to see the obvious respect of her friends last night as they gazed, open-mouthed, at her transformation. And the others, the ones who mocked and scoffed at her behind her back? Well, they could go to hell.

Her foot hit something resting on her blankets – her stocking! She sat up more quickly than was perhaps wise given the amount of cider she'd put away and grabbed for it. It was just a little thing made of red binca and clumsily embroidered with an angel and her name but it held her earliest memories of Christmas. The stocking was a kind of taster for the main event, filled with one or two presents to keep her quiet until it was time to get up. Such a device was obviously redundant these days but her mother insisted on keeping up the tradition. It was sweet, really.

Clare put her hand inside and pulled out a satsuma. Honestly. Who ever thought that fruit would do as a present? Diving in again she found what looked like a bottle, wrapped in shiny gold paper. Talc. It was bound to be. Clare almost didn't open it but then she couldn't resist. She was right and her heart sank a little. People must actually use talcum powder or else why would they still sell it? However, the only place Clare had ever put the vile stuff was on Sebastian's bum on those rare occasions that she'd changed his nappy.

The second present was also tube-shaped but much smaller. Lipstick. Clare pulled off the lid and twisted the perfect column until it stood as tall as its casing. It was a pretty pale pink, almost iridescent like the inside of a seashell. Clare tested the shade on the back of her hand. It was so pale that she almost couldn't see it. She had never worn pink lipstick in her life. This must be the Clare that her mother wished for, a feminine Clare that liked pretty colours and smiled passively when people spoke to her. The actual Clare must be such a disappointment.

Sometimes Clare would catch her mother just staring at her. There seemed to be a sadness in her eyes, as if her second child dismayed her. That was hardly surprising. Clare knew she was a disappointment to her parents and that she caused no end of trouble. She sometimes wondered if she even belonged in this family. She would play out a little fantasy in her mind in which she'd been accidentally swapped for another baby in the hospital. Maybe her real family was out there somewhere? Perhaps she'd be a better fit with them and not cause as much trouble as she did in this one. Actually, she liked causing trouble, revelled in it even, but from time to time she wondered why she couldn't just accept things like the others did. Why was she constantly pushing at boundaries, overstepping marks? It was almost like there was something in her that made her do it, her own personal self-destruct button.

Clare got out of bed, and as she did so she caught a glimpse of her black hair in the mirror. For a second she was shocked by her own reflection, not really understanding who it was in her bedroom with her.

Then she remembered. The contrast between the Clare who used rose-scented talc and wore pale-pink lipstick and the angry-looking young woman that she saw in the mirror made her want to cry.

By the time she got downstairs, the others were milling about in the kitchen.

'Now that Seb understands Christmas,' Anna was saying, 'can we open the presents before breakfast? I mean, Christmas is all about the children, really.'

'Nice try, Anna,' said Clare as she strolled in.

'Now then, Anna,' said their father from the sink, where he was washing the best glasses ready to be set on the Christmas table. 'You know the Bliss family traditions as well as I do and there will be no tampering with them, two-year-old family members notwithstanding. Presents come after breakfast.'

Anna groaned and swept Sebastian up to sit on her hip.

'Well, can we at least get on with breakfast, then?'

Clare smiled to herself. For all that Anna was thirteen, she was still just a kid herself. Seb didn't care about presents. It was Anna who couldn't wait. Their mother came in and Clare saw her recoil slightly when she saw her hair, much as Clare herself had done earlier, but then she gathered herself quickly. Clearly Clare's new hair wasn't going to feature in the Bliss family Christmas celebrations.

'Shall we sit down? Now, how do you all want your eggs? I'm doing scrambled or poached.'

The thought of an egg made Clare feel nauseous after last night's cider.

'No eggs for me, thanks, Mum. I'll just have cereal and toast.'

Their mother didn't really approve of cereal, believing that her children should have a proper cooked breakfast, but since Sebastian had been born things like bacon for breakfast had fallen by the wayside. Her mother shook her head and tutted quietly but she passed Clare a box of Rice Krispies.

Christmas Day trundled on in the way of all their Christmas Days. Presents were opened and squealed over, crackers were pulled and her mother enjoyed more sherry than she usually drank, and now they were all sitting around the dinner table half-heartedly passing the cheese board to one another. Sebastian had fallen asleep with his face on the highchair tray but no one could be bothered to move him to his bed. Miriam was recounting a convoluted tale about something that had happened at college. Clare wasn't really listening but she tried to look as if she was. She liked these times, when they were all together and having fun. Yes, she enjoyed stirring things up and breaking a few of the pointless rules that circumvented her life, but when they were all getting along together it was easier to feel like she belonged. She hung on to those precious moments.

When she looked round, Anna was staring at her.

'Did it hurt?' she asked.

Clare was lost.

'Your nose,' Anna clarified. 'Did it hurt when you pierced it?'

Trust Anna to spoil stuff. Everyone always said that it was Clare who caused the trouble but when it all kicked off you never had to look very far to find Anna. To retain this light-hearted mood, Clare should just ignore her or change the subject, but part of her was too proud of what she'd done to overlook the opportunity to talk about it, no matter what the consequences might be.

'Yeah,' she said. 'It hurt like hell.'

Her mother threw her a warning glance.

'Heck,' she corrected herself.

'Why a perfectly intelligent person would choose to ram a piece of stainless steel through her nose is a total mystery to me,' said her father. 'You'll probably have a scar for life.'

Clare shrugged.

'And all in the name of fashion,' he added, shaking his head.

'It's not fashion, Dad,' piped up Anna. 'I read an article on it in the paper. Punk is all about anarchy. That's right, isn't it, Clare?'

Anna, clearly proud of her knowledge, looked up at Clare, waiting for her confirmation. Clare didn't care about all that ideology stuff. As far as she was concerned, her new look was all about the shock factor. The politics of it didn't interest her. However, she was smart enough to know that if she made it look like she was standing up for something her father would at least give that a grudging respect. After all, wasn't that what he had always taught them?

'Yeah,' she said. 'It's about breaking free, striking out against the establishment.'

'Punk is basically being anti-things,' sighed Miriam, like she was way too mature for that kind of silliness. 'Anti-state, anti-society. I mean, what is the point of it? If you get rid of the rules, then society just collapses into chaos.'

'Well, duh,' replied Clare. 'That's kind of the point.'

'I think it's all very worrying,' said their mother. 'What was that awful song? The one about being an Antichrist? It made me chilled to the very bones of me, so it did.'

'That would be the Sex Pistols,' said their father. 'Such a talented bunch of young men.' The sarcasm oozed out of him as he spoke.

'Yeah, but that's it,' said Clare. 'Their talent is in having no talent. It's ironic, Dad.'

'It's the Emperor's New Clothes, that's what it is. They set out to exploit the youth and now they are sitting pretty on the proceeds.'

'Except Sid Vicious,' said Anna. 'I don't suppose he's looking very pretty by now.'

Their mother's eyebrow knitted themselves together as she struggled to follow the conversation.

'He's dead, Mum,' explained Miriam gently.

'Oh, may all the saints bless us. Don't be speaking ill of the dead, now, Anna.'

'They're all imbeciles,' said their father dismissively. 'And I can't understand why you, an intelligent young woman, would want to nail your flag to their mast, Clare. I mean, look at you. Your hair looks like something from a fancy dress shop, your clothes are basically rags and you have a nappy pin stuck through your nose. How exactly is that going to bring down society?'

Clare could feel her anger building but she tried to swallow it back down. Using every ounce of self-restraint she could muster, she kept her voice calm.

'It's about rising up against the establishment, Dad,' she said. 'Look at this country. We have strikes every day, there's no work. Do you remember when Mum had to queue up for bread? Capitalism isn't working and your generation is doing nothing about it. It's about time someone took action.'

'And sticking a nappy pin through your nose is going to solve all that, is it?' mocked their father.

'Frank, Frank,' their mother said, touching his arm. 'Let's not do this. It's Christmas Day.'

'At least I'm doing something!' Despite her best efforts Clare was shouting now, but what was going on here? She didn't care about the punk movement. Not really. She just liked the look and yet here she was getting herself into a massive argument defending it. She should stop, turn it all into a joke, but she couldn't. This was just the same as everything else. No one showed her any respect. She did something interesting or courageous and instead of congratulations she got ridicule. Their father never treated the others as badly as he treated her. It wasn't fair. If Clare was being entirely honest, she didn't really like the way her hair had turned out and the pin was killing her. She'd do anything to just take it out and forget about the whole thing. But if she did that her father would just smile at her smugly and say that he had been right all along, and she wasn't going to give him the pleasure of that.

Clare pushed away from the table. She caught sight of Anna, smirking at what was unfolding in front of her.

'Oh, Clare,' said her mother. 'Please sit back down. We're having such a lovely day. Let's not spoil it.'

Let's not spoil it? Why did her mother always do that, pretend to turn everything round so that the blame lay with them all? It was obvious that the only person spoiling things around here was her. Again. Everything was always her fault. She could never win.

She stalked out of the kitchen and slammed the door behind her. As she stomped up the stairs she could hear a wail rising up from Sebastian, who had clearly just woken up. That would be her fault as well, no doubt.

SEBASTIAN – 1985

I

'Are we nearly there yet?' asked Sebastian.

Anna, sitting next to him in the back of their old Volvo, tutted and rolled her eyes. Nobody spoke. Sebastian was feeling a bit sick, but not so bad that he might actually chuck up the Jubilee Pancake that he had wolfed when they'd stopped for lunch. It was more the kind of feeling that just sat there in the background, reminding him that they had been in the car for ever. Nobody answered.

'Can I open the window a bit?'

Immediately his mother's head spun round and she looked at him quizzically.

'Are you feeling all right, Sebastian? You're not feeling sick now, are you? Shall I get your father to stop the car?'

Stopping the car would be great, he thought. Then he could get out and get rid of the pins and needles that had been slowly creeping up his foot. But then if they did stop, they might never get there.

'No. It's okay,' he said, smiling his best charming smile at his mother. 'I'm fine. Well, I feel a bit queasy but I'm not going to be sick.'

He liked the word queasy. It was new. He had heard Anna use it. He liked how it stretched out on his tongue and made his lips leap to attention. He mouthed it to himself now – queasy, queasy, queasy. The more he said it, the less it sounded like a proper word.

'What are you saying, Pumpkin?' his mother asked. 'I can't hear you. Frank, could you take these bends a bit slower? You'll have us all green behind the gills, so you will.'

'Just want to get there,' said his father grimly, but he slowed the car down a little.

'Are we nearly there?' Sebastian tried again.

'Not long now, little man,' said his father. 'The last sign said it was five miles. It just takes a bit longer to cover the ground on these little roads.'

'So, can I open the window?' he asked again.

'I suppose so, if it's entirely necessary,' said his father.

'No,' said Anna at the same time.

Sebastian ignored his sister and turned the handle round half a turn so that a two-inch gap appeared at the top. He sat up in his seat to try to get the breeze to hit his face but the fresh air was running over the top of his head. He turned the handle again. Another two inches of air appeared.

'Mum. He's got the window wide open. It's freezing and it's messing my hair up.'

Sebastian looked at Anna's hair. Her fringe was combed so that it stood upwards and she had so much hair gel and spray on it that he was sure he could wind the window right down and it wouldn't even wobble. Anna raised her hands to her fringe and began teasing the roots with her fingers. Sebastian loved Anna's hair. When she'd had a bath and it was clean, it hung down her face, a chestnut curtain all shining like a mirror. But when she had finished 'doing' it, the shine was all gone and the fringe stuck up from the top of her head like a bird's nest. Sometimes Anna tied a spotty scarf around her head and pulled the towering fringe out. He liked that too. Today, though, her hair was plain.

'Sebastian, could you just put it back up a bit, there's a lamb?' his mother asked gently.

Sebastian turned the handle the smallest amount that he thought he could get away with. The glass crept back up the door frame. Anna threw him a look that said 'I'm on to you. You'd better watch out!' but she didn't speak.

The car slowed down and his father swung into a left turn. Sebastian recognised the hoardings along the road now. They showed pictures of caravans with hills and lakes in the background and an over-smiley family with rosy cheeks and blond hair. They really were nearly there. Around the next bend and there were the familiar white gates. Sebastian always thought it looked a bit like a fort with the archway over the road and the little wooden box where the man who checked who was coming in and out sat.

Daddy pulled the Volvo up at the window and spoke to the man.

'A very good day to you, Charlie. We find you well, I trust. Is it busy yet? We set off early to beat the crowds but I'll bet that old devil Thornbury has beaten us to it.' His father was laughing as he spoke to the security man.

Charlie ran his eyes over the list in front of him.

'There are a few arrived already, the Thornburys included. You'd have to get up early to beat them, Mr Bliss.'

His father laughed.

'Right. We'd better get this show on the road, get unpacked, all shipshape and Bristol fashion and what have you,' his father said. His mother raised an eyebrow. It was her that did the unpacking.

'Can I get out here and walk down to have a look at the lake?' asked Anna.

'What about the unpacking?' his father was in the middle of saying, but his mother put a hand on his arm and said, 'Yes, Anna. That's fine. Don't be too long. I'll need you to go to the shop for a few bits once we're sorted.'

Anna nodded her head without smiling and then she flung the car door open and set off down the road towards the trees at the bottom. His father tutted.

'Leave her be, Frank,' his mother said. 'She'll perk up once we get settled in. It's not much of a holiday for her with us and her little brother. It's a miracle she's here at all.'

'Well, there was no way she was staying at home by herself, not after last time. And now that Clare's gone . . .'

His father stopped talking and looked down at Sebastian.

'Let's not start all that again,' said his mother. Sebastian was disappointed. He wasn't really sure what had happened the last time they'd visited the caravan and left Anna at home and no one seemed prepared to tell him. He would just have to keep listening.

Dad pulled the car away from the gate slowly and at the first fork in the road turned right, which was the way to their caravan. Sebastian was sure that he could find it blindfolded. You followed the road down, past the patch of grass with the pond, and then took the second turning on the right next to the copper beech tree and then up the hill to the fourth van on the left.

'There she is,' said his mother as they turned at the copper beech and the caravan came into view. 'Oh, may the saints preserve us! Just look at that roof! We're going to have to do some cleaning whilst we're here, Sebastian.'

Sebastian smiled. He liked going up the ladder to pull the leaves out of the gutters. Anna didn't.

His father pulled the car on to the hardstanding at the side of the caravan and switched off the engine. He let out a sharp sigh.

'Let the holiday commence!' he said, and got out of the car. 'Hope you've brought your thermals, Mother!' he said. 'It's pretty parky out here.'

'Always a bit of a gamble at Easter, the Lakes,' said his mother, opening her door. 'Do you remember how it snowed that time?'

They always talked about the time it had snowed. Sebastian had only been three or four and he wasn't really sure that he did actually remember it. His blurry memories were all mixed up with photographs of him wrapped up in a blue jacket and a red bobble hat and the stories that the others told of that year.

'No snow in the forecast this year,' said his father confidently. 'But you never know what those hills might hold in store for us.' He threw a pretend scared look up at the black mountains in the distance, opening his eyes really wide and hunching his shoulders over.

Sebastian laughed.

'Now, where are those keys?' he said, and started patting all his pockets. Sebastian smiled at the familiar game. Even though it was pretty babyish, he liked to join in for his father's sake.

'That one!' he said, pointing at the breast pocket of his father's jacket. His father comically searched each pocket in turn without luck until he finally came to the one that Sebastian had pointed to in the first place and produced the key with its cork keyring dangling from it.

'Why didn't you tell me to look there in the first place?' he laughed, and Sebastian laughed too. His father tossed the keys at his mother. She caught them with her left hand and then slotted the key into the lock. The door opened smoothly.

Inside the caravan everything looked orange as the weak sunlight shone through the woven curtains. It was cold and smelled musty, as it always did when they first arrived. It was Sebastian's job to open the curtains. He took his trainers off, leaving them on the mat at the door, and squeezed past his mother so that he could let the light in. He kneeled up on the benches to reach the curtains, pulling them carefully from the top as his mother had shown him and not from the bottom where they were likely to come free from the tracks.

'Shall I start bringing in the stuff?' asked his father.

'Yes. That'd be grand. We'll be done in no time,' said his mother. 'And then you can go down to the shop and get some milk for a cup of tea, Pumpkin.' Sebastian loved going to the shop on-site because his father often gave him five pence to spend as long as he didn't tell his mother or let her catch him chewing Bubbly.

His father brought the bags and boxes from the car and piled them up in the doorway. Sebastian passed them to his mother, who decanted the contents into drawers and wardrobes until it was all away. He then passed the empty bags back to his father, who shut them up neatly in the boot of the Volvo. This job used to be done by Miriam and Clare but now it was his job.

His mother was just putting the Rich Teas in the biscuit barrel above the kettle when Anna reappeared.

'Shoes!' shouted Sebastian at Anna as she tried to come in without taking them off.

'All right. Keep your hair on,' she said sharply, but she slipped her pumps off.

She came in and slid herself on to the bench seat behind the dining table.

'Any chance of a cup of tea?' she asked.

'Sebastian is just going to get the milk. Do you want to go with him, Anna?'

Sebastian flinched. Going to get the milk and his sweets by himself was one of the highlights of his holiday and having his big sister with him would rob him of this chance.

'No, thanks,' said Anna, and Sebastian relaxed. 'I'll just kick around here for a bit. It's dead out there. There's no one around except the Thornburys.'

Another of Sebastian's favourite things about coming to the caravan was that they always saw the same people. There were caravans for ordinary tourists to borrow but most of the families on the site had their own static caravans, like they did. Some of them visited every weekend, he knew. His family didn't. It was too far, and there was always something happening at home at the weekend. They came every holiday, though, and that was when most other people came.

'I thought you liked Colin Thornbury,' his mother asked Anna.

'That was before he turned into a lecherous toad with wandering eyes and hands to match,' Anna said. Their mother threw her one of her warning faces, although Sebastian wasn't sure why. He hadn't noticed a swear word in there. Maybe 'lecherous' was rude? He would have to try to remember to look it up later on. He had packed his *Collins Pocket Dictionary* at the bottom of his satchel. One problem with being the youngest child was that he often had no idea what was going on around him, so the dictionary came in very handy. He wondered briefly what wandering hands were and his mind skittered off to *The Iron Man*, which they were reading at school. That had a wandering eye in it too, come to think of it. It didn't seem that that could be what Anna meant, though. Sebastian knew Colin and there was nothing odd about his appearance – at least, there hadn't been the last time they'd met.

'And you've always got along with little Laura,' his mother continued.

'That was when we were kids. She's only fifteen and she just doesn't get it.'

Get what? Sebastian thought, and wondered whether other families spoke in this kind of code that he wasn't old enough to have the key to yet.

'Well, I know the Rosses will be coming and the Bakers. And anyway, haven't you got revision to be done?'

Anna groaned.

'Give me a break, Mum. We've only just arrived.'

'Even so,' his mother said knowingly and then carried on putting the mini boxes of breakfast cereal into the cupboard over the sink. Sebastian loved the cereal variety packs. They only ever had them when they were here. His mother said they were far too expensive to buy the rest of the time but they fitted so neatly into the little cupboards of the caravan that they were allowed (although there was only one packet and once they were gone they were gone). There were other small things too that they bought at a special supermarket on the way that seemed to sell only tiny things. Little bottles of ketchup, half-sized jars of Nescafé. It made Sebastian feel like a giant, or at the very least an adult. At home they had economy-sized everything. Even though Miriam and now Clare had left home, his mother still seemed to shop as if they were a family of six. Maybe she hoped they would call in for tea at the drop of a hat and she wanted to be prepared. No chance of that, though. He hadn't seen Clare for ages.

'I'll go get the milk, then,' said Sebastian, anxious to run his errand before it got snatched away from him. 'Do you need anything else, Mummy? Can I have some money, Dad?'

'Just the milk at the moment, Pumpkin,' his mother said. 'Have you got some change, Frank? I've only got notes.'

His father rattled around in his trouser pocket and pulled out a handful of change. Sebastian eyed it greedily.

'How much will it be?'

'More than at home. That site shop is very expensive. It shouldn't be more than 25p, I wouldn't have thought.'

Dad picked out three shiny ten-pence coins and handed them to Sebastian.

'Usual deal?' asked Sebastian hopefully.

'Okay,' replied his father. 'But don't tell your mother!'

'Don't tell me what?'

'I can't tell you!' laughed Sebastian, and stuffing the coins into his pocket he headed for the door.

'And put those trainers on properly,' she shouted after him. 'If you break the backs down there'll be a holy bother.'

Sebastian wriggled his feet into his trainers and stuffed the laces down the sides.

'Tie your laces!' his mother shouted. 'You'll break your neck.'

Was there nothing she didn't see?

He set off down their road and when he got to the copper beech he turned right towards the centre of the site. The lake was in front of him, the water sparkling in the early-morning sun. There were some dinghies out already and a couple of the large boats that had rooms tucked away underneath the water out of sight were bobbing up and down on their moorings. Sebastian wanted to sail but so far his father had always said no. Maybe this holiday they could hire a boat and have a go. It didn't look very difficult. All you had to do was sail up and down and shout instructions at your crew when you wanted to turn. He was pretty sure that they could master it quickly.

He reached the shop and went inside. Even though he loved coming to the shop, he always got a little bit nervous as he walked in. It was run by the Macintosh family, which seemed to be made up of girls with red hair and big chests. If Mrs Macintosh or the oldest girl was serving there was no problem, but there were also the twins. He cast a nervous glance at the counter. Two red-headed girls were standing there. His heart sank.

He picked up a bottle of milk and checked the price – twenty-four pence. That meant he could spend his five pence and still have change. The penny sweets were by the till. He sidled over, trying to look small and unimportant.

'Hey! Look who's back,' said the nearest twin. Sebastian didn't look up.

'Who?' asked her sister.

'It's that little lad with the posh name. What's your name again?'

Sebastian contemplated ignoring them but he was the only one in the shop.

'It's Sebastian,' he said quietly, without looking up from the sweets.

'That's it,' said Twin One. 'Like that poofter on the telly. 'You got a teddy bear, then?'

'No,' replied Sebastian, although he had.

'You here for the holidays?' Twin Two asked.

Sebastian thought that was pretty obvious but he didn't want to make them cross so he just nodded his head.

'You brought those sisters of yours with you?'

'Just Anna.'

'That's good. We won't have to lock our boyfriends away, then, eh, Mary?'

Twin One nodded. Sebastian had lost track of which of them was speaking, mainly because of his refusal to make eye contact.

'She's a right slapper, your sister.'

'Yeah, that's right. A proper little goer.'

Sebastian had no idea what they meant, nor which sister they were talking about, but he knew it wasn't nice. This was annoying. He was going to have to rush his sweet selection just so that he could get out of there. He grabbed two Bubblies, a Juicy Fruit and two Black Jacks and thrust them forward to be totted up with the milk. It was a bad choice. Bubbly was banned and his mother would spot the Black Jacks on his teeth but there was nothing he could do. He needed to get out of there.

The twin that was serving dropped each item into a white paper bag. He heard them hit the bottom one by one.

'That's twenty-nine pence, please,' she said.

He handed over his coins without making eye contact. She dropped them into the till and handed him his penny change.

'Say hello to your mum and dad,' the other one said. 'And your sister.'

She was smiling but there was something about her look that he didn't like. Her eyes reminded him of the snake in *The Jungle Book*.

'Thanks,' he mumbled and, picking up the bottle and the paper bag, walked out into the sunshine. He could hear them laughing after him although he knew that they couldn't be laughing at him. What had he done?

Outside and away from the door, he put the milk down and looked at his selection. He would have to eat the Juicy Fruit now. The trip back was too short to allow the other two. He was cross with the twins, making him rush his choice like that. Still, they were here all week so there should be a chance for another errand, and next time he would choose a moment when the twins weren't working.

He picked up the pint and set off back towards the van, allowing the Juicy Fruit to melt slightly on his tongue before he could resist no longer and began to chew.

As he walked, a squirrel ran out in front of him, looked at him and then scampered up a tree at the roadside. He had learned at school that grey squirrels had seen off all the native red ones and so weren't very popular. He felt a bit sorry for the squirrels. He wondered what the twins had meant about his sister and which sister they had been talking about. It was bound to be Clare. It was always Clare. He thought he might ask his father but something made him cautious. Maybe he'd ask Anna, if she ever stopped being so cross all the time.

II

It was later in the day that Sebastian overheard another conversation that left him confused. They had eaten lunch and had all wandered down to the edge of the lake for a stroll. Sebastian had taken his fishing net and an old bucket. It had a picture of three cheerful little fish and a smiling shark on it. It was probably a bit babyish for him but it still held water okay.

Sebastian, in his wellies, with his jeans rolled up to his knees, stood in the shallows and tried to catch the minnows as they swam past. It was harder than it looked and the long handle of his net kept getting in the way, but every time he went to scoop water with his hands, his mother would shout at him to keep dry.

His parents were standing at the water's edge just behind him, looking out at the boats that sailed back and forth.

'I don't know what to do, Frank,' his mother said. 'It's been over three weeks since I've heard anything from her. I'm worried sick, so I am.'

'She is so selfish,' replied his father, and Sebastian, curious to know more, tried to listen without turning round and looking.

'Has Miriam heard from her?'

'No. I don't think so. Not when I rang her on Thursday, anyway. She said I shouldn't worry and that no news was good news.'

'Well, that's probably right. And she is an adult.'

'She's only twenty-two! I know that technically that counts but how much does she know? I mean, really.'

'She's flighty and headstrong but she's not stupid. She'll not do anything daft,' said his father.

Sebastian assumed that his father had bent down to pick up a stone because one came skimming by him, hit the water five times and then broke the surface and disappeared into the black lake. The fish near him scarpered.

'But she already has, Frank. Done something daft. I mean, what was she thinking of?'

'Well, she wasn't thinking, was she? And that's the problem. She never does. She's a law unto herself, that one.'

Sebastian was pretty sure that they were talking about Clare. She had come back from poly at Christmas as usual and then there had been a massive row and she'd left again. Sisters were always coming and going. Sebastian was used to it. But this time his parents seemed to be more worried than usual.

'Have you caught anything there, young man?' his father asked, and Sebastian turned round, relieved that he could stop earwigging.

'Not much. A few tiny little things but no real fish. I don't think this is a good spot.'

'A bad workman blames his tools, son.'

'I'm not! It's just that there aren't any fish here. I think they like shady bits best.'

'Why don't we wander over there, to where those trees are over-hanging,' said his mother. 'Don't forget that spade.'

Sebastian collected his belongings and set off down the beach, try-ing not to get too far ahead in case there was more information to overhear.

'I know where she is,' his mother continued. 'She put the address on that postcard. I could just hop on a train and make her come home.'

'And what good would that do?' asked his father.

'Well, at least I'd know she was safe, for one thing.'

'If she wasn't safe, I'm sure we'd have heard.'

'How do you know, Frank? A man like that?'

'A man like what? Honestly, Dorothy. He's not an ogre!'

'But how do you know?!' His mother's voice was getting louder and louder. Sebastian no longer had to strain to make out her words. 'How can you possibly know what kind of man he is? We've met him once.'

'Well, like I said before, we have to credit her with some common sense.'

His mother sighed loudly. It sounded like she might be crying but Sebastian didn't want to turn round.

'I'll ring Miriam again after six. See if she's heard anything.'

'Good idea. And in the meantime, stop worrying. We're supposed to be on holiday.'

After that they stopped talking about Clare. Sebastian was pleased. For someone who was never there, she did seem to cause an awful lot of bother.

He stood at the edge of the lake and looked hard into the khaki water. The shadows cast by the overhanging trees made it difficult to see but then, as his eyes focused on the dark, he could just make out the thin shapes of small fish darting in and out around each other.

'Dad! Look, there are loads here.' He tried to manoeuvre his net but it was just too unwieldy so he bent down and lowered the bucket into the water as slowly as he could, hoping that the fish might swim straight in. He didn't have to wait for long. Soon two small minnows had crossed the threshold and, quick as a flash, he righted the bucket and pulled it to the surface.

'We'd better invite some people over to the van tonight,' his father laughed. Sebastian had no clue what he was talking about. 'Well, we'll never consume all that fish without help!'

'Dad! You can't eat them. They're too small.'

'Oh, leave the poor boy alone, Frank,' laughed his mother, and Sebastian was relieved that the tears of a moment ago seemed to have dried up.

Sebastian thrust the bucket below the water line once more, hoping that more fish could be tempted to swim in before the existing captives swam out.

'What we need,' he said decisively, 'is some bait.'

III

It wasn't fish for tea in the end but bacon and a kind of fried potato mush that his mother got out of a crinkly silver packet, like food for spacemen. Anna had turned her nose up at it to start with.

'This is my holiday too, I'll thank you to remember,' his mother had said when Anna complained. 'I want the food to be easy. And this is easy.'

Once Anna had stopped moaning and actually tried the potato mush, they had all decided that it tasted remarkably good for packet food. They washed up and stowed all the crockery back into the little cupboards. His father told them constantly how it was important to be tidy in such a small space but Sebastian noticed that it was always his mother who did the tidying.

Then the four of them sat down at the dining table to play cards before bed. His father had a can of beer and his mother a glass of sherry. Anna and he didn't have a drink. Sebastian thought longingly of the remains of his paper bag but knew that they would have to wait until tomorrow.

'Beggar My Neighbour?' asked his mother.

'Do we have to play that?' asked Anna. 'It's boring.'

'Well, it's nice and straightforward for Sebastian but we could play something more complicated if you like.'

Sebastian was about to say that he was more than capable of playing a complicated game when there was a loud banging on the caravan door.

His parents looked at each other in confusion. Then, before anyone had had time to open it, the door burst open and there stood Clare. She had a suitcase in her hand, which she dropped at her side. It landed with a thud on the floor, making the caravan wobble just a little. She wasn't wearing a coat. This was just the kind of rebellious act that Sebastian had come to expect from his sister.

'Hi, Mum. Dad.'

Nobody spoke and then everyone spoke at once.

'What are you doing here?'

'Clare, my angel. Are you all right?'

'This should be good.' This last was Anna, who put down her hand of cards and leaned back in her chair.

'I thought you'd be here,' Clare said. 'I rang Miriam to check,' she added. 'We're nothing if not creatures of habit, us Blisses.'

'Clare. Come in. Sit down.' His mother pushed Sebastian along the bench until he nearly fell off the other end. 'Can I get you anything? A cup of tea? A glass of sherry, maybe?'

'No, thanks. Well, maybe a cup of tea, actually. It's freezing out there.'

'Where's your coat?' his mother asked, and Sebastian felt pleased with himself that he had already noticed. 'Anna, please would you make your sister a cup of tea.'

Anna was about to object but a look from their father closed her mouth. Instead she just tutted and slid her way out of her seat into the tiny kitchen area. Clare immediately sat down in the space that she'd vacated.

'So? Have you had a nice day? What did you get up to?' Clare asked. This wasn't right, Sebastian knew. He hadn't seen his sister since Christmas and now she had turned up at the caravan in the middle of the night with no coat. Something was most definitely up.

Nobody spoke. The kettle filled slowly, the sound of the running water getting higher. Anna plugged it in and flicked the switch.

'Well?' she asked.

'I'm sure Clare has plenty to tell us but let her have a cup of tea first,' said his mother. Sebastian could hear a wobble in her voice that wasn't normally there. 'I think it's time for bed, young man.'

Usually, he would have objected. It was not quite eight o clock and he was on holiday, but something told him that he should do as he was told with the minimum of fuss.

'Okay,' he said, proud of his grown-up attitude. 'Will you come and kiss me goodnight?'

'Of course. Don't forget to do your teeth. You'll need to be getting all those sticky sweeties out of them, so you will.'

How did she know about his little white paper bag? Was there anything she didn't see?

When the family came to the caravan, he and Anna shared the double bed in the little room at the back. When all six of them had slept there they had needed to turn the benches at the table into a bed too but these days his parents slept on the bed that came out of the sofas. Sebastian pulled his clothes off quickly, bundled them into a pile of sorts and thrust them into the bottom of the tiny wardrobe. He hopped into his pyjamas and then went into the little shower room to clean his teeth. The rest of them were talking now but it was not the relaxed and easy kind of chat that he was used to at home. His mother was asking stiff questions about Clare's journey. His father still hadn't spoken.

He spat out the toothpaste, rinsed his toothbrush and then went back to the bedroom.

'I'm ready,' he said as he passed through the kitchen area.

He snuggled into his sleeping bag. It was dark blue but it had flowers on the inside because it had belonged to Anna originally. It was cold but he rubbed his feet backwards and forwards really quickly and soon he began to warm up. His mother stuck her head around the door.

'Goodnight, sweetheart,' she said, and leaned over the bed to kiss him. The room was so small that she couldn't even walk up the side of the bed to reach him. As she backed out, she was replaced by his father.

'Right then, my little soldier,' he said. 'Let's get some good sleep, for tomorrow we go in hunt of the snark. You know what a snark is?'

'Of course,' replied Sebastian proudly. 'Where will we hunt?'

'Hither and thither,' said his father. 'Hither and thither.'

He reached out and ruffled Sebastian's hair and then shuffled back out and closed the door firmly behind him. That was a shame. Sebastian had been hoping that they would leave the door ajar so that he could hear their conversation. He lay very still. At first he could hear nothing but as his ears began to tune in, he found he could make out what they were saying, more or less.

'Well,' came his father's slow, muffled voice. 'To what do we owe this honour?'

'Oh, Frank,' said his mother. 'Can't you see she's exhausted? The main thing is that she's all right. You are all right, aren't you, Clare? Though it is a surprise, you turning up like this, out of the blue.'

There was a quiet moment. Sebastian could hear Anna saying something but he couldn't make out her words.

'Be quiet, Anna,' said his mother sharply. 'If you haven't got anything constructive to say then you can go to bed.'

'It's eight o clock!'

'Well, you'd better be quiet, then.'

There was no talking again for a bit and then someone began to cry. Sebastian listened hard to try to tell who it was. Crying didn't happen often at home but he supposed this must be Clare.

'Oh, darling,' said his mother. 'Come here. There, there. Let it all out and then you can tell us what's happened.'

There was some muffled sobbing for a while. Sebastian turned himself round in bed so that his head was nearer the door. There was no keyhole for him to peep through but at least the words were clearer from there. He thought about climbing out of the window, sneaking round the outside of the van and looking in through the big window at the back, but then he remembered that they had already drawn the curtains. And anyway, that would mean he would be able to see but not hear. It was probably better to be in here where at least he could kind of follow the conversation.

Clare's sobs seemed to be slowing down. Then there was a big sniff. His father would have offered Clare his big white handkerchief at that point, Sebastian felt sure. He was right. He could hear Clare, or someone, blowing their nose as if they were done with crying. More silence. He wished he could see their faces.

'I've left him,' said Clare.

'Oh, Clare,' said his mother.

'You've done what?!' said his father. He sounded more cross than concerned.

'I've left him. I never want to see him again. I told him. I said, I'm packing my bags and I'm never coming back. And then he said I wouldn't dare. And so I did.' More crying.

'Will you slow down, Clare,' said his mother. 'Have you had a little tiff? That happens all the time when you live together. It's only natural. It can't be all hearts and romance every day.'

His father seemed to be making a choking kind of sound.

'The hearts-and-romance stage normally lasts longer than a couple of months,' he said.

'Shhh, Frank! Well, whatever it is, I'm sure it can be sorted out.'

Sebastian thought he heard Anna snort but it could have been a sound coming from outside.

'It can't,' said Clare. She sounded pretty sure. 'It's over. I have left him and I'm never going back.'

There was silence again.

'If she's coming back then she can't have her room back. She'll have to have the little one at the back that I used to have.'

'Anna, I'm warning you,' said his mother. She was starting to sound cross. 'Clare, darling,' she said more gently. 'Why don't you start at the beginning and tell us what's happened and then we can work out how to fix it.'

Sebastian thought that Clare would say that it couldn't be fixed and that this conversation was going to go round in circles for ever, but luckily she began to move on.

'It was fine to start with. We rented this little flat just off the North Circular. It was a bit scruffy but it was warm.'

'Is that the address that you sent to me, then?' asked his mother. She needs to stop interrupting, thought Sebastian, or Clare would give up.

'Yes. Rodney was having to drive huge distances because all his customers were up north. So a lot of the time he would have to stay in motels and work said that they wouldn't pay for that because it was up to him if he chose to work in Yorkshire and live in Watford.'

'I'm not surprised. Damn fool idea,' said his father, but he must have said it quietly because Sebastian had to strain to hear him and only really got the gist from his father's tone of voice.

'So you've been living down there in some grotty little bedsit all by yourself?' asked his mother.

'It wasn't grotty and it's a flat not a bedsit, but, basically, yes. Well, only during the week. Rodney was there at the weekend. I got a job in a café so I was working most of the time that he was at work.'

There was more mumbling from his father. Sebastian couldn't quite catch what he said but he thought he heard 'decent education' in and amongst the words.

'Frank. Please.'

'Anyway, it was all going okay. I mean, it wasn't great but it was okay. Then yesterday, I was turning out his pockets so that I could wash his trousers.'

Sebastian was certain he heard a snort that time but Clare continued.

'I was turning out his pockets and I found a receipt from Da Mario's on the High Street at home. It was for two pizzas, a bottle of red wine and a side of garlic bread.'

Clare paused so that the full significance of this discovery could sink in. It didn't seem to be doing so.

'I'm sorry, love. I don't really understand . . .'

'Well, don't you see?! He'd taken her. Out for dinner. Just the two of them.'

'Who?' asked his father.

Yes, who? thought Sebastian.

'Her, of course. Linda. His bloody wife.'

She'd be for it now – she'd sworn in front of their mother. But no one seemed to notice.

'Oh, Clare,' his mother said now. It sounded like someone had let all the air out of her.

'Right. Let me see if I've got this straight,' his father interrupted. 'Rodney, the man who you as good as eloped with, the man who left his wife and two small children so that he could run away with you not four months ago, has met his wife and the mother of his children for a pizza and a bottle of wine.'

'And garlic bread,' said Anna. 'Don't forget the garlic bread.'

'Anna!' warned his mother.

'And, no doubt,' his father continued, 'to discuss the arrangements for the upbringing of his children or some other important domestic detail. And on the basis of this, you pack your cases and hotfoot it back to Mummy and Daddy, disturbing their perfectly pleasant holiday to boot.'

Sebastian wasn't sure he understood quite what his father was getting at but it felt like he should burst into applause at the end of this speech, so dramatic was it.

'Frank!' said his mother in that tone she used when she didn't approve. 'Honestly, Clare, don't listen to him. We're delighted to see you, so we are, and you can come home any time you need to. You know that, don't you?'

'As long as you don't want your old room back.'

Sebastian heard a thudding sound which he thought was probably someone clattering Anna.

'But, Dad, listen. That wasn't it,' continued Clare. It was getting easier and easier for Sebastian to hear as their voices got louder. 'Obviously he has to see Linda and make arrangements for the children. It was the fact that he had done it without telling me that pissed me off.'

'Clare! Language!' This was Anna as well, he was pretty sure.

'So you just upped sticks and walked out?' asked his father.

'No! Will you just listen. Mum. Tell him.'

'Frank, can you not let the poor girl speak?'

'So, I asked him about it when he got home. I showed him the receipt and told him that I'd found it in his trousers, not that I was snooping or anything.'

'Although it sounds like you were right to snoop. Sneaky love-rat Rodney, eh?'

'Anna! Be quiet.'

'I wasn't bloody snooping. I was expecting him to have a go at me for being unreasonable or something but he just stood there and burst into tears.'

Someone, Sebastian had to assume Anna, sniggered.

'He did what?'

'He cried, Dad, and then it all came out.'

At this point Sebastian was pretty sure that Clare had started to cry again because there was lots of sniffing and he heard his father's handkerchief being employed again.

'Take your time, Clare. What did he say?'

'He said that he'd made a terrible mistake. That he should never have left Linda for me and that he'd made such a mess of things. And then he said' – and here there was another huge trumpet into the handkerchief – 'and then he said that he was really sorry but he was going to go back home . . . Home. He called it "home". To me! That he was going back "home" and was going to try again with Linda. He said she was prepared to forgive him and would take him back for the sake of the children.'

'Oh, Clare. My poor baby.'

More nose-blowing.

'So that's it, then?' his father asked. He sounded cross now. 'What were you? His midlife crisis? I've got a good mind to drive down there and give that jumped-up, forty-something waste of space a piece of my mind.'

'And what good would that do?' his mother asked. 'The main thing is that Clare is here with us, safe and sound. She did exactly the right thing. You did exactly the right thing, love.'

'Oh, Mum. I feel so stupid.'

'I'm not surprised!' chipped in Anna. Sebastian could not believe that she was still being allowed to sit there and hadn't been sent to bed.

'I thought it was love and that he would get a divorce and we would get married. And all the time . . .' Here Clare dissolved into tears again. It sounded terribly sad, all this being an adult.

'Well, it sounds like you've had a very narrow escape,' said his father. 'First thing Monday you can get in touch with your tutor and see if they'll take you back. You might be able to catch up. How much have you missed – ten weeks, give or take? If not, they might let you defer a year and go back in September, although you got in by the skin of your teeth in the first place so they may not be that keen. Either way, it's going to leave a yawning gap in your CV. There are going to be some difficult questions to answer . . .'

'Frank. Can you just stop trying to fix everything? Please! All that can wait. The main thing is that Clare is back and she's safe. Why don't you nip across to The Boater's for a pint and I can settle Clare in?'

His father made a humph kind of noise.

'In fact, why don't you take Anna with you.'

'I'm up for that,' said Anna. 'Will you buy me a drink?'

'Okay,' said his father. 'But this isn't finished. Not by a long chalk.'

Then there was the sound of shoes and coats being found and put on and finally Sebastian heard the caravan door bang shut. After that things went quiet and Sebastian felt his eyes getting heavier until pretty soon he didn't hear anything else.

IV

Sebastian didn't hear Anna climb on to their bed and zip up her sleeping bag but she must have done because when he opened his eyes the next morning, there she was. She was lying very close to him so that he could smell her slightly bitter breath. He drew his hand out from the depths of his sleeping back and started to flick at her eyelashes with his finger. Her eyes looked as if they might open but then she just turned her head and slept on.

Sebastian couldn't understand how girls could sleep for so long. His sisters would sleep all day if his mother let them. This thought reminded him of what had happened the previous evening. Clare had just turned up out of the blue and cried. Sebastian hadn't been entirely sure where Clare had been. He had gathered over the last few weeks that she was not where she should be but whenever he had asked questions his parents had changed the subject. And now it appeared that she was no longer where she had been and was back with them.

As well as a tendency to sleep for long periods of time, he had noticed that girls ran very complicated lives. He assumed, as he was a boy, that his life would be far more straightforward when he got to be a grown-up.

Because he could no longer reach Anna's eyelashes, he tried tugging on her hair. Not all of it – that would be asking for trouble. Just a couple of strands. Enough to be irritating but not enough that she would automatically blame him. At first there was no response but after a while she groaned and rolled on to her back.

'These beds are so uncomfortable,' she said without opening her eyes. 'And my feet are freezing.'

'You can see your breath,' said Sebastian. 'Look!' And he breathed out as hard as he could so that the air in front of him formed itself into a little cloud.

Anna groaned again.

'I don't know why we come to this godforsaken caravan in the middle of the winter when we have a perfectly warm house.'

'Technically it's spring now,' chipped in Sebastian.

'I don't care what it is. It's flipping freezing. I'm not getting up until it's warmed up a bit.' With that she pulled her head down inside her sleeping bag and disappeared from view except for the very top of her hair.

'Morning, you two,' came a voice from the other side of the flimsy door.

'Mummy, would you be a darling and make me a cup of tea? I may die from hypothermia if I have to leave my sleeping bag.'

'Anna, you're making such a fuss, so you are. There's barely a chill in the air. Not like that year—'

'—when it snowed,' they chorused.

'If you're making tea . . .' came Clare's voice. They must have had to make up the extra bed for Clare.

'Honestly, you're all bone idle,' said his father through the wall. 'But if you are making tea, Dorothy, I wouldn't say no to a cup.'

'Okay,' said his mother. 'Here's the deal. I will get up today and make you all tea but tomorrow one of you can do it.'

'I vote Anna for tomorrow,' said Clare.

'All right. Anything just so long as I don't have to get out of bed today. What's the forecast, Dad?'

His father always knew what the weather was going to do. He would consult charts, examine the wooden barometer that was stuck on the inside of the door and read the countryside signs. Cows gathering, fir cones opening and various sorts of birdsong could all give clues as to what was about to arrive, according to his father.

'I do believe that it's going to rain today, sure as eggs is eggs.'

'Great. That's just perfect,' said Anna as she burrowed herself still deeper into her sleeping bag.

'Well, those lakes don't just fill themselves, you know.'

His father said this every time they complained about the weather. Anna groaned, and Sebastian decided that it would be a good day to practise his tree-climbing, particularly if the sudden reappearance of Clare was going to keep his naturally cautious mother busy. Maybe he could try for a boat trip too.

Later, when they'd had breakfast and cleared away, Sebastian was sitting at the dining table with Anna. The others had donned water-proofs and gone for a wander into the village. Anna was doodling on the corner of the newspaper, a never-ending spiral that twisted round and around itself so that Sebastian could no longer see where it had started.

'Anna?'

'Yes.'

'Is Clare all right?'

'Yes. Why?'

'Well. I didn't know she was coming.'

'No. None of us did.'

'So why did she?'

Sebastian was taking a gamble. He would need to pretend that he hadn't heard anything of the previous night's conversation. If he let anything slip that might give him away, then Anna would probably clam up and he'd be no further forward.

Anna didn't say anything for a few moments. She sucked on her lip, her pen continuing to trace the spiral.

'Clare's made a mistake,' she said eventually. 'Quite a big one, as it happens. And now it's all gone wrong and so she's had to come running back to us with her tail between her legs.'

Sebastian thought this was a bit harsh but then Anna never did take any prisoners.

'What kind of mistake?' he ventured. This was a genuine question. For all that he'd overheard the night before, he still didn't really have any idea of what had gone wrong.

'She thought she was in love but she was just in lust.'

Sebastian didn't know what being 'in lust' was either but he didn't want to clarify things in case the interruption made Anna stop talking.

'And it turns out that her new man felt the same way. She's better off without him. He was far too old for her anyway.'

'Who was? Rodney?'

Anna stopped doodling and looked straight at him.

'Were you listening last night?'

'No,' he said, and then, 'Well. Maybe a little bit. So who is Rodney anyway? Stupid kind of name, whoever he is.'

'He's some salesman who thought he was in love with Clare and then thought better of it. If you ask me, she's had a narrow escape. Tied down with a married man who's twice her age and with brats in tow. And her only twenty-two? It's not how I envisage my life panning out, I'll tell you that for free, little brother.'

'So, will she be coming back to live with us?'

'I think she's supposed to be going back to poly but I'm not sure they'll take her. If they won't then yes, she'll probably come home.'

Sebastian was quiet as he contemplated this. He liked it at home with just him and Anna. Whenever Clare was there, there were rows. Miriam had never caused any bother when she'd been around but trouble seemed to follow Clare about.

'Are Mum and Dad cross with her?' he asked.

'A bit. Well, I think Dad is. Mum is just glad that she's okay. Everyone knew that she'd made a mistake but we just had to wait until Clare worked it out for herself. Anyway, it turns out that old Rodney was a spineless git so she's worked it out faster than we thought.'

Outside, it looked like the rain was easing and there were more people moving about the site, all dressed in dingy waterproofs and wellies.

'I need to get on with some revision now, Monkey. If they get back and I'm not hard at it there'll be hell to pay. Can you find something to do?'

Sebastian nodded his head and wondered what a git was.

CLARE – 1990

I

Clare stood in the playground and waited for River to come out of school. It was bitterly cold and her thin jacket did almost nothing to keep out the biting wind. It didn't help that the zip was broken. She pulled it tighter around herself, tucking her hands under her armpits. The chill was rising up through her feet too, the thin soles of her Converse pumps providing very little insulation. She hopped from one foot to the other but then decided that she must look stupid and so stopped. Most of the other mothers were huddled in a little group near the shelter. They didn't look cold in their warm boots and thick anoraks. They looked totally without style but they didn't look cold.

A shriek of laughter went up from the main gaggle of women. A couple of the others turned round to see what the hilarity was all about but Clare didn't. She wouldn't give them the satisfaction of knowing she was curious. In fact, she wasn't curious. She really didn't care what they were finding so very funny. She ignored the small nagging voice that told her they were laughing at her. Why would they be? She hadn't done anything to draw attention to herself and even if she had, what did she care about a bunch of stupid women who had nothing better to do with their time than drink coffee and bitch about people they knew fuck all about. Clare didn't know that they did this but they definitely looked the sort.

Come on. It must be time for the bell to go. The waiting here on her own was the downside of getting here early but she was making a real effort now after River had complained to her.

'Mrs Slaughter gets cross if you're late, Mummy,' he'd said, his pale eyes wide. 'She said that it's rude to make her wait for you. Please could you try to get there when all the other mummies do so I'm not left on my own.'

Mrs Slaughter can damn well wait, Clare had thought. That is what she's paid for. But River had bitten his lip as he spoke and Clare had felt a sting of shame. It wasn't her little boy's fault that she couldn't get to school on time to pick him up. She had no excuse, anyway. It wasn't as if she had a job. Most times she was late simply because she lacked the motivation to drag herself away from whatever mind-numbing crap she was watching on daytime TV when the clock reached 3 p.m.

'I will try extra-hard,' she had said to him, taking his little hand in hers as they left the playground, last again. She had given it a little squeeze and River had squeezed back. See. She could do this being-a-mother thing. She just had to stay focused on it. And she had been making a real effort. She hadn't been late all week, and when Mrs Slaughter had released him, he had come skipping across the tarmac towards her with a big smile on his face. It gave her a warm feeling, seeing him smile like that, thinking that she was just as good as all those other mothers. She wasn't, of course. You just had to look at her own mother to see what a piss-poor job she was doing with River. But she was trying and that had to count for something, didn't it?

To her left, another woman was standing on her own. Clare gave her a sidelong glance, not wanting to accidentally make eye contact with someone she didn't know. It was Rochelle, the mother of River's little friend Joshua. Clare waited for a moment to see if she would come and join her but she showed no sign of moving. If she was going to fit in here Clare could see that she was going to have to make the running herself. She took a deep breath and sidled over.

'Hi,' she said when she got close enough to be heard. 'How are you doing? River so enjoyed playing with Josh the other night.'

Rochelle gave her a tight little smile and nodded.

'Yes, they were having a fine old time playing soldiers,' Clare continued.

Rochelle shuffled a little on the spot and bit her lip.

'Boys just love shooting stuff, don't they?' asked Clare. 'My little brother was just the same when he was their age.'

'Actually,' said Rochelle, her eyes not looking up from the ground, 'we don't encourage that kind of play. I'm not sure it's healthy. And Joshua doesn't have any toy weapons.'

'What, no guns? All boys play with guns.'

'Not Joshua,' said Rochelle. She threw her head back with a defiant little shake. 'I've told everyone not to buy him any.'

Clare was starting to get just a little irritated.

'Well, he certainly knew what to do with River's. They were having a proper battle. It was just a bit of fun, though. I mean, it's not like they're real or anything.'

Rochelle nodded slowly. 'And is it true that you let them watch a *Rambo* film?'

Clare smiled. 'Yes. River loves them. We've got all three on video.'

Clare was proud that she had managed to get hold of an ancient video recorder. A friend of Anna's had been throwing it out and so it had found its way to Clare's flat along with a selection of videos. There was no way she would have been able to afford that on her own but she was pleased that River could have a video recorder just like his school friends.

'You do know that it's an eighteen certificate?' Rochelle said, her voice dropping into a whisper so that the other mothers couldn't hear her.

'Well, yes, but they don't really understand it. River just likes the blowing-things-up parts.'

'But they're four years old,' said Rochelle.

'That's why it doesn't really matter,' said Clare. 'They're so young they don't know what's going on, not really.'

'Dave and I were very unhappy about it,' continued Rochelle, 'and I spoke to some of the others and they agreed.'

Clare felt the world shift under her feet. So they had been bitching about her behind her back. She'd felt it. They were all so bloody superior with their flashy cars and their holidays in Majorca. She knew that they looked down their noses at her, a single mother with no sign of the father and barely a penny to her name. None of that was River's fault, though. That was what made her angry. The fact that they took it out on him.

'Oh,' Clare said. She wasn't sure what else to say. 'Okay. Well, next time Josh comes round I'll put a different video on. Does he want to come for tea tonight?'

Rochelle shook her head. 'It's his piano lesson tonight.'

'Well, how about tomorrow, then?'

Rochelle's cheeks went scarlet. 'He's . . . erm . . . busy tomorrow too.'

Oh. Clare could see what was going on here. She wasn't good enough for them. They didn't want their little darlings kicking round with River because he was the wrong sort of child, from the wrong background.

'Well, fuck you,' said Clare, and Rochelle's jaw fell open. 'I wouldn't want your stuck-up little brat to play with my beautiful boy anyway. He definitely doesn't need morons like you in his world.' She was shouting now and the other mothers turned to see what the commotion was about. Clare didn't care. She was on a roll. 'I wouldn't let River play with your precious son if he was the last child on the planet.'

That told her, thought Clare, spinning round away from Rochelle, a smug smile on her lips.

River was standing right behind her, having been released to her by Mrs Slaughter. His little face was a picture of concern as he tried to work out why his mummy was shouting at his friend's mummy.

'River, baby,' said Clare. She felt about two inches tall. 'I didn't see you standing there.' She knelt down so she was at his eye level. 'Have you had a good day?'

'Why did you say that I couldn't play with Josh?' he asked. His eyes were brimming with tears.

Clare took his hand and tried to lead him away but he wouldn't move and just stood looking between her and Rochelle, his forehead creased.

'I like Josh,' he continued. 'He's my friend.' And then he started to cry but he still stayed stubbornly on the spot. Clare could feel the eyes of the other mothers on her. She flicked a V-sign at them. She could hear the gasp and then the twittering voices as she yanked at River's arm to make him move.

'Mummy, that hurt,' whined River, but Clare just had to get out of there and she ignored his complaints as she pulled him across the playground and out towards the street. She could hear the hushed voices of the other mothers whispering behind her back as she left.

II

It was freezing in the flat. The storage heaters were supposed to come on at night but you could only feel the feeble heat that they produced if you leaned your back against them, and then the draughts coming through the floorboards outweighed any benefit from the low-level warmth.

River had gone to sleep. He had cried all the way home from school, perking up only a little bit when she used the last of that week's spare cash to take him to McDonald's for tea. There hadn't been enough money for her to eat as well so she had made do with a scorching cup of bad coffee and a couple of stolen chips. He had seemed fine, but as he was falling asleep he started to cry again.

'Why did you say those horrible things to Josh's mummy?' he asked her, confusion written across his open little face. 'Now he won't want to be my friend, ever. And he'll tell the others and then no one will be my friend. And it's all your fault, Mummy.'

And it was true. She should have kept her temper. She should have just accepted Rochelle's point of view and moved on. They were all entitled to make their own choices about how to bring up their children. So Rochelle didn't want Josh playing with guns. Well, that was her choice. Clare wasn't sure now why she had taken it as such a personal affront. Actually, who was she kidding? She knew exactly why. Rochelle's objections hadn't really been about the guns or watching *Rambo*. Anyone could see that. No, this was all about how she, and consequently River, didn't fit in. They wore the wrong clothes, ate the wrong food and clearly watched the wrong television, and whilst the majority would tolerate her up to a point, there was definitely a line that she wasn't supposed to cross. Except that she had. She had skidded over it in a burning car with no brakes. Again.

River had been at school for less than a term and already she had messed things up. He hated her. The other mums hated her. The teachers probably did too. She was a crap mother. Could she give him up for adoption? The thought skittered across her mind but she pushed it away. Instead, she opened the second bottle of Thunderbird. It didn't taste quite so bad as the first bottle now that her taste buds had been numbed. Soon the rest of her would be numbed too and she wouldn't have to think about any of it until tomorrow. She pushed herself closer up against the heater and slopped the wine into her glass.

The phone rang. She'd ignore it. It would be her mother or Miriam and she couldn't bear speaking to either of them right now. She only had a phone because her mother paid the call charges. How pathetic was that? Her own mother. Clare just wanted to make herself as small as possible so that this sick feeling in the pit of her stomach would disappear. Maybe if she just stayed here the world would melt away? The ringing phone jangled her nerves. They must know that she would be here – where else would she be? So they would also know that she was ignoring them. She didn't care. She just sat there, working her way down the bottle.

When she woke up it was 5.30 a.m. The flat felt like an igloo and the empty bottles were lying upturned at her feet. Her head was thumping and her mouth was dry. When she tried to move her neck and shoulders they felt stiff and uncooperative. What day was it? She thought hard and concluded that it was Saturday. No school, thank

God. If she could stand she could get herself to bed. River would be up soon but if there was no sign of her, he would just get on with things on his own. He'd had plenty of practice. Feeling sick and swaying slightly as she got to her feet, she stumbled across to her bedroom and fell on to the sheets, still tousled from the day before.

Next time she woke it was to a gentle knocking. She couldn't place the sound so she rolled over, set on ignoring it, but then she heard voices. River's cheerful chatter and another softer tone.

'Mummy's in bed so I made myself breakfast and now I'm watching cartoons,' said River proudly. Clare couldn't hear what the other person said. She should go and see who it was but she couldn't find the energy to drag herself from the bed. If they wanted her they would come and find her. She groaned and rolled over, looking for a glass of water or in fact any liquid at all, but there was nothing within reaching distance.

Another knock, closer this time.

'Clare? Are you awake? Can I come in?'

It was her mother. Shit. Now they would all know just how very crap she was. The empty bottles were still on the floor where she'd left them and River was careering about the flat like some gypsy urchin. She was twenty-eight years old and her life was a disaster.

The door opened and her mother's face partially appeared, peering round the edge as if she were afraid of what she might find. Clare buried herself deeper under the covers, hiding her head. She couldn't bear for her mother to see her like this. They all thought she was a waste of space and now here she was, proving them all right.

'Oh, Clare,' said her mother. 'Heavens preserve us now.' Her voice was gentle and kind with no hint of judgement. She crossed the room and came and sat down on the bed. Clare felt the mattress sink as the springs gave way. She buried herself deeper under the duvet. 'What's going on here, love?' asked her mother, gently lifting the duvet up to reveal Clare cowering beneath. Clare's instinct was to snatch it back down, to preserve the dark world she had created for herself, but she knew that was both childish and pointless. Having found her in this state, there was no way that her mother would just turn round and leave without satisfying herself that Clare was all right.

Clare flinched from the light. She felt sick with shame. The T-shirt that she slept in was stained and smelled vaguely of vomit. Her hair hung in rat-tails and she could only imagine what yesterday's make-up would have done to her face.

'I'm okay,' she said, despite all the evidence to the contrary. 'I'm just having a bad day. I'll be fine in a bit. Thanks for coming and all that but there's no need to worry.'

She closed her eyes again.

'River is so grown-up these days,' said her mother, totally ignoring all the other aspects of Clare's life that might merit comment. 'He's made his own breakfast, he was telling me, and him only four. You should be very proud of him, Clare, so you should. It's so important to be independent.'

God bless her mother. She always managed to find the positive. Of course River was independent. It was either that or starve some days.

'Thanks,' she said in a voice so quiet that it barely sounded at all.

'Now, let's get you up and dressed. Shall I run you a bath? I'm sure you'll feel much better with some clean clothes on you.'

There was nothing clean in the flat. She had neither the money nor the inclination to go to the laundrette. Despite this, Clare let her mother help her sit up on the edge of the bed. Her mottled legs were a mess of bruises – some fresh and purple, others raging yellows and blues. She tried to pull the T-shirt down to cover them but there wasn't enough fabric to do the job.

'And then we can all go down to the supermarket and get you some bits,' her mother continued. 'I'm sure there must be some treats that River would like.'

Clare knew how this went. She had been here before. By 'bits' her mother meant to fill her entire kitchen with food, as it was obvious that she was incapable of doing this for herself. Then she would set about cleaning the flat and finally they would go out for tea as a 'treat' for River. It was the same every time. It was all so humiliating. Clare didn't move. She closed her eyes tight against the horror of it all.

'You don't have to do that, Mum. We'll be fine.'

'But I want to. If a mother can't come and look after her own child, then what's the world coming to?'

The irony of this statement was either lost on her or she chose to ignore it.

'I've really fucked things up this time,' said Clare. She saw her mother flinch at her use of an expletive but that couldn't be helped. 'I had a screaming match with this cow of a woman in the playground. She was being so fucking smug and patronising and I just saw red. Who do they think they are to judge me like that? Stupid bitches.'

'Well, I can remember well enough how hard it can be, looking after a child on your own,' said her mother. 'It's so tough and you feel like the whole world is out to get you.'

Clare had not heard her mother talk like this before. She had always been so perfect, with no chinks in her armour. It was hard to believe that life had ever been tough for her, not tough like it was for Clare.

'Yeah, but you had Dad,' Clare said, her tone dismissive.

'Your father was away with his work. I spent a lot of time on my own. And it was hard, bringing up four of you. I felt like I was chasing my tail most of the time, trying so hard to do the right thing but not always being sure what that was.'

Her mother reached up and stroked Clare's hair. Clare's first reaction was to pull away but then she found that she quite liked the slow, reassuring strokes down her matted locks.

'There was a time,' her mother continued, 'when I didn't know which way to turn either. Miriam was a baby and your father gone and I really wasn't coping. I slipped too, Clare. So I understand what it's like. I really do.'

Her mother's voice cracked and Clare finally opened her eyes. Her mother was clearly struggling to hold back her tears.

'You just have to do your best,' she continued. 'Keep putting one foot in front of the other until you get to the other side. You'll get things wrong, Lord knows I did. But you just have to learn from it and keep going. It will all work out, eventually.'

Clare doubted that. She had no real qualifications, no job, a child that she couldn't look after and no one to lean on.

'You have to stop the drinking, though, Clare,' her mother added quietly. 'That's not going to help anyone.'

Clare bristled. How much she drank was entirely up to her. It was the only way she could get through the pain and no one was going to take it away from her.

'I'm fine, Mum,' she said briskly. 'We're fine. We just had a bit of a setback yesterday but we've had worse. And River's okay. He's doing well at school and he's got some little friends . . .'

She stopped. He'd had friends. She had pretty much scuppered that for him with her outburst yesterday. Well, what did that matter? They would move house. There were other schools. They could start again somewhere else. The council could sort her out with a flat in a different town. Or perhaps abroad, India maybe, and he could go to school with the local kids, run around barefoot in the sun.

'It's not just about you any more, Clare,' her mother was saying. 'You have to do what's best for your son. That's what I've always tried to do for you. Even though I made mistakes, I always had you at the front of my mind.'

What was she talking about? thought Clare. Her saintly mother hadn't put a foot wrong in her life. What did she know about fucking things up? She had absolutely no idea what Clare was going through, the guilt that she felt every day at the mess she'd made of everything. And then there were her bloody siblings, who'd never fucked anything up either. Well, they could all just piss off. She didn't need them. She didn't need anyone. Something hardened in her heart.

'Actually, Mum,' she said, 'River and I have plans for today so it's probably best if you just left us to it. Thanks for coming and all that.'

She stood up too quickly, her head spun and she saw stars.

'Say hi to Dad for me,' she added as she walked with as much dignity as she could muster in her dirty T-shirt towards the bedroom door.

River was sitting on the floor in the lounge, about a foot from the TV screen. At his side were an upturned cereal bowl and a can of Coke. He was still wearing his pyjamas. The Bliss children would never have been in their pyjamas later than 8 a.m. Her mother spoke quietly.

'Let me help, Clare,' she said. 'You don't have to do it all on your own.'

But Clare ignored her. She held open the door to the flat until her mother crossed the threshold.

'Bye, Mum,' she said, and then she closed the door.

DOROTHY – 1996

I

Dorothy wept as the reporter read out the names of the dead.

'Can you believe this shooting, Frank?' she said when she had managed to compose herself a little.

Frank looked up from his paper. 'In Scotland? It's a tragedy.'

'All those poor little mites. Just imagine how frightened they must have been. Such a pointless waste of life. A whole community's future wiped out. Just like that. And there'll be no justice. Turning the gun on himself like a coward.'

'They should have strung him up.'

'And that brave teacher,' Dorothy continued. 'Throwing herself in the firing line to save her class. It's shocking. And those that didn't die will be scarred for life. Nothing in Dunblane will ever be the same. Never.'

Frank shook his head. 'It is, as I said, a real tragedy. What's for tea?'

Dorothy wiped her eyes with a cotton handkerchief and then stuffed it back inside her sleeve. Why did tragedy never seem to touch men the way it touched women? It was like they were wired in a totally different way. The futile loss of sixteen children, sixteen families decimated, and he was worried about his stomach.

'Fish,' she said.

'Are we doing food on Sunday?' asked Frank.

Dorothy noticed the plural pronoun and raised an eyebrow.

'Just a finger buffet. And a cake, of course. You can't have a birthday without a cake. I'm going to do a Black Forest gateau. That's always been Anna's favourite since she was a little girl.'

Dorothy had such fond memories of Anna helping her bake, the way her little tongue stuck out as she stirred the mixture, being careful not to slop it out of the bowl, how she licked the spoon mid-stir when she thought Dorothy wasn't watching.

'I'm sure she'll love it. And are we expecting a full complement?'

'I think so. Plus Sebastian's new girlfriend if she can bear us until Sunday. And I think Clare is bringing Dicken.'

Frank tutted. 'He's a waste of space, that one. A potter? What kind of a job is that?'

'Dicken is a good man, Frank. You shouldn't be so hard on him. Clare could do a lot worse.'

'She could do a lot better. Why can't she pick someone normal for a change? You know he's got his nose pierced. What kind of man wants to stick a bead on a pin through his nose?'

'Well, Clare did that too, remember, so we're in no place to criticise. You're to be nice to him, Frank. I don't want anything spoiling Anna's day.'

Frank rustled his paper and disappeared back behind it.

'We need to get that box of old toys down from the roof for Rosie and Abigail. I'm sure Miriam will be after bringing some things of theirs from home but other people's toys are so much more interesting. Miriam said that little Abigail is quite steady on her feet now.'

'Mmmm.'

'I'm not sure what River will find to do. Ten is such an in-between sort of age, so it is. Maybe Sebastian can show him those cartoon books he used to collect. I do worry about that boy.'

'Who?' came Frank's voice from behind his paper. 'Sebastian?'

'No! River! A child needs some stability in its life. He gets pushed around from pillar to post so often. It can't be good for him. If Clare would just settle to something . . .'

'It'll do the lad no harm. Character-building. And it's none of our business, anyway. Clare's a grown woman. How she chooses to live her life is up to her.'

'Well, I hope Dicken sticks around for a bit. It's good for River to have a man in his life, especially at his age. It's important he has a good role model.'

'A potter with a nose piercing?'

'Oh, be quiet, Frank.'

Dorothy worried about all her children but Clare was still the one that had her lying awake at night. There had been a string of men, each less suitable than the one they replaced. Lord only knew which of them had been River's father. Dorothy had once screwed her courage to the sticking-place and asked Clare outright. It had not gone well. Clare had screamed at her, accusing her of interfering, of inflicting her values on her. She had been left with the clear impression that Clare didn't actually know which one of them had fathered her son. Just thinking about this made Dorothy's heart beat faster. Thank the Lord that her own parents hadn't been around to see how Clare was turning out. She could virtually feel the breeze that was coming off her father spinning in his grave. She couldn't help but wonder, though. Was there a reason why Clare was so troubled when the others were settled? Dorothy had thought about telling Clare of her suspicions more than once over the years. She had seen how much pain her daughter was in, comparing herself and her many failings to her siblings. Would it help to know that there might be an explanation? Dorothy couldn't decide and always stopped shy of saying anything, worried that it might do more harm than good. She would tell Clare, though, eventually, before it was too late. She owed her that. Dorothy just had to wait until Clare was a little bit stronger.

'Is Anna not bringing anyone?' asked Frank, cutting through her internal monologue and bringing her back to the here and now.

Now here was another worry. Anna wasn't getting any younger. She needed to stop working so hard and get on with finding herself a nice young man to look after her.

'Not that I know of,' she said, shaking her head sadly. 'And I'm sure she would have said. Thirty years old and still single.'

'Now that really is a tragedy,' said Frank. 'Anna will make someone a perfect wife. What happened to the one that came here that Boxing Day? What was his name?'

'Justin? I don't know where he disappeared to. The whole thing just seemed to peter out. Miriam said he was quite keen. She was certain he'd propose but then Anna was so off-hand about it all that the poor wee boy lost his nerve, so he did.'

'Well, if he wasn't the one for her . . .' said Frank. 'Anna knows her own mind. Always has done. She won't go settling for second best.'

'Sometimes you have to compromise, Frank. I mean, I married you, didn't I?'

Frank lowered his newspaper and frowned at her over the top. She couldn't see his mouth but she could tell from his eyes that he was smiling. If her daughters could just catch themselves a good man like she had done . . .

'And what's that supposed to mean?!' Frank asked.

'All I'm saying is that if Anna doesn't choose someone to marry soon, it will be too late.'

'Too late for what, exactly?'

'You know. Children and things.'

'Children and things? What kind of things?'

'Oh, Frank, do you have to be so difficult? You know what I mean plain well. She's thirty years old already. If she doesn't meet someone and settle down soon then . . .'

'She'll die an old maid, eating cat food and surrounded by back copies of the *Reader's Digest*. Don't be ridiculous, woman. She's fine. If she meets someone then all well and good, and if she doesn't then she will be perfectly all right by herself. Better that than ricocheting from man to man like her wayward sister.'

The front door banged and a voice called 'Hi' from the hall.

'Hello, Sebastian, love. We're in here.'

There was the sound of a heavy bag being dumped on the floor and then Sebastian strolled in.

'Hi, Ma. Pa.'

He walked over to Dorothy and gave her a kiss on her pink cheek.

'Don't I get one of those?' asked Frank.

'What do you think?' asked Sebastian as he bounded over the back of the sofa and landed on the cushions with a bounce.

'Don't jump on the furniture! And take your shoes off. Honestly, you've been gone five minutes and already you've forgotten the way things are done around here.'

'When's tea? I'm starving.'

'You're not expecting to be fed as well, are you?' asked Frank. 'Isn't that what your grant's for?' Dorothy knew he was only half joking.

'It's fish, or it will be if I can shake myself. I'll go and put it on in a minute. Is Tessa not with you?'

'Yes, she's here.'

Sebastian turned to the door as a tall willowy girl with dark, shiny hair walked into the room. Lord but she was a beauty. Dorothy felt a ripple of pride that Sebastian had managed to find such a lovely girlfriend. For a moment she was lost for words but then she remembered herself.

'Tessa,' Dorothy said, rushing across to the girl. 'How lovely to meet you.' She went to give Tessa a hug but Tessa pulled away so that Dorothy had to make do with a pat on her shoulder.

'Nice to meet you too, Mrs Bliss,' she said tightly. There wasn't much warmth to her, Dorothy thought, but she supposed it must be a bit intimidating, meeting them all in one weekend. She'd make allowances for now. She smiled broadly at her.

'Oh, but you must call me Dorothy. And this is Sebastian's father, Frank.'

Frank looked up from his newspaper and Dorothy was sure that he did a double take. She hoped Tessa hadn't noticed but she suspected that she had. Tessa gave him a little half-smile and a nod.

'Hi,' she said baldly.

Dorothy felt a little thrown. She'd been expecting a little bit more enthusiasm. It wasn't that Tessa was rude exactly, but she gave off an air of superiority that made Dorothy feel uncomfortable. She turned her attention back to Sebastian.

'And how's the course going, Sebastian?' she asked. 'Have you written any good essays lately?'

'It's Maths, Mum. We don't do essays. We do sums!'

Dorothy was feeling stupid now but she ploughed on, hoping that she wasn't blushing too much.

'Well, I'm looking forward to hearing all about it. Has that boy in your flat settled in a bit better now?'

'Watty? No. He's still crying himself to sleep.'

'It's such a shame for the wee lamb. It's not easy leaving home. It's a big adjustment.'

'He just needs to grow a pair.'

'Sebastian!'

'I've brought my washing home, Mum. You don't mind, do you? I was going to stay and do it but then I thought that would be less time with you two so I just bundled it all into a bag and brought it back.'

Frank snorted from behind his paper.

'That's fine, dear. We've plenty of time to run a couple of loads through the machine.'

Tessa moved so that she was standing right next to Sebastian and began to play with the lobe of his ear as he talked. It was all a bit unnecessary, Dorothy thought, but she tried to ignore it.

'So, who's coming to this shindig?' asked Sebastian.

'It's more of a gathering than a shindig. It'll be just us and I thought I might invite Marjorie and Malcolm.'

'God! Do you have to?'

'Well, is it not a bit rude to leave them out? They'll be hearing us through the wall.'

'Let them listen. Please, Mum. Don't invite them. Anna will hate it and it is her party.'

'Well, maybe I won't. It might look a bit like an afterthought anyway.'

'Is Clare bringing Dicken? He's a good bloke. I like him.'

'We think so, don't we, Frank. And Miriam and Richard and the girls, obviously. And Anna and Melissa and that's the lot. Oh, and River.'

Sebastian sighed. 'I won't have to entertain him, will I?'

'Well, there's no one else for him to play with. He's not interested in his cousins. They're far too small. And he is your nephew.'

'He's a pain in the backside, that's what he is.'

'Don't say that, Sebastian. He's a nice boy, just a bit unsettled. It can't be easy, always being on the move.'

'Last time he came, he completely destroyed that Airfix model of mine. It took me months to make that. Months!'

'Sure that was an accident.'

'It so wasn't. He threw it down the stairs on purpose to see if it would fly even though I told him it was just a model. And Tessa's here too, remember. I can't leave her to cope on her own with the sisters. Freak Boy will just have to entertain himself.'

'Don't speak about your nephew like that, please, Sebastian,' said Frank sternly. 'If you haven't got anything nice to say then you can keep it zipped.'

'Okay. Sorry. But honestly, Mum. Don't make me look after him.'

'Well, we'll see how things pan out. Perhaps he'll bring something to do.'

'Right, then!' said Sebastian, bouncing up from the sofa in one easy movement. He's starting to look like a man, thought Dorothy, and part of her mourned that cherubic little boy with blond curls that she would never again bounce on her knee. 'We're going to take my stuff upstairs. Am I in my room?'

'We've not let it out just yet,' said Frank. 'We thought we'd wait until your second year!'

'Oh, ha ha!'

'Yes, dear. And I'll put Tessa in Anna's old room.'

Dorothy registered the glance that passed between her husband and son but there'd be none of that business under her roof. 'I've changed the sheets,' she continued, 'and there's a clean towel on the bed. If you want to bring your washing downstairs, Sebastian, I can make a start on it and then I'll get on with the tea.'

Sebastian and Tessa left the room and disappeared upstairs, Sebastian's bag thumping against the steps on the way.

'It's nice to have him back,' said Dorothy. 'The house feels so empty without him.'

And then, when she was sure that they were out of earshot, she added, 'Tessa seems nice?'

It came out as a question, and Dorothy realised that she was looking for confirmation from Frank.

'She's a looker, certainly,' Frank said, shaking his newspaper and folding it neatly into quarters. 'I'll bet she doesn't take any prisoners.'

Before Dorothy had chance to ask him what he meant, he stood up.

'Right. Is there just time for a quick stroll before tea?'

This was Frank's code for a trip to the pub for a pint and a chat.

'I suppose so,' she replied reluctantly. 'But if you're not back by half past six, you'll be fishing yours out of the bin.'

'Yes, Ma'am.'

Dorothy heard the front door shut and Sebastian walking about overhead. She smiled. It was going to be a lovely weekend. Or at least she hoped it would be.

II

'Who the hell eats salmon-paste sandwiches?'

'Shut up and keep spreading!'

Sebastian and Frank had got a production line going for the finger buffet whilst Dorothy coordinated operations, although she was sure it would have been easier just to do it all herself. Tessa had disappeared back to Anna's old bedroom and Dorothy had so far resisted the urge to go and check that she was all right. Perhaps she was working, although it seemed more likely that she was lying low. Dorothy got the impression that Tessa didn't think that much of the Bliss family so far. She tried to put it from her mind. She had enough to deal with already.

'Have you finished the ham ones?' she asked.

'Yes, Ma'am. All present and correct, Ma'am!' said Frank with a salute which flicked salmon paste from the knife that he was holding and into Sebastian's hair.

'Dad! Watch what you're doing. That's gross.' Sebastian began to part his hair to find the stray lump of paste.

'Do you have to do that near the food, Sebastian?' Dorothy was beginning to lose patience.

'What do you want me to do? Leave it there for later?'

'Don't be ridiculous, love. I just meant that it's not very hygienic to be playing with your hair just where you're making the sandwiches.'

'Well, it's not very hygienic to be flicking food around the place but I don't notice you telling Dad off.'

'No insubordination in the ranks!' said Frank 'Be quiet or I shall issue you with a regulation hairnet.'

'Could you not just concentrate, please?' said Dorothy. 'They'll be here any minute and I still haven't got changed.'

'You go and make yourself even more beautiful, my darling, and me laddo and I will finish the sandwiches.'

'Well, if you're sure you can be trusted,' said Dorothy doubtfully. 'Can you cling-film the plates when they're done and pop them in the fridge? And then there's the crisps to be put in bowls. They're in the pantry. Don't put them all out. I'll save some in case we have to rustle up some more food later on.'

'You see that?' asked Frank to Sebastian. 'Always planning ahead, that's your mother. You can learn a lot from her, Sebastian my son.

'Oh, for the love of God, will you not just get on with it?' said Dorothy, but she was smiling. How could she not? Her men were here in her kitchen and all was right in the world. Or at least, that's what she was hoping.

She made her way upstairs and into their bedroom. Her dress, all pressed and ready to go, was hanging on the outside of the wardrobe door. She cast a critical eye over it. It was a deep azure-blue with a fine black stripe and enormous shoulder pads, which looked even larger as it hung on the hanger. She had picked out some huge blue earrings to go with it but now she found herself wondering whether it wasn't all a little bit much. Shoulder pads were very dating. Everyone would know that the dress wasn't new. They made her look slim, though, and who cared if it was an old dress. It was only family coming. Well, and Tessa. She really wanted to make a good impression there for Sebastian's sake but she could already picture her son's girlfriend turning her pretty nose up at her outfit. And there was Dicken, of course, but he wouldn't notice what she wore, let alone sneer at it.

She opened the wardrobe, scanning its contents before declaring it all unfit for purpose. There was nothing else suitable unless she chose something more casual and she really did want to make an effort for Anna's special day. The dress would have to do. She slipped her stripy apron over her head and undid the cord of her dressing gown. Having bathed earlier, she was already wearing her magic pants, which squeezed at her stomach uncompromisingly. She peered at her image in the dressing table mirror, which, as it was only small, meant that she could only take in parts of herself at a time. It was a good job. The magic pants were great at flattering her tummy but the extra displaced flesh just seemed to splurge out at the edges. For a more convincing trim outline, she was going to need more than just magic pants.

She pulled a slip out of her top drawer and stepped into it. Then, removing the dress from the hanger, she lowered it over her head, taking care not to mess up her blow-dried hair. She fastened the buttons as far as she could up her back and straightened the belt. Then she stepped into her black court shoes and examined herself as best she could in the tiny mirror. Well, it wasn't great but it was as good as she could manage. She sat at the dressing table to begin doing her make-up.

There was a knock at the door.

'Mum? Can I come in?'

'Anna! Is that you? I didn't hear you arrive. Come in! Come in!'

The door pushed open and Anna appeared. She was wearing jeans and a faded sweatshirt.

'Happy birthday, darling.'

Anna bent down to kiss Dorothy on the cheek.

'Thanks, Mum. I hope you don't mind that I'm here a bit early. I was a bit lonely all by myself. Do you need a hand with those buttons?'

Anna gently fastened the dress up the back.

'You're not that early. The others will be here in a few minutes. Are you going to get changed up here?'

'I wasn't going to get changed,' said Anna. 'It's only us, isn't it?'

'But you've got jeans on, Anna. You can't wear jeans. Not to your own thirtieth birthday party.'

'Why not?'

'Well, you ought to at least look like you've made an effort.'

'I have made an effort. I got dressed! I've brushed my hair. I've even got lipstick on!'

'Oh, you know what I mean, Anna. And Sebastian's Tessa seems . . .' Dorothy hesitated, not wanting to seem disloyal. 'Seems very particular.'

'She's just a student. She won't care what we're wearing,' replied Anna.

Dorothy decided to let Anna make her own mind up. It was probably just her feeling inferior and nothing to do with Tessa at all.

'Even so, love,' Dorothy said. 'Will you not make a bit of an effort?'

'Well, I haven't brought anything else with me, Mum, so that's that. Honestly. I'm thirty years old. Can't I decide what I want to wear to my own party?'

'I suppose so.' Dorothy bit her tongue. She should be pleased that her lovely daughter wanted to spend her big day with her family. That would have to be enough.

She began to apply foundation to her face. 'I swear I have more wrinkles every day,' she said. 'I'm not sure if this stuff makes them look better or worse.'

'You look great, Mum.'

Dorothy didn't look too closely at her daughter as she said this. If Anna was flattering her then she would rather just not know. She was sixty-five, for God's sake. She should lower her expectations a little. Her own mother had considered herself old at this age but she still felt like a young woman. Well, she did in her heart. It was a slightly different story in her knees.

The front door banged.

'Oh, who's that now?' Dorothy said, flustered anew. 'I haven't got my face on and the towel needs changing in the downstairs loo and Lord only knows what those boys are up to in the kitchen.'

'Don't panic. You stay here and finish your make-up. I'll go and head whoever it is off at the pass. Dad will give them a drink. Are the clean towels in the airing cupboard?'

Anna left in search of towels and Dorothy continued with her face, carefully drawing on her eyebrows and reddening her cheeks. Was the dress too much after all? Perhaps she should change it? Maybe everyone would be as casual as Anna. She didn't want to look overdressed. Oh! What the heck! She was ready now.

By the time she got back downstairs, Miriam was standing in the kitchen, Abigail swinging from her arm in a car seat. She had made an effort with her clothes at least, and Dorothy relaxed a little. Miriam looked tired, though, her skin a little grey and all the life gone from her hair. She would speak to Richard at a quieter moment, make sure that he was doing his fair share with those granddaughters of hers. Small children were not easy. Dorothy remembered Miriam when she was Abigail's age. Hadn't she nearly killed her once when she was teething? Unbidden, her mind took her to the café on the corner, to StJohn who had been there for her when she had been at her lowest ebb. Even now, she could still picture his thoughtful eyes. She hadn't seen him for so many years but her memories of that time were still sharp. After their meetings in the park that spring when Miriam was small, the two of them had become so close for a while. Too close, maybe. StJohn had provided her with something that she had needed so badly, something that Frank couldn't give. It was hard to put her finger on exactly what it had been. Compassion, perhaps? Understanding certainly. He had shown her that just because she hadn't taken to motherhood like a duck to water it didn't make her a bad mother. Of course now, more than thirty years later, Dorothy understood that being a good mother was about more than stopping a child from crying or doing endless jigsaw puzzles with them, but back then she had judged herself against those benchmarks and found herself lacking. StJohn had taught her to be gentler on herself.

Guilt rose up in her now, though, and she felt her cheeks burn at the memories. She busied herself with the glasses and hoped that no one would notice the glow that was radiating from her. Yes, Miriam needed to be nurtured right now or who knew what might happen. She would definitely speak to Richard.

'Hi, Mum,' Miriam said. 'You look nice. Richard's just bringing stuff in from the car. Rosie has fallen asleep so I thought we could leave her for ten minutes and then give her a poke. She'll be less of a handful if she's had a sleep. I'll feed them both early, if that's okay with you. Then I can relax and Richard can look after them for a bit. It's his turn, I reckon.'

'I don't mind taking a turn,' said Anna, breezing in from the hall, towel in hand. 'I love my little nieces, don't I?' she said in exaggerated tones to Abigail, who beamed and raised her arms to be picked up.

'Can I take her out of there?' Anna asked.

'You can if you're prepared to deal with the consequences,' Miriam said sternly. 'Once she gets free of those straps there'll be no getting her back in!'

'Well, maybe we can leave her be a little bit longer,' said Anna. 'How are you, sis?'

'Exhausted. As usual,' said Miriam with a weary smile.

'How's work going?'

'The kids are fine. They're quite pleased to have me back. Not sure the supply teacher was up to much. But my head of department seems to have forgotten my name and keeps fixing meetings for the early evening, which I can't make because I have to get back to the nursery in time to pick the girls up. It's really unfair of him. The male staff members don't have a problem. In fact it probably suits them to avoid bath time at their houses, but for us working mums . . .'

'There'll be none of that Women's Lib talk in my house,' said Frank as he walked into the kitchen. 'How are my two favourite girls?'

'Excuse me!' said Dorothy, pretending to be affronted but also slightly irritated that Frank had interrupted Miriam. She saw Anna about to take Frank on but Miriam shook her head at her.

'You, my darling, are no girl,' Frank continued. 'You are all woman.' He threw his arms around Dorothy's waist and spun her round on the spot.

'Frank! Stop it. Put me down,' said Dorothy, patting her hair back into conformity.

'Ew. Get a room, you two,' said Sebastian as he strolled into the kitchen, towelling his damp hair.

'Hi, Seb.'

'Hi, little bro. How's it going in the big grown-up world of university?'

'Great, thanks. Lots of beer. Lots of gigs. Not much work.'

'Sebastian,' chipped in Frank. 'Now don't you be telling tales of your debauchery in front of your mother. You know how she worries.'

'Joking, Dad. Just joking. It's going really well, actually. My tutor thinks I have natural talent and flair.'

'And unlimited modesty,' said Anna, punching him gently on the arm. 'Seriously, though, Seb, if a flair for Maths is something you aspire to then that's all good.'

Dorothy felt her heart swell a little. Here they were, her beautiful children, all grown-up and teasing each other. If only this cheerful mood could be sustained for the whole afternoon. She would cross her fingers but her joints were so stiff these days that it wasn't really an option. She crossed them in her head.

'And where's this girlfriend that we've been hearing all about? I want to meet her so I can tell her what a nasty little scrote you were when you were growing up,' laughed Anna.

'She's just upstairs. She'll be down in a minute,' replied Sebastian.

'Have you met her, Mum?' asked Anna with a wink. 'What's she like? Quick! Tell all before she gets here.'

What should Dorothy say? That she found Tessa aloof and standoffish and ever so slightly patronising? No. Of course not. She would leave the girls to reach their own conclusions.

'She seems like a lovely girl,' she said neutrally.

'And she's a looker,' said Frank.

'Dad! Women's rights really have passed you by, haven't they?'

'I'm just reporting what I see like the good journo that I am.'

'She's fabulous,' Sebastian chipped in. 'And considerably more beautiful than any of you lot,' he added with a smirk.

Anna swung her arm around and clouted her brother across the head, narrowly missing Abigail, who was watching with great interest from her car seat.

'Honestly,' said Dorothy, 'do you lot never stop? What will Tessa think of us?'

Tessa chose that moment to appear, leaving Dorothy madly replaying the last few sentences in her head to see if they had said anything that she could be offended by.

'And here she is,' said Sebastian proudly. He crossed the room so that he was standing next to her and put his arm protectively around her shoulders. Tessa leaned into him and gave them a languid wave. She reminded Dorothy of a Siamese cat.

'Sisters,' he said, 'this is Tessa. Tessa, this is, well, everyone.'

'Except Clare,' said Anna.

'Well, yes. Except Clare. She is coming, isn't she?' Sebastian looked at Dorothy, who nodded.

'She is indeed. Now, Anna, if you're not going to get changed then can you put that clean towel in the cloakroom and the rest of you can help me move the food into the dining room. Ah, Richard. Good to see you. How are you?'

Miriam's husband shuffled in carrying a plastic mat under one arm and a bag overflowing with disposable nappies in the other.

'Hello, Dorothy. Hello, siblings. Can I put these bottles of formula in the fridge?'

'Help yourself, Richard dear. Shift the other things around. You can pass me a plate of those sandwiches when you're in there, make some space. Frank, will you get these good people a drink? They'll be parched, so they will.'

'Coming right up. Water all round? Only joking, only joking. We have red, white, beer or lager, or some rather iffy sherry that's been in the cupboard since Adam was a lad.'

Everyone shouted out their orders and soon they were standing, glasses in hand, around Abigail, whose eyes were drooping as Sebastian rocked the car seat with his foot.

'So, Anna, daughter of mine, how does it feel to have reached the heady heights of thirty years of age?' asked Frank.

'Old,' said Anna. 'Well, not old exactly. More like the world should start taking me seriously.'

'And does it? Take you seriously, I mean.'

'Not entirely.'

'Well, I propose a toast,' said Frank, raising his half-empty glass to the ceiling. 'To Anna, my beautiful and intelligent daughter, who must henceforth be taken seriously by all and sundry, on the occasion of her thirtieth birthday. Health, wealth and happiness.'

'Health, wealth and happiness!' chorused the others.

The kitchen door swung open.

'Well, this is all very cosy, I must say,' said Clare.

'Clare! My darling girl. We were just toasting the birthday girl,' said Frank.

Clare looked at them each in turn but didn't smile.

'So I see.'

No one spoke. Sebastian scuffed his trainer against the floor.

'Someone get Clare a drink!' said Frank. His voice sounded over-loud all of a sudden.

'Coming right up,' Sebastian leaped in. 'What would you like, sis?'

'Red wine,' said Clare.

'We were just asking Anna how it felt to have hit thirty,' said Miriam.

'And,' said Clare, 'how does it feel? Pretty shit, going by my experience.'

Dorothy flinched. She blinked slowly and bit back her instinct to pull Clare up for her language.

'Pretty much like twenty-nine, if I'm honest,' said Anna. 'Only with more celebrating!' She raised her glass and everyone laughed awkwardly.

The door swung again and in strolled Dicken. He was a shortish man with a full beard and a round belly that sat above his belt, as tight as a drum. He was wearing a jumper with stripes of rainbow colours which ran violet to red rather than the other way. Its effect was discon-certing and Dorothy found herself staring at it.

'Not quite the thing, eh, Mum? Dicken's top?' snapped Clare. 'Well, Anna hasn't exactly made an effort, has she?'

'Don't be silly,' said Dorothy. 'It's a fine sweater, Dicken!'

Anna leaned in to kiss Dicken on the cheek. 'How lovely to see you again,' she said sweetly. 'How are you?'

'Well, I'm still breathing,' laughed Dicken. 'Happy birthday.'

'Thanks.'

'It's all getting a bit congested in here,' said Dorothy. 'Shall we move next door where there's a bit more space?'

'Then it'll just be congested in there,' said Frank. 'No one told me that when I had four children they would all grow up and take up so much space.'

The group laughed again but the tension hovered around them all.

Clare, having taken a hefty swig from her wine, looked up and Dorothy saw her notice Tessa.

'And who's this?' Clare asked, nodding sidelong in Tessa's general direction.

'I'm Tessa,' said Tessa, her head held high and her shoulders back, and Dorothy thought again what an enviable air of confidence the girl had about her.

'Right,' said Miriam, taking control as she always did and leaving Dorothy feeling slightly redundant. 'You lot go through, then, and I'll stay in here and feed the girls. Richard? Could you bring Rosie in from the car. She should be awake by now. And Sebastian, stop rocking Abigail or we'll have no peace later!'

There was a general shuffling around as people made space for each other.

'Drink, Dicken?' asked Frank.

'I'll take a beer if you have one, thanks, Frank. Very civil of you.'

'And I'll have another red wine,' said Clare.

No one commented but Dorothy was aware of Sebastian trying to catch Anna's eye. She ignored him.

'No River?' asked Frank as he ripped a can from the plastic linking it to the others and passed it to Dicken.

'No. He wasn't keen on coming so I said he could stay at home.'

'On his own?' asked Dorothy. She really mustn't interfere but ten was far too young to leave a child alone. If she wasn't careful, someone would report her to Social Services.

'I think he said his friend was coming. He didn't feel all that welcome here, after last time.'

Sebastian played with a lock of Tessa's hair and didn't meet anybody's eye.

'Oh, now, don't be so silly, Clare,' Dorothy said, and then, when Clare bristled, wished that she'd chosen her words more carefully. 'Of course he's welcome. It was only a toy and it didn't even matter, did it, Sebastian?'

She threw a warning glance at Sebastian.

'No,' he answered on cue. 'It didn't matter at all.' His voice was flat and must have sounded totally unconvincing even to Clare.

'Right. We'll go through, then,' said Frank, and started to usher his family out of the kitchen.

'Do you need any help, Miriam?' asked Anna as she left. Dorothy saw her cock her head in Clare's direction and pull a face at Miriam.

Miriam shook her head, her eyes wide, and then turned her attention back to Anna.

'That would be great, Anna,' she said in a voice that sounded overly cheerful. The kitchen door closed behind the others. Dorothy busied herself in the pantry, leaving Miriam and Anna in the kitchen with baby Abigail.

'This has the makings of a disaster written all over it,' said Miriam in hushed tones, though loud enough for Dorothy to hear. 'Did you see how fast she downed that wine? Do you think she and Dicken have had a row in the car? They didn't come in together and there was a definite atmosphere.'

'Well, Dicken seemed all right. I think it's just her. It didn't help that she walked right into the middle of Dad's toast. She'll have thought that we'd started without her.'

'Well, we had! She needs to grow up and stop being so sensitive all the time. So we started without her. It's a party, for goodness' sake. People arrive when they're good and ready. What do you think of Tessa?'

'Hard to tell,' said Anna. 'She doesn't give much away, does she? She's gorgeous, though. They make a very handsome couple. I just hope

Clare doesn't kick off in front of her and scupper things for Seb. You know how she can be when she's had a drink and if she's already feeling got at . . . Right, I'd better go through before she thinks that we're hatching a plot against her as well.'

'Sebastian's in there.'

'Yes, but he's a boy. He can't read atmospheres like we can. I'll go and try to smooth things over. Here. Pass me that bottle. She might lighten up when she's had a couple more drinks.'

'I'm not sure that's such a good idea,' said Miriam doubtfully, but Dorothy noticed that she passed Anna the bottle anyway.

'You will come through, won't you? I don't want to have to deal with her all by myself.'

'Of course. I'll just get these two sorted and then I'll be right there.'

Dorothy came out of the pantry and as she didn't comment on her daughters' musings, they clearly thought that she hadn't heard them.

'You coming through, Mum?'

'Yes. In a mo. I'll just check that the food's all ready.'

As Anna opened the door, Richard appeared with a sleepy-looking Rosie over his shoulder.

'This may take some time,' he said, tickling the soles of his daughter's feet to try to rouse her.

'Bless her,' smiled Anna. 'Wasn't life straightforward when you were two?'

In the lounge, small groups seemed to have formed. Sebastian was talking to Dicken, who nodded at him as he spoke, Tessa stuck to Sebastian like glue, not speaking to anyone. Clare was balancing on the arm of the sofa and talking to Frank. Anna sat herself next to Frank. Dorothy busied herself with bowls of crisps, not wanting to sit down in case she inadvertently said something wrong. It was so easy to set Clare off and she so didn't want to spoil Anna's party.

'Bring those over here, Mum. I'm starving!' said Sebastian, and she immediately felt better for having something to do.

As the afternoon wore on and things seemed to be going well, Dorothy felt herself relax a little bit. Everyone was happy enough and Abigail and Rosie were being delightful. Grandchildren were such a blessing, she thought. It was disappointing, though, that River hadn't come. She wondered whether it was really at his instigation or whether Clare was keeping him away for some reason of her own. It hurt her to think it but holding him back was the kind of thing that Clare might think up as punishment for some imagined wrong. It was so difficult to form any kind of relationship with River as she saw him so rarely and there was generally a row of some kind when he was there. She would try to talk to Frank about it when they had all gone. Maybe they should invite River to stay on his own in the holidays? Clare had always refused in the past but it might suit her to have a little time on her own with Dicken.

Dorothy was just fetching the trifle when she heard raised voices in the lounge.

'That's right. You take their side. You always do.'

It was Clare. Of course it was. Her voice was shrill and ever so slightly slurred.

'Oh, don't be daft, Clare,' replied Dicken. He was speaking in a slow, calm voice as if he were reasoning with a child. 'I was just saying—'

'I know exactly what you were saying. It's what you always say. You sound like my bloody mother. You should learn to live a little, lighten up, have some fun.'

'You're making a show of yourself,' replied Dicken.

'Like you'd care. You used to be fun, Dicken Ezard, but now you're just like all the others. Booooring.'

Dorothy hurried into the lounge. Clare was just upending another bottle of red into her glass. She was sitting on the coffee table with her feet on the sofa. Dicken was staring thunderously at her from his place on the nearby armchair.

'I think we should leave,' he said, making to stand up, 'before you totally ruin what was a pleasant afternoon.'

'You leave if you like, Mr Boring-Britches,' said Clare in a sing-songy voice. 'I'm having a perfectly delightful time here in the bosom of my lurverly family.' Her words dripped with sarcasm. 'Look. There's super-duper grown-up Miriam with her sensible husband and her two-point-four children. And Anna the Perfect who can do no wrong. Although you haven't found yourself a man yet, have you, sis? That's a bit of a blot in your copybook. And lovely, handsome Sebastian with his puppy-dog eyes and his big brain. And then there's me! Clare the Social Embarrassment. Clare who everyone wishes would go away because she's just soooo difficult to control.'

Dorothy put the trifle down on the table.

'Clare, love,' she said, 'would you not like to go and have a little lie-down? You can use your old room. Would you like to do that?'

'No, I bloody would not!' shouted Clare. 'What am I? Ten? Honestly, Mother. You're as bad as the rest of them. When the chips are down, you just can't help yourself, can you? I know. Let's just patronise Clare. She might shut up then and stop embarrassing us all. Well, I know. I know what you all think of me. I'm not stupid. I can see it in your eyes. The pity. Poor old Clare. Just can't seem to get her life on track. Always crashing from one disaster to another. A son with no dad. No money. No job. A crap, hippy boyfriend. Well, that's me, so you'd better all get used to it. I've had enough of having to be constantly apologising for myself. And I've had enough of you. And I've had a bloody bellyful of you, Dicken Ezard! So you can all go to hell!'

'Clare!' shouted Frank, standing up and taking a couple of steps towards his daughter. 'Don't you dare talk to your mother like that.'

'What are you going to do, Daddy dearest? Take me over your knee and knock the living daylights out of me? I'm a bit big for that kind of thing now, aren't I? Don't worry. I'm going. I shall just take this . . .'
She grabbed wildly at a half-empty wine bottle, almost knocking it over

but then catching it at the last moment. 'And I'll leave you to enjoy your lovely little party. Happy birthday, Anna the Perfect. Many happy returns.'

Clare lurched towards the door. Dorothy's stomach lurched too. She looked at Dicken in desperation, hoping for him to provide a solution, but he just shook his head slowly.

'Better let her alone for a minute,' he said as he drained his glass.

'But where will she go? We can't let her wander off on her own. Not in that state. Anything might happen to her.'

The front door banged shut so loudly that the house shook.

'She'll not go far,' he said. 'I've got all the keys and her cash.' He patted his jeans pocket reassuringly.

'Oh, Dicken,' said Anna. 'I had no idea. How long has she been like this? I thought she'd cut back on the drinking.'

'It comes and goes,' said Dicken with the resigned air of someone who had seen it all. 'There's no telling what'll set her off. Sometimes she can have a drink and she's nice as pie. And others . . .' He flicked his head towards the door. 'Well, you saw for yourselves.'

'Is she getting any help at all?' asked Anna. 'I mean, AA or something?'

'She can't see that she's got a problem and until she does . . .'

'She's a liability,' said Miriam, holding Rosie to her chest and rubbing her hair gently. 'There, there, Princess. Don't you worry. Mummy's here.' Rosie could be heard sobbing gently. 'I've had enough of her. I really have. She spoils everything. Well. She's done it this time. She's burned her bridges, as far as I'm concerned. That was her last chance.'

'Oh, Miriam,' said Dorothy, aghast at her daughter's suggestion. 'You can't say that. She's your sister. You can't abandon her. You mustn't.' Dorothy couldn't bear to let this happen. Her beautiful family seemed to be ripping apart from the inside.

'I really don't see that I have much choice, Mum,' said Miriam. 'You've seen what she's like. She's got a self-destruct button a mile wide and there's nothing that any of us can do to help. I'm really sorry, Anna, but I'm going to take my girls home now so that they don't get any more upset. It's been lovely, Mum. Thank you.' She gave Dorothy a quick kiss on her cheek and Dorothy felt the tears pricking at her hot eyes. 'Richard. Can you help me collect our stuff, please?'

'I'll go and find her,' said Dicken, standing up with a sigh. 'Thanks for a lovely party. Sorry about . . . Well, you know.' He shrugged. 'And happy birthday, Anna.'

Dicken let himself out and five minutes later Miriam and Richard were also gone. Sebastian and Tessa stayed where they were having watched the party unravel around them. Dorothy wished that Tessa hadn't been there to witness what had just happened but right now she had bigger things to worry about.

'Oh, Anna,' she said with her hand over her mouth. 'What on earth should we do about her?'

CLARE

I

Who the fuck did they think they were, the patronising bastards? How dare they talk to her like that, like she was a child incapable of understanding the adult world, when in fact it was them that had no idea what was really going on here. They sat there with their perfect little lives and thought that it was appropriate to criticise her, to offer their trite platitudes, as if everything would be all right if only she would do what they said, follow their advice.

It was ironic, really, almost enough to make Clare laugh out loud. There they all sat, offering their half-baked solutions, and not one of them would know a real problem if it knocked on the door and invited itself in for tea. They had all pootled along in their blessed little existences, never once having to deal with one tenth of the amount of shit that had been thrown at her. They had no fucking idea. Miriam in her cosy little marriage with her two angelic children and her nice, boxy house that was just like the nice, boxy house next door. What did she know about pain and suffering? How could Saint Miriam even begin to comprehend how crap Clare's life could be?

And bloody Anna. Clare tried to spit at the thought of her sister's name but the wine had made her lips numb and she couldn't seem to get up the necessary amount of power. Instead of firing a satisfying ball of phlegm at the pavement, the spittle got caught around her tongue and ended up on her chin. She wiped it away with the back of her hand. Bloody Anna with her charmed bloody life. Thirty years old and still not put a single foot wrong. How could that be? Why did things fall at Anna's feet in beautiful gift-wrapped boxes when Clare had to stumble across broken glass just to get the most basic of tasks done?

Fuck. How was she going to get home now? Dicken was still at the party. She was either going to have to sit here outside the house until he came to find her or go back in. She remembered another time when she'd stormed out as a teenager after some row or other only to have to storm back moments later because she didn't have anything on her feet. This was just fucking typical of her. She couldn't even storm out properly. Now she was stuck here with no money and no wine and no one to talk to. It was all crap.

She sat on the wall and swung her legs backwards and forwards until she heard the front door open, voices saying thank you, good bye, sorry. There they were again. Apologising for her. Still, precious Anna's precious party had crashed and burned pretty quickly after she'd left. They might all hate her but she still called the shots in the Bliss family. This thought made her smile.

'Are you going to sit there all day or are you coming home with me?' Dicken was standing at her side. He put a steadying arm on her shoulder but she shrugged it off.

'Party all finished?' she asked. 'Oh, that's a shame. Don't suppose you picked up any booze on your way out? That lot won't be needing it until Christmas.'

'You're a disgrace,' said Dicken, turning and walking away from her. He had a hole in his cords, near the pocket where his wallet must have worn away the fabric. She could see the pink cotton of his boxers.

'And I can see your pants,' she shouted after him, but he didn't turn back. In the old days that would have made him smile. Her refusal to follow social norms was one of the things that he said he loved about her. Now she seemed to irritate him just like she irritated everyone else.

She was going to have to get home somehow, though. She slid herself down from the wall and trailed after him like a chastised child.

'Wait,' she called to his back. 'I'm coming.'

But he didn't turn round.

ANNA – 2000

I

'How long will she be in hospital exactly?' Anna asked.

There was a pause at the other end as her mother considered her answer.

'Three or four days,' her mother replied. 'A week at the most.'

'A week! What will I do with a teenage boy for a week?'

'Oh, come now, Anna,' her mother said. 'Is it so very much to ask? He's your nephew and he needs somewhere to stay whilst Clare is away. Miriam would help but she's got her hands full with the girls. He could stay here with us but that won't be much fun for the lad. Your father is far too cantankerous for house guests these days.'

Anna knew that she was the obvious choice but still her mind struggled to come up with other solutions.

'What about Seb and Tessa?' she asked. 'I know their flat is only tiny but the two of them are so totally joined at the hip that they must barely take up any space. There'd be plenty of room for River.' She was only half joking.

'Oh, now, don't be silly,' her mother replied. 'You couldn't swing a cat in that flat. The two of them live on top of each other as it is. Not that they seem to mind. It's a joy to me to see Sebastian so happy. I'm not sure I've ever seen two young people so much in love.'

Anna bristled. She knew her mother's comments about her loved-up brother were not designed to be a criticism of her but she couldn't help but take them like that. There was Sebastian, love's young dream, and her, older by eleven years and still resolutely single. It wasn't that Anna resented her brother's happiness per se but did they all have to rub her nose in it so hard? Every time she saw Seb and Tess it became more and more obvious that they were totally devoted to one another. If every other person on the planet disappeared in a puff of smoke, the two of them probably wouldn't even notice. And if Anna was being completely honest, wasn't she just a teensy bit resentful of Tessa? Since she'd been on the scene a gap had opened up between herself and Sebastian which Anna had found difficult, especially as she wasn't entirely sure what Seb found so entrancing about the girl. Anna would have to get used to it, though. Sebastian and Tessa were clearly soulmates, whatever that was.

'Okay,' she said to her mother. 'River can come here, if he must.'

She'd been boxed into a corner. It was nothing short of a divine power, this talent her mother had for making things happen the way she wanted them to. Dorothy had decided that Anna would have River whilst Clare went into hospital for a routine operation and lo, it came to pass. Anna had absolutely no say in the matter.

'But I don't know what to do with teenage boys,' she complained. 'I don't know what to talk to him about or anything.'

This was true. With no children of her own, Anna had always found the world of the child a mysterious and slightly scary place. Whenever she spoke to her nieces it was in a patronising tone that even she was horrified by. She could see them merely tolerating her stilted attempts at conversation just long enough until they could sidle off and get back to other, less tedious pursuits. But at least her nieces were girls. She had been a girl herself once. A boy was a whole different kettle of fish.

Anna could hear her mother sigh down the phone.

'For the love of God, Anna, just feed him, make sure he goes to school and comes back at night. How hard can that be?'

And so here they were, day one. River had been delivered to her house after school and Anna had taken a couple of hours off work to make sure that she was home when he arrived. She didn't know why she'd bothered, though. She had set River up in her spare room and he hadn't shown his face again since. A heavy silence fell over the house. She had expected raucous music or at the very least a TV turned up loud, but there was nothing. Whatever he was doing up there, he was doing it very quietly.

Should she go and check on him? Was that what the responsible person in loco parentis would do? She didn't want him to think that she was spying on him and yet that was exactly what she would be doing. And didn't she have a right to? He was a guest in her house, after all. She needed to make sure that he wasn't coming to harm.

God, she could kill Clare. It was so like her to do this. Expect everyone to hold her life together for her when she couldn't cope. No sooner had this thought escaped but Anna reprimanded herself. This wasn't Clare's fault. Her condition might have been exacerbated by the drinking but that was far from certain. It was just one of those things, nobody was to blame, and Anna was doing what any reasonable sibling would do by helping out in a crisis. She could still kill her, though.

She opened a packet of Penguin biscuits and tipped a couple out on to a plate. Then she filled a glass with squash and dropped a couple of ice cubes in for good measure. What about a straw? Too much? Maybe? He was fourteen, not four. She put the whole lot on a tray and made her way upstairs. Standing for a moment outside the closed bedroom door, she strained to hear anything that might give her a clue as to what he was up to. Maybe he was smoking, or taking drugs, or maybe he had shimmied down the drainpipe and the quiet she could hear was the silence of his absence. He was Clare's son, after all.

With her heart in her throat, Anna gave a cursory knock and flung open the door as if to catch him in whatever terrible act he was indulging.

River was sitting on the bed, propped up against the headboard. He was reading a book. Of all the possible scenarios that had crossed Anna's mind, reading hadn't been one of them. Anna was so relieved that she almost laughed. He looked up briefly as she came in and then his eyes dropped back down to his book without acknowledging her.

'I thought you might like a snack,' she said.

No response.

'Are you hungry?'

Nothing.

She set the tray down on the bedside table.

'What are you reading?'

He twisted the front of the cover so that she could read the title.

'*Hitchhikers Guide*?' She nodded appreciatively. 'Good choice. Dad, your grandad, used to read that to us – well, me and then your Uncle Sebastian. He used to do all the voices. We loved it.'

Anna stopped. River's eyes didn't lift from the page and Anna felt immediately guilty. Who would have read to River? Certainly not Clare. And how insensitive to talk about being read to by your father when River didn't even know who his father was.

'I usually have tea around seven,' she said, changing the subject abruptly. 'Is that okay with you? It's pasta tonight but I can make something else if—'

'Pasta's fine,' said River, still without looking at her.

Anna felt like she was being dismissed from her own bedroom. She'd have forced him talk to her if it hadn't been for the fact that she had nothing to say. His rudeness was actually saving them both a lot of effort. So that was fine. If he wanted to be rude then two could play at that game.

'I'll see you downstairs at seven, then,' she said, and left him to it.

The cheek of the boy, she thought as she set the table. She had put herself out for him. She'd taken time off work, for God's sake, and he was too rude to even attempt to have a conversation with her. She'd ring

Miriam later, sound off to her about their uncommunicative nephew. Miriam would understand, especially when her daughters were such sociable little creatures. They were always at least prepared to chat with Auntie Anna, no matter how awkward it might be. No, River was something else – a chip off the old block, that was for sure.

By the time seven arrived, Anna had worked herself up into a frenzy over the unacceptable behaviour of her nephew and was determined to beat him at his own game. Yes, it was childish, but who was here to see? At least it would make her feel better.

She was about to shout up the stairs when he appeared, silent as a ghost, in her kitchen.

'Sit down,' she said, gesturing at the table. River took the chair nearest the wall and sat, staring at his place mat. When she put the plate of pasta in front of him she was almost disappointed to hear a quiet but distinct 'Thank you.' Well, that made no difference. Just because he had a modicum of manners, it didn't mean that he could undo the damage.

Anna put her own plate down and sat opposite him. The room was painfully quiet and she wished she'd thought to put some music on. If she stood up to do it now it would just look awkward, like she didn't want to talk to him. Well, she didn't. At least she would be being honest.

For a moment or two they each concentrated on their food. He didn't seem to be a fussy eater, so that was something. Maybe when you lived with Clare you had to learn to eat whatever was put before you? Behind them the central heating boiler hummed.

'Did you have a good day?' Anna asked, weakening first despite her determination not to.

River shrugged. 'Was okay,' he said.

'Do you like school?' Anna persisted.

'Suppose.'

'What's your favourite subject?'

He shrugged again. 'I like reading,' he said without making eye contact.

'Me too,' said Anna. 'Have you read all the Douglas Adams books?'

'At least five times each,' he said. Finally, he looked up, and was that the hint of a smile?

'There was a TV series when I was around your age,' replied Anna. 'Of *Hitchhiker's Guide*. It was "must-see" viewing.'

He nodded but his face fell flat again.

Like pulling teeth, thought Anna.

II

It was Valentine's Day but Anna wasn't expecting a deluge of cards and roses from men declaring their undying love for her. Just one would be nice, but when the post hit the mat it was immediately apparent that this year was going to be just as disappointing as the last. Not one silly pink envelope peeped out from beneath the catalogues and takeaway menus. When she'd been a girl, her father had bought the three girls a card each and every year. They'd always known it was from him but Anna had still counted it proudly as she totted up her card count. Clare always received the most, of course.

'I could paste the walls with mine,' she used to say, and it wasn't far from the truth. The boys always seemed to know how to push at that open door. A couple of times Anna had even got a card from Malcolm next door but those had gone into the bin without being displayed. Cards from your father were one thing, cards from a total loser like Malcolm Connors were quite another.

And here she was again, twenty years later with neither man nor card to display. She wondered if River had anyone to send a card to. Did teenagers still do that kind of thing? She had no idea but she liked to think that it was one of those quirky little traditions that would never go out of fashion. Surely you could never be too sophisticated to get a thrill out of knowing someone found you attractive? Would he have cards waiting on his mat at Clare's squat? It seemed unlikely. They hadn't been living there so long and Anna couldn't believe that River would advertise his address. School probably didn't even know where they'd moved to. As a girl Anna had used the phone book to look up her beaux, but any admirers of River's would have to try much harder than that to track him down.

It had been an odd morning. The pair of them had overcome a slightly awkward moment on the landing on their simultaneous journeys to the bathroom, she in a dressing gown and he wearing only a pair of boxer shorts. He might be only fourteen but he definitely wasn't a little boy any more and Anna had made a mental note to hang a bathrobe on the back of his bedroom door before tomorrow. He had not appeared for breakfast with her but when she had shouted up the stairs to say that she was leaving for work, he had come downstairs, fully dressed in his school uniform.

'Help yourself to anything you can find in the kitchen,' she had said as she left. 'See you tonight.'

As she drove to work, Anna played out a little fantasy in her head where she had a partner and a child or two. It wasn't that far-fetched. She was only thirty-three. There was still plenty of time for her to fall in love and settle down. It would be good, though, oh gods, if it happened sooner rather than later. No point playing chicken with her ovaries.

When she got home, a smell of frying onions was wafting from the kitchen and River was standing at the table chopping veg. He was wearing her stripy apron, a gift from her mother one particularly uninspired Christmas.

'Thought I'd cook,' he said without meeting her eye. 'Curry. Is that okay?'

'Great. Can I help?'

River shook his head and continued to chop.

'You like cooking, then?' asked Anna, desperate to mine this potentially rich seam of conversation.

'Have to eat,' he said.

'Is your mum still a . . .'

'Terrible cook?' He looked at her and grinned. His eyes had that fire that had also sparked in Clare's when she was a girl. 'Yeah. I learned to cook when I was pretty young. It was either that or live off Pot Noodles and beans.'

'I don't like cooking much,' Anna said. 'It hardly seems worth it when there's only me. I survive on jacket potatoes, mainly. Sebastian is hopeless too but he doesn't care. Miriam can cook.'

'Course she can,' said River, and then immediately looked as if he wished he hadn't. Clare was speaking through him as clearly as if she had been in the room with them. It tickled Anna.

'Will you go and see your mum tonight?' she asked, but at the mention of his mother River closed back down.

'Dunno. Hate hospitals.'

'Well, maybe tomorrow,' she suggested, and River shrugged.

The curry was delicious – a perfect blend of spices with just the right amount of heat. Anna was very impressed.

'That was fabulous, thank you,' she said when the last mouthful was gone. 'Do you want to be a chef when you leave school?'

River shook his head. 'God, no. I'm going to do something that makes shedloads of cash so I never have to live on someone else's floor.'

Who could blame him? What kind of a childhood had he had so far, pulled from pillar to post by Clare on her eternal quest for that thing that she lacked. Anna had lost count of the number of schools that River had been enrolled in, only to be moved on when Clare had grown tired of the place or fallen out with the teachers. The only consistent thing in his world so far had been inconsistency, as Clare ricocheted from one disaster to the next. And yet, despite all that, he had the makings of a pretty decent human being and was showing no sign of following his mother down the path that she had taken. In fact, when you looked at it, it was a miracle he was here at all.

'You do know that we're all here for you, don't you, River?' asked Anna, but as she spoke the words, she felt how hollow they sounded in her mouth. Who was she kidding? Recently the three of them had only really paid lip service to their duties as a sibling as far as Clare was concerned. If they'd spent half as much time helping Clare as they had moaning about her then maybe things might be different. That said, they had tried at the beginning, before it became obvious that Clare had no intention of ever accepting help. Since River had been born, though, Clare had distanced herself further and further from them. Yes, they kept track of where she was living, at least most of the time, but it was as if Clare had decided that bringing up River was up to her and nothing to do with the rest of them. And now Anna was beginning to get the same independent vibe from River. Whatever he achieved in life, he was going to do it off his own bat with no help from anyone else.

River didn't reply.

DOROTHY – 2014

I

Dorothy's heart was breaking as she watched Sebastian weep. His sons, barely four and two and with no real understanding of what had just happened, were trying to comfort him. Theo, the eldest, had clambered on to Sebastian's lap and was now reaching up to pat his back, a gesture no doubt learned in times of his own distress from his mother, Tessa. Little Zac, totally bewildered by this horrible reversing of roles, sat still as a statue next to his father, his head inclined so that their bodies touched at all points.

'It's not right,' Sebastian said, shaking his head in disbelief. 'I mean, it's not fair. How can it be fair? Look at them. They're so young. How can they go on for the rest of their lives without their mummy?'

Dorothy felt instinctively that such openness in front of the boys was not a good thing but knew that to suggest that to Sebastian would be futile. He and Tessa were bringing their children up so differently from how she and Frank had done it. The divisions between child and adult were far less marked these days. '*Pas devant les enfants*' seemed to have no part to play in this world of modern parenting. Still, it couldn't be good for the boys to see their daddy in such obvious distress.

'Shall I take the boys to watch some television?' she asked, but Sebastian pulled the boys in closer to him and shook his head. Tears rolled down his face unchecked.

'But why, Mum? That's what I don't understand. What purpose can it serve?'

Dorothy had no answer. She might have blamed it on God's mysterious ways but she knew better than to do that now. God was of no comfort to her in times like this and He certainly wouldn't be helpful to Sebastian. Instead she just shook her head.

'I don't know, son,' she said, horrified at the shallowness of her words but not knowing what else she could say that might be better. 'It's all so wrong. A horrible accident. Nobody's fault.'

Sebastian looked up at her then, his eyes red-raw and puffed up to mere slits.

'It was my fault,' he said. 'She asked me to take the lights down and I didn't do it. If I had, then . . .' Guilt, horror and realisation flooded over him in a tidal wave of pain. He made a deep, guttural sound and buried his face in his hands. Theo set to rubbing his shoulder still harder, his little face fixed, determined to make things better.

'It was nobody's fault,' Dorothy repeated sternly. 'It was an accident and nothing you could do would have made any difference.'

'But if I had just done it then she wouldn't have had to.'

'You mustn't blame yourself, Sebastian. You know that once Tessa got an idea in her head there was no stopping her.'

Sebastian almost smiled. It was true. Dorothy had rarely met a more free-spirited, headstrong woman than her daughter-in-law. If Tessa decided that something needed to be done, then she would move hell and high water to do it.

'But what am I going to do without her?' His face crumpled again. The realisation of what now lay ahead kept crashing over him in waves. 'I can't do it on my own. I just can't go on. What am I going to do, Mum?'

Dorothy had no idea what he was going to do but she knew that he had no choice.

'You will go on, son. You will go on for the sake of your boys. You will be there for them every day so that they can live their lives without their moth—'

Dorothy's voice cracked but she took a deep breath and swallowed back her tears. She had to be strong here for her boy. She'd be of no use to him if she collapsed into a mess of weeping and wailing.

'Come on, boys,' she said to break the tension. 'Shall we go out to the park?'

'Yes!' squealed Theo excitedly, and then remembered the sombre mood and stopped smiling. 'Can we, Daddy?'

Sebastian wiped his eyes with the heel of his hand.

'I think that's a fantastic idea,' he said, his voice falsely bright. 'Are you sure, Mum? Can you manage?'

'Of course I can,' replied Dorothy. 'I brought you four up in a park! Right, let's go get your shoes and coats on, boys.'

Her grandsons wriggled their way down from the sofa and charged off in the direction of the hallway to retrieve shoes from the enormous messy pile that lay there, Tessa's amongst them. Should she pick Tessa's shoes out and put them elsewhere, Dorothy wondered. She dismissed the thought. The house was full of Tessa and her things. She couldn't remove all of it and she wouldn't want to. No, Sebastian was going to have to find his own way of coping with all that she'd left behind her.

Coats and shoes on, Dorothy ushered the boys out of the door.

'We'll be back in an hour or so,' she called back. 'Will you be all right?'

'Yep,' came Sebastian's strangled response.

She took a boy by each hand and set off towards the park. They made slow progress, Dorothy aware of every one of her eighty-four years but determined not to let Sebastian down. Had she been too ambitious? Well, what if she had? She was going to have to dig deep. They could go on the slides and the roundabout and then she'd take them for one of those hideous blue ice drinks that they liked so much. The main thing was that Sebastian got some time to gather himself, deal with the shock that accidental death trailed in its wake.

The park was busy despite the early hour, filled with exhausted-looking women and small, bouncy offspring. The boys seemed torn between racing away from her and staying close by. They were all at sea, the poor little mites. Dorothy could feel tears threatening again but she had to hold herself together for the boys' sake.

'Who wants to go on a swing?' she shouted, and followed as quickly as she could whilst the boys raced pell-mell to climb up. Her breath was short in her chest and her hips screamed out in pain but somehow she got them sitting side by side on the swings. Pushing was easier than walking, at least.

They would get through this, she thought, together like they always had done. 'Team Bliss', that's what Frank, may he rest in peace, had always called them. And they were a team when the chips were down. The girls would flock around Sebastian now, protecting their baby brother from further harm. The question was whether Sebastian would let them help him. He was proud and had always been determined to come out from under the wings of his sisters. That's where Tessa had been so magnificent. She had given him things to be proud of in his own right. Oh, this was all wrong. Someone so young and vital as Tessa being taken so soon. Tears welled in Dorothy's eyes again.

'Push us! Push us!' came the cries from the boys, waiting not that patiently on the swings.

Dorothy swallowed back her emotions and obliged.

II

'I just don't know what to say to him, Miriam,' Dorothy said, the tears, held back in front of Sebastian the day before, now trickling down her wrinkled cheeks. 'He is entirely broken. He thinks it's all his fault when it was just a horrible accident.'

Miriam filled the teapot with boiling water and then carried it to the table and placed it down on the cork mat.

'Well . . .' said Miriam, and Dorothy knew exactly what she was going to say next. She willed her not to. Sebastian felt bad enough as it was without them making it worse. And it wasn't his fault. How was he to know that Tessa would climb the ladder when she was on her own? Thank the Lord the boys had been out with Sebastian and hadn't had to find their poor mother lying spread all over the patio like a broken doll. It was a small mercy but even small things seemed important at a time like this.

'And he won't be separated from those boys,' Dorothy continued. 'I managed to get them to the park for an hour but when I offered to have them overnight, he just clung to them and wouldn't let them go. I'm not sure it's healthy for the wee boys, Miriam, to see their daddy upset like that.'

'We have to let him find his own way through,' said Miriam. 'He'll ask for help when he's good and ready.'

Dorothy wasn't so sure but she felt relieved that Miriam was there. She wouldn't let anything happen to Sebastian. She would look after her baby brother just like she had done since she'd been not much more than a child herself.

Dorothy sank lower into her chair. She was so tired. Every one of her eighty-four years was sitting heavy on her shoulders. Recently she had started to feel that she'd had enough. She hadn't been sure how she would carry on after Frank had died but she had found resources from deep inside herself and picked herself back up, as much for the children's sake as for her own. Now, though, she wasn't sure she had the strength for any more.

The day before, the day when she'd heard the terrible news about Tessa, she'd had a funny turn at home, coming over all dizzy for a moment, and she'd had to sit down, her left arm numb until she'd rubbed some life back into it. It was nothing serious, she was sure. Probably just the shock. Balance had been restored quickly enough and by the time she had taken the boys to the park she had felt normal again. Now, though, she could sleep for a week.

'We'll have to draw up a rota,' Miriam was saying. 'You, me and Anna can take it in turns to help out. I'm sure Tessa's friends will be there too. I'm not sure who they are. Maybe we can work it out at the funeral . . .'

Miriam chattered on, in full organisational mode, but Dorothy had stopped listening. What would they do, the four of them, when they found out about her secret? It surely wouldn't be long now before the truth came out. She wasn't going to live for ever, after all. She had written that letter years ago, certain then that unburdening herself was the best thing to do. Now, though, she wasn't so sure. What good would it do to unsettle them all, especially when Sebastian had so much to deal with already? This would be a terrible time to land an extra trouble on them all. Maybe it would be better not to let them find out at all? Perhaps she should just get rid of the letter, rewrite her will and take her dreadful secret to the grave?

'What do you think, Mum?' Miriam asked, cutting across her thoughts.

'Sorry,' Dorothy replied vaguely.

'About where we should have the wake for Tessa?'

Did Miriam never stop? Couldn't they just have this one terrible moment of peace without her having to make plans?

'I suppose that'll be for Sebastian to decide,' she said.

'But he's hopeless,' Miriam objected. 'Maybe if I rang round a few places, got an idea of costs. Do you think that would help? It wouldn't take a minute . . .'

But Dorothy wasn't listening.

ANNA – 2014

I

Anna pulled the car on to the gravel driveway of the nursing home and nosed it forward into the last parking space. Someone had parked their car skew-whiff and their front tyres were trespassing. Anna had to park far too close to the wall and then, because there wasn't enough space to open the door, shuffle across so that she could get out of the passenger's side.

It didn't matter what time of day she came to visit her mum. The car park was always full. She doubted that many, if any, of the residents still owned cars and there never seemed to be enough visitors inside to correlate with the contents of the car park. It must be the staff. Or maybe people parked here, pretending to be visiting, and then wandered down into town like they did at the supermarket. Surely no one would be that cheeky?

On the lawn in front of the house someone had placed an optimistic scattering of tables and chairs but Anna had never seen anyone using them. There were also some rickety-looking sun-chairs on the patio, their faded cushions split to reveal the sponge padding inside. Anna wondered exactly what her mother's exorbitant fees were spent on. It certainly wasn't the soft furnishings.

A couple of residents were sitting together on the patio in a companionable silence and looking out across the lawn. Mr Argyle raised his trilby to her as she walked past.

'Hello there, young lady,' he said. 'Lovely day for it.'

Anna wasn't sure exactly what he meant. Today seemed no different from any other day. Was 'it' referring to something special or just the daily grind of getting through one's life?

'Indeed,' she replied non-committally.

'She's inside,' he continued. 'In the big day room. I'm not sure she wanted to come downstairs today but there's no arguing with that male nurse. He's like a force of nature. I once tried to tell him that I like to take my bath in the evening and not the morning. You wouldn't believe the to-do it caused. Over a little bath. Ridiculous. We may be old but we're not entirely gaga. Well, some of us are.' He nodded at his companion, who was swaying her head in time to some music that only she could hear. 'But I'm old enough and ugly enough to know when I like to take my bath. I said to him, I said, "Look here, Kelvin. I've been having my daily bath in the evening since my mother ran the water for me and I'm not about to change now just because it happens to fit in with your schedule. There may be some that's happy to have their baths in the morning but I'm not one of them. You need to redo your list."'

'And did he?' asked Anna, more out of politeness than interest. 'Redo his list, I mean.'

'No. He jolly well didn't. But that didn't make a jot of difference. I just took my bath when I chose, just as I always have. I can see the sense for some of the residents. Old Elsie here, and your dear mother, of course. But those of us who still have the full picnic should be allowed to make our own choices. This is supposed to be a care home, with the emphasis on care.'

Anna didn't like it when the residents moaned about life at the home. They had left the selection of their mother's new home pretty much up to Miriam. A quick decision had been required. Oak's Reach had had an available room and the manager had answered Miriam's questions satisfactorily.

'Are we sure about this?' Sebastian had asked. 'I mean, I know she needs a lot of attention but a nursing home? Is that what we want? Is that what she would have wanted?'

'Are you volunteering?' Clare had asked.

Sebastian had looked at his feet.

'Well, I'm not sure I can take Mum on. Not right now. Not with everything.' He had looked broken for a moment and Anna had been angry with Clare for being so heartless, but there had been little point picking her up on it. 'You have a spare room, Miriam,' Sebastian had suggested when he'd recovered himself.

'Yes, and I'm at school all day. Or are you suggesting that I give up teaching so that I can nurse our mother?'

'No, no. Of course not. I just want to make certain that we've thought through all the options before we commit.'

'He's right, Miriam,' Clare had said. 'It's not just the place. There are the fees to think of. All Mum's savings are going to get eaten up by this.'

'Well, there's not much to speak of.'

'No, but after all that bloody scrimping and saving for years it seems such a waste to pass it direct to a home when she's got all of us who could do the job much cheaper.'

'Well, I don't see you volunteering either, and anyway, why shouldn't she spend her money on somewhere appropriate to live?' Anna had said. 'It's not like she has much else to spend it on.'

'No, but . . .' Clare had paused, eying them from behind her curtain of dirty-looking hair. 'Well, I was kind of hoping that some of it would come to us but we'll never get our hands on it if it all gets blown on care fees.'

'She hasn't died, Clare,' Miriam had snapped. 'You can't go divvying up her stuff whilst she's still with us.'

'I didn't mean that. It's just that surely it would be better if what she has comes to us rather than lining the pockets of some care home owner.'

'That'll be the care home that's providing the care that you don't want to provide, will it?'

Clare annoyed Anna when she got like this. Yes, she needed more money – which of them didn't – but did she always have to make it feel so grasping, so grubby?

'For God's sake, Anna. Don't be so bloody holier-than-thou all the time. I was just making sure that we'd thought through all the possible avenues before we sign on the dotted line, and you have to paint me as some ungrateful, money-grabbing bitch—'

'This is getting us nowhere,' Miriam had said. 'Mum needs care. She needs it now. Oak's Reach seems nice. It's got all the necessary facilities and it has a room spare. I know it's not ideal and none of us would have it as our first choice but I really don't see that we have any alternatives. So, do we sign the papers or what?'

And so they had signed the papers and Dorothy had been moved from the hospital by ambulance with the battered handbag and clothes she'd been standing up in when she'd had the stroke. And it had been okay. It really had, but when the likes of Mr Argyle complained, Anna was forced to check their decision in her mind.

But what was the issue here? Mr Argyle was old. Old people complained and the source of the complaint was the timing of a bath. It was hardly abuse, was it?

'Well, it sounds like you got it sorted out in the end,' said Anna with a friendly wave as she started to move slowly towards the front door. 'Anyway, I'd better go in and see how she is. Enjoy your . . . your afternoon,' she added.

'My son was a pilot in the war, you know,' said the swaying lady.

'No, Elsie. That was your father. Your son works in a bank,' said Mr Argyle and he raised his eyebrows at Anna. She smiled and let herself in through the heavy wooden door.

Inside there was a smell of disinfectant. It wasn't unpleasant as such; they did well to hide the stench of decay here, but there was always an artificial scent hanging heavy in the air. If it wasn't Dettol then it was some synthetic lemon air sweetener. Anna longed to throw open the windows and let the fresh air in but that would drop the ambient temperature below what was optimal for the old and infirm, so instead she breathed through her mouth and tried not to think about it.

Kelvin was bustling through the hallway with a pile of cardboard bedpans in his arms. He nodded at her as he passed but didn't speak. She didn't mind. The staff were quick enough to tell her if there was a problem with her mother and she didn't feel the need to make small talk otherwise. Behind him was Adele, the day manager. She was a whole different kettle of fish.

'Well, hello there, Anna,' she said, smiling widely. Anna objected to Adele using her Christian name. It seemed overly familiar somehow – Anna was a client, after all – but being called Miss Bliss seemed wrong as well. She probably just didn't like Adele.

'Your mother is very well today. She's had some lunch and she's up to date with her medication. She's just relaxing in the Dale Suite at the moment.'

Adele took great pride in knowing where her 'guests' were at any given moment but she was the only one who gave the rooms their allotted names, as if the home were a smart hotel. The Dale Suite was actually the big day room that Mr Argyle had referred to and could only possibly be referred to as a suite because of the folding screen that might be pulled across to make two small rooms but absolutely never was.

'Thanks,' said Anna.

'Would you like a cup of tea?'

'No, thanks. I can't stay long.' Anna had an irrational dislike of the pale-green institutional crockery that was in use at Oak's Reach, although she couldn't quite put her finger on the problem.

'Righty-ho. Well, if you have any questions I'll just be through here,' Adele said, and then bustled off, speaking to the next person that she came across almost before she had finished talking to Anna.

Anna stood on the threshold of the Dale Suite and cast an eye around for her mother. Old people all seemed to look the same. It didn't help that they never seemed to be wearing their own clothes. She recognised a cardigan that Sebastian had bought their mother for Christmas on a tiny, birdlike woman who sat in a wing chair by the radiator. It might not be the same one, of course, but it looked like it and it was clearly too large for the woman who wore it.

She continued to scan the room until her eyes landed on her mother. She was sitting by herself on a small sofa between a window and a birdcage. Inside the cage were two blue budgies. Anna had forgotten all about budgies until she came here. The birds had played no part in her life since she was a child yet here they were, bouncing between perches and twittering, and she wondered how they could have got lost in her mind.

Her mother appeared to be asleep. Her eyelids flickered and a high-pitched whistle sounded with each of her shallow out breaths. When she was asleep like this she looked just as she always had done. In repose her face seemed gentler, the deep wrinkles that cut across it less pronounced. It was when her eyes were open that Anna sometimes struggled to see her mother as she remembered her.

She pulled up a chair and sat next to her. The budgies hopped from perch to perch, chattering away to each other. A crocheted blanket, which someone had placed on her knees despite the stifling heat in the day room, was slipping down and Anna reached out to catch it and put it back. The movement of the fabric against her tights made her mother stir and she opened her eyes, smiled at Anna and then closed them again.

The blanket was made of hundreds of granny squares stitched together in bright jewel colours with a stark black border. Miriam had taught Anna how to make them when she was a child. It had taken a while as Anna had kept pushing her hook through the wrong space, causing her work to unravel before her eyes, but gradually, with Miriam's patience, she had mastered it and soon she'd been churning out squares like there was no tomorrow, snaffling lengths of wool from wherever she could find them. Now, though, she couldn't remember what had happened to them. She felt sure she would have remembered a blanket so she must never have got round to sewing them together, typically moving on to the next thing before the first was finished. They would probably find them stuffed in a bag somewhere when they started the job of clearing the house.

'It's a shame,' said a voice at her ear, making her jump.

'I'm sorry,' said Anna, turning her head towards the voice.

An old lady stood at her shoulder. She was still quite tall, for an old person, and she stood with her head erect although she was leaning on a stick for support.

'It's a shame,' she repeated. 'What's left of a person after a stroke. I wonder if they might not be better off dead.'

Anna was taken aback at her bluntness and also wasn't sure that she agreed with her. For a moment she struggled for a response.

'I don't think we can say that,' she managed.

'Don't you?' the old woman said sharply. 'What kind of a life is that?' She nodded at Anna's mother. 'Sitting in a chair hour after hour with no hope of improvement, wondering whether it will be apple pie or jam roly-poly for pudding. Hoping that someone will visit, going to bed disappointed, with no prospect of ever getting back to the life that you once had, the life when things were yours for the taking, when you could wake up in the morning and choose how you would pass the hours.'

'I don't agree,' Anna said, realising as she spoke that she did have an opinion on this difficult issue.

'Of course you don't. That's because you want your mother here, with you. You can't imagine the emptiness of a post-stroke life, of old age even. Try it now. Try to imagine.'

'I don't need to imagine,' said Anna. 'I know what it's like. I do talk to my mother, you know. And we've spoken to the doctors. She's in no pain and she does seem happy.'

'That's true enough,' conceded the old lady. She spoke so quietly that Anna struggled to hear her over the racket coming from the budgerigars.

'But if she could choose, if she could truly choose to carry on like this day after day or to let go and leave, what do you think she would pick? What would you do?'

Anna didn't reply.

'There are no choices here,' continued the old woman. 'Even I make no choices and I'm still relatively able-bodied. They lay my clothes out for me, they present me with food, they tell me when I should go to bed. It's a cliché to say that the aged are like children but it's true. Where is the dignity in a life like this? No matter how successful you were in life, no matter what you did or how much respect you gained, when you are incapable of controlling your bladder or eating without spilling food down your chin then all is lost. The memory of what you once were is totally overshadowed by what you have become.'

Anna still said nothing as she contemplated what had been said. Hot tears were threatening and she tightened her jaw to stem the flow. Then the old lady reached out and touched Anna gently on the arm. Anna could see her veins, blue through her paper-thin skin.

'Don't get upset, dear. It's just the ramblings of a decrepit old woman. And what I say can't change anything. Your mother survived her stroke, for good or for ill, and there's nothing that we can do about that until something else happens and changes things.'

When Anna didn't comment the old woman withdrew her hand and began her slow progression across the room towards the dining room, where the chink of teacups being rattled was starting to be heard. Anna watched her go.

Her mother made a spluttering sound at the back of her throat but then continued to sleep. Anna picked up her hand from where it was resting on the blanket and wrapped it gently in her own. The fingers, once so strong, were now fragile, the skin on them wrinkled and loose. The wedding band, worn thin from years of wear, hung from her third finger. Only the swelling of the joints prevented it from slipping off and being lost.

Was the woman right? Would it have been better if her mother had been taken when the blood clot hit her brain? That was surely nature's intention. If it hadn't been for the quick thinking of the woman in the queue behind her in the supermarket, would her mother have died there and then on Asda's tiled floor?

No. What was she thinking? Her mother's life here wasn't so bad. Most days she was perfectly lucid. Yes, her speech was a bit slurred and the names for everyday objects often eluded her, but she could generally get her meaning across. By using a mixture of hand gestures, facial expressions and the words that had stayed stuck in her memory banks for reasons that Anna could not fathom, the two of them could have decent conversations. They were just painfully slow.

Her mother's eyes flickered open again and this time she was awake. Anna gave her hand a squeeze.

'How are you today, Mum?' she asked. 'You look well. It smells like it was fish pie for lunch. That must have been a treat. I know how much you like fish pie. Do you remember how much I hated it when I was little? Dad used to make me eat it and I'd spit it out. I must have been a nightmare.'

Dorothy gave her hand a little squeeze and smiled weakly. Did that mean that she too could remember Anna's fussy dining habits? Anna hoped so. She pressed on, not wanting to leave the silences that she found so hard to deal with.

'I quite like it now, fish pie. I mean, I wouldn't choose it from a menu but if someone served it to me at their house I could manage a portion without spitting it out. I must be growing up after all.'

Dorothy smiled again. She looked so weary, Anna thought, as if merely existing was getting too much for her. Maybe the old woman was right?

'I spoke to Miriam this week,' Anna continued resolutely. 'She's well. She says she'll try and get over here at the weekend. It's a bit busy at their house, she said. Rosie is taking her driving test next week and she's nagging Miriam to take her out every minute of the day. Miriam said that it's exhausting but Rosie's absolutely determined to pass first time. Can't think where she gets that from!'

Another squeeze of the hand. Dorothy loved to hear news about them all and good news was the best sort.

'Miriam says she drives well. The instructor expects that she'll pass but you can never tell, can you? I thought I'd pass first time but I got that wrong, didn't I?'

'You . . .' her mother started, taking care over the word as if the mere act of shaping her lips to sound it out was an effort, '. . . were not patient.' She took a deep, rattling breath before she could continue. 'You rushed at it.'

It was true. Anna had been desperate to pass her test and unwilling to hear that she wasn't ready. She smiled fondly at her mother.

'No,' she said. 'Not patient at all. And Sebastian's good, I think. Holding up, anyway. He still won't ask for much help but me and Miriam do what we can. I think he's okay. It's hard to tell but I think he is.'

'Thank you,' said her mother. Anna knew that this was for the help she gave to Sebastian, help that her mother could no longer offer. The stroke had come not three months after Tessa's accident and Anna knew her mother felt that she had somehow let Sebastian down, which was utterly ridiculous. 'And Clare?' asked her mother, her tone expectant.

'I haven't been able to get hold of Clare this week,' said Anna. She hated lying to her mother but there was nothing to be gained by telling her that Clare had totally fallen off all their radars yet again. 'I'm not quite sure where she is,' she continued. 'There was talk of her going to stay with River for a few days so she might be there. I left a message on his answerphone but he's not got back to me yet. Or she might be with her friend Louise. She often gives her somewhere to stay if, well, if she needs somewhere.'

Did her mother know how bad things had got with Clare? Could she sense it by some spooky maternal instinct? Anna knew that was ridiculous and it was probably her reticence to provide any news that made her mother anxious for more information. What would be the point in telling her the truth, though, that Clare appeared to be caught in a downward spiral that no one could pull her out of? Her mother would just worry and there was no need to put her through that.

'Anyway, I'm sure she'll ring me when she gets a minute,' continued Anna breezily, even though she had rarely felt less sure of anything in her life.

'Would you like a cup of tea?' asked a voice just behind her, making her start. It was the tiny care assistant whose name Anna didn't catch when she was first introduced and was now too embarrassed to ask.

'Not just now, thank you. Mum? Would you like one?'

Nothing. Anna wondered sometimes whether her mother chose to play dumb so that people left her alone.

'I think we're fine, thank you,' Anna added. As the tiny woman withdrew, her mother took hold of her arm and squeezed it with a surprising strength, her gnarled fingers quite white with the effort.

'Anna,' she said breathily. 'There's a will.'

Anna's heart jolted. She didn't want to be talking to her mother about death and wills. That she hadn't got long left was obvious to both of them. What need was there to draw attention to the fact? They would find the will when the time came.

'Don't worry about that now,' she said, stroking her mother's hand, which was still gripping her arm urgently. 'We'll find it.'

'No,' said her mother, and the sharpness of her tone seemed out of place in this soft space. 'You must get it, Anna.' She was breathing even more heavily now, each word clearly a huge effort to pronounce. 'Don't let the others read it.'

Anna was confused.

'Why not?'

Her mother's eyes bored into hers. Even though their colour had faded to a milky tan from their once chocolate brown, they still held the steely determination that Anna recognised.

'There's a letter with it,' her mother continued. 'For Clare. Don't give it to her.'

'But . . .'

'Dorothy's eyes were closing now with the effort of speech. 'She's not strong enough. She mustn't know.'

'Know what?' Anna asked. 'Mum. What are you saying?'

Dorothy flopped back against the cushions of the chair, her energy spent. Her eyes were closed now and she looked as if she might be sleeping but for a crease that cut deep between her eyebrows.

'Promise me,' she whispered. 'Burn them.'

ANNA – 2015

I

Anna couldn't believe that a month had passed since her mother's funeral. Miriam, in true eldest-sibling fashion, had taken control of everything, including replying to the many letters of sympathy that had been sent to them and, in some cases, to their mother – as if she shouldn't have to miss out on hearing how truly sorry people were at her demise. Anna wondered how the senders expected these letters would ever be read, the recipient being dead and all, and checked to see if they were from the more mentally infirm of her mother's friends, but there seemed to be no correlation. Maybe writing to the dead person herself was quite common? Anna had no idea.

Miriam had said that they should split the letters between the four of them so that the task of replying would seem less daunting. She had then redistributed Clare's allocation between the other three, just to be on the safe side.

Anna's little pile had sat, accusingly, in the corner of her kitchen for well over a fortnight but now she was going to have to do them because she'd told Miriam that they were ready to post, just waiting for stamps. Miriam would find out soon enough if they never hit a postbox. Her network of spies was legendary.

When she finally set to with a packet of bland thank you cards and a biro that both worked and didn't spit ink, she discovered that she'd got off quite lightly. Hers were mainly from well-meaning members of her mother's WI who she'd never met and so she could reply in simple platitudes that required almost no emotional investment. She plucked the top one from the pile. It had a picture of a bunch of lilies on the front with the message printed in some curly, seventies-style font. Inside, the quavering handwriting expressed the writer's deep sorrow for the loss of her mother. She squinted at the name, which the sender had helpfully written in block capitals under her signature. Vera Brown. The name meant nothing to Anna. 'Dear Vera,' she began. 'Thank you so much for your kind thoughts at this sad time. We are all very grateful. Kind regards, Anna Bliss.' She dithered over adding a kiss, almost did and then decided against it. One down. Loads to go.

'This is bloody ridiculous,' she said to Margot, who had leaped up and was sitting, purring in her lap. 'Miriam is an idiot. Surely no one expects a reply to a sympathy card, do they?'

Once she'd actually started, though, she got into a rhythm and soon the pile of envelopes was taller than the pile of cards. She picked up the last one. This card was altogether classier than the others. There was no silver gilt or curly lettering here, just a simple image of a single rose. The handwriting, whilst a little wobbly in places, showed signs of having been flowing and elegant once. Anna looked at her own cramped lettering and felt a little envious. Her eyes dropped to the bottom to see who had sent it. StJohn Downing. The name meant nothing to her but then she didn't know all her mother's friends. She quickly scanned the message. It covered the same ground as the others. Terribly sorry to hear of your loss . . . She was a wonderful woman . . . My thoughts are with you, etcetera, but there was something about this one that seemed more heartfelt, as if whoever StJohn Downing was, he was genuinely moved by her mother's death.

Anna plucked another thank you card from the packet and penned her standard reply. She signed it, addressed the envelope and pulled the white strip from the flap. Whatever happened to licking envelopes. Too unhygienic in these days of anti-bacterial everything. She slapped the last letter down on the top of the pile with the satisfaction of a job if not well done then at least finished. She fished the card from StJohn Downing out of the pile and dropped the rest into the recycling bin. She'd ask Miriam about him, see if his name rang a bell with her.

With the letters done, the next and far more daunting task was now hanging over the four of them like a raincloud at a barbecue.

'We need to sort the house,' Miriam said when she rang. 'And soon. It's no good to anyone just sitting there empty.'

Miriam was in sergeant-major mode yet again. It was great that she took control but Anna wished she would slow the pace down, just a little bit. Throwing away what was left of their mother was hard enough without running it like a military campaign. There was no point suggesting this to Miriam, though, not if you wanted her to carry on being in charge. Anna took a deep breath. 'I know.'

'And then there's the will . . .'

Anna's heart did a little leap. 'What will?' she asked. The will that's sitting on my kitchen table under a pile of magazines and old invoices? she thought. Oh, that will.

'Well, there must be a will,' Miriam said. 'Mum wouldn't have died without leaving a will. But I've been to the bank and the solicitors that Dad used and they are both denying all knowledge. So, I'm assuming it must be in the house somewhere.'

'Maybe there isn't one,' said Anna, grateful that this conversation was taking place over the phone so that her sister couldn't see her squirming. She closed her eyes as she spoke, as if not being able to see anything would make the lies easier to tell.

'Don't be stupid, Anna. Of course there's a will. We just have to find it. It'll just split everything four ways, I assume.'

Anna fought the urge to make a joke about being the favourite and so getting the lion's share. Sebastian might find that kind of thing funny but Miriam wouldn't.

'Okay. Well, we can keep an eye open for it when we're at the house.'

Nausea rose in her throat. How long could she realistically keep this up? If she could just persuade them that there was no will then they would stop looking and she wouldn't have to confess a) that she had it, b) that their mother had asked her and not one of them to retrieve and burn it, and c) that she hadn't actually carried out her mother's wishes.

Anna wasn't sure why she hadn't destroyed the will and the letter when her mother had been so emphatic that she should. Curiosity? That was certainly part of it, but something in Anna's gut told her that whatever was in the letter, it was information that should not be lost. Maybe now was not the right time for it to be revealed but Anna's instinct told her that Clare had a right to know whatever it was that her mother had first wanted to tell her and then to conceal.

'Perhaps Mum had the stroke before she got round to writing one?' Anna suggested, but it sounded feeble even to her. They both knew that Dorothy would never have left something like that to chance. 'And Dad's solicitors definitely haven't got it?'

Anna could almost hear the silent tut that came down the line from Miriam, could visualise her rolling her eyes. 'No. I already said. Anyway, I was thinking that if we got together next weekend we could make a start. I've rung Sebastian and he can get someone to mind the boys so I just need to get hold of Clare . . .' Miriam's voice tapered off.

'Where is she at the moment?' Anna asked gently.

'I think she's at Louise's again but I'm not sure. They had that row, didn't they?'

'What about River?'

'Don't get me started about that ungrateful little so and so.'

Anna could hear her sister fighting to control her temper.

'He said that he doesn't know where Clare is at the moment and he can't be held responsible for her actions.'

'Well,' Anna had said cautiously, 'he does have a point. No one can help Clare unless she's prepared to help herself.'

'But he's her son!'

'Perhaps it's just self-preservation? It can't have been easy being brought up like that.'

Miriam didn't speak for so long that Anna began to wonder if the connection had been broken.

'Well, anyway, I'll get hold of her somehow and tell her to be at Mum's on Saturday morning.'

When Saturday dawned, Anna woke up feeling that there was something unusual in the offing. Then, as she lay there listening to the rain beat against her bedroom window, she remembered that it was the day of her mother's house clearance and the brief fizz of delight was replaced by a heavy sense of dread. She snuggled back under the duvet, reluctant to have the day begin by getting up. Margot was curled in her habitual place on the pillow next to her and Anna pressed her nose to Margot's little black one.

'Morning, Margot,' she whispered in case some hidden surveillance equipment might overhear her talking to her cat and mark her down accordingly. Margot responded to the sound of Anna's voice by purring gently but didn't open her eyes.

In the kitchen, whilst waiting for the kettle to boil, she flicked idly through a magazine. Fresh-faced and beautiful young models smiled out at her from every glossy page. It would make much more sense, thought Anna, if they used models who actually had wrinkles to advertise these products. Every one of her forty-nine years hung heavily on her this morning. The kettle came to the boil and she poured the hot water on to the coffee grounds, enjoying the rich aroma that always seemed to smell better than it actually tasted. She carried the cafetière to the table, took a mug carefully from the overfull draining rack and a carton of milk from the fridge. Margot padded through and nuzzled her head against Anna's legs, demanding food.

'Here you go, old girl,' Anna said to her as she poured the little crunchy cat biscuits into an earthenware bowl.

'I'm not looking forward to today.' Margot was focused on her food and didn't appear to be listening. 'Miriam will be tetchy, Sebastian morbid and God only knows how Clare will react. Do you think I could just go back to bed and forget all about it? Do you? Do you?' She rubbed the cat's ears affectionately but Margot was most unresponsive and continued to munch her way through her breakfast.

'You're not really being very sympathetic. I don't know. Call your-self my friend!'

Anna sat back at the table and poured the coffee. The steam rose until she added the cold milk. Cupping the mug in her hands, she pulled her knees up and wrapped her robe around them until she was bundled up like a little cocoon. By the bread bin was a pile of post that needed sorting out. It was where she put everything that she didn't quite know what to do with or couldn't be bothered to deal with on first opening. She hadn't tackled it for some time and knew that it should be on her list for the coming week. There was nothing too dreadful in it – no red bills or store card accounts that needed urgent attention. It was all for filing or transferring to her diary. All except the large manila envelope that was hidden at the very bottom, which was invisible to anyone who gave the pile a casual glance but had been on Anna's mind almost constantly since the day she had retrieved it from her mother's house six weeks before.

II

When Anna got to the house, Sebastian was already there, sitting on the garden wall, swinging his legs. It was as if the last thirty years hadn't happened.

'God! How many hours have we spent sitting on that wall?' Anna asked as she locked the car and walked towards him. 'I used to pretend it was a horse. You couldn't do that now,' she continued, peering over into the garden where brambles and bindweed had taken over and were sprawling up the stone. 'You'd cut your legs to ribbons. I thought someone was supposed to be doing the garden,' she added.

'Yes. I did too. I think Miriam had a word with some boyfriend of Rosie or Abigail. Can't remember which one. I hope she didn't pay him up front. It doesn't look like he's done anything for months.'

The small front garden, once their mother's pride and joy and indicator to the passing world of a state of order that continued into the house, was unkempt and overgrown. There was no longer any lawn – Sebastian had covered it over with black plastic and gravel when mowing it became problematic – and the borders seemed to consist mainly of tall yellow-flowered weeds with the odd head of stock or hydrangea poking resolutely through.

'Oh, how your mother loved that garden,' came a voice from next door, the implied criticism as sharp as if she'd voiced it directly. Mrs Connors stood on her doorstep, hairnet covering her curlers and a housecoat straining over her ample bosom.

'She did indeed, Mrs Connors,' replied Sebastian politely. Anna was grateful to him. He offered no excuses for what were clearly, in Mrs Connors' eyes, their shortcomings but looked at the garden as if it were a grave.

'You here to sort the house, then?' asked Mrs Connors.

'That's right. It's a big job but we can't put it off for ever.'

'I could send our Malcolm round if you need an extra pair of hands.'

'No, thank you,' said Anna quickly before Sebastian had chance to prevaricate. This was going to be difficult enough. The last thing they needed was Mrs Connors's spy in the ranks. 'We'll be fine just us.'

'You all coming to help, then?' continued the neighbour, looking down the street for signs of more arrivals.

'That's right,' said Anna briskly. 'In fact, we'd better be getting on. Have you got the key, Seb?'

Sebastian looked sheepish.

'I thought you'd have one,' he replied.

'Damn,' said Anna, and then wished she hadn't. Mrs Connors was watching with interest to see how this pickle panned out. She would of course hold a key herself but she wasn't about to volunteer it and pass up an opportunity to make Anna squirm.

'Actually, I'm pretty certain Miriam is bringing hers,' said Anna, turning away from Mrs Connors and pulling a face at Sebastian.

As if on cue, Miriam's car pulled up alongside the gate and Miriam got out.

'You've got the key, haven't you, Miriam?' she asked quickly. Anna could see Miriam gearing herself up to reprimand them but then, glancing quickly at the tableau before her, Mrs Connors's eager eyes ready to pick fault, she changed direction.

'Yup,' she said. 'As we arranged.' Anna chanced a wink at Sebastian.

Miriam scrabbled around in her bag and produced a brass key on a plastic fob. Anna saw 'MOTHER' printed in Miriam's neat handwriting.

'Here we are,' she said. 'Shall we go in? Nice to see you, Mrs Connors,' she added but did not make eye contact with her. She put the key in the lock and opened the door and, with barely a hesitation, made her way into the dark hallway with Anna and Sebastian following close behind. Anna closed the door firmly.

'She's such a witch, that woman. I shall be delighted when we never, ever have to set eyes on her again.'

'Oh, she's not that bad,' said Miriam. 'She used to be quite nice when I was little. She was great when you were born, Sebastian. I think she's just got old and grumpy with age.'

'I'm not surprised, spending her entire life living in that house with that socially disastrous son of hers. Honestly, she couldn't wait to have a go at us about the garden.'

Anna stopped, remembering just too late that it was Miriam who had made the arrangement with the ineffectual teenage gardener.

'Yes. I must have a word with Harry about that,' Miriam said, not rising to the bait.

They stood in the hall. It was fusty, as if the air had been stagnant for too long. With all the doors closed there was very little light coming in, and the dirty windows compromised what there was.

'Come on,' said Sebastian. 'Let's go through.' He opened the door into the lounge.

The lounge also felt empty and uncared-for. The tired-looking sofas seemed to radiate the smell of years of meals eaten from a tray, and dust had settled thickly on every surface. On the wicker coffee table a peace lily drooped, its leaves dried and yellowing.

No one spoke. Outside, Anna could just make out the tinny tune of an ice-cream van in a neighbouring street.

'Did you manage to get hold of Clare?' asked Sebastian. 'Is she coming?'

'I spoke to her yesterday,' said Miriam. 'She's back at Louise's for the time being. She said she'd get here if she could.'

Anna had no doubt that Clare would come. If there was treasure to be found, Clare would want to be a part of the search party.

Sebastian walked over to the mantelpiece and picked up a tarnished silver photo frame.

'Look at us,' he said. 'So innocent.'

'Well, you were,' laughed Anna. 'You could only be six months old in that picture. God, it wasn't half a shock when you were born. We had no idea!'

It was old family history but whenever it came up they always responded the same way.

'Proper shock for me,' said Miriam. 'What with my pivotal role in your arrival on to the planet. I saw things that day that a sixteen-year-old should never have to see!'

'I still struggle to believe that Mum had no idea,' said Sebastian, following the well-trodden path.

'Oh, believe it, little bro. It was one hell of a shock. I really think she thought her childbearing days were well behind her. I remember that look on her face when I found her in labour. There was no way that she knew. And you know what she was like. Even if she was in denial, she would have made some sort of plan. She wouldn't have been able to help herself. There would have been baby clothes secreted about the place somewhere at the very least. There was nothing. Absolutely nothing. You wore pink for the first week!'

'It's like something you'd read about in a teenage magazine,' said Sebastian. 'Still, it's always served me well at dinner parties.'

Miriam walked to the grimy window and looked out on to the street beyond.

'All those people enjoying themselves right outside this window and Mum in labour on her own upstairs. Unbelievable.'

She stood quietly staring out.

'Things were never the same after that,' she said in a voice so quiet that Anna had to strain to catch her words. 'I had to give up my dreams of drama school for a start. And Clare . . .' She let the words hang in the air between them.

'I'm not sure that's right,' said Anna gently. 'Dad had already said no to the drama school thing. Even if Sebastian hadn't come along with his constant squawking demands for food and clean nappies . . .' She smiled at Sebastian, her baby brother and now a good foot taller than her. 'You'd never have gone to London. And Clare. Well, I know I was only young but even I could see that she was bent on self-destruction. Well, maybe not self-destruction exactly. But she was already well and truly off the rails. I suppose Sebastian's arriving might've meant that Mum and Dad took their eyes off the ball a bit but I can't see how they could ever have controlled her, short of locking her in her bedroom – and even then she'd have just shinned down the drainpipe and escaped.'

The front door opened and banged shut, making Anna jump. When Clare sauntered into the lounge it couldn't have been more obvious that they'd just been talking about her.

'Started without me?' she asked with a sneer.

'No,' said Miriam. 'Not at all. We haven't started at all. We were just chatting – reminiscing, really – about that day when Sebastian was born.'

Clare seemed to relax a little. 'Right in the middle of that bloody street party! Jesus, brother. You knew how to make an entrance! Some woman came to find me. I can't remember where I was. Off with some lad or other. Anyway, she found me and she said, "You'd better get yourself back home", and I said, "Why?", and she said, "Cos your mum's just had a baby!" I thought she was mad. A baby! At Mum's age. People went on about it for months. We were the talk of the bloody town.'

Clare sat down heavily on the sofa and a fine cloud of dust rose into the air. Anna risked a quick glance at her sister. The thick make-up that she was wearing couldn't hide the dark rings under her eyes and her hair was lank and lifeless. There were food stains down the front of her T-shirt. One of her ballet pumps had a hole in the side through which Anna could see the greying skin of Clare's foot.

'So, what's the plan?' said Clare.

Miriam turned from the window and came to sit next to Clare. Anna sat on the high-backed chair by the fireplace and Sebastian stayed where he was, like some Victorian father in an old-fashioned photograph.

'I haven't really given it much thought,' said Miriam, and Clare rolled her eyes.

'Liar!' she said. 'Miriam, arch planner extraordinaire, not given it much thought? Yeah, right.' She winked at Miriam.

Miriam raised her eyebrows at her sister.

'Well, maybe a bit. How about we each take a room, see if we can find anything that might have any value or anything sentimental. Then we can divvy that stuff up and get a price from the house clearance people for the rest.'

'Sounds sensible,' said Sebastian. 'And we can see if we can turn up the will while we're at it.'

'I thought there was no will?' asked Clare.

'Well, we're not sure that there is,' said Miriam. 'There's no sign of one, but it just doesn't ring true to me that Mum wouldn't have made one. I know there's not much to leave, really, but I'm sure she would have sorted it out after Dad died. Just bear it in mind, anyway.'

Anna looked down at the floor so she didn't have to meet anyone's eye.

III

'Right, well, how about Anna and I do downstairs and you two take upstairs?' suggested Sebastian, and when no one objected he continued, 'We can make a start in the dining room, Ans.'

Clare followed Miriam up the stairs and Anna opened the door into the dining room to be immediately punched in the stomach by a hospital-style bed. Her heart raced when she saw it and her throat thickened.

'God, that was a shock,' she said when she felt sure of her voice again. 'I'd completely forgotten that that was in here. Where did it come from? Won't someone be wanting it back?'

Sebastian put his hand to his mouth, breathing steadily and deeply. Anna could see on his face the strength that it was taking to compose himself and she wished with all her heart that she could close the door and protect him from the memories of death and dying. 'I've no idea,' he said after a moment. 'Miriam will know.'

The bed was stripped, the clean sheets and blankets folded neatly in a pile at its foot. The mattress had a plastic top sheet.

'I'm so sorry, Seb,' said Anna. 'We can leave this room to the others if you like.' Sebastian just shook his head and so she went in.

The dining table had been folded and pushed in against the sideboard. The chairs were stacked in twos in front of the window. On the mantelpiece were some curling get-well-soon cards and a crystal vase which, thankfully, someone had emptied and washed. The thought of being greeted by dead flowers was almost more than Anna could bear.

Sebastian was still looking at the bed.

'The stroke was the beginning of the end,' he said. 'Until then I thought Mum would go on for ever and die peacefully in her sleep when she was a hundred and ten. She was always so active. I never imagined anything slowing her down.'

Anna nodded, not quite trusting her voice not to break if she spoke. Sebastian continued.

'I mean, it's so brutal. To be left virtually immobile and with next to no speech. I can't imagine what it must have been like for her. If I get like that, Ans, you have to promise to have me shot. Or take me to Switzerland or something because I'm telling you now, there will be no way that I'll want to continue living.'

'There was a woman at Oak's Reach who said much the same to me,' said Anna quietly. 'But I don't think I agree. At least she stayed in her own home until almost the end and she knew what was going on around her. Her mind stayed pretty sharp. And she had us.'

Anna paused and her eyes were drawn again to the bed. She pulled her gaze away.

'Right!' she said decisively. 'If there's anything in here worth keeping then it'll be in the sideboard, so we're going to have to shift that table out of the way so that we can open it.'

Taking one end each, they managed to manoeuvre the mahogany table far enough away from the sideboard to open the drawers and cupboard doors, but the space was tiny and they had to squat down in the gap with the two pieces of furniture towering over them.

Anna opened a cupboard, twisting her arm so that it didn't bang on the table behind her. Inside was stacked the best china, which was only ever used on Christmas Day and even then with extreme caution. Carefully she removed a soup bowl from the top and turned it over to look at it.

'It's Wedgwood, this service, but I've no use for it. I almost never entertain. I wonder if Miriam might want it? I suppose you have all the plates you need.'

Sebastian half-smiled. 'I think Tessa had it covered. I sometimes think we could eat our dinners for an entire month without ever having to do any washing-up.' Sebastian stopped.

'You're doing so well, Seb,' Anna said gently, reaching out to touch him lightly on the shoulder. 'I'm so very proud of you.' Sebastian bit his lip and nodded but he didn't meet her gaze. 'We'll leave the Wedgwood here and ask Miriam about it. I wonder if I ought to make a list?'

She delved further into the cupboard and found various glass sundae bowls, all with a fine patina of dirt. There were some tarnished silver cruets and a little silver mustard pot with a blue glass insert and a tiny wooden spoon.

'I used to love that spoon when I was little,' said Sebastian. 'I even tried to whittle one myself once. It was rubbish.' He laughed at the memory and Anna was pleased to see his customary cheerful exterior restored, even if it was merely a veneer. 'This drawer is just the best cutlery, you know, that stuff with the bone handles. And this one, if I remember correctly' – he opened the drawer with a flourish – 'is full of . . . yup. Napkins.'

'How do you think Clare looked?' asked Anna, reaching in the back of the cupboard and pulling out some Pyrex serving tureens. 'Just now, I mean,' she added, though no clarification was needed.

'Not bad at all,' said Sebastian. 'Surprisingly well, in fact. I thought she'd been going through a bad patch but I certainly didn't see any sign of it.'

Anna had probably asked the wrong sibling. She was pretty sure that Miriam would have seen Clare as she had done, down at heel, doing her best to keep up appearances but with a distinct undertone of neglect.

'And she's sober,' added Sebastian. 'I was a bit worried that she wouldn't be. I know it's first thing in the morning but that doesn't really mean anything, does it?'

'Yes. I agree, so that has to be a good thing. Do you think that we ought to offer her the house again, just to stay in until it sells?'

Sebastian thought for a moment and then slowly shook his head.

'No. She was so angry last time I'm not sure we should risk it again. I don't really understand it. You'd think that she'd jump at the chance. A place to stay, fully furnished and rent-free.'

'And full of painful memories and with the heavy disapproval of her family to cope with?' added Anna. 'I can see why she wouldn't want to be here. I'm not sure I would if I were in her shoes. And I suppose if we are looking to sell, it'd be better if the place was empty. The last thing we'd need is the estate agent showing people round and discovering Clare on a bender.'

Sebastian smiled weakly.

'I asked her to come and stay with us, you know, before Tess died,' he said. 'It was a bit of a hard sell to Tessa but the boys were up for Auntie Clare to come to visit and we've got a spare room. But she turned me down outright. Just said thanks for the offer but she was perfectly all right the way things were. I'd quite like to have her around now. Anything is better than the silence. Daren't ask her, though. I don't think I could bear her to reject me again.'

Anna felt a little wounded at learning that he had asked Clare to stay. She'd always thought there was something special between her and Sebastian. They were the little ones, she the reputed favourite and Sebastian the baby of the family. They had always stuck together but maybe Sebastian felt differently. Maybe he saw all his sisters as equals. 'Perhaps you should ask her again,' said Anna, even though she hated the idea of Clare hurting Sebastian any more.

'Maybe. I feel so guilty. I keep thinking that I'll wake up one day to a phone call from Miriam telling me that she's been found face down in a ditch somewhere. Or worse.'

'All we can do is be there for her if she needs us. Just ask her. Is it still tablecloths in that big drawer at the bottom?' she added, moving back on to less emotionally charged ground.

'Looks like it. Do you think I need to take them all out so I can tell Miriam that the will isn't in there?'

'Probably or she'll only make you look again. Oh, look!' Anna pulled her hand out from the back of the cupboard. She was holding a tiny china lady in a blue crinoline skirt. 'How I loved this when I was small. It used to be on the mantelpiece in the lounge.'

Sebastian gave the ornament a cursory look.

'Is that the one that Clare broke by throwing it at Miriam? Before my time, that was.'

'Yes. Look. You can still see where Dad glued her little arm back on.' There was a clear dark line encircling the arm, the yellowing glue visible in lumps. 'He didn't do a great job, did he? I wonder if the others would mind if I took it?'

'I doubt it. It's not like anyone's missed it in the decade or so that it's been stuck in that sideboard!' laughed Sebastian. 'I wouldn't claim it as your valuable item, though.' He winked at her and in that moment looked just like the boy that he once had been.

'Well, it's worth the world to me,' said Anna, and she put the lady gently on top of the sideboard.

'I'm not sure there's much else in here. Shall we move on to the kitchen?'

'Yes. I could do with getting out of here anyway. That bed . . . It's giving me the heebie-jeebies.'

Anna stood up, her knees creaking slightly, and negotiated her way out of the space between the table and the sideboard.

'I think the table's worth a bob or two,' she said. 'We should per-haps get a valuer round before the house clearance people come. Just in case,' she added.

'If there is no will,' said Sebastian, 'how will it work? Will we just divide everything by four?'

Anna felt a flush creep across her cheeks. She ignored it and Sebastian didn't seem to notice.

'I suppose so. We'll sell it all and then split the proceeds. I think it'll take a while, though. It'll have to go through the solicitors and everything. We can't just sort it out ourselves.'

'I'm sure we could,' said Sebastian. 'I mean, who'd know?'

'I don't know. It might make selling the house more difficult or something. Let's just hope we find it.'

Anna could feel her cheeks burning and turned away so that Sebastian wouldn't see. Obviously they'd never find the will, what with it being hidden at her house and all. Still, she had to behave as if she was just as much in the dark as the rest of them so that nobody became suspicious. If it weren't so awful having to lie, she thought, all this sub-terfuge might be quite good fun.

They left the dining room, Sebastian closing the door behind them, but not before Anna took one last look at the stark white bed.

IV

The kitchen looked far more as Anna remembered it. The scrubbed-pine table stood in the centre, waiting to be set for tea, and her mother's selection of aprons hung on a hook by the back door where they had always been. It too had the damp, sad smell of the rest of the house.

'I'll be glad when we get out of here,' she said. 'It's so depressing.'

'Oh, I don't know,' said Sebastian. 'Once it's sold we'll have no way of connecting with the memories. It'll be like a part of our childhood will have been lost for ever.'

He ran his hand over the dints in the scullery door frame, where their father had chipped lines to record their height.

'And that's not depressing?!' Anna laughed.

She opened a couple of kitchen cupboards but the contents were sparse. More crockery, some glasses that had come free with petrol and never seemed to break, a tin of Bird's custard powder, a box of Cup-a-Soup.

'Mum never really moved into the twenty-first century, did she?' Anna said.

'Well, you know what they say. Once a Cup-a-Soup drinker . . .'

'I'm glad you're with me. It was awful when I was here by myself.'

Anna stopped, frozen to the spot. Had she given herself away?

'When were you here by yourself?' asked Sebastian without looking up from the drawer that he was riffling through.

'Oh, a while back. Mum wanted me to find something for her. Some underwear or something.'

Sebastian seemed to accept this and didn't question her further. Relief washed over her. She definitely wasn't cut out to be a spy.

Upstairs, they could hear the low hum of voices.

'I wonder if those two are having any more luck?' he asked.

'I doubt it. I can't think that there is anything here of any value. Whatever there was disappeared years ago.'

Sebastian looked up quickly and Anna met his gaze defiantly.

'Well, it did. There's no getting away from it. Most of the stuff that Mum and Dad had that was worth anything has gone down Clare's throat at some point over the last thirty years.'

Sebastian didn't reply. Had she gone too far? Probably.

'Is there anything you'd particularly like?' she asked him, because it was obvious that he wasn't going to join her in a slagging-Clare-off session. 'From the house, I mean. Sentimental stuff?'

'Not that I can think of. I've got Dad's dress watch and his shirt studs. I would like something of Mum's but there's nothing that springs to mind. She did say I could have her engagement ring. Do you remember that? She was worried that it would cause a row between the three of you. I assume it's still kicking around somewhere. She wouldn't have sold it, would she?'

'You'd better ask Miriam. I think she has the stuff that came back from the home after . . . There'll be her wedding ring too, although it was worn so thin that I'm surprised it hadn't snapped.'

The steady trudge of footsteps could be heard coming down the creaking stairs.

'Stand by your beds,' said Sebastian and winked at Anna. For a moment he looked just like their father. She grinned back. Some things, like her bond with her brother, would never change.

Clare came in first and Anna could see Sebastian eyeing up the holed shoes and dirty clothes that had failed to make an impression on him when she'd first arrived. Clare seemed to notice his lingering gaze and stared at him as if challenging him to comment. Of course he didn't.

'Any luck?' asked Anna.

'With what?' asked Clare. 'No will. No valuables. Bit of a waste of time all round.'

'I wouldn't say that,' said Miriam. 'There's that lovely little water-colour in the back bedroom – the one of the Alps – and there's some cut glass. A couple of perfume bottles that I think were Granny's and a crystal vase which is quite nice. I'd quite like the watercolour if no one else has their eye on it.'

'That's fine by me,' said Sebastian. 'I was just saying, Miriam. What happened to Mum's rings?'

'I've got them at home, and her watch. I think that's Cartier. I'm not sure.'

Sebastian paused, nodding slightly before he said, 'It's just that Mum always said that she'd like the engagement ring to come to me. Do you remember?'

'No,' said Clare, an upward inflection in her voice suggesting that she thought this to be unlikely. Anna's heart sank. Poor Sebastian. Why could Clare not just have remembered that or at least pretended that she had? What difference would it make to her whether Sebastian had the ring or not?

'Well, she did.' Sebastian pressed on bravely. 'I remember quite distinctly. She said I should have it because she couldn't split it between us all and she couldn't choose between the three of you.'

'I don't remember any such thing,' said Clare, her hands on her hips. 'Why would she want you to have it? It's not like you can wear it or anything.'

'I'm just saying what I remember. I don't want a fight. If no one else remembers, then we can just forget it.'

'It is the kind of thing that Mum would have said,' said Miriam. 'If we could only find a will she would surely have put this sort of stuff in there. It's not so important for the house and whatever we get for the furniture. We can just split that four ways. But actual bequests. She might have left something for my girls.'

'Oh, they're all circling now,' said Clare, rolling her eyes and jutting her hip to one side just like she had done as a teenager. 'The vultures. No doubt Sebastian will want a share for his boys as well.'

'That's not fair, Clare,' said Sebastian. 'I only mentioned the ring because Anna asked me if there was anything in particular that I'd like. It really doesn't matter.'

'I don't think you're being very kind, Clare,' said Miriam. 'And you've got River, anyway. Don't you want him to get something too?'

'Not especially. He barely ever saw Mum. He couldn't even be bothered to turn up to the funeral. And anyway, he keeps telling me how well he's doing on his own without me so I see no need to share my share, whatever that turns out to be, with him.'

There was a silence whilst Clare's words sank in. Clare, seeming to realise that she had stepped over some line of appropriate behaviour, looked at her feet, appeared to see the hole in her shoe and then looked up again defiantly.

'Let's not row about it,' said Anna before Miriam had the chance to cut in. 'Not here. This is hard enough without us all falling out. We'll keep looking for the will and if it turns out that there isn't one, we can decide what to do then. In the meantime, we need to take anything that we don't want to go to the house clearance people so that we can get the rest of it valued. There's the best china through there, Miriam, if you fancy it.'

'I notice you don't ask me if I'd like the china,' spat Clare.

'You don't have anywhere to put it,' Miriam spat back. Anna threw her a silencing look.

'Just because I don't have a mortgage on a nice little suburban semi like you, sis, doesn't mean that I should miss out on the divvying-up.'

'Miriam does have a point,' said Sebastian. 'What would you do with a set of Wedgwood china? If Miriam likes it and can give it a home then I can't see why she shouldn't have it.'

'She should leave it to get valued with everything else,' said Clare, 'and then she can knock the cost of it off her share.'

'Oh, now you're being ridiculous,' said Miriam. 'I would like the china. It's lovely but I don't want it if it's going to cause all this bother.'

'Is there anything that you want, Clare?' asked Anna. 'There's the bone-handled cutlery and there's some nice damask table linen that's barely used.'

Clare looked at Anna, the disgust barely concealed. 'Damask table linen? For God's sake. What the fuck am I going to do with damask bloody table linen. I haven't even got a table.'

'I was just saying, trying to even things out a bit. If you don't want it then that's fine but you don't have to be so aggressive about it.'

'Here we go! Nothing changes. First chance you get, you lot gang up on me. It's always the bloody same. I can see you sneering. Notice the hole in my shoes, did we, Sebastian? Makes you feel uncomfortable, does it, to see someone with no cash?'

'Don't start all that, Clare,' said Miriam. 'I wouldn't put it past you to have worn those shoes on purpose to win the sympathy vote. You're working. I know for a fact that you have shoes without holes. I've seen them. You managed to dress the part for the funeral, after all.'

'Oh, get down from your high horse. Who are you to come across all superior? You've always been the same, thinking that you're better than the rest of us, but you're not that fantastic. A teacher? What is it they say? If you can't do, teach?'

'Stop it! Both of you,' said Anna as she tried to stop the situation spiralling out of their control. 'This is getting us nowhere. We'll get the house and contents valued and then we can take it from there. It's not like we can get our hands on anything now anyway. It'll take months going through probate. The whole point of coming today was to see what there was of sentimental value . . .'

'Sentimental and valuable, you mean.'

'Clare. You're just making this whole thing so much worse and there's no need. Nobody wants to rip you off. We'll divide whatever there is four ways. If Miriam and Sebastian want to pass some of their share on to their kids then that's up to them.'

'Well, you would say that, wouldn't you, Anna, seeing as you have no kids. You'll end up the best off.'

'Now you're being ridiculous. I thought that was your idea, how you wanted to do it. Honestly, Clare. You're completely impossible sometimes.'

'Well, if that's how you feel there's no point me sticking around.' Clare turned on her heel and made for the door. 'You can do what the hell you like. You always fucking do.'

'Clare!' shouted Miriam after her. 'Don't be silly. Come back.'

But the front door opened and then slammed shut.

'Mrs Connors will be having a field day,' said Sebastian.

'I so didn't want that to happen,' said Miriam.

'It's not your fault,' said Anna. 'It couldn't be helped. She's completely unreasonable. She always has been. She thinks that we're all out to get her and nothing that we can do will convince her otherwise.'

'She was fine upstairs,' continued Miriam. 'We were just chatting about all sorts of stuff. It was nice.'

'It's the money that set her off,' said Sebastian.

'Well, that's a joke. There isn't any money. It all went trying to dig her out of the various holes that she's got herself into over the years. She just won't see it. She is totally paranoid.'

'I think that kind of goes with the territory,' said Sebastian.

'Well, I'm sick of it,' said Miriam. 'We're just trying to do what's right and if she can't see that then it's her loss.'

'Will you ring the valuer or do you want one of us to do it?' asked Anna, desperate to stop the conversation turning back to the lack of a will.

'I'll do it,' said Miriam. 'She already thinks I'm out to get her. No point you two catching it as well.'

'Come on,' said Sebastian. 'Let's shut up here. I think that's enough for today.'

'I hardly dare ask but can I take this?' Anna held up the mended china lady.

'God, I'd forgotten all about her,' said Miriam, smiling fondly at the little statuette. 'Yes. You take her. It's not like she's worth anything. Not after Clare threw her at the wall!'

They all trooped out and Miriam locked the door after them. Mrs Connors was in her front garden, no longer in her housecoat but with her curlers still peeping out from under her headscarf.

'Get it all sorted out, did you?' she asked.

'Yes, thank you,' said Anna curtly, and pulled the garden gate smartly shut.

V

Anna looked at the envelope in front of her. It looked innocuous enough. Manila, foolscap, of a standard quality. In fact, there was nothing to mark it out from any other envelope that she might have about the place. Nothing except the label that had been stuck, not quite straight, across its front. Anna pictured a harassed secretary trying to get the post out before the end of the day.

'The Last Will and Testament of Mrs Dorothy Bliss – Private and Confidential.'

Miriam would do her nut if she knew Anna had it. Even though this whole situation was a nightmare, Anna couldn't help smirking. All that hunting and speculating and cursing and the will had been here on her kitchen table the whole time. Well, it was kind of funny. Kind of.

She drained her cup of tea but kept her hands cupped around the mug, trying to eke any last vestiges of warmth from it. This was no good. She had to do something. She put down the mug and picked up the envelope, feeling its weight in her hands. The flap was stuck down but if she worried at its edges she could work it free without tearing it. Gently she pulled until the glue gave way and it opened. She tipped it upside down and out fell a document tied up in pink ribbon, and a sealed white envelope.

The will. It had lain here for the six weeks since she had retrieved it from her mother's house but she hadn't looked inside the envelope until now. Her mother had told her to destroy it, so opening it had felt like a betrayal, but she hadn't been able to bring herself to burn it either. She was caught in a limbo of indecision. So she had done the thing that felt right to her and just ignored it.

Now, though, after her day at the house with her siblings, and with her mother dead and buried, her curiosity was nipping at her. What if she read the will but not the letter? At least that way she would know what her mother had intended and might be able to nudge things along in that direction.

Of course, she could just tell the others. They would be cross that she'd had the will and not mentioned it and no doubt there would be some jibes about her being asked to get it because she was the favourite, but it might not be too bad. But then, she didn't know what was in the letter to Clare. Whatever it was, her mother had changed her mind about telling Clare. So by rights, if Anna produced the letter, she would be going against her mother's dying wishes. Could she, in all conscience, do that?

She would read the will and then decide. That was the best way forward, wasn't it? She pulled at the ends of the ribbon, untying it and opening the will out flat. Then she started to read. Her eyes flicked over the legal jargon, settling on the parts that she could understand. The estate was to be divided between the four of them. There were some specific bequests too. Her mother had remembered her promise to Sebastian. Anna could hear her mother's voice, its Irish lilt never really lost despite almost a lifetime in England. Her engagement ring was to go to him just as he'd said. Other bits and pieces of jewellery and china were evenly spread between herself, Miriam and Clare. There were sums of £1,000 for each of the grandchildren.

She read on and there it was, almost at the end. The will made specific reference to an appendix, a letter to Clare Elizabeth Bliss. Shit.

Anna sighed. Well, now she had a massive problem. How could she destroy the letter to Clare without getting rid of the whole will? She could hardly tear out the offending page. 'I'm sorry, Miriam, but I think the mice got at that bit.' Or could she?

She examined the will with a calculating eye. Could she remove the page and fake the less important parts that would also be lost? No! Of course she couldn't! What was she thinking? That was a ridiculous plan. The only way she could do it would be to rewrite the whole thing and forge the signatures, but then the paper would be all wrong and the solicitor's stamp would be lost. What was she, some kind of gangster? No. Forging was not an option. She either kept the will as it was with the letter or she burnt the lot as her mother had told her.

Anna sat back in the chair to consider her options. Margot meowed hopefully at her feet and was ignored.

What would happen if the will never hit light of day like her mother had wanted, if she just carried on pretending that there wasn't one? Sebastian would lose the ring. It was obvious after yesterday that Clare would never agree to his having it. He'd be disappointed but he could always buy the ring out of his share of the proceeds of sale, as they'd discussed yesterday. He had money. The ring itself wasn't valuable. He could live with that. The grandchildren would each lose their legacies. They were nice windfalls but not enough to make any difference to their lives. The rules of intestacy would then ensure the remainder of her mother's wishes would be put into effect. It wouldn't be a total disaster.

Anna picked up the second document, a white envelope with 'Clare Elizabeth Bliss. To be opened in the event of the death of Dorothy Bliss. PRIVATE.' written across the front. And it still was private. Anna had opened the will because her mother had died. That was the way of things even if this particular arrangement was less than conventional. And, Anna justified to herself, she couldn't help seeing the will when she opened the envelope (even if she did have to untie the ribbon to read it!). A sealed letter was a different matter. She picked it up, running her fingers around the sharp edges, and then stabbed the point of the corner into the fleshy pad of her forefinger.

She knew what she should do. Her mother had told her to burn it. Her instructions had been clear and unequivocal. The problem was that without knowing what the letter said, Anna couldn't decide whether what her mother had told her to do was for the best. It might just be a reprimand from the grave for all those years that Clare had wasted. Maybe her mother had just wanted to give her one last piece of advice and then thought better of it. If it was something as simple as that then surely it would be fine to give it to Clare. Yes, she'd be pretty cheesed off about it but it would mean that the rest of the will could be actioned.

But what if it wasn't that? What if the letter was something that might do harm to the already fragile Clare? That, after all, was what her mother had implied. And then what? If Anna read the letter she'd know what it said. Even if she destroyed it she would always know something that the rest of them didn't. Could she bear that? She didn't know if she could.

What a bloody mess!

Margot leaped up on to the chair next to hers, purring noisily for attention, making Anna jump.

'So, what would you do, cat, if it were your problem?' Anna asked her.

Margot didn't reply but nuzzled her nose into Anna's open hand, requiring her to rub along her tiny skull to her ears. Anna ran her hand quite roughly over the soft fur and Margot purred contentedly.

'Thanks,' said Anna. 'That's really helpful.'

She was in danger of being overdramatic here. The chances were, it was just a letter to Clare, trying to steer her back to the straight and narrow. A fat lot of good that would do now. Clare was fifty-three. The path of her life was well and truly set. Nothing that their mother could say would make a difference to that.

'Maybe it isn't even from Mum?' Anna said to Margot, who was now plucking at her jeans with her claws. 'Maybe Dad wrote it and gave it to Mum for safe keeping?'

The typing on the envelope gave her no clues. However, a letter from her father struck her as less likely.

'Or maybe it isn't from either of them? Maybe it's a bequest from someone that I don't even know that was only to come into effect on Mum's death? Now I sound like a detective-story writer, Margot.' She really should stop talking to her cat.

Anna lifted the envelope up to the light but the quality vellum gave nothing away. Shaking her head, she put the white envelope back into the manila one and returned it to its place at the bottom of the pile by the bread bin.

She stood up, dislodging Margot, who mewed in objection but then settled herself back down in a ball to go to sleep.

'It's all right for you,' said Anna. 'You don't have to grapple with these complicated moral issues. You just have to eat, sleep and catch vermin. Nice life, Furball.'

Grabbing her keys and her phone from the work surface, she left the house and stepped out into the leafy street. The heatwave was over, brought to a dramatic conclusion by a spectacular electric storm a couple of days after they'd buried her mother. Now the summer seemed to be building itself up to be not bad but not outstanding. It was warm enough for no jacket but no cardigan might be rash.

She set off, not really knowing where she would go. The object of the exercise was to clear her head, think though the possibilities, make a decision.

She found herself walking in the direction of the small municipal park that was nestled at the end of the street between the school playing fields and the new housing estate. It would be busy at this time on a Sunday with families and dog walkers and lovers. Usually it was a place that she might avoid at a weekend but today she wanted the comfort of strangers around her to help her with this decision.

Clare was in her head. Of all her siblings, Clare was the one that she'd always felt the least close to. When they were children it was always Clare and Miriam that were together. Anna had scampered along after them but they had never really let her into their gang. After Sebastian was born everything had changed at home. Mum was always tired, Miriam was cross and Clare had just floated away without anyone really noticing. By the time they realised she was missing, Clare had broken her old life. Then she dropped out of poly, had River, started drinking. It was sad but there was nothing Anna could have done to fix things. But now she maybe had something. Would whatever was in the letter make a difference?

On a grassy hill in the centre of the park, a young boy was trying to fly a kite. There was a bit of a breeze, enough to float a lightweight kite like the one he had, but the child was on his own with no one to help him launch it. Anna watched as he laid the kite carefully on the grass and then backed away from it, unravelling the string as he went. Just as it seemed he had enough string to secure a successful take-off, someone would run over it as it hid in the heavy grass, twisting it into a knotty muddle and he'd start all over again. Perhaps he has no siblings, she thought, no one to be there for him. She couldn't imagine life with no siblings, although sometimes she wished she could. Parents should be made to sign an agreement before they have more than one child, Anna thought, just to make sure that they understood their responsibilities. Even treatment for all, no favourites, real or imagined, and definitely no secret letters left in wills.

'Need some help?' Anna shouted across to the boy as he began to lay the string out yet again.

He looked up at her, taking her in, rating her for potential danger signs. Either she looked safe enough or his frustrations were stronger than any warning signals she was giving off. He nodded his head.

'Shall I try and launch it for you?' she asked, walking towards where the red-and-orange kite was sitting on the ground.

The boy nodded again. Anna lifted the kite. It had been a very long time, decades probably, but instinctively she knew what to do. The boy continued to let out string, backing away from her.

'I think that's enough now,' she shouted to him. He was quite a distance from her. 'You need to get it in the air first and then let out more string when it finds the thermals.'

The boy looked at her like she was a simpleton. Obviously, he didn't need kite-flying lessons, just someone to hold the thing.

'Sorry.' She smiled. 'Right. Are you ready?'

The boy still didn't speak. You mustn't talk to strangers but it can be all right, in certain circumstances, to use them to launch your kite, it seemed. He turned away from her and started to run. Anna ran too and when she judged that they had enough speed, she launched the kite into the sky. The boy, feeling the tension on the string, turned and pulled at it to coax the kite up into the space above him. It flew beautifully now that it was up there. Anna watched as he let more and more string out and it soared upwards until it was little more than a red spot above them.

'She's a beauty,' she shouted out to the boy. 'Look at her go!'

The boy raised a thumb in salute to her and then turned his attention back to his kite.

Anna walked back down the grass towards the path. She knew what she was going to do. Clare couldn't make things work on her own. Just like the boy with the kite, she needed help. It was up to Anna to do whatever it took to help her sister and if that meant breaking her promise to their mother then that's what she would do.

VI

Now that she'd decided to read Clare's letter, Anna couldn't get back home quickly enough. She didn't run exactly but her walk was focused and precise. Anyone watching her might have thought that she was late for an appointment. She got back to the house, let herself in and retrieved the envelopes from their hiding place. The envelope containing the letter to Clare was well gummed down. She was about to steam it open when it occurred to her that she could always just replace the envelope afterwards. She was turning into a secret agent here.

She slid a knife into the top corner and sliced through the paper. The letter slid out of the envelope obligingly. It was the old-fashioned ivory Basildon Bond paper that her mother had always used. That, together with her mother's tidy handwriting, wobbled Anna for a moment. She closed her eyes to steady herself, breathing deeply through her mouth. She could do this. She opened her eyes again. The letter was dated February 2012, so her mother must have written it not long after her father had died.

Anna took a deep breath and began to read.

My darling Clare,

This is a hard letter to write and I have fretted over whether to write it for many years. You know what a worrier I've always been! For a long time, I thought I would just tell you. But as the years went on, there never seemed to be the right moment. I nearly told you a couple of times but then something always happened. It was so noisy in this house when you were all young. There was never two minutes' peace.

Then I thought I'd wait until your Dad died. I don't think he knew and of course I hated holding secrets from him but this felt like something I should keep to myself. And you were a bit of a challenge, weren't you, Clare? There was always some drama or other going on in your life and I decided, whether for good or bad, not to add to your worries.

But in the end, I feel in my heart that you need to know and so I'm writing you this letter which I shall put with my will and then you'll find it after I've died. I know you'll think that's a cop-out but I'm afraid it's the best I can do.

After Miriam was born, I had a bit of a difficult time of it. Babies are hard work. Nobody ever tells you that. I struggled with all four of you, to be honest, but first and last were particularly difficult: first because I had no idea what I'd let myself in for and it frightened the life out of me, and last because having Sebastian was such a shock that it took me a while to get over it.

Anyway, your dad was away with work a lot during the week and I was left on my own with a new baby, not coping. I'm not trying to make excuses, Clare, I'm just trying to tell it like it was so you can understand. I used to go to a café for a cup of tea in the afternoons, more to get out of the house than anything, and there was a man who was sometimes there. He used to sit at a table near the window reading his paper and drinking strong black tea. One day we struck up a conversation about something. I can't remember what. It really doesn't matter. After that I started to bump into him and then we arranged to meet in the park quite often, just to talk. I really enjoyed our chats. He seemed to understand me, how hard I was finding life. He'd listen to me weep and wail about how awful it all was without ever judging me. He was a wonderful listener.

Then one day he bought a proper picnic – a blanket and some sandwiches, a pork pie and what have you. And a bottle of wine. I wasn't used to drinking. With your dad never home and Miriam so small, I had got out of the habit and it was the middle of the day.

Anyway, the wine went straight to my head. I was as giggly as a schoolgirl. I never meant for it to happen. I don't think he did either. It was just one of those moments and what with the drink and me being so low . . . But I loved Frank and I knew that I would never do anything else to hurt him so I told the man I couldn't meet him again and tried to forget all about it. He understood that. He knew that I was in my marriage for keeps. I missed our chats, though, missed him.

When I found out I was expecting, I was beside myself. I had no way of knowing who the father was for sure and of course there was no one to talk to except the man. He was amazing when I told him, so kind when he could have been so cruel. But in the end, I knew there was a good chance that you were Frank's baby so I just carried on as if nothing had happened. And I loved you, Clare, right from the start I loved you.

I wish I'd had the courage to talk to you face to face about this, to tell you myself, but as the years went on it just got harder and harder. You looked so much like Miriam that no one ever questioned it. Why would they? I was a perfectly respectable married woman. But then you started to kick back in a way that the others never did and I began to wonder whether there was something special about you, my darling girl.

None of this matters to me, Clare. You are my baby. You always will be. I couldn't have loved you any more than I have. But I know that there are tests and things that you can do nowadays and I think you ought to have the choice to find out for yourself.

I didn't see the man again after you were born. He moved abroad not long after that but he used to write to me occasionally, just to make sure that I was okay. His name was StJohn Downing.

My darling Clare, I love you more than you can ever imagine. You must never doubt how much you were wanted and treasured. But I can't in all conscience go to my grave with this secret. I owe it to you to tell you the truth.

Your ever loving

Mum x

VII

Shit.

Anna sat with her mouth open and stared at the kitchen wall. Shit. She didn't know what she'd been expecting when she opened the envelope but it wasn't that. Her mum had had an affair. No, not an affair exactly. More like a one-afternoon stand. Her mum! Her Irish Catholic salt-of-the-earth mother had had sex with someone that wasn't her husband. If Anna hadn't read it in black and white in her mum's handwriting herself then she'd never have believed it.

Really, though, that particular piece of tittle-tattle was just the aperitif, the warm-up act before the main event. The actual story was much, much worse. Clare might not be their full sister. Clare! Anna couldn't take it in. The four of them were a gang, a gang that fought like cats and dogs, who could cheerfully have murdered one another at various points, but a gang nonetheless. It couldn't be right that Clare wasn't Dad's daughter. She looked so much like Miriam. People used to mistake them for twins when they were young. They had obviously been swimming in the same gene pool. Hadn't they?

But what if they hadn't been? What if the shared looks were only half the story? Could Clare and Miriam look alike without them being full biological sisters? Cousins often looked similar, after all. Maybe there were differences between Clare and the rest of them but no one had noticed them because no one had been looking.

And, of course, there were some differences. Despite her appearance, Clare had never been quite the same as the rest of them. She had kicked against what they accepted. She had personality traits that none of them shared, a different set of values, an alternative moral code. Anna had always assumed that that was just how Clare had turned out, but what if it had more to do with nature than nurture? What if the more challenging aspects of what made Clare Clare were nothing to do with Frank and everything to do with StJohn?

Shit.

Anna knew at once that she had made a massive mistake in reading the letter. What was she supposed to do now that she knew the whole sorry story? This was definitely one of those moments where something that seemed like a great idea at the time went on to become a full-blown regret the instant it was too late to change it. Why hadn't she listened to her mother? Her mother had made her promise to burn the letter so why hadn't she? Anna knew exactly why. It was because, as usual, she thought she knew best. She was the favourite child and so it stood to reason that she could do no wrong. And now look. She'd unlocked the biggest Pandora's Box that her family was ever going to face and all because she thought she knew better than her mother.

She felt sick. She read the letter through again, just in case she might have got the wrong end of the stick the first time. She hadn't. The only doubt here related to exactly who Clare's father was.

Slowly the panic started to subside and Anna began to think clearly again. There was only one thing for it. She would do what she was supposed to have done in the first place. She would destroy the letter like her mother had told her to do. And the will would have to go too so that there was no reference to the letter ever having existed. That wasn't so hard. The others would just have to accept that their mother had gone to her grave without writing a will. They wouldn't like it but what could they do? And Anna's punishment for not doing as she was told would be to carry the secret all her life and never be able to tell anyone. All she had to do was burn the documents. And yet . . .

Anna turned this idea over in her mind. There were worse things, she supposed. People kept secrets all the time. Her mother had carried this one with her for fifty years, for goodness' sake. Anna would do the same. The others need never know. And the chances were that Clare was Frank's child anyway. Presumably her parents had been having sex more regularly than just once in a park. Anna deliberately chose to ignore what the letter said about Frank working away and Miriam being a difficult baby. Those factors would have had absolutely nothing to do with the chances of Frank being Clare's father. Absolutely nothing. Shit. Shit. Shit.

VIII

When Anna had come up with her solution to the problem that she had accidentally created, it had seemed like a brilliant idea. She would visit StJohn Downing, have a look at him, see if he could possibly be Clare's father, and then leave. How hard could it be? She had the excuse of her mother's recent death. He'd sent them a note, after all, with his address helpfully included. It was a shame she'd already posted her reply but that couldn't be helped. She'd go round and introduce herself, get the measure of him and then leave, and if he looked nothing like Clare she could stop feeling guilty, destroy the letter and get on with her life. It was a simple plan.

Now, as she stood on the street outside his bungalow, the plan felt less bulletproof. She was tempted to turn tail and drive home but then she'd have to live without ever knowing. She wasn't sure she could do that either. After all, it was her insatiable curiosity that had got her into this mess in the first place. And anyway, how hard could it be? A brief conversation with an elderly man who was expecting her. She could manage that for the greater good, couldn't she?

StJohn Downing's bungalow was small and neat. It was surrounded on all sides by a garden which, on first impression, looked just like any other, but which on closer examination was filled with unusual and exotic plants. The hedge that separated it from the next house along was bamboo and there were tall structural shrubs in the borders that Anna didn't recognise. There was no grass either, just paving and waves of gravel raked into curling patterns. No grandchildren, then, thought Anna as she imagined what destruction her nieces and nephews would wreak on such regulated order. The front door was a dark, bold red with the house number painted on to it in an Asian-style font. If it weren't for the fact that she had the address written clearly on a piece of paper in her hand, Anna would have thought that she had come to the wrong place. It really didn't look like the kind of house where a man in his eighties would live.

She walked up the drive, stood on the doorstep and rang the bell before she had the chance to change her mind again. Moments later StJohn Downing opened it. He was very old, that much was obvious from his face. His wrinkles reminded her of the concentric circles in the gravel, cutting deep and even furrows across his face. His hair still grew strong and white with no sign of receding but his eyes were hooded and very dark. If Clare's genes were in there, then they were buried pretty deep. He was also in a wheelchair, which Anna hadn't expected. It wasn't your run-of the-mill standard-issue kind of chair: more lightweight, state of the art, expensive.

'Good morning,' he said. His voice was still strong despite his appearance and had a hint of a local accent. 'Do come in, Anna.'

He reversed the wheelchair skilfully to allow Anna to step inside and then indicated a room on the right.

'Please. Go through.'

Anna did as she was told and found herself in a light and airy sitting room which was full of green, healthy-looking plants. It looked like something you'd see in a magazine, very minimally furnished with grey cord chairs and a pale wooden floor. On the walls were some block prints and line drawings of long women in elegant kimonos. She was getting the Japanese vibe loud and clear.

'Sit down, please, Anna. May I call you Anna?' he asked politely.

'Er, yes. That's fine.' She was never quite sure about the alternative. Miss Bliss? Honestly!

'Can I get you a drink? Tea, perhaps? Coffee? Something cold?'

Given the decor, Anna wondered whether the tea might come with a ceremony attached. She fancied coffee but she was curious. Again.

'Tea would be great,' she said. 'Do you need any help?' she added awkwardly and then instantly regretted it. This was his house. He could presumably make drinks without too many problems.

'I think I'll be fine,' he said, and the chair hummed away to the kitchen.

Anna was perching right on the edge of the seat. She pushed herself back into it and tried to look relaxed and confident, neither of which she was feeling. The house was gorgeous, not at all what she had been expecting. She looked for signs that there might be someone else living here but there were so few things out on display that it was difficult to find any clues at all.

She could hear the kettle being boiled in the kitchen, cupboards opening and closing.

'Your house is lovely,' she shouted through. 'Have you lived here long?'

'No. Not so very long. I did some travelling in my younger days but when my lifestyle had to change, I decided to settle down and I came back here. I'm not sure why, other than one tends to be drawn to one's roots, doesn't one? Especially when you get to be as old as I am.'

He appeared at the door with a tray resting on his lap. Anna half-stood with a view to relieving him of it but he had got to the table and set the tray down on it before she had the chance to move.

'Are you from round here originally, then?' she asked.

'Questions so soon and I haven't even poured the tea,' he said. 'It's green – sencha. I hope that's to your taste.'

Anna preferred builders' with plenty of milk but she nodded as if sencha, whatever that might be, was her absolute favourite.

StJohn poured the tea into white bone china bowls and then wheeled across and gave one to her without a drop being spilt. She wasn't sure that she had as much control. Her hands were shaking madly. She concentrated hard on not slopping into the saucer. He then went back to his spot by the table and turned the wheelchair round to face her.

'So, you're Anna,' he said, and looked at her as if he were examining every detail of her face. 'Dorothy's girl.'

'Yes. That's right. Dorothy's third girl, actually,' she added. And possibly Frank's third too, she thought, although that particular fact was rather up in the air at the moment.

Anna had sort of planned out what she wanted to say but now that she was here, she found herself suddenly and inexplicably shy. This wasn't like her. She could generally hold her own in conversation but then this wasn't a general kind of conversation. And he was so closed, giving nothing away. Did he have an idea what she was here for? Probably, but there was no way Anna was going down that particular avenue. She just had to stick to the plan, scan his face for any traces of Clare and then forget all about him.

'Thank you so much for your letter,' said Anna, her voice gushing out over-loudly in the peaceful room, her words tripping over one another. 'It was very kind of you to write. We all appreciated it a lot.'

'I was so sad to hear that your mother had passed away. She was a fine woman and I was most fond of her. You must all be very upset about her loss.'

'We are,' said Anna, feeling her throat thickening a little. 'But it wasn't a surprise. She'd had a stroke, which meant that she couldn't look after herself, so by the end it was almost a blessing.' Anna's conversation with the old woman in Oak's Reach flew through her mind. 'I mean, a blessing for her. Not us,' she added, flustered now. 'Obviously, we were all devastated.'

'Obviously,' said StJohn. There was something about the way he spoke that Anna found disconcerting. He made her feel young and foolish, like a senior and not very tolerant don at university.

'And your father?' he continued.

'He died a while before. Cancer. It was very quick. Mum had been on her own for a few years.' Anna thought she could hear an accusation in her voice which surprised her. What was she trying to say? If you thought so much of her then where were you when she was left all alone? But if StJohn noticed it, he didn't react.

Anna took a sip of her tea to fill the awkward silence. Green tea really wasn't her thing. It was so thin but she had to get to the bottom of the cup out of politeness if nothing else. She seemed to be perching on the front of her chair again. She tried to shuffle back without spilling the tea. There was no table nearby where she could put it down. She had another sip. She seemed to have lost all ability to speak. God, what was happening to her?

Eventually, StJohn filled the silence.

'And you have three siblings, is that right?'

Grateful to be on familiar territory, Anna perked up.

'Yes. Miriam is the eldest. She's an English teacher. Then Clare.' Years of having to explain away Clare meant that Anna had fine-tuned her replies to almost nothing. 'Then me. I'm single. No kids. And then Sebastian. He has two little boys. They're a handful. All doing well,' she added as if she were having to justify their lives to this total stranger. It was only a little lie.

StJohn nodded his head and then took some tea, giving Anna the chance to snatch a closer look at him. She searched his face for anything that might give her a clue but found nothing obvious. Maybe something around the eyes, the mouth? It was so hard to tell. With a face as old as his, all clues were buried deeper than a cursory look could dig.

As if conscious that he was being examined, he lifted his eyes from his teacup and looked straight at her.

'And why are you really here, Anna?' he asked.

Wow. She hadn't seen that coming. She could feel a blush rising up her neck. It was all she could do to stop herself squirming in her seat or wrapping her legs one around the other. His question was so direct, so knowing. She took a deep breath.

'Well,' she began slowly. 'I wanted to say thank you, obviously, for your letter. From all of us, I mean. It's very kind of you to write and everything. And also . . .' She paused. To see whether you could be the father of my wayward sister. She didn't say this last part out loud.

He looked at her expectantly but didn't prompt her.

'And,' she continued, 'if I'm totally honest, I suppose I was curious. I mean, there aren't so many of Mum's friends still alive and those that are I've either known all my life or at least know where she picked them up from. You were a bit of a mystery. Your letter arrived out of the blue and it made me wonder, that's all.' Whilst she had been talking, her eyes had been flitting around the room, but now that she was quiet she focused on his face, but there was nothing to read, or at least nothing that she could see. His dark eyes remained fixed on her.

'Ah,' he said. 'I see.'

That was it. Nothing else. Anna didn't speak, giving him a gap in which to give her more details, but nothing came. He just continued to look at her. If it weren't for his behaviour thus far she might be tempted to think that he was losing his marbles but actually it was all too apparent that StJohn Downing was entirely in control of his faculties. Was he really going to give her nothing?

'Have you read your mother's letter?' he then asked, his directness making her start. 'The one she wrote to Clare about me?'

His gaze didn't falter. Anna felt like he had opened up her skull and was staring straight into her brain, watching it work, knowing all her most private thoughts. It was very disconcerting. There would be no beating about the bush, which Anna liked, but she still felt slightly wrong-footed by his question. Yet wasn't this exactly what she had come here to find out about? In an instant she decided to just follow his lead and see where he took her.

'Yes,' she answered simply.

'And Clare?' he asked.

Anna shook her head. 'Only me. Mum told me to burn it but I . . .' She shrugged. 'Well, it didn't feel right and so after Mum died and I read it and . . .'

'And now you are stuck in no-man's-land not knowing which way to go?'

He had hit the nail on the head. Anna nodded.

StJohn looked out of the window and watched the swaying bamboo for a moment.

'Would it help if I told you my side of the story?' he asked, without moving his focus from the plants.

Would it? Anna wasn't sure. Her need for information was what had got her into this mess in the first place. But then again, wasn't that why she'd come here? To learn something new. Oh, what the hell? In for a penny and all that.

'Yes,' she said quietly. 'Please.'

StJohn took a deep breath as if he were settling himself into the task ahead.

'So,' he began. 'Let's start with what you already know.'

'Not much,' said Anna, bringing her mother's letter to the front of her mind. 'You met Mum in a café. You got close. You had one . . .' Anna paused. She could feel her cheeks starting to burn. God, this was awkward. They were talking about her mother having sex with this stranger. '. . . one . . .'

StJohn just nodded and Anna, grateful that she didn't have to say it out loud, moved on. 'And that was about it. Mum had the baby. She told you. You moved away and we got on with the rest of our lives. Is that pretty much it, in a nutshell?'

He moved his wheelchair over to the table and poured himself some more tea from the bone china teapot. He raised it in Anna's direction but she shook her head. Then he went back to where he had been and by the time he had repositioned himself, he seemed to have what he wanted to say straight in his mind. He began.

'I never married,' he said. His voice was quiet but clear. 'I never could. After I had met your mother, no one else seemed to compare. She was a good woman and totally devoted to your father. For her, what happened between us was an accident, a wrong turn taken in a period of great unrest. It was the only time, as far as I know, that she was ever disloyal to any of you. But for me, it was the sweetest, most precious part of my life, and no one has ever come close to matching it.'

Anna watched him closely as he spoke. He placed his elbows on the armrests of his wheelchair and made a pyramid of his hands, the tips of his fingers resting on his lips. A triangle, thought Anna. How very apt.

'After we made love,' he continued, and Anna tried hard not to squirm at his frankness, 'your mother knew at once that it had been a mistake. Not us being friends,' he added quickly. 'There was nothing wrong with that. It was a little unconventional but that was all. But we should never have . . . I should never have . . . Anyway, Dorothy was determined that we must never allow it to happen again. We met one last time in the park. It was a vile day, grey and drizzly, and we sat on a bench looking out at the grass rather than facing one another as Miriam slept in her pram. Dorothy explained how much she loved your father, that what we had done had been a terrible mistake, but there was no need for her to say any of it. I knew it all. I had been listening to her talk for weeks. I knew how much Frank meant to her.'

His voice was even quieter now and Anna felt herself craning forward to catch his words.

'And that might have been it,' he continued. 'A drunken mistake, instantly shoved under the carpet and never mentioned again, just like thousands of other encounters. But we are talking about Dorothy. She was such a good woman and she understood how hard it was for me. When Clare was born she wrote to tell me. Neither of us could know who Clare's father was and so what was there to say? I never saw the child so I couldn't tell you if I felt drawn to her by some parental instinct, and Dorothy didn't send photos. I think that would have been too much of a betrayal for her.'

StJohn turned his head and looked out at the garden again and Anna saw his hand sweep briefly across his eyes. He took a deep breath through his nose, letting it out slowly through his mouth as he gathered himself.

'Not long after that I moved to Japan. Japanese gardens had always fascinated me so I decided to go and learn from the Masters. And that was it. A new start away. Dorothy knew where to find me if she needed me but she rarely got in touch and it wasn't for me to contact her. The last time I heard from her, it was to tell me that she had left a letter for Clare with her will. And that, Anna, is it.'

He looked straight at her now. His eyes were fascinating, Anna found, mesmerising somehow as they held her gaze. She could see why her mother might have been drawn to him. Anna pulled her stare away first.

'It's such a sad story,' she said without really thinking. 'God, I'm sorry. That was thoughtless of me.'

'Yes, possibly.' He gave her a resigned half-smile. 'But true nonetheless. The discovery and subsequent loss of your mother has been the greatest sadness of my life, but over the years I have come to terms with it. And it is lovely to meet you, Anna. I can see your mother in your face so clearly. It is a shame that I will never meet Clare but—'

'You could meet her,' Anna interrupted, her mind racing with the possibilities, but StJohn was shaking his head.

'No,' he said firmly. 'Your mother was sure that that was the wrong thing to do. You say she told you to destroy the letter before she died?'

Anna nodded sheepishly.

'Well, that's what you should do, Anna. She had decided that there was nothing to be gained by telling Clare now and I agree. I am an old man. Both your parents are dead. What would Clare do with that knowledge except let it eat away at her?'

'But doesn't she have a right to meet you?' asked Anna. 'I mean, there is a chance that you are her biological father.'

'How I hate that expression,' StJohn said. 'Biology is just chemicals. Your sister's father was Frank. I have no claim over her. Maybe, eventually, the secret will reveal itself, when the time is right. But not now.'

Anna couldn't see how the truth would come out if only she and StJohn were aware of it, but she didn't labour the point.

'And now, if you don't mind, I would like to be on my own,' said StJohn.

Anna jumped up.

'Yes, of course. Thank you for seeing me and telling me about Mum.'

'You're welcome.'

He started to manoeuvre his wheelchair towards the door.

'And I think it would be best if we didn't meet again, Anna. If you don't mind. I have spent a lifetime putting this out of my mind and for my own sake I would like to continue to do that.'

Anna nodded. He was right. She had the whole picture now. Her curiosity was sated. She would carry her mother's secret to her own grave and the identity of Clare's biological father was a detail that none of them needed. As StJohn had said, what difference would it make? Her father had always been Clare's father and that was that.

'Goodbye, then,' he said as he opened the door to let her out.

'Goodbye.'

Anna turned and walked down the path. She didn't turn round but she could feel his eyes following her, watching her leave.

IX

Anna hated the gym. What was the point of it? Well, she knew what the point of it was: she had to stay in her favourite jeans somehow. Also, she kept reading magazine articles about all the hideous things that were about to happen to her body. Hot flushes, sleepless nights, mood swings, osteoporosis. The list just went on and on. With all these battles on the horizon, the least she could do was invest a bit of her time in preparation, but she did it with extremely bad grace.

She stepped up and down, up and down. It was relentless. She must surely be halfway up Everest by now – at Base Camp at the very least. She cast a sideways glance at the machines on either side of her. The man on her right looked like he might have a heart attack at any moment and droplets of his sweat kept flicking on to her machine. On to her as well, no doubt, but she couldn't bear to think about that. The woman to her left looked like a gazelle. Anna sighed inwardly, ignoring the wobble that she felt in her thighs each time they pushed down, and stared at the data screen. She could get off in ten, nine, eight . . .

Climbing down with her quads burning, she went in search of a different machine of self-inflicted torture. The rower, maybe? That wasn't too excruciating and at least it generated its own breeze.

So now what, she thought as she pulled hard and sure on the handle with long rhythmic strokes. Seeing StJohn Downing the day before had clarified her thoughts. The letter to Clare had to disappear. This morning, as she was having her breakfast, Anna had extracted the will from the envelope in the pile on her table, where it had been hiding in plain sight. She was hoping for a light-bulb moment, something that she hadn't thought of before that would allow her to keep the will and not the letter, but nothing had come to her. The two documents were totally joined at the hip.

The man on the stepper slid off and virtually collapsed in a soggy, hot pile on the floor. That cannot be good for him, Anna thought. The gazelle woman was still going with even strides, looking like climbing to the moon would be a breeze for her.

This whole situation would be so much easier if she could just talk to one of the others. Miriam would know what to do and Sebastian would at least pull sympathetic faces if she brought it up with him, even if he didn't actually tell her what would be best. Anna knew that that wasn't an option, though. The fewer people who knew the truth the better, especially if the decision was not to tell Clare. Anna was on her own.

She realised that she was rowing more and more slowly until eventually she just stopped. Enough deliberating! She would destroy the letter and the will today. It might mean that Sebastian would lose his right to their mother's engagement ring but surely that was better than Clare losing her identity. And anyway, making sure Clare never found out was what her mother had wanted her to do, wasn't it?

Now that she'd finally made the decision Anna felt immediately better and started to pull again on the rower with long sure strokes. The breeze bathed her face. This was easy when you knew how.

She worked her way round the rest of her programme feeling as light as air, which was more than the weights did. Mission accomplished, she ticked the box on her programme with a flourish, tucked it back in the box on the gym instructor's desk and headed for the showers. As she let the hot water run over her skin, she congratulated herself on a decision well made. She could deal with holding a secret. She had broad shoulders.

As she got dressed, she checked her phone for messages. There was a missed call and a text from Miriam.

'*DISASTER! Washer dead. No clean knickers. Help!!*'

Anna smiled. It was so rare that Miriam ever asked for help. She punched in a reply.

'*Cavalry to the rescue. Use mine. No worries. Xxx*'

She pressed send and seconds later . . .

'*Thank you xxxxx You are an angel. Maybe still there when you get home?*'

'*Yes. Home around 6.30. See you then xx*'

Leisurely she packed her kit back into her bag, brushed her hair, thought about what she might cook herself for dinner. There was a chicken breast in the fridge, some nice salad— The thought struck her like a bolt of lightning. Her entire body went cold. Adrenaline pricked in her fingers and at the base of her neck. The will! It was just sitting there on her kitchen table where she'd left it that morning. The letter to Clare was still hidden under the pile of magazines and bills but the will was lying there.

Anna's breath came in quick short gasps. What should she do? She could hardly ring Miriam and tell her that the washer wasn't working after all. Or ask her to ignore the document handily marked 'The Last Will and Testament of Mrs Dorothy Bliss' that was just waiting to be read. Anna's heart was racing. She needed to get home as quickly as she could to try to avert disaster.

She grabbed her bag and ran for the door.

There was an outside chance that she would get to her house before Miriam did but it was more likely that Miriam had had her car packed and ready to go when she sent the text and would be well on her way by now. There was nothing else for it. She would just have to cross everything and hope that Miriam just put the clothes in the machine and then left.

Anna drove home as quickly as she dared but as she turned on to her street she saw Miriam's car parked outside her house. Anna reversed her car into the space next to Miriam's. One of her tyres was on the pavement but there was no time to sort that out. She abandoned the car and raced to the house, fumbling for her house keys as she went.

The front door banged behind her.

'Hi, Miriam. Did you find the washing powder and everything . . .?'

There was no reply. Anna opened the kitchen door, her heart in her mouth. Miriam was sitting at the table. In front of her was the will, open at the last page. Anna didn't speak. She wasn't sure that Miriam had even heard her come in. Her eyes were scanning over the legal niceties of the signature page.

'Miriam,' said Anna after what seemed like an eternity but was probably only a matter of seconds.

Miriam turned to look at her. Her mouth was open, her eyes questioning.

'Anna, what's this?' Her voice was gentle, as if she were trying to take on board what she had just read.

Anna swallowed.

'It's Mum's will.'

'And why have you got it? I'm not sure I understand. Did you go back to the house after we'd left? Did you think of somewhere we hadn't looked? Why didn't you ring me when you found it?'

Anna took a deep breath. This was her way out. She could just lie, let Miriam believe that she'd had a sudden and lucky flash of inspiration. She could just pretend that the letter wasn't with it and then none of the stuff about Clare need ever come out and she could go back to living her simple, straightforward life. The chance was just there in front of her. One lie and it would all be over. She couldn't believe she hadn't thought of this before. But as the thoughts flew around her head she saw something change in Miriam's face, a kind of understanding that started small but grew and finally took hold. Anna had hesitated too long.

'You knew!' said Miriam accusingly. 'You knew about the will. You had us crawling all over that house and all the time you knew where it was.'

Anna opened her mouth to speak but Miriam wasn't finished.

'And we had that enormous row with Clare. About how we should divide everything. With Sebastian and the ring and me and that china. And my girls. They get a gift each. Oh, Anna! How could you?'

'Look, Miriam. I didn't know. Well, I knew that I had the will, obviously. Mum told me where it was and asked me to go and get it. But I didn't know what was in it. Well, not then. I hadn't read it then. Honestly.'

This was all going too fast. Anna's head spun as she tried to work out what to tell Miriam and what to keep to herself.

'Why on earth didn't you say?' said Miriam, standing up and waving the will in the air in front of her. 'What possessed you to keep quiet? You could have just brought it along to the house and we could have all opened it together. Why didn't you do that, Anna?'

'I don't know. I didn't know what to do.'

'What do you mean, you didn't know what to do? It's not hard.'

Then Miriam's face changed again and now her eyes were cold and accusing as she stared at Anna. 'Oh, I get it,' she said, nodding slowly. 'You wanted to check what was in it first. This is starting to make sense now.'

'Miriam. Calm down,' said Anna. 'You sound like Clare. You've got it all wrong.'

'I don't think I have. You were worried that Mum might have done something that would water down your share and so you decided to sit on the will and let us all think that there wasn't one whilst you worked out whether you'd be better off with or without it.'

'That's ridiculous,' said Anna, and it was. Of all the reasons she could possibly have for hanging on to the will, that was the most ludicrous. Surely if she just stayed calm then Miriam would realise that?

'Oh, is it?' replied Miriam, not sounding at all calm. 'Well, it doesn't seem that ridiculous from where I'm sitting. In fact, it's all starting to make perfect sense.'

Anna's mind was racing. What should she do? She couldn't let them find out about the letter. That decision was made. Her mother, StJohn and she all believed that giving Clare the letter would be a disastrous mistake. And if she mentioned it now, then there would be no reversing. Miriam would want to tell Clare and Sebastian in the interest of honesty and then it would all be out in the open. No, it was better to keep quiet and face the full wrath of Miriam to protect her mother's secret.

But how could she explain her behaviour without giving Miriam the whole picture . . .?

'I didn't tell you about the will,' she said, still trying to concoct a feasible story as the words tumbled out of her mouth, 'because . . . because I thought you'd all think it was strange that Mum told me where the will was and not any of you. I know you all think that I was her favourite, which isn't true by the way, so I thought that if you knew that she'd asked me to get it then you would all think badly of me. And see! I was right!' Anna could not keep the triumphant tone out of her voice, although it was more to do with her relief at having come up with something half plausible. 'I was going to hide it,' she added, the final cherry on the cake, 'so that one of you would find it, but then . . .'

She nodded to the will lying on the table. Anna could almost see the cogs turning in Miriam's head as she tried to make sense of what she was hearing, and for a moment Anna thought she had convinced her. But then Miriam spoke again.

'But we were having that enormous row,' she reasoned, her eyes narrowed. 'You could have stopped all that. You could have brought it all to an end with one simple sentence. "I have the will." Surely that would have been more important than you worrying about all this crap about favourites?'

Anna looked at her feet. What could she do? She was completely snookered. Now all that remained was for her to keep quiet and hope that it all blew over quickly.

'Sorry,' she said.

'Well, I don't know what to think,' said Miriam, standing up and pushing her chair noisily across the floor. 'The others are going to go mad when they find out. Sebastian will be cross but Clare will be absolutely livid. And I will tell them, don't you worry about that. I shan't be playing any snake-in-the-grass games like you've been doing.'

'I'm sorry,' said Anna again. 'I really didn't mean to cause any bother.'

'Well, what did you think would happen, Anna? Honestly? I'm leaving now. I'll send Richard round to collect the washing later. And I'm taking this' – she waved the will at Anna – 'with me. I'll ring you when I've spoken to the others.'

Miriam picked up the will, the envelope and even the pink ribbon and made for the door. She hadn't seemed to register the missing letter, Anna thought, but of course she would when she thought about it, and then Miriam would be on at her about that too. Anna would just have to make out that the letter wasn't with the will when she took it. More lies but what could she do? She couldn't let them see the letter to Clare. She would protect them from that, no matter what it cost her.

As Miriam was leaving, she turned to look at Anna.

'I can't tell you how disappointed I am in you, Anna.'

Anna hung her head. Miriam sounded just like their mother and somewhere Anna was sure she was shaking her head in disappointment too. After all, Anna had let them all down – Miriam, Clare, Sebastian and her mother.

Miriam left with the will, banging the door behind her. The washing machine went into its spin cycle. The letter to Clare was still safely hidden.

Anna opened a bottle of wine.

CLARE – 2017

I

The backbeat of next door's music pulsed in time with the throbbing in her head. Clare looked at the clock. It was officially the middle of the night. Surely they had to sleep eventually, her neighbours? They'd probably gone out and just left it banging through her wall, searing through her nerve endings without giving it a second thought. Clare tried banging on the wall again but it was a half-hearted gesture. It wouldn't make any difference, even if they were in. Never once had they turned the noise down after she'd asked. Last time she went round, the girl – twenties, white-skinned, black-haired and eyes that were barely open – had laughed at her. Actually laughed. It was a good job that Clare was sober or the girl would have come away from that little encounter without any teeth.

She was wide awake now, not that she'd truly been asleep at any point. She turned on the TV and let the late-night dross wash over her. There was no point wasting any more energy on the situation. She would play her music as loud as it would go tomorrow at breakfast when the girl would probably be trying to sleep. The justice of this plan appealed and Clare smiled to herself despite it all. They'd move on before too long anyway. Clare knew the type. She'd been the type once. Living in the moment, thinking only where the next drink, hit, whatever was their particular poison was coming from. Looking at the girl, it was probably the drugs that would be her downfall and that tended to happen faster than with booze. You could be dependent on alcohol and still breathe for longer.

And Clare wasn't really worried about her neighbours. In fact, she was just pleased that she finally had some. This was her place now and she was going to hang on to it. Her days of begging favours and squatting on people's floors were behind her. This was a new start. She'd been off the booze for sixth months now and although she considered having a drink every single day, in fact every single hour of every single day, so far the answer had always been no. It felt good. She was in control of her life for the first time in decades. She didn't even have to put up with Miriam and that 'concerned' thing that she did because, for once, Miriam had nothing to be concerned about. Clare Bliss was sorted. Life was, if not exactly sweet, then at least not bad. She even had a bit of a job at the local bakery. It was only cash in hand – a real job would mess up her benefits – but she turned up when they wanted her, more or less on time, and it felt good to have someone relying on her. She hated the expression 'in a good place' but really, she kind of was.

When the doorbell rang the next morning, she didn't hear it over the din of the music that was pumping out of her ancient CD player, through the walls and straight into the jugular of the girl next door, or so she hoped. It was only when she saw Anna's face peering through the window that she realised that there was anyone there. She went to open the door, taking the chain off and pulling back the bolts smoothly.

'How can you stand that racket?' asked Anna as she came in, fingers plunged into her ears.

'It's revenge,' said Clare, and Anna smiled wryly. Clare turned it down a little bit. 'What are you doing here?' she asked, suddenly suspicious. In spite of herself, she flicked her eyes across the flat, checking out what kind of state it was in, but it was straight-ish and this was Anna, not Miriam.

'I bring post,' Anna said with a smile. 'It was sent to my house for you. Maybe whoever it is doesn't have your new address.'

Clare was confused. Their mother's house was long sold, the contents divided between the four of them as per the will. Clare could think of no one who would either be wanting to write to her or use Anna as the messenger. Well, there was River, of course, but letters weren't his style and anyway she'd made sure that he always knew where he could find her even if he rarely bothered to look.

Clare turned off the CD player. She could resume torturing the girl next door later. 'What is it?' she asked before she'd even got Anna to sit down or offered her a drink or any of the things she knew she was supposed to do now that she had a home of her own.

Anna dug around in her bag and pulled out a white envelope. She handed it to Clare.

'No idea,' she said.

The envelope was addressed to Miss Clare Bliss, care of Anna at Anna's house. It was typewritten and franked and the envelope was heavy and textured, expensive-looking. Clare weighed it in her hand for a moment, considering it.

'Maybe it's "the" letter. The long-lost letter from Mum's will,' she said, although this seemed very unlikely.

'Only one way to find out,' said Anna. She was blushing, Clare noticed.

Clare picked at the corner of the flap and then put the envelope down on the sofa next to her. It was bound to be bad news. It always was. Well, she didn't want to know. Life was running smoothly for her at the moment. She didn't need anything tipping things out of balance.

'Well?' asked Anna, looking at her, her eyebrows raised in expectation. 'Aren't you going to open it?'

No. Clare didn't think she would. She hadn't asked for a letter. She had no need of anything. She didn't want to know. Then again, what if it was something to do with that mystery letter that her mother's will had mentioned? That had never turned up, despite a vigorous search, and Anna had continued to deny all knowledge of it even though she'd had the will. There was something very fishy about that whole situation and Clare wasn't sure she believed Anna, but there was nothing any of them could do. They'd just had to accept Anna's dodgy story. And also, why had someone sent this letter to Anna and not her? That was annoying. It was probably because she had been of no fixed abode for such a long time. Still, it rankled. Maybe she would open it, just to see what it was.

Clare grabbed the envelope and tore the flap open, yanking the letter out by the corner. The paper was as thick and luxurious as the envelope. She flicked it open and began to read. When she got to the end she was no wiser. Someone, a solicitor it appeared, wanted to talk to her about something and she had to ring their office to make an appointment. She looked up, pulled a face at Anna, read it again.

'Well?' asked Anna, after Clare had read it for a second time. 'What is it?'

'Fuck knows,' said Clare, and passed the letter over, watching as Anna read it for herself. Anna's face switched from interest to shock to . . . What was that last expression? Fear? No. Too strong a word. Anxiety, then. Clare couldn't quite work it out but something wasn't right here and Anna definitely knew more about this than she did. Clare wasn't going to give her the satisfaction of asking, though.

'Will you go?' Anna said.

Clare shrugged. 'Might as well. Got nothing to lose.'

'Do you want me to come with you?'

Clare thought about this for a moment. She didn't need Anna trailing along after her getting in the way. She didn't need any of them. She never had done. She was surprised, therefore, to hear herself say, 'Yeah. That'd be good.'

II

The building wasn't like anything Clare had ever been in before. The front, four or five storeys high, was all glass and you could see people rushing about inside like rats. She hated places like this, smug and self-important and full of people whose lives had turned out exactly the way they wanted. She was in the wrong place. Who cared about the letter? Whatever they wanted to tell her, she didn't need to know. She turned on her heel to head back the way she'd come and walked slap-bang into Anna.

'Is this it?' Anna asked, and Clare noticed that she tactfully avoided mentioning that Clare had been going in the wrong direction. 'Have you been in yet?'

Clare shook her head.

'Right, we'd better or we'll be late,' Anna said. 'Unless . . .' She stopped and stared, with what Clare took to be a meaningful look, into her eyes. 'Well, we don't have to go in. Not if you don't want to.'

Anna linked her arm with Clare's, an odd enough gesture between the two of them, and pulled her away from the smart-looking doorway. It was such a subtle movement that Clare thought for a moment that perhaps it was subconscious, but it was definitely there. Clare eyed Anna suspiciously. The casual way that she suggested they abandon ship, the gentle tugging, whether intentional or not, in the opposite direction. Something was off here; it didn't feel quite as it should. Clare knew all the tricks. She'd not spent a lifetime getting herself out of tight spots without being able to manipulate a situation. Anna was an amateur next to her, although it wasn't a bad effort.

Anna didn't want her to go in. Clare was certain of it. So, Anna must know something about this that she didn't. That probably meant that it was something that Anna didn't think would be 'good' for her. Her siblings were all the same. They each thought they knew what was for the best, wanting to prove how much better they had organised their lives than she had. The reasons for this sense of self-congratulation had always been a mystery to Clare. What the fuck did they have to be so very pleased about? Miriam was a teacher. A teacher, for God's sake. If ever there was a job that showed a lack of imagination, it was that. She wasn't even sure what Anna did. Something for a charity? And Sebastian? Well, he was doing a bit better than the other two but not by much. Had none of them noticed that she was an adult? She had actually made it to her fifties. Admittedly, she'd not always followed the straightest path to get to where she needed to go but she'd got there in the end and she'd done it without any of their help. She wasn't about to take Anna's advice now.

Clare tugged back on Anna's arm. 'No, it's fine. Let's go in,' she said, hoping that her voice sounded like this wasn't something that was making her heart pound.

Was that a little flicker of disappointment across Anna's face? Yes. She did believe it was. Good.

They walked up the marble stairs and into the air-conditioned calm of the reception space. If Clare had to pick one word to describe the space it would be 'clean'. The walls and floor were white and glossy and the reception desk a sharp red. Even the strategically positioned foliage which screened off the lift doors looked fresh. Clare didn't think she'd ever been anywhere that looked less like a solicitor's office. She whistled under her breath and Anna shushed her.

'This is one hell of a gaff,' she said as she ran her hand along a mirrored wall. Her fingers left a trail. She saw Anna wince as if she were a child so she put her fingers in her mouth and then did it again. This time the mark was significantly bigger.

'Clare,' hissed Anna. 'Must you?'

Before she had a chance to tell Anna that yes, she must, the receptionist interrupted.

'Can I help you?' she asked, and although Clare was ready for some full-scale disapproval, her voice was friendly, which threw her a little. For a moment she forgot why they were even there but then good old Anna stepped up to smooth over her inadequacies.

'My sister has an appointment with Caitlyn Bear,' she said. 'It's Clare Bliss.'

The friendly reception woman smiled and nodded and directed them to some modern-looking red sofas, all skinny legs and low-profile cushions. Anna sat down but Clare paced about trying to find something to relate to. She failed. She glanced at Anna, who was flicking through some brochure or other. She looked completely at home, like she spent half her life in this kind of place. Maybe she did. What did Clare know about Anna's world?

The lift doors opened and a young woman in a navy suit and heels emerged, did a quick scan of the space and then walked towards Anna with hand outstretched.

'Miss Bliss?' she asked.

Clare watched as Anna lost her cool for a moment. She looked flustered and a bit unsure. Maybe the ever-perfect Anna had limits too, Clare thought, and the thought pleased her.

'Yes, but it's my sister Clare that you want,' replied Anna. 'Clare?'

Clare eyed the woman, taking in her expensive suit, her classy haircut, the quiet self-assurance that radiated off her.

'Yep,' she said after a moment. 'That's me.'

The solicitor put out her hand to shake Clare's but Clare didn't offer her own, and so the solicitor had to drop hers awkwardly to her side.

'Would you like to come with me?' she asked.

Anna stood up but Clare put her hand up to stop her.

'Thanks, Anna, but I think I can go in by myself. I'm a big girl now.'

Clare saw the look of surprise and then disappointment cross Anna's face and enjoyed it. That would teach her to be so transparent. If there was something here that she didn't think Clare should know then Clare was going to find out what it was on her own. That way Anna and the others would have to second-guess what had been revealed. Anna looked like she might object but then seemed to think better of it. She could hardly insist on coming into the meeting with her.

'Back soon,' Clare said with a wink.

III

'Did you find us all right?' asked the solicitor. Clare had forgotten her name already, not that it mattered. It was such a stupid question, given that they were standing side by side in the lift, that Clare didn't reply. The solicitor flicked at her fingernails to fill the silence. Clare watched the numbers light up on the control panel as the lift rose. When the doors opened, the solicitor showed her down a corridor to a room at the end. Clare was expecting it to be her office but actually it was a meeting room with big glass panels and views of the street below.

'Coffee?' asked the solicitor. Her tone was slightly less friendly now.

Clare could hear Miriam in her ear. It wouldn't do any harm to be polite to this woman. It might even be in her best interests. She smiled widely.

'That would be great. Milk and three sugars, please.'

She felt sure that the woman's eyebrows lifted just slightly but she prepared the coffee to Clare's instructions and passed it over to her. Clare took the cup and sat down at the round table on which was sitting a slim black folder. Whatever this was all about must be in there, Clare thought.

The solicitor put a pen down on the table and looked directly at Clare. She was younger than Clare had thought. Very young, in fact.

Barely old enough to be out of school. How long did it take to become a solicitor these days? Maybe she wasn't a solicitor at all. Perhaps she was the office junior. That would be right. No one would bother sending an actual solicitor to deal with someone as unimportant as her.

'Now, Miss Bliss, do you know a gentleman called StJohn Downing?' the solicitor/office junior asked.

Clare shook her head. The name meant nothing to her.

'He is, or was, a client of ours. Sadly, he died recently, leaving his estate in our management.' She tapped the black folder.

Clare's mind raced. Was this going to be one of those situations that you saw in the films where someone inherited a fortune from a stranger? Well, Clare was up for that. Bring it on. Inheritance without all the effort of grief. Excellent.

'Mr Downing left us a letter to be delivered to you in the event of his death. I have that letter here.' She opened the folder and took out an envelope. It was made of the same heavy paper that the letter summoning her here had been printed on. The solicitor/office junior glanced at her nervously. 'I have to tell you,' she said, 'that the contents of this letter are highly personal and may come as a shock to you. Because of this, you can either take the letter away with you and rearrange a further meeting for another time or open it now. It is entirely up to you.'

Clare thought of Anna waiting in the reception downstairs. Had she known what was coming? Was that why she offered to come with Clare?

The woman was staring at her expectantly and Clare realised that she had to reply. Without even considering it she said, 'I'll open it now. My old dad always said that there's no time like the present.'

The woman nodded and handed the envelope over. Clare could feel her heart beating faster but she didn't want to give anything away. She hoped the woman couldn't see that her hands were trembling. She opened the envelope. Inside there was a letter, handwritten in blue-black ink in a curling, old-fashioned script.

'Dear Miss Bliss' it began, and Clare felt her stomach lurch. Did she really want to read this now? Shouldn't she at least take it home with her? But then again, what could it possibly say that would do her any harm? StJohn Downing would just be some kindly benefactor, maybe a childless distant relation that she'd never heard of. It wasn't like she had the names of all her relations at her fingertips. Miriam would know who this bloke was. She could just ring her . . .

She looked down at the letter in her hand, took a deep breath and read on.

> I trust this letter finds you well. If you are reading it
> then you can assume that the same cannot be said
> for me.

He has a sense of humour, then, this Downing guy, thought Clare.

> Depending on who has told you what over the years,
> you may or may not have heard of me. I was a friend
> of your mother's for a brief period in the 1960s. After
> that, I travelled extensively in the Far East and we were
> unable to see each other, but I kept a watchful eye over
> you all, and particularly you.

Clare could feel the eyes of the solicitor on her as she read. Her hands were really shaking now so she put the letter on the table so that the woman couldn't see.

> I never formed any other attachments over my life and
> so I have been left with the thorny problem of what
> to do with my estate. I have considered charities as a
> backstop but have concluded that more good could
> possibly be done closer to home.

245

Which brings me to the nub of the issue. Your
mother told me, Clare, that there was a question over
your paternity . . .

What? Clare's eyes skipped back over what she had just read. A question
over her paternity? She felt adrenaline prickle in the ends of her fingers
and her chest tightened as if she'd been running. She read on.

I appreciate that that is a very bald statement, particularly if it has come as a surprise to you, but I'm afraid
I could think of no way of introducing the subject
in a gentler fashion. There has always been a chance
that you were the product of one especially tender
and unique encounter beneath a spreading oak tree.
Statistically, I gather, the odds are stacked against it –
I assume this is why your mother chose to keep it to
herself – but theoretically it is a possibility. As I mentioned, I have no other offspring. You, Clare, might
be all that I leave in this world to show that I was ever
here. Equally, you may not.

If it weren't for the pressing conundrum of what
to do with my estate, I would have gone to the grave
with this mystery unsolved, leaving the question of my
progeny up to the gods, but the practical part of me
needed to know that the product of a lifetime's work
would not simply be handed to Her Majesty.

So, I came up with a solution. If it can be proved
beyond reasonable doubt that I had a child then that
person shall inherit. If not, then the estate will be left
to a charity that assists other children in the Far East
who find themselves without parents to protect them.
Whether you wish to put in a claim is entirely up

to you. However, I have left instructions that such a claim must be made within one month of today's date.

I am sorry if this letter has caused you any unrest but sometimes keeping secrets has unforeseen circumstances.

Yours, with the very greatest of respect,
StJohn Downing

Fuck. Clare looked again at the letter but the words were swirling on the page. She looked up at the solicitor.

'Is this for real?' she asked.

The solicitor nodded.

'As Mr Downing says in his letter, our instructions are that if a legitimate claim is made on the estate then that person will inherit.'

Clare stood up and paced backwards and forwards. The room wasn't large. Six steps and she was at the wall, six steps back.

'And this claim,' she said. 'If someone wanted to make it, how would that work?'

'There would need to be a DNA test which would prove the matter beyond reasonable doubt. Mr Downing has left a record of his own DNA for comparison purposes. As you will have seen, there is a deadline for the submission of such a claim of a month from today. Can I get you anything, Miss Bliss? A glass of water, perhaps?'

Clare shook her head. A skin had formed on the top of her coffee but she picked it up and drank it, the sugar hitting her system quickly.

'And how much money is there?' she asked. 'Just what are we talking about here?'

The solicitor opened the folder again, ran her finger down a list of figures and said, 'As at close of business yesterday, the estate was worth approximately one point two million pounds. Obviously there will be inheritance tax to pay on that, bringing the sum closer to six hundred thousand, although until the property is sold it is difficult to give an exact amount.'

Clare felt sick. This was too much to take on board. More money than she'd ever had, but at what cost?

She needed air. The cold coffee lay heavy on her stomach. She had to get out of there.

Without saying goodbye to the solicitor, she grabbed the letter and then left the room. She could hear the solicitor calling after her but she didn't stop. She ran down the corridor to the lift and banged the lift buttons. The lift was on the ground floor. She couldn't wait for it. She made for the fire escape and bounded down the stairs, her footsteps echoing in the tiled space. At the bottom she burst out into the reception. Anna was still sitting where she had left her. She looked up as she heard the door opening.

'That was quick,' she said. 'Was everything . . .? Clare?'

Anna stood up but Clare rushed straight past her and out into the street, knocking into a couple who were coming in. Then she set off up the road at speed. She didn't know where she was going. She just needed to put as much space as possible between her and that room. On the next corner there was a pub, pink and white petunia trailing from dripping hanging baskets around the door. She didn't think, just marched straight in and ordered a double vodka tonic. It didn't even touch the sides.

IV

Anna was less than ten minutes behind her but already Clare was on her third drink. The barman hadn't batted an eyelid, just served her in the same glass. After her few dry months, the joy of the alcohol hitting her system was like welcoming a long-lost friend. She couldn't take on board what had just happened so the best thing was to blot it out. It was a tactic that had worked for her all her life. There was no reason to reject it now.

She heard Anna sigh as she came in and saw her sitting at the bar. She was such a disappointment to her family. She always had been. Had they always known that she wasn't one of them, not really? Was that why they were so fucking perfect and she had always felt like a reject, like the ugly duckling who didn't quite belong but was sort of tolerated?

'Shall we sit down over there, Clare?' Anna said, her arm gently on Clare's shoulder, steering her away. Again.

Clare allowed herself to be moved, holding her empty glass tight into her chest. They sat at a table in a window a little away from the main space. Clare banged her knee on the cast-iron table leg as they sat down and pain shot round her body. Anna signalled something to the barman over her head.

'I need another,' said Clare.

'In a minute,' said Anna. 'First, tell me what happened.'

Clare didn't have the words to explain. She thrust the letter that she was still clutching at Anna.

'Double vodka,' she called out to the barman.

Anna took the letter, smoothed it out on the table and began to read. Clare watched her face. What was she expecting to see when her sister discovered that they were less sisterly than they'd thought? Clare watched carefully but there was nothing. No reaction. It was just like before, when Anna had tried to talk her out of going.

'You knew,' said Clare slowly. 'You fucking knew and you never said.'

It was all starting to make sense now. The way they patronised her, that kind of smugness that they all had when she was around them, the silent raising of eyebrows when they thought she hadn't seen. They all knew and had never said. They had just pretended that she was one of them but all the time . . .

Anna was shaking her head but Clare pressed on, the pieces all starting to drop into place.

'You all knew. No wonder I'm such a fucking embarrassment to you all. I thought it was just Clare the walking disaster who can never make anything go right, but no. It's Clare who's not really one of us, who we can make excuses for, knowing that she doesn't really belong. Christ, I'm an idiot, but I see it all now.'

'No, Clare. You're wrong,' Anna said, her eyes wide and panicky. 'I did know about StJohn Downing but only after Mum died and I didn't tell the others. I promise.'

'And you didn't think you ought to mention it to me,' spat Clare. 'Just a little thing, not that important. You see, you might be illegitimate. That man, the one that brought you up. Well, he might not be your dad after all. Funny how things turn out, isn't it?'

Clare needed another drink. 'Vodka,' she shouted at the barman who was cleaning glasses at the other end of the bar and seemed to be ignoring them. 'NOW!'

'Don't, Clare,' said Anna gently, like she was talking to a child. 'That isn't going to help.'

'How the fucking hell would you know what would or wouldn't help me? I've always had to help myself. It's always been the same. You three, you tolerate me. No more. You've put up with me because we were family and you had to. Well, guess what, my little pretend sister. We're not family so you don't have to tolerate me any more.'

Clare looked up at Anna and saw that she had tears streaming down her face.

'And there's no need to feel responsible for me any more either. That'll be a relief, I bet. Half-sisters don't need to mop up after each other, do they? You can just piss off back to Miriam and Seb. Tell them that all their troubles are over. They'll be delighted. One less thing to worry about. The alcoholic nightmare of a sister can be cut free and left to rot.'

'Stop it! Stop it!!' Anna was shouting now. 'It's not true, Clare. That's not how we feel. And this' – she pointed to the letter – 'this won't make any difference. It doesn't matter what any test says. You are our sister and you always will be.'

For one moment, Clare grasped on to Anna's words, like a drowning man flailing for a life raft. Did she mean it? Would it really make no difference to them who had provided the sperm at her conception? But then she shook her head.

'Oh, fuck off, Anna. Leave me alone. Where's that fucking drink?'

Clare stood up. Well, if they weren't going to serve her in here then she would have to go and find somewhere else. She headed for the door, her head swimming slightly as she gathered pace. She expected to hear Anna following behind her but no one came. This is it, she thought as she crashed out into the street. I'm finally on my own.

V

When Clare woke up she found, by a miracle, that she was not in a ditch somewhere but safely at home. She hadn't made it as far as the bed but at least she appeared to be in one piece and without any bruises or other scrapes. Her head was pounding, though, and her mouth was dry. She needed a drink but there wasn't anything here. She'd been so careful not to buy anything, not to have anything close by where it could call out to her from inside cupboards, tempt her back to the place she'd just escaped. And now what had she done? All that work, all those AA meetings, the sheer bloody humiliation of exposing her considerable flaws to a room of strangers, and all for nothing.

Clare groaned and rolled on to her side so that her head was level with the coffee table. Just twenty-four short hours ago she had been in control of her life for once. A place of her own, a job and a clear head. Things that seemed so simple for the others but had been almost impossible for her to achieve. Well, she wasn't ready to let all that go. It didn't matter how bad things got. She had made a deal with herself and she owed it to herself to hang on.

The letter was sitting on the coffee table. It was considerably less pristine than it had been. She must have screwed it up at least once and there was a rusty-coloured drink ring on one corner. She tried to remember where she had been, who she had shared her tale of woe with, but the information wasn't there, great chunks of her evening missing as they so often had been in her life, the memories not stored in her databanks. It was yet another night that she'd lost and would never get back.

And then there was Anna. Clare felt a twinge of guilt. She could pretty much remember what she'd said to Anna. Poor Anna. Oh well. Fuck it. It was probably no more than she deserved. After all, she'd known about this Downing bloke all along and decided to say nothing. Playing God with Clare's life.

Well, her life was nothing to do with them any more. It was up to her. She could just take the test and inherit the money. It was obvious even to a blind man in a dark room that it would turn out that this stranger was actually her father. In fact, that would explain her whole life – every wrong step she had taken, every disastrous decision, every catastrophic mess that she had made could be linked back to this one, secret fact. She was predestined to fail. She had been an accident from the very outset. Of course a fact like that was going to affect her life, her karma. No wonder things had worked out the way they had. Some part of her, some deep-hidden section of her heart, had always known there was an answer, a reason for her failures, great and small. And now she knew what it was.

Clare sat up carefully. Her head was banging but it was bearable. She tried to think clearly. This could be a good thing, the start of something new. She could take the test, claim the money and run far away where the rest of them would never find her, not that they'd want to. They'd be relieved to have her off their backs. She could just hear Miriam now. 'Well, it's all worked out for the best. We always knew, though, didn't we, that there was something about Clare . . .'

Did her dad know, Clare wondered? Her lovely, funny, big-hearted father – did he know that his wife had cuckolded him with a passing stranger? No. She couldn't believe it. He had always treated Clare fairly, looked out for her and welcomed her back no matter how much she screwed stuff up. Would he have done that for a child that he had no claim over? No. Of course not. This must have been her mother's dirty little secret. And then Anna's.

She needed a drink but tea would have to do. She even had some milk. She stood up, swaying slightly as she reconnected with gravity, and then moved into the tiny kitchen. Anna was already in there and Clare jumped. Her sister/not-sister was sitting on the rickety stool that Clare had rescued from a skip, staring out of the window watching the children run in the alley behind the block.

'I wish I had a child,' she said, which was so random that Clare didn't think she'd heard her properly. 'I always thought I would have. It was in my life-plan but then it just never happened. I even wondered for a bit about having one on my own. Women do, don't they? But I just wasn't brave enough and now I'm too old.'

'You can have mine,' said Clare, ignoring the surprising fact that Anna was in her kitchen, had been there all night quite possibly. 'He clearly doesn't want me in his life. Have you drunk all the milk?'

'I'm so sorry, Clare,' Anna went on. 'I should have told you about StJohn Downing but I just thought it would be better if no one knew. I mean, it doesn't make any difference whether you're Dad's girl or not. You're still our sister.'

Anna was looking at her now and Clare could see that the rims of her eyes were crimson.

'Easy for you to say,' said Clare. 'From your place up there on the marble pedestal.'

Anna made a sound somewhere between a laugh and a sigh. 'There's plenty of milk,' she said.

Clare pottered about her kitchen boiling the kettle and finding the teabags and all the time Anna watched her. Clare quite liked it, liked that she could entertain her sister in her own home like a totally normal person. It had been such a long time coming, this self-sufficiency.

'What are you going to do?' asked Anna, bringing Clare crashing back down to earth.

'Honestly?' asked Clare. 'I have absolutely no fucking idea.'

MIRIAM – 2017

I

Miriam stood and stared at the poster for a long time, absorbing all the information that she could glean from it. She'd read *Dancing at Lughnasa* when she was at university. She couldn't remember much of the play. Something about a big Irish family of mainly sisters who keep falling out over the best way to behave. It all sounded horribly familiar. And wasn't the eldest, Kate, an upright teacher with crushed life ambitions? She'd be perfect for the role. She might even get away with her age, given kind lighting, and she'd barely have to act at all. The part surely had her name written all over it. There was dancing, which might be more problematic, but she could probably master that. How hard could it be to jig about on the stage with wild abandon? Miriam sighed. Not that hard when she was seventeen. Possibly more challenging now.

She didn't often let herself think about what might have been if she had gone to RADA after that fateful summer when Sebastian was born. Even though her father had said no to the audition when she'd first mentioned it, she was pretty certain that she would have won him round eventually, one stage of the process at a time. First the application, then the audition. By the time the start of term arrived, she would have convinced him that a daughter on the stage was his life's ambition and that he had never wanted anything more. Of course, there was always the very vague chance that she might not actually have been offered a place, but when she was dreaming about this alternative life of hers she never let that fact cloud her vision.

Did she still have it, that drive to perform? At college she had got involved in various serious but instantly forgettable productions, and at work the annual school play had fallen into her remit until the school had appointed a sickeningly keen newly qualified drama teacher. But as for treading the boards herself? It had been a while. Since the girls had been born there never seemed to be any time. Well, now that they were at university themselves maybe the time had come for her to claim back her life?

She read the details on the poster again. Auditions were being held later that week for this 'new and exciting production'. She scribbled the phone number down on the back of a supermarket receipt which she found in her bag. She would think about it.

It was nearly time for her shift at the Help the Aged shop and she liked to be there on time so that she would be allocated to work on the till and not sorting the donations. Going though bags of discarded belongings was still difficult, even though it had been a couple of years since the four of them had stripped their mother's home like a plague of locusts. Nothing had been left by the time she and the house clearance firm had finished. That was the idea, of course, but it still seemed so very brutal to remove everything that had once created their home. All that remained when she locked the door for the final time was the makeshift height chart that their father had carved into the scullery door. It broke her heart to leave it behind. If she could have cut the wood out and replaced it with a new piece she would have done. She had even toyed with the idea of doing some sort of rubbing of it, like you did of brass on a gravestone, but Richard had told her that she was being ridiculous. He was right. They were middle-aged adults now and no one needed to know how tall they had been when they were five. But still . . .

Her phone started to ring and she screwed her nose up in irritation. She was nearly at the shop. She didn't have time for interruptions. The phone had got itself trapped in the lining of her handbag and by the time she extracted it, the caller had rung off. It had been Anna. Miriam would ring her back later but then it rang again. Anna.

'Did you lose your phone in your bag again?' asked the familiar voice when Miriam answered. 'I always ring twice. You never get to it in time on the first go. Why don't you put it in your pocket? Or on a string round your neck?'

'Oh, ha ha,' she said. 'No one ever rings me except you and Richard. The girls just text or send pointless emoji that I can't see without my specs and then can't decipher.'

'Listen,' said Anna. 'Something's happened. We need to talk.'

'Well, can it wait?' asked Miriam. She had reached the shop and was now standing with one hand on the door ready to push it open. 'I'm just about to start at the shop.'

'I suppose so but it's important. Can you meet me tonight? I'll ring Seb too.'

'And Clare?' asked Miriam, but somehow she knew the answer to that.

'No. I'll explain when I see you.'

They made a plan for later and Miriam finally got into the shop just in time to see her co-worker claim her place at the till with a smug smile. Donation bags it was, then.

They met later at Sebastian's as he hadn't been able to get a sitter at such short notice. Even before Miriam was in the house she could hear that Theo and Zac were neither in bed nor showing any signs of wanting to go there. Sebastian's approach to a bedtime routine had always differed from her regimented one, but since he had been on his own, it seemed to have fallen away entirely. Anna had told her that the boys usually fell asleep where they dropped and then had to be carried to their beds. It was no way to bring up children in Miriam's opinion but then Sebastian had enough on his plate and the boys were delightful, if a little boisterous. They had such a large measure of their mother's care-free spirit running through their veins. They looked far more like Tessa's side of the family too – dark with chocolate-drop eyes and smooth, caramel-coloured skin.

She rang the doorbell and told herself not to judge.

Anna opened the door, still dressed in her work clothes and looking like she needed at least a week's sleep at once. Zac skidded down the hall behind her on his knees, closely followed by Theo, who was brandishing a lightsaber. Neither boy looked like he would ever need to sleep again.

'Come in,' said Anna. 'We're in the kitchen.' She pulled her face into an expression that suggested that Miriam should prepare herself.

Sebastian's kitchen was not like Miriam's. The table was still laid for the evening meal, the plates left abandoned. The area around the sink was piled high with what was certainly more than one day's washing-up and the sink was full of pans. On the floor was a basket overflowing with laundry. Miriam couldn't tell if it was clean or dirty but she suspected dirty. One corner was entirely taken over by a carpet of footwear: mainly trainers but also school shoes, wellington boots and one roller skate. A supermarket bag-for-life was disgorging its contents on one work surface and another was piled so high with paperwork that the stacks were starting to topple. Miriam bit her tongue.

Anna started to clear a corner of the table so that they could at least sit down without putting their elbows in the remains of whatever had just been consumed. Miriam started to move the plates across to the sink area but Anna shook her head. Sebastian was very touchy about anything that suggested that he wasn't coping. They had run into that particular obstacle before. The things that were important to Miriam, like order, tidiness, even cleanliness, didn't matter to Sebastian. They hadn't mattered to Tessa either but people forgot that. It wasn't that the house looked like this because Sebastian had no wife. It had always looked like this.

Miriam piled the plates on top of each other, pushed them to the opposite corner of the table and turned so her back was to the sink.

'Right,' they heard Sebastian say in the hall. 'I have to have a chat with Aunts Miriam and Anna so can you leave us in peace and try to keep the noise down so we can hear each other speak. Can you do that?'

There was no anger in his voice. He reminded her of their dad, although Sebastian's turn of phrase was far less floral.

'Okay,' he said as he came into the kitchen. He was smiling broadly. 'I reckon we've got about twenty seconds before—'

'Can we watch a movie?' asked Theo as he careered into the kitchen using the other roller skate as a skateboard.

'Yes. But only if it's approximately age-appropriate and you don't make too much noise.'

Satisfied, Theo rolled back out into the hall.

'Drink?' asked Sebastian, getting a bottle of beer from the fridge and flicking the cap off with his thumb. 'I have white wine, beer or tea. No coffee. I forgot we'd run out.'

'Wine, please,' said Anna, and Miriam nodded.

'So,' said Miriam when they all had a drink, 'what's happened?' She looked at Anna expectantly but Anna was picking at a thread on her jacket sleeve and wouldn't meet her eye.

'It's very complicated and you're not going to like it but could you try to stay quiet until I get to the end and then we can discuss it.'

Miriam looked at Sebastian, who was nodding gently.

'Okay. Let's have it.'

Anna took a deep breath and ran her fingers up and down the stem of her glass.

'So,' she said. 'I got a letter for Clare from a firm of solicitors acting for a friend of Mum's. He had died and his solicitors wanted to see Clare.'

'What?' asked Sebastian. 'Just Clare? Why did they want . . .?' Anna put her hand up to silence him. 'Sorry,' he muttered. 'Carry on.'

'So, Clare went and they gave her a letter. Basically, it seems that there's a chance that this friend of Mum's might be her father.'

Miriam wasn't sure that she'd heard her properly. 'What? What did you just say?'

'Miriam. Please,' said Anna in exasperation. 'Just let me get to the end of it. So this bloke has said that Clare will inherit all his stuff if she can prove that she's his daughter. She has to do a DNA test.'

Sebastian whistled. 'Bloody hell. So that means . . .' He crinkled his brow as he thought through the consequences of what Anna had just said.

'That means,' said Miriam, 'that either he's a lying toe-rag or Mum had an affair.'

Miriam brought an image of their mother into her mind. She was old, grey-haired, as she remembered her last. She dug deeper into her memory for the Dorothy of fifty years ago, a young and vivacious Dorothy who might have had her head turned by someone who wasn't their dad, but there was nothing there.

Sebastian took a swig of beer and then said, 'So how did Clare react?'

'Pretty much like that,' said Anna, nodding towards his bottle. 'I found her in the pub. She was in a state, not really knowing what to do.'

'No.' Miriam sighed. This was a blow. A sober Clare was a rare and precious thing. 'And she'd been doing so well. You didn't leave her there, did you?' she asked, panicked now at the thought of what might happen to an unsupervised Clare with the possibility of money behind her. Miriam had seen Clare on a bender and was hoping that it was something that she would never have to deal with again.

'Of course I didn't,' said Anna, her tone indignant. 'She wouldn't speak to me so I kind of stalked her until she was too drunk to function and then I took her home.'

The three of them sat there staring into space. Sebastian spoke first.

'Well, it would make a lot of sense,' he said. 'I mean, if . . .' He looked at them awkwardly, clearly hoping that they would understand what he was saying without him actually having to voice it.

'No, it wouldn't,' Miriam heard herself say. 'Clare is a troubled person but that's just who she is. It doesn't mean that she has some stranger's genes. How could you say that, Seb?'

Sebastian looked like he was going to argue but then thought better of it.

'What's she going to do?' Miriam asked Anna. 'She's not going to take this test, is she?'

'Honestly? I have no idea. She was okay when I left her – I mean, not drinking or anything – but it seemed like it hadn't hit her, not really.'

'How much money are we talking?' asked Sebastian.

'About three quarters of a million net, the solicitor reckoned.'

Sebastian whistled again. 'That would make one hell of a difference to her.'

'As long as she didn't drink it,' said Miriam.

'She's doing really well, Miriam. Or she was before this blew up. I don't think she'd want to go back to how things were before.'

'I'm not sure she'd be able to help herself.'

Anna poured them more wine, even though Miriam had barely touched hers. Then a thought crossed Miriam's mind. 'Do you think this is what was in that letter that we never found? The one in the will?'

'I bet it is,' said Sebastian, nodding enthusiastically. 'Mum must have been going to tell Clare and then changed her mind at the last minute. What do you think, Anna?'

Miriam saw something flicker across Anna's face, the hint of a blush on her neck, and in that moment, Miriam knew. There had always been something odd about that whole will business, the way Anna had had it hidden at her house, the missing letter that they all had to pretend had never existed. At the time, Miriam had been furious with Anna for withholding it, self-righteously demanding that she explain herself, but what if . . . Miriam winced as she realised that Anna must have been protecting Clare. If she knew what was in the letter then perhaps she had decided that it was better if Clare never found out. Destroying both the will and the letter would have caused a bit of hassle but a lot less damage than telling Clare the truth. But she had messed all that up by finding the will and then charging about with it like a bull in a china shop.

'Maybe,' said Anna quietly. 'I don't know.'

Miriam knew then that she was right, that Anna had known, at least since their mother had died. Poor Anna for carrying this horrible burden by herself.

'The real question,' said Miriam loudly, trying to direct attention away from Anna, 'is how we go about supporting Clare. This must have come as such a shock to her and it's more than enough to put her recovery back months. I vote we go see her, make sure she understands that none of this makes any difference to us.'

Sebastian looked at her thoughtfully.

'The thing is, though, Miriam,' he said, 'it kind of does make a difference, doesn't it? I mean, she'll only be our half-sister. That's quite a big thing.'

Miriam couldn't believe what she was hearing. How could Sebastian think like that? This was Clare they were talking about. She was about to reply but there was no need. Anna was on it.

'That is the most ridiculous thing you've ever said, Seb,' said Anna. She was virtually shouting at him. 'It makes no difference whatsoever. She's still Clare, our sister. What if she'd been adopted? Would she not have been our "real" sister then either?' Anna put air quotes around 'real' and sneered at Sebastian. 'We were all brought up by the same parents in the same house. As far as I'm concerned that makes her our sister. End of.'

Miriam was surprised by the response of both her siblings. Sebastian was usually so easy-going about things and there had never been any love lost between Anna and Clare. It must be the shock, although if she was right about Anna then this wasn't exactly a shock to her.

'The most important issue' – Miriam tried again – 'is Clare. When did you last see her, Anna?'

'This morning. I stayed over so I was there when she woke up. We had a cup of tea and then I left her to it. She was fine.'

'I think one of us should get over there, just to make sure.'

A scream went up from another part of the house as Theo and Zac grew tired of their film.

'Well, I can't go,' said Sebastian. 'I need to stay here with the boys.' He looked relieved.

'I'll go,' said Miriam. 'I'll go right now.'

She stood up and Anna stood up with her.

'I'll come too,' she said pointedly. 'We'll give her your love, shall we, Sebastian?'

'Oh, come on,' said Sebastian. 'Don't be like that. I'm just saying . . .'

'Well, don't,' said Anna. 'Bye, boys,' she said as she let herself out of the front door, but she didn't wait for a reply.

Sebastian shook his head.

'What did I do?' he asked. 'I mean, it's true. If she has a different dad then she's not our proper sister, is she?'

Miriam sighed. 'For someone so smart, brother dear, you can be remarkably dense sometimes. I'll ring you tomorrow.'

She reached up and gave her brother a kiss on the cheek and then followed Anna out.

II

'I'll drive,' Miriam said as Anna dug around in her bag for car keys. Anna didn't object, maybe thinking of the wine she'd drunk, and Miriam waited as she climbed into the passenger seat in silence.

Miriam pulled the car smoothly out of Sebastian's drive and turned on to the main road. Clare's flat was on an estate on the other side of town. It was dark now and the headlights of cars coming towards her flared. She hated driving at night. She was getting old.

'You didn't have to be that hard on Sebastian,' she said to Anna once they were on their way. 'It was a shock for him. I'm sure once he's had time to come round to the idea he'll see that it doesn't make any difference.'

They stopped at traffic lights and Miriam turned to look at Anna, who was staring out at the road ahead, her jaw tight.

'It wasn't a shock for you, though, was it?'

Anna turned her head and then shook it slowly, eyes downcast.

'The letter was with the will?'

Anna nodded. There was a silence as the lights turned green and Miriam pulled out into the traffic.

'So,' prompted Miriam, 'are you going to tell me how you ended up with the will or is it a secret?'

'Well, it was a secret,' replied Anna, her voice spiked with indignation. 'Bloody hell. What a mess.'

Miriam waited. There was no point pushing Anna. She would share, given time. She didn't have to wait long.

'It was Mum,' Anna said, staring resolutely out of the windscreen and not turning to look at Miriam. 'She asked me to go and find the will and the letter and made me promise to burn them.'

Miriam felt her lips tightening. Even after all these years, the fact that their mother had asked Anna to collect the will and not her rankled. She was the eldest. She had sacrificed her life to the task of fetching and carrying for her mother and then, when something important, something significant, needed doing who had her mother asked to help her? Anna! The play poster from earlier flicked into her mind. She would definitely audition. There was still time to do what she wanted for once in her life. She wasn't dead yet – not quite, anyway.

'But you didn't do it,' Miriam said, hoping that Anna didn't sense her irritation and clam up.

'No,' replied Anna, shaking her head sadly. 'I meant to. I was going to but then your washer broke down and you found the will before I had chance. It was just luck that you didn't see the letter. So, I decided it would be better for everyone if I just kept my mouth shut.'

Anna took a deep breath and Miriam could see that she was fighting to control her emotions. That was Anna all over, always in control, never giving anything away. It was good to see that some things did have the power to touch her after all, to pierce her ice-maiden exterior. Immediately Miriam felt guilty for thinking like that. Poor Anna. They had all been so vile to her about the will and she had just been trying to protect Clare from the truth.

'Oh, Anna,' said Miriam. 'I'm so very sorry. That must have been horrible for you, knowing that massive secret and not being able to say anything. But . . .' Miriam paused. 'Why didn't you just do what Mum asked in the first place?'

Miriam tried to keep the accusation out of her tone. Actually, Anna had only had to deal with all this on her own because she had overridden their mother's wishes. In many ways, it did kind of serve her right.

They turned into Clare's estate. A gang of small boys was playing chicken in the street, standing on the white line until their car approached and only at the last minute diving for the kerb. Miriam resisted the urge to blow the horn at them. There was nothing to be gained from drawing attention to yourself here. In the distance, a blue light flashed in the night sky and a siren sounded and then faded away.

'So? Why didn't you?' Miriam asked again as they pulled up in the parking area outside Clare's block.

What would she have done if it had been her? Well, if her mother had asked her to destroy the documents then that's what she would have done. Without question. Unread. Eldest child. Always the rule-follower.

'I wanted to know what it said, of course,' said Anna sharply. 'I know you wouldn't have read them, Miriam, but I'm not you. I just couldn't resist.'

Just like Pandora, thought Miriam. Anna lifted her head high as if she was expecting a fight but Miriam wasn't going to give her one.

'And would you have told Clare?' Miriam asked, her voice barely above a whisper.

Anna turned in her seat and looked straight at her. Miriam could see her eyes flashing in the darkness.

'No,' she said. 'But now it turns out that I went through all that for nothing because that bloody man has written to Clare from beyond the grave and spilled the beans anyway.'

They sat there a moment longer, each thinking through the implications of what they had just said. Then there was a shout in the street behind them. Miriam opened the door to get out and then stopped, half in, half out of the car as she took in the scene. Clare was walking down the middle of the road, her arms akimbo as she tried and failed to balance on the white line. She had a wine bottle in each hand.

'The. Leith. Police. Dismisseth. Uth,' she shouted. 'See. I'm not pissed. I can walk. I can walk in a straight line. And I can say the Leith Polith. Fuck it! No I can't!'

She broke into laughter, a manic sound that could just as easily have been crying.

'Shit,' said Anna, and ran from the car to where Clare was turning circles in the middle of the road. She put her arms round their sister and steered her gently towards the pavement. Clare seemed to resist at first and then, when she realised who it was, allowed herself to be moved along.

'It's my baby sister. Anna the Favourite. Well, she was my sister. Now we're not all that sure, are we, Anna the Favourite.'

Anna spoke to her. Miriam couldn't hear what she said but then Clare looked in her direction and pointed at her with one of the bottles.

'There she is,' she shouted. 'My other not-sister. That's the bossy one. That's right, isn't it, Anna?'

Anna pushed down on Clare's arm and started steering her towards the staircase that led up to the flats. Miriam checked the street for potential car thieves, although she wasn't sure what good it would do, flicked the central locking and followed them up.

The flat was surprising tidy – much better than Sebastian's place. Yes, there were signs of a recent decline – a pizza box on the floor, a couple of upturned wine bottles on the coffee table – but the place was basically clean. Maybe things hadn't slipped too far yet, Miriam thought. If they could just get Clare back from the brink.

Anna went into the kitchen and started to fill the kettle. Miriam was surprised at the ease with which Anna moved about the place and felt a stab of jealously. Had Anna spent more time here than she had? Was there a growing bond between her and Clare that Miriam didn't share? No. She was being ridiculous and anyway, what did it matter if she and Clare had found a level that worked. It had been a long time coming.

Clare flopped down on the sofa, laying herself out along its length, and stared up at the ceiling. Her lower legs dangled off the armrest.

'Tea?' shouted Anna from the kitchen as the kettle started to bubble.

'Can't we do better than that?' asked Clare. 'Have you not brought a bottle or two with you? Can't have a proper family reunion without a bottle or two.' She sat up and pointed at Miriam. 'One. Two,' she continued, pointing at the kitchen door. 'There's one missing. Where is my not-brother? Where's Sebastian? We need the full set for a proper family party. Ring him up, Miriam, and get him to come and bring some booze.'

They were going to get nowhere tonight, that much was obvious.

'Sebastian's at home with the boys,' explained Miriam, conscious that she was using her teacher voice.

'Ah, yes,' said Clare, nodding sagely. 'Dead wife.'

Miriam winced at the way that Clare casually mentioned the one subject that she and Anna tripped delicately around.

Anna appeared with three mugs of steaming tea which she put on the coffee table, moving the bottles and stowing them out of sight under the sofa. 'You've run out of milk,' she said. The tea was varying degrees of brown. Miriam instinctively reached for the one with the least milk even though she hated black tea, for was it not forever her role to play the martyr, not that anyone ever noticed the sacrifices she made?

'So, Clare,' she said. 'Anna told me about the letter from the solicitors . . .'

'Now there's a turn-up for the books,' said Clare with a stagey wink. 'Might not be your actual, total flesh and blood. Didn't see that one coming, did you?'

'Could I look at it?' Miriam continued. 'The letter. Please.'

Clare nodded and then began looking around with exaggerated movement like a mime artist but the longer she looked without the letter appearing the more anxious she seemed to become. 'It was here,' she started muttering under her breath. 'It was right here on this table.

I had it and then I read it and then I had it and then . . .' Then she hit her hand to her forehead with such force that it made Miriam jump. 'The little bastard,' she said. 'That low-down, shitty little bastard.'

Miriam looked at Anna but she shook her head. She had no idea either.

'Who?' asked Miriam. 'Who do you think has taken the letter, Clare?'

Clare was swaying slightly in her seat but her eyes were cool and focused.

'River.'

III

'How sharper than a serpent's tooth it is to have a thankless child.'

Miriam liked that she generally had a quote at hand should the need for one arise. Not that it often did. Her children just rolled their eyes at her when she tried to drop them in, rarely even breaking their conversational stride to acknowledge it, let alone asking where the quote might have come from. School was worse. Not only the students but her fellow teachers looked dismayed when she employed a salient quotation, as if it were just one more thing that they had to absorb. Time was when she could quote entire pages of Shakespeare, chunks of epic poetry, even the odd stanza of modern verse, but not so much now. What was it they said? You had to use it or lose it. Maybe it was too late for her to audition for the Friel piece?

She pulled her wayward mind back to the current problem. Had River really taken the letter or had Clare, as was far more likely, just left it somewhere? What would River want with it anyway? They didn't even know for sure that he'd visited his mother that night. He hadn't been near for months, according to Clare. Miriam didn't think much of her nephew. Anna had always said that the way River cut himself off from them was simply a product of the chaotic upbringing that he'd had, that his faith in the Bliss family had been gradually eroded as Clare rejected offer after offer of help from them. Miriam was less inclined to be charitable to him. She had never seen the side of him that Anna professed was there, this gentler, more open nature that was apparently buried deep down. Still, there was no reason to connect the missing letter with him. That made no sense. No. Clare would have taken it out in the pub and then left it on the table or in the ladies' loo. Miriam sighed. Did she always have to be responsible for everything? Was this the burden of the eldest child until the end of time? Secretly, of course, she knew she loved being in charge and would be devastated if they all turned round and started fixing things for themselves.

Well, River or no River, the letter was gone. She and Anna had had a good poke around Clare's flat after she had passed out on the sofa and it definitely wasn't there. She thought about trailing round Clare's usual haunts but then abandoned the idea. No need to advertise her sister's failings. The best bet would be to contact the solicitors and just get another copy sent, although probably there'd be some data protection rule that meant that Clare would have to do that for herself. Perhaps if Miriam stood over her, made her make the call—

'Miss?' said a voice, pulling Miriam back to the here and now. Year 9, bottom-set English. One of Miriam's bigger challenges. It was Charlie Bennett with his hand up.

'Yes, Charlie,' she said with practised patience.

'I don't get it, Miss. What's the point of reading this book about something that never happened? If a plane did go down on an island then air traffic control and satellites and stuff would find it. And there's the black box too, Miss.' Charlie looked round at his classmates for approval.

'Yes, Miss,' said Shelley Keane. 'And where are all the girls? It's stupid that it's just boys.'

'Well, Shelley. That's an interesting point. How do you think the story might have been different if it had been girls that were stranded and not . . .'

The bell cut across her and the class stood up, scraping chairs across lino before she had chance to finish her sentence. Whatever happened to respect for the teacher? In her day, nobody would have dared to move until the class had been dismissed. A lot of things were different from how they'd been in her day. She felt old.

The class poured out of the door, a few of them turning to say goodbye to her as they left.

'Finish chapter ten for homework,' she called after them, knowing that they would pretend they hadn't heard her.

As she packed her marking into her bag she decided that she would have to go back to Clare's. She dug her phone out and texted Clare. '*Coming round now. Are you in?*' She'd go whether Clare replied or not. Someone needed to keep an eye and it had better be her. Anna would still be at work so there'd be no need to trouble her with it. She'd pick some milk up on the way and then she and Clare could have a proper talk about what Clare was going to do.

Forty minutes later she was ringing the bell on Clare's door with a pint of semi-skimmed and a packet of chocolate chip cookies. She'd had no reply to her text but now she was here she could hear a TV blaring, although that might be coming from next door. She was just ringing again when Clare appeared on the landing. She was wearing her work tabard and carrying a plastic bag filled with hot dog rolls. She looked a bit rough but she was sober.

'God, not again,' she said, but she was smiling.

'I brought supplies,' replied Miriam, holding up her purchases. 'Contrary to what you obviously believe, I am not a total write-off. Not yet, anyway.'

Clare retrieved a key and let them into the flat. The curtains were still drawn at the lounge window but the thin fabric simply diffused the light rather than blocking it. The flat looked fine. There was no sign of any tumbling from wagons. Clare opened the curtains and pulled her tabard over her head, throwing it carelessly on to the back of a chair.

It missed and slithered to the floor. The urge to pick it up and fold it neatly was so strong that Miriam had to turn away and busy herself with the biscuits.

'Tea or coffee?' asked Clare. 'I assume you've brought that stuff because you want a little chat and not just for my store cupboard.'

Miriam flinched just a little. There were never any social niceties with Clare. She said what she meant without any concern for anyone's feelings. She'd always been the same and it had always got her into trouble, particularly with their father, who had valued good manners over almost everything. Of course, he might no longer be their mutual father. She was finding this all so very unsettling. God only knew how Clare was coping.

'Coffee,' replied Miriam. 'And there's no need for your attitude. I've come to make sure that you're okay and to see if you want to talk because you're my sister . . .' Oh God. There she went again. This whole situation had long tentacles that had the capacity to reach out and strangle everything she had ever known. '. . . And that's what sisters do,' she finished, hoping that Clare wouldn't make another sarcastic comment, but Clare, it seemed, had had enough.

'Coming right up,' she said, grabbing the milk from Miriam's hand and disappearing into the kitchen.

'How's work going?' asked Miriam through the wall.

'Well, it's shit. Obviously. It's a shit job that pays shit money and could be done by a monkey with half a brain,' replied Clare, but there was something in her tone that told Miriam that she was actually quite proud of it.

'Do you work with nice people?' continued Miriam, giving Clare the chance to confess to enjoying it just a little bit.

'They're all right,' she said.

'I think it's great that you've got yourself a little job . . .' Damn. Why did she have to say 'little'? It sounded so patronising, so 'big sister' of her. No wonder Clare got so angry with them all. There had always been more than a sniff of superiority in the way that they had dealt with Clare over the years. They didn't do it on purpose, or at least she didn't – Anna had her own agendas – but somehow most things she said to Clare seemed to be painted with a liberal layer of smug. For once, Clare didn't seem to pick up on it. She came in with two mugs, the steam coming off the top emphasising the chill in the room.

'Yeah,' she said. 'It's cash in hand so you can't ask for much but it's a nice place and they treat us fair.' She placed the mugs down on the table and sat down with a humph. Miriam offered her a chocolate chip cookie.

Miriam had been trying to think of conversational opening gambits all the way there but as it turned out she needn't have worried. Clare needed no prompting.

'Well, this is a bit of mess,' she said. 'The black sheep of the family might turn out to be half goat.'

Miriam shook her head and laughed. 'That is the worst metaphor . . .'

'Thus spake the English teacher. I've been thinking about it since I got the letter. As I see it there are two possibilities. Either I am Dad's daughter or I'm the illegitimate lovechild of this Downing bloke. Do we know anything about him, by the way? The name means nothing to me.'

For a moment Miriam wavered but it was important, wasn't it, that they were all honest with each other? Lies would just breed more resentment. 'Anna met him,' she said.

Clare nodded as if this was totally expected. 'Of course she did. How very Anna, always right in the centre of any drama.'

Miriam thought that Clare was probably describing herself more than Anna but knew that it would do no good to say so.

'He wrote when Mum died. His letter was on Anna's pile to reply to and then later, she went to say hello.'

Clare eyed her. Her stare reminded Miriam of a seagull's, steady and intent and ready to pounce on a stray chip at any minute.

'She went to see if I looked anything like him, you mean,' she said. It wasn't a question.

Miriam shrugged. 'Quite possibly, but I don't know because I'm not Anna and she didn't tell me. Or Sebastian, before you ask. She's been carrying your secret all by herself for all this time.'

Miriam felt the need to defend Anna. It seemed odd to her to side that way but then this whole situation was pretty odd. Clare shrugged this away like it was nothing, but that wasn't fair. It was a massive burden for Anna to carry by herself, something that she'd done entirely for Clare. There was no point raising this, though. Clare might not see it like that, not yet anyway.

'So,' continued Clare as she picked at her ragged fingernails, 'as I see it I either pretend none of this happened and carry on as before or I get the test done and find out. Whether I accept the money – well, that's a third thing, I suppose.'

How did Clare do that? She always managed to surprise Miriam. If they'd been put on some hideous game show where they had to second-guess each other's actions, Miriam would never have said that Clare might take the test but not the cash. That was the kind of considered reasoning that she might expect from Sebastian. Anna would probably find out, take the money and just not tell the rest of them. She really wasn't sure what she would do if faced with this conundrum. But Clare? She definitely had her pegged as taking the money and having it spent within six months.

'And,' began Miriam tentatively, 'what are your thoughts?'

Clare sat back in the chair and stared up at the ceiling. She was quiet for so long that Miriam wondered if she'd drifted off.

'I reckon,' she said eventually, and Miriam felt herself shift a little forward in her chair, 'I reckon that I have no fucking clue.'

SEBASTIAN – 2017

I

Sebastian was sick of his sisters. They always knew best and they never failed to inform him of the fact. It had been the same since the day he'd arrived, late on the scene after their mother's phantom menopause. He'd always been babied by everyone – spoilt, really. The family dynamics had shifted with the appearance of a fourth child and a boy, no less. His mother, he knew, had struggled to regain her equilibrium for a while and so his father and Miriam had stepped up to the plate. He knew now that Miriam had resented that but at the time he didn't think it was odd that his sister was more his mother than his mother was.

By the time he'd hit his teenage years, his mother was back in control, but somehow those early years at home seemed to have given his sisters the right to burrow into his life even though he was now forty and more than capable of running things for himself.

God, he missed Tess. She would have known what to do now, would have said the right thing to both him and The Stryxes, her name for the sisters collectively. A stryx was a kind of owlish vampire favoured by the Romans, Tessa had told him. She'd read Classics to his Maths and was always colouring their lives with mythological creatures. Sebastian had never asked her about the specific characteristics of a stryx but he knew her well enough to know that it wouldn't be an endearment.

Sometimes in the early days he'd felt the need to defend his siblings, but then Tessa would make him laugh about something they'd said and he would suddenly see them through Tessa's eyes: three middle-aged women, each with their own complicated issues, who argued constantly amongst themselves but couldn't seem to steer clear of one another. Tessa had always managed to keep them at a distance with a nonchalance that Sebastian marvelled at. She'd smile her wide, open smile at Miriam as Miriam explained some trivial issue regarding the family and then totally ignore what had been said and do what she thought was best for Sebastian and her boys. And she had always been right.

The house was horribly quiet. Theo and Zac were in the lounge and, as far as he could tell, asleep. He would have to sneak in and carry them up to their beds at some point but not right now. Sebastian sank into a chair at the kitchen table. This was where he felt closest to Tessa. Even though their bedroom was where they'd shared more intimate moments, it was here, at the heart of everything that happened to them, that he felt her with him.

'What do you think, Tess?' he said out loud. He often spoke to her when he was alone. It felt natural, like she could just be behind him stirring something on the stove or flicking through a travel magazine planning a madly exotic holiday that they'd never take. 'I'm right, aren't I? Of course it makes a difference if Clare has a different dad to the rest of us. Part of the connection that holds us all together will be lost. It's like, I don't know, like ivy clinging to a wall. It's still attached if you cut away some of the roots but the connection's not as strong. Actually, that's not a great analogy, but you get what I'm saying, don't you? If she's only half my sister, then her catastrophic life is only half my problem. I won't have to keep making allowances for her, will I? Does that make sense?'

Was this what he thought? It had certainly been his gut reaction when he'd heard the news but could he sustain it? Anna and Miriam didn't share his concerns. He was out on a limb but . . . It was his limb. He was entitled to hang on to it if he wanted.

He heard Tessa's voice in his head, full as it always was of light and laughter. 'Once a stryx, always a stryx,' she said. 'You're stuck with her.' And Sebastian was irritated by her refusal to side with him entirely. Since when did Tessa support the sisters over him? But he knew the answer to this. It was ever since she stopped being his wife and instead became the voice of his conscience, speaking to him in those moments when he wasn't sure which way to turn.

It was so hard making decisions by himself. There had always been his sisters and then Tessa to make things happen around him. He remembered how she'd planned their wedding, making it feel like it was their dream day when in fact he had had very little say in what happened, not that that mattered. Her ideas had always turned out to be exactly what he wanted in the end.

She had been desperate for a *Midsummer Night's Dream* wedding, in a wood not far from home.

'I want candles in the trees,' she had said, her dark eyes shining. 'And I want everyone to sit together in a clearing, like we're all fairies. We don't need chairs or anything. We can get a huge tarpaulin or some- thing and I . . . No, wait. We can have little stools, like milking stools.'

'Where from?' he had asked. 'Milking Stools R Us?' He'd been mocking her but only gently. They had always had to cut through the mad parts of her ideas before they got to the golden core. 'Chairs would be better. And then you could wrap vines and stuff round the backs.'

She had nodded, visualising how it would be. 'Yes, that's good. And we can read beautiful poems. And Miriam's girls could be flower fairies. Are they too big for that, do you think? How old are they again? We should have got married five years ago when they were tiny.'

'But you hadn't said yes then,' Sebastian had said, laughing fondly at her now. He had proposed endlessly since they had first met at uni- versity but Tessa had taken her time in accepting him. She had waved his objection away with a flick of her hand. 'And I don't think it's actually legal to get married in a wood,' he had added. 'Doesn't it have to be in a structure of some sort?'

Tessa had looked crestfallen for a moment but then bounced back. 'We could build a tree-house. I don't know how much it would be but I bet it's cheaper than hiring some posh country-house hotel. And then we could get married in there and then come down the steps afterwards to some wonderful, ethereal music and re-join our guests. And we could be barefoot . . .'

'In a wood?!'

Not all her ideas had worked out but they had gone ahead with the wood and she had been barefoot, stepping lightly on a green carpet that they laid in lieu of an aisle. And she had found a harpist to play and Rosie and Ellie had been bridesmaids with little wings sewn into the backs of their dresses. At ten and seven, Miriam had said they were too old for that kind of nonsense but when the girls had seen their gauzy golden frocks they hadn't objected. They'd been ready to do whatever Tessa asked. That was what Tessa had been like. Everyone had wanted a piece of her, for her to turn her attention on to them so that they could bask in the golden light that shone from her.

Everyone except his sisters. Miriam had thought she was silly and frivolous, that she spent Sebastian's money too freely without ever seeming to make any financial contribution herself. Anna had been stiff and cold with Tess, even when Tess had made an effort to try to win her round. The two of them had been as bad as each other, Sebastian thought, each circling around but refusing to commit to a proper relationship for fear of losing face. The fundamental problem had been that they were too alike but Sebastian would never have told them that. 'Don't worry about it,' he'd said to Tessa when yet another meeting had gone awry. 'I think she's just angry that you've taken me away from her.'

He hadn't really thought about it when he made the comment but looking back afterwards he wondered whether he had hit the nail on the head. He and Anna had always been a gang and now he had Tess instead. Or as well. That was how he saw it.

And then there was Clare; Clare who disappeared for months on end, Clare who forgot the boys' birthdays and sometimes even that the boys had been born at all, Clare who had been so far down the neck of a bottle that she had missed Tessa's funeral. When the hideous accident had stolen his beautiful bride and the mother of his handsome boys, where was his sister? Finding herself in the Shetland Islands, living on a croft and drinking whisky.

'That's not a good enough reason, Seb,' Tessa whispered in his ear. 'You can't abandon your sister because you think she abandoned you. If she takes the test and you have different blood she will still be your sister.'

Sebastian put his head in his hands.

'Do you know what I hate about you, Tessa Bliss?' he said to the air.

'That I'm always right?' replied the Tessa in his head.

CLARE – 2017

I

She knew it was here somewhere. Through all the lovers, the flat-shares and the rough patches spent on strangers' floors, the box had always stayed with her, like a talisman. Or a dead weight around her neck, depending on how you looked at it. She had lugged it from place to place, never losing connection with it. She had even paid for a left-luggage locker when she set off on that ill-fated trip to India, to make sure that the box and its contents were safe and not exposed to prying eyes.

As far as she knew, no one had ever peeked. She couldn't guarantee it but she was hopeful that no one would be interested in the random ramblings of a middle-aged woman.

The storage cupboard in the hallway was absolutely fine as long as you didn't open the door, which, of course, brought with it a number of problems. Gingerly she pulled the handle down and inched the door towards her. She could feel something giving way and falling into the widening gap. She stepped back and let it clatter to the floor. Ironing board. Why did she have an ironing board, for God's sake? Did she even have an iron?

Once the ironing board was out of the way, it was easier to see the remainder of the cupboard's contents, which were mainly underused cleaning apparatus, screwed-up plastic bags saved because the Green

Gestapo made you feel so bad about throwing anything away these days, and boxes full of stuff she never looked at but couldn't quite get rid of. It was as if holding on to them made her believe that one day she too could have a life like other people, filled with stuff she didn't need stored in cupboards she never opened.

The box was on the floor in the middle and not that difficult to access because it wasn't that long since Clare had last dug it out. As she tried to lift it and wriggle it past everything else that was in the way, she felt her back twinge threateningly. God, how she hated getting old. Once extracted, she carried the box to the lounge and sat it on the coffee table, which still had the remains of her little tea party with Miriam scattered across it. She ditched mugs on to the floor and lifted the box's lid.

At the sight of the notebooks inside, she suddenly felt calmer. Here they all were, her babies, guarding the secrets of her life and keeping them safe from harm. There was no regularity to the books; mostly they were whatever she could lay her hands on at the time. The earlier ones were exercise books filched from unlocked stationery cupboards at school. After that there were one or two black Moleskines. She must have had some money then and ideas of grandeur for her words, but that phase hadn't lasted long. Mostly they were cheap shorthand note-books, the springs at the top all bent out of shape and the paper so thin that you could only reliably write on one side and still read it. Recently, since she'd had her job at the bakery, she had bought herself a pack of three slightly more substantial books filled with graph paper like the French used. Two were still pristine, waiting for her to fill them with her thoughts.

Clare lifted an exercise book from the box reverentially. On the front, in the box usually reserved for Pupil Name, Teacher's Name and Class, she had written 'Clare Bliss. 1980. Private and Confidential. Keep out. That means you Miriam!!!!!' As a matter of fact, Miriam hadn't even known about Clare's books. If she had she would have searched for them endlessly. Recording her life was Clare's secret.

She opened it at a page about two thirds of the way through the book and began to read.

Saturday 15th March

Well, we did it! The earth didn't move or anything but what can you expect? Fireworks to start fizzing everywhere?!! It's a start though and I'm sure that we will improve with practice!! He's much more gentle than S****. It was like he wanted to make sure that I was enjoying it too, which was a first for me. Usually they are in and out so fast that I hardly notice! Nothing to write home about either for all their big talk. God – boys are full of crap sometimes. But with P*** it was different. He's bloody boring though. I said we should nick some cider and take it down the river but he came over all goody-two-shoes on me. Might be good in the you-know-what department but I'm not sure we're going anywhere. I'll hang on for a bit before I bin him though. I can always get my kicks with M ****** and the others when P*** isn't around.

Clare smiled with affection at her younger self. It sounded like she was enjoying herself, at least. She had no idea who these coded references were referring to. You'd think the names would be etched on her memory but they were lost. She flicked forward.

Wednesday 14th May

I hate Anna. She never gets in the shit. It doesn't matter what she does – she always gets away with it. It pisses me off. Tonight she was late back and missed

tea. Did Mum even bat an eye? No she just put Anna's
in the oven to keep warm. If that had been me it would
have been World bloody War 3 but Anna just floats
around taking the piss. It's not fair. She's only 14 for
God's sake. [Clare liked how even in her fury she had
given 'God' a capital G and an apostrophe.] If that had
been me when I was 14 then they'd have locked me
in my bloody bedroom for a week. But no. Princess
Anna gets to do precisely what she bloody well likes.

Clare could tell from the marks that the pen had made across the paper
that she must have been pretty angry when she wrote it. Even now she
could remember how unjust it had seemed that Anna got such special
treatment. At the time she'd been convinced that it was always her
singled out for punishment. Had she been right after all? Were they
harder on her because she didn't quite belong?

She picked another book out at random. 1995. The Dicken years.
A wry smile fluttered across her lips. God bless Dicken. He'd tried so
hard with her. He'd been so kind and forgiving and for a while there
Clare had truly believed that she had at least a few redeeming features.
In the end, though, she had driven him away like she did with everyone.
He'd even been good with River, for God's sake. He'd been a keeper. She
should have seen that at the time.

She flicked the cover but didn't open the notebook. She usually
enjoyed engaging with the Clare of days gone by so she could make
believe, if just for a moment or two, that the ensuing years hadn't been
squandered. But reliving all this old stuff would get her nowhere now.
All those decades spent chasing round after that elusive something.
God knows what it was. She never caught it. She barely even spotted
it. It was always just out of sight, a shadow turning a corner a few paces
ahead of her. If things had turned out differently . . . well, who knew
how her life might have been.

She should have been a journalist like her dad. Like Frank, she meant. (This not-knowing business didn't half make life complicated.) Frank had loved words. They had dripped from his lips like honey from a spoon. Often he'd spoken as if he were on a stage, his words a performance rather than merely a means of communicating his thoughts. When any of their friends had come to the house, they had always been drawn to him, pulling up front row seats for whatever was coming next. Of course, Frank had liked a drink too. That's what journalists did back then: sat in smoke-stained rooms drinking whisky and comparing stories, competing as to who had netted the biggest fish. No wonder she liked a diary and a drink, she thought. Like father, like daughter. And then she remembered that maybe Frank wasn't the father she'd always believed him to be and she felt sick.

Shit. She needed a drink. How was she supposed to deal with this new, fiendish turn of fate sober? Frank. StJohn. What the fuck did she care? Neither of them had turned out to be much use to her. She had careered down the wrong rabbit holes all by herself.

Bloody stupid to dig the box out too. It always made her miserable. The fondness for her younger self soon festered into loathing when she remembered the reality and that invariably sent her in search of a drink. There was nothing in the flat, though. Miriam had seen to that. Clare had pretended not to notice when her sister had discreetly poured what was left of her wine down the sink. She hadn't objected. The recent relapses had been a response to the shock, nothing more. Now, though, she could barely believe she had been dry for so long. That wasn't her. Clare Bliss who was incapable of doing or creating anything positive. She wasn't sure why she'd ever thought she deserved a fresh start here, why it would be different.

When these thoughts settled on her darkening mind, Clare knew how she was supposed to banish them. All those AA meetings had equipped her with the necessary strategies for seeing off her demons. She closed her eyes, took a deep breath. She'd got this. She would put the box away before anyone appeared. (Since she'd got the letter, there seemed to have been a plethora of unexpected guests.) Then she would tidy the flat and she could decide what to do after that.

The front door banged. For fuck's sake. Could they not leave her alone? She'd had more than enough sibling concern. But none of them had a key. That meant that this could only be . . .

'Hi, Mother,' said River.

II

Clare took in her son. He looked like he had just stepped off a shoot for Hugo Boss in his sharply creased chinos, a crisp shirt open at the neck and a jacket that looked as if it had cost more than she would earn in a year at the bakery. He was a handsome man, if she did say so herself, and the fine lines that had started to appear after he'd turned thirty last year just added to the overall effect. She had always thought his eyes had that same guarded quality as hers, though, perpetually on the lookout for trouble.

'You're not still writing those diaries?' he asked her. He was smiling but Clare recognised the mocking base notes in his voice. He had no time for reminiscing. 'You're moving forwards,' he always said, 'so why keep looking behind you?'

Clare started to pack the notebooks back into the box, anxious that what was written inside them should not be open to River's scrutiny. He had probably helped himself to them over the years. She supposed it was naive to think that he'd never looked, but there was no point in giving him an open invitation.

'Any chance of any dinner?' he asked, looking doubtfully towards the kitchen.

Clare knew that there was nothing to eat barring half a tin of baked beans and some eggs. The shop had been next on her to-do list. If she told River this, though, he would just assume that she had been too badly organised to feed herself. That might have been true in the past – River had had more than his fair share of meals cobbled together from whatever could be scavenged – but no more. This time Clare had run out of food in the way that ordinary people ran out of food – simply because she hadn't got round to buying any yet. Of course, River wouldn't believe that.

'Not unless you're planning on taking me out,' she said, meeting his eye defiantly.

She saw his nose turn up as he cast his eye around the flat and she felt her spine stiffen. One of the things about not drinking was that it heightened her awareness of other people's responses to her and it hurt. Sometimes it was almost enough to send her back to where she'd been, to that delicious oblivion that it created.

'Okay,' he said. 'Where? I'm not going to that bloody horrible pub.'

'There's a pizza place on the high street, if that suits.' She wanted to make some snotty comment about it matching his high standards but she held back.

'That'll do.' He looked her up and down, taking in her tired hoodie-and-jeans ensemble.

'I'll just get changed,' she said before he had a chance to suggest it. Picking up the box, she carried it into the bedroom, tucked it behind the bed where it couldn't be seen from the door and opened her wardrobe. The laundrette was another job on her list but her better jeans weren't too bad and her blue top was clean. That would have to do. It was only River and, despite his fancy clothes and all his airs and graces, they both knew where he'd come from.

When had River started making her feel so inadequate? Maybe he always had and she hadn't been switched on enough to notice? There must have been a time when he respected her. She was his mother, after all. And she was proud of him. He had done so well, you just had to look at him to see, despite the shaky start that she had provided, or possibly because of it. River had probably taken one look at the mess she'd made of her life and decided that he would do things differently. He didn't have to make it quite so obvious that he was peering down at her, though.

She pulled a comb through her hair, trying to tease some volume into it, but without a great deal of success. A little bit of red lipstick completed the look. What was it Coco Chanel had said? 'If you're sad, add more lipstick, and attack.' Well, she wasn't sad right now but it wouldn't hurt to be prepared.

When she went back into the lounge River hadn't even risked sitting down.

'Right. Shall we go?' she said, heading straight for the door as if it had been him who had kept her waiting and not the other way around.

The restaurant, Giovanni's, was stuck firmly in the twentieth century. The walls were panelled in wood stained dark by a rich patina made up of thousands of olive-oiled fingerprints. Yellowing photographs of fifties film stars hung at jaunty angles, illegible signatures scrawled across their faces. The tables were covered in red cloths and paper napkins sprouted from the wine glasses.

'You have a booking?' asked Giovanni or someone masquerading as him when they approached the desk. Clare shook her head.

'No matter, no matter,' the Italian said, and showed them to a booth in the far corner.

They sat and as he lit the candle Giovanni eyed them knowingly, like he had the measure of this relationship between an exhausted-looking middle-aged woman and this beautiful young man. 'He's my son, for God's sake,' Clare wanted to shout, but part of her was amused by what she suspected was going through the other man's mind.

'So, how's work?' she asked when they had ordered. She didn't really understand what River did as a job – what parent did? Something in computers, she thought, but whenever she'd asked him about it she hadn't listened properly to his answer. He ignored the question.

'I saw the letter,' he said.

Ha! She'd known it was him who had nicked it. She raised her eyebrow at him.

'That letter was private,' she replied.

'Shouldn't have left it lying around for anyone to read, then,' he said. 'So Grandpa Frank wasn't actually Grandpa after all.'

Clare felt stung. 'Of course he was. He was my father, whatever else might have happened. I don't care who this Downing bloke was to Mum. It doesn't change a thing.'

'But it does, though, doesn't it?' said River, opening a paper packet of breadsticks, sniffing the contents and then putting it back into the bread basket. 'There's this money that he seems desperate to leave you for a start.'

That was River all over. Straight to the point. No messing. She'd give him three seconds before he—

'How much is it, anyway?'

Bingo.

'Oh, not much,' she said without looking at him. 'They did say but I can't quite remember.'

Who did she think she was trying to kid? Honestly, she sounded like Dorothy.

River didn't even challenge her. He just stared at her, eyebrows raised until she was forced to reply.

'One point two million,' she said under her breath. River whistled. 'But there's tax and shit to take off that. I won't actually get anywhere near that much. A bit over half, I think. Well, if I did the test and he turned out to be my father, that is.'

River sat back in his chair and considered her through narrowed eyes.

'But you are going to take the test?' he said. 'I mean, why wouldn't you, not when there's all that money up for grabs.'

Clare picked up the breadsticks that River had rejected and pulled one out, breaking off the end and putting it into her mouth. It was soft.

'I haven't decided yet,' she said. 'I'm still thinking about what to do.'

She hadn't realised until this moment that she still hadn't decided.

'But, Mum, it's a no-brainer. You take the test. If you're not related then who cares, and if you are then it's jackpot time.'

And was it that simple? Could she take the test and use the result simply to get her hands on the cash? Certainly the Clare of yesteryear would have done. When she was River's age she might have gone straight from the solicitor's office to the testing centre without giving it a second thought. But now . . .?

'I'm not sure I want to know,' she said quietly. 'If Dad wasn't my dad, I mean. If the others are only half-brothers and sisters.'

'There's no point worrying about those idiots,' interrupted River. 'What the hell have they ever done for us other than taking the moral high ground and looking down on us.'

This wasn't true. Clare knew exactly how much they had all done for her and River and had continued to do even when she had made things impossible for them. They had stood behind her, if not quite shoulder to shoulder then certainly with a bucket and a blanket. River didn't know how hard they'd tried to help over the years, but she did.

'Don't say that,' she said. 'Miriam and the others have been brilliant. They've looked out for me all my life, even when I made theirs hell.'

River scoffed. 'That's not how it looked from where I was sitting,' he said. 'Yes, they said all the right things, sent a bit of cash from time to time, but did any of them ever actually give us a roof over our heads? When we were crashing from hostel to B&B and back again, did any of them ever actually do anything that would help? Did they hell.'

Clare could understand how River thought this. They had never moved in with any of her family other than for the odd night here and there, but River didn't know how many times they had offered a permanent home and how many times Clare had rejected them, generally with an insult and very little grace. She was ashamed of how she had behaved, how she had thrown their offers of help straight back at them. And taking this test, wouldn't that be the final kick in the teeth? It would be like saying that she didn't want to be part of their gang, that a windfall meant more to her than all the past fifty years. And really, truly, it didn't.

Anna had said it didn't matter what the results were, that nothing would change, but of course it would. If it turned out that they didn't have the same father, then surely the sense of sibling responsibility that had made them do all that stuff would take a bit of a knock. None of that was her fault, of course, but she wasn't sure she could live with it. When she had stopped drinking and managed to stay dry (apart from the wobble after the solicitors), she had begun to see things differently. She really wasn't sure that she should go delving around in the past, especially when she might not be able to deal with what she found. And no amount of money was worth sending her back into the hell that she'd just got out of. Suddenly, and with a clarity that was totally alien to her, Clare knew exactly what she would do.

'This is nothing to do with you, River,' she said, looking him straight in the eye. 'It's my decision and I'm not going to take the test.'

River sat forward in his chair so fast that it made her jump and she felt herself pulling away from him. 'Like hell it is,' he hissed. 'It might have escaped your notice, but I am your son and I'm already pretty lacking in the relations department, you never being entirely sure who my father is and all that. So, if this means that I might actually not be as closely hitched to the few relations that I thought I had then I have a right to know. Are you even my mother? At this rate I'm going to end up with no family whatsoever.'

Just for a moment, the defensive, secretive boy that he had once been, that she had created, stared out at her fearfully, but then the adult River was back, with that confident, unemotional persona that he had built for himself without her help.

'Don't be ridiculous,' she said, shaking her head at him. 'You know that I'm your mother. And your father? Well, there's not much we can do about that. But the others – they are part of you whether you like it or not and I'm not about to stab them in the back for some stupid little inheritance.'

'One point two million pounds is not some stupid little inheritance,' said River. He was almost shouting now and people turned to look at them. 'Think what you could do with that money. You could buy a house for a start and then you wouldn't have to worry about renting some council shithole among all the other losers and dropouts.'

'What's wrong with my flat? I like it,' Clare said defensively as the image of the girl next door and her incessant noise bounced up and down in her mind's eye.

'And you could invest some in me, in my business. Yes, I'm doing great by myself, but think what I could do with some real money behind me. And all you have to do is take a bloody DNA test. I mean, for God's sake, Mum! How hard can it be?'

The waiter arrived with the pizzas and, sensing the tension, put them down and retreated without even brandishing his ludicrous black pepper mill.

'I'm sorry but I'm not taking that test,' Clare said. She surprised herself at how calmly her voice came out, how calm she felt. 'I know that it's a lot of money and that it might be useful but some things are just more important.'

Had she really just said that? Clare Bliss, wastrel, drunkard and general waste of space, was rejecting the possibility of a massive wad of cash for the greater good. Somewhere deep inside her, a tiny little drum was beating proudly. She'd got this. For once in her troubled existence she had made a decision based on more than what was right in front of her nose and she was doing the right thing. It felt good.

It felt so good that when River stood up and stormed out of the restaurant she still knew she was right and she even managed a little smile.

ANNA – 2017

I

'She's only gone and taken the test!' Miriam shouted down the phone at Anna. Anna held the handset a little bit further from her ear. 'After everything she said. All that rubbish about family being more important than cash. It obviously meant absolutely nothing to her. I don't know why I expected anything different, really. I mean, leopards and spots and all that.'

Anna was struggling to find a response. 'Are you sure?' was the best she could do. She'd been certain that Clare would ignore StJohn Downing's proposal. Actually, that wasn't completely true. She couldn't have called it either way when Clare first found out about the terms of StJohn Downing's will, but there was something different about Clare now, an easiness, a sense of certainty. Clare was still unpredictable but it was like things had fallen into place for her and she knew who she was supposed to be. The flat, the job, all of it.

'Do you know, I used to dream that I was adopted,' Clare had said when the two of them had last spoken a couple of days earlier. 'I know everyone does that, builds up stupid little fantasies that they don't belong where they've ended up. I was certain, though. Do you remember when Dad broke that story about those boys who got muddled up at the hospital?'

Anna hadn't but she'd nodded anyway, not wanting to break Clare's flow. It was so rare, this intimacy. Anna hadn't wanted to waste a second of it.

'Well, that was what had obviously happened to me. In my head, anyway. I even got as far as the bloody hospital to ask them. Fuck knows what I'd have said. Was there another girl born the same day as me? Could I have her address so I could check out her family, see if it's any better than mine?'

They had been walking along the towpath by the canal. When they'd been kids, this place had been out of bounds, too derelict, too dangerous. Now it had been cleared up with some environmental grant or other and the most dangerous thing likely to happen was getting knocked into the water by a passing runner. Anna had kept an eye on where she was putting her feet, just in case.

'I invented myself a whole bloody life,' Clare had continued, and Anna had felt her heart hurt both for the pain that Clare must have felt when they were growing up and for the fact that until now she'd never even noticed. 'It was perfect: the life I would have had if they hadn't sent me to the wrong bloody house.'

Clare had made a noise: a laugh, a sigh, Anna hadn't been sure.

'What was it like?' she'd asked, not really wanting to hear about her sister's fantasy life away from the rest of them but desperate to hang on to this new, open Clare for as long as she could. Clare had shrugged.

'Christ, I can't remember. Some bollocks. And now look at me with my dodgy genes. I might not have been that far off the mark.'

Clare had winked at Anna but she'd looked so hurt, so deeply crushed, that Anna had wanted to grab her sister and just hold her tight. Clare, however, must have seen something in her expression. Anna had hoped it wasn't pity but whatever it was, Clare had pulled down the shutters and the moment was gone.

'Anyway,' Clare had continued as if nothing had been said, 'I've decided. I'm not taking the fucking test.'

And that had been that. Discussion over. Anna supposed it was possible that she might have changed her mind again, must have done if what Miriam was saying was true. Swapping and changing was Clare all over, after all, and Anna shouldn't really be surprised by a change of heart, but she was.

'Of course I'm sure.' Miriam was now shouting down the phone. 'Like I'd make something like that up.'

The full implications of what Miriam was telling her started to dawn on Anna. If the test was positive, what would that mean for her? She found herself testing the two options in her mind to see how she might react to either. Did she fall in the Sebastian camp or the Miriam one? Should a diluting of their shared genes make a difference? No, and yet . . .

'And?' she asked.

'And what?' Miriam sounded tetchy and irritated and Anna wondered if she was trying to do two things at once.

'And what were the results?'

'Oh! Well, I don't know that. She's still waiting, apparently. It takes a few days to get them back from whichever lab they've gone to.'

All was not lost yet, then. There was still a chance that the result would be negative and they could go back to how they'd been before all this happened. Except, of course, the burden of her secret would be lifted. A negative test result would mean that their mother had had no need to worry, there needn't have been a letter to hide and the last few years of crippling guilt could have been avoided. Marvellous. And, of course, there would be the small matter of knowing that Clare had been happy to abandon her family in favour of cash.

'Did you go and see her at the flat?' asked Anna. 'Was she okay? No sign of any more drinking?'

Anna was surprised to feel her fingers crossing themselves unbidden.

'What?' said Miriam, clearly still distracted by something else. 'Just put it in that corner out of the way,' she added to whoever was distracting her. 'No. I haven't been back to the flat since that night we went. I bumped into River in town. He told me.'

Ah. River. Anna hadn't seen her nephew for a while but if he'd been around then it must only have been to see Clare. He rarely came back these days. Her mind skittered back to the self-contained boy that had come to stay with her all those years ago. Even then he'd been shaping his own way in life, knowing that if he didn't he'd probably end up following his mother into that black abyss where she'd spent such a lot of her time. And it had worked for him. He'd made a good life for himself but he'd done it by focusing entirely on himself and his own needs. Still, who could blame him, really?

'Listen,' said Miriam. 'It's all happening here. New tiles being delivered. It's a nightmare. I have to go. I'll ring again soon. Can you check in with Clare? Have you got time? I'd do it myself but . . . No! Those are the wrong size. For God's sake! Did no one read the order form? I've got to go, Anna . . .'

And with that Miriam abruptly cut the line. Anna yanked open the fridge door and, grabbing a bottle, she unscrewed the lid and poured herself a large glass of wine. She was cross. She'd believed Clare this time, had had faith in her, and yet again she'd been let down. She should have known better. Miriam was right. Clare was just Clare. She'd never given two hoots for the rest of them. She had done precisely as she pleased her whole life. Anna had been naive to think that anything would change now. The chance to get her hands on all that cash was clearly too tempting and Clare wouldn't care what she had to go through to get there.

Anna knocked the wine back and poured herself a second glass.

CLARE – 2017

I

Was she too old to take up exercise, Clare wondered? Her running days were definitely behind her but she was pretty sure she could still manage something. She wasn't that bloody old! The girls that she worked with did a spin class and made it sound, if not fun exactly then at least effective. There must be one nearby. She'd ask them where they went. Maybe she could even tag along one night.

In her brave new post-drinking world she had masses more energy than she'd had when her body was constantly trying to filter out the toxins that she kept pouring in. An exercise regime? Clare Bliss worrying about her fitness levels? She rolled her eyes. Oh my God! She'd be having her nails done next! Her jeans were getting a bit tight, though. That's what came of working in a bakery and consuming her calories in solid form. Life, it seemed, was just one denial after another.

Clare did feel healthier, though. She liked this new leaf. It kept changing colour, getting brighter and brighter. As she packed bags of burger buns into boxes ready to go out she felt positively cheerful. She tried a little whistle to express her new status as a happy person but it came out shrill and tuneless and so she stopped. Maybe she could have a party? Nothing big, just the family. She'd never had the space before but now she had the flat. She could get some crisps and stuff, some pop for the kids, no alcohol of course but the others wouldn't mind that, not for one night. They'd be driving, anyway. It would be great to do something nice for them for a change.

Yes, she could have sausage rolls and maybe get some frozen party food to heat up. By the time her shift ended, Clare so was so full of ideas that she felt like she might actually float down the street. Her phone vibrated in her pocket and she pulled it out. Anna.

'Hi. Listen, Anna, I've had a great idea. What about a party at mine . . .?'

'You think that's a good idea, do you?' Anna's tone was sharp but her words weren't. Was she drunk? 'Turn your back on us all and then invite us round for a little get-together on the proceeds. Great plan, Clare. Fucking brilliant.'

She was drunk. Anna never used the F-word sober. Clare was immediately unbalanced, her good mood of moments before evaporated and her heart snapped back shut like a Venus flytrap.

'Chill, will you, for God's sake. It was just a thought. And you don't have to come if you think it's such a crap idea. I can have the fucking party without you.'

Clare cut the call, her heart racing. Who did she think she was? Princess bloody Anna with her superiority complex and her 'you're a walking car crash' attitude. Well, she could get lost. Clare didn't need her. She didn't need any of them. She'd spent her whole life doing things by herself, making her own decisions, and nothing was going to change that. They could go to hell, the lot of them. She'd move away, get a new flat, a better job. She'd show them, the sanctimonious bastards. This was the start of something fantastic for her.

But even as these thoughts crossed her mind she knew it wasn't true. Yes, she was holding things together for now, but she was hanging on by a thread. It had only taken the reading of that letter from StJohn bloody Downing to send her spiralling off course. Move away and start again. Who was she kidding?

She let herself into the flat. Flyers for pizza delivery places and Indian takeaways sat on the floor. She would normally have just left them there but that was the old Clare. This new, improved Clare picked up junk mail and threw it away. She bent down and gathered them up. Underneath was a letter. It was in a white envelope so nothing from the state. It was addressed to her. In the top left-hand corner there was a logo in green lettering. 'Lancaster Laboratories' underlined with two spiralling lines that looked a lot like a rollercoaster track.

Confused, she looked at the envelope again but there was no doubt what it was. This was obviously a letter from the DNA lab but why would they be writing to her? She hadn't contacted them, let alone sent them a sample, so they wouldn't even know who she was.

It took her less than ten seconds to work it out. The lab had clearly tested someone's DNA and if it wasn't hers then that left only one person who could possibly prove a link between her and StJohn Downing. River.

Fury grabbed hold of her and shook her. How dare he? How bloody dare he?! He knew she'd decided not to take the test. They had talked about it, she had explained how she felt, made it perfectly clear. And yet, despite all that, he had totally ignored her wishes and gone ahead anyway. Clare's jaw tightened as she thought it through. He must have sent the sample in pretending it was hers. Maybe he'd even taken something from her. She thought of all those police dramas. A glass with her saliva on the rim, a hair stolen from her hairbrush. The little shit.

But he couldn't get the lab to reply to him. It was one thing providing the sample pretending to be her but another getting the actual results. It was her details that the solicitor had. The letter was always going to come here. So what was his plan? To sneak in when she was at work and pick it up without her knowing? But he couldn't get his hands on the money. It was left to her, not him. So he must be planning to tell her what he'd done at some point. Maybe he was going to get the result and then present it to her as a fait accompli. No point not claiming the money now, Mum, when the test's already done. Was that his plan?

She'd fucking kill him. She'd throttle him and then chop his body up into little pieces and feed it to the street dogs. Clare took her shoe off and threw it at the wall and then threw the other after it. She screamed her frustration out into the stale air of her flat and it felt good so she did it again.

But then she took the envelope and sat on the sofa staring at it. So now what? Suddenly, she could feel how thin the veneer of resolve that she had wrapped herself in really was. She could scratch it off with her fingernail and it would just be the old Clare underneath. Because despite it all, the flat and the job and the sobriety, she would never amount to anything. She had been a waster all her life and in this envelope was the reason why, the explanation, everything that they had all known but never said out loud. The thing about Clare was that she just didn't belong.

She dropped the envelope on the floor and wept.

II

She must have fallen asleep because when she woke up it was dark and the streetlight outside her window glowed orange though the glass. It took her a moment to remember that she hadn't been drinking. She moved her head delicately but there was no pain or sickness. Yes, she was lying on the floor in her flat, but there were no bottles surrounding her.

Then she remembered. The letter was still where she'd left it, unopened. With shaking hands she picked it up and with one decisive movement slit the top of the envelope with her finger. Then she pulled the letter out and opened it slowly. Her eyes ran up and down the words without taking anything in. Her breath wouldn't come. It stuck in her throat as her heart pounded in her ears. She swallowed and tried to control her breathing, remembering the techniques that she'd learned in India all those decades ago. Then she forced her brain to concentrate on the words.

> We have now completed our calculation of the probability of paternity as requested. Based on an analysis of fifteen independent autosomal DNA factors Mr StJohn Downing has been excluded as the biological father of Ms Clare Bliss.

She read the sentence again and then the full letter. The words swam round in her head and it took three readings before she was sure that she understood. StJohn Downing was not her father. That's what it was saying, wasn't it? Her father was her father and her siblings were her siblings and all the horrible confusion thrown up by StJohn Downing meant nothing.

Clare took a moment to register what she was feeling but she couldn't quite pin it down. What was it? Relief? Joy? Something altogether less straightforward? Yes, the situation was as they had always believed it to be but so many questions would have been answered if it she had had a different father, had originated from a different gene pool. It might have given her the excuse that she needed for the disaster that she had made of her life so far. She would have been able to say that she was so different, so much less successful than the others, because she had been dealt a different card. Maybe a part of her had been hoping for exactly that scenario?

But that presupposed that Downing had passed on genes that had influenced her lifestyle choices, forced her to turn down the wrong alleys. Nature not nurture, was that what she was claiming? That none of the decisions that she had made had been her fault, that she had been genetically predestined to fuck everything up. Yet from everything Anna had told her, it sounded like this StJohn Downing was a perfectly decent bloke. Even if he had been her father, he wouldn't have been responsible for the litany of mistakes that trailed after her. No. Sooner or later Clare was going to have to accept that the only person responsible for how things had worked out was her. She had screwed her life up all on her own.

Clare heard a key being slid into the lock, the front door opening and then her son stood in the doorway, his shape silhouetted by the light in the hallway.

'It's negative,' said Clare without introduction.

'Shame,' he said. 'Worth a try, though, eh, Mother?'

Then he turned and let himself out of the flat.

She couldn't blame him, not really. He was just looking out for himself, for them, in the only way he knew how. It wasn't just herself that she'd damaged through her mistakes.

Clare looked at the letter one more time, just to be sure. She should let them know. They would want to know, wouldn't they? Then again, they didn't know that River had sent the sample off. She could keep it to herself, another secret. But she knew she wouldn't. She wanted to share it with them, her siblings. She rang Miriam's number.

ANNA – 2017

I

Anna drew a line in Mulberry Magic around her lips. She'd started to notice that if she didn't use a lip liner the overall effect was less convincing. It didn't seem fair but there were lots of things about getting older that she wasn't keen on. This was just the latest in a long line.

She stood back from the mirror and took in her appearance. Not bad, she supposed, for a woman the wrong side of fifty, and anyway, it would have to do. The taxi taking her to the restaurant would be here in a couple of minutes. It had been a while since the four of them had been out together without partners and children in tow. This particular evening had been Miriam's idea. A celebration of their life so far and of bringing Clare back into the fold. Not that she'd left the fold for long. In fact, if it hadn't been for Sebastian's little outburst, nothing would really have changed and Clare didn't even know about that.

Miriam was already sitting at their table when Anna arrived. Of course she was. She just couldn't help herself. Never late for anything, her self-imposed standard of excellence.

'I've ordered some poppadums and a tray of pickles,' she said as Anna sat down. 'And a jug of mango lassi,' she added with eyebrows raised.

Anna would have sold a sibling for a beer to go with her curry but Miriam, as always, was right to avoid it.

The other two arrived shortly afterwards. Was Sebastian looking slightly sheepish or was Anna imagining it? Clare definitely looked much better. Maybe this time she really would sort herself out. Anna wasn't going to hold her breath, though.

They ordered food, all declaring that lassi was exactly what they fancied and wasn't Miriam clever for thinking of it. They chatted and bickered and argued their way through the meal like they were still teenagers. It didn't matter how old they were. The dynamics between them were set into the very workings of the universe itself. Nothing would ever change that. It was solid, a certainty, a given.

It wasn't until they were scraping round the bowls with the remains of the chapattis that the subject of Clare's paternity finally came up.

'It wouldn't have made a difference, you know,' said Miriam as she wiped her mouth with her napkin.

Sebastian busied himself with the remains of his rice and didn't meet anyone's eye. Anna held her breath. Not this. Not now, when everything was going so smoothly.

Clare looked at Miriam and shook her head.

'For fuck's sake, Miriam,' she said. 'You talk some shite. Of course it fucking would. I'd have been loaded for a start.'

Miriam was about to reply when she saw the twinkle in Clare's eye. That was the thing about Clare. You never knew what she'd do next.

ACKNOWLEDGMENTS

The Thing About Clare began life as a short story and was then a stage play before it grew into a novel. Having four children of my own, I have always been fascinated by the relationships between siblings, especially as I only have a brother myself. The dynamics and loyalties amongst my four are constantly shifting and they often seem to be part of a secret gang that no one else can join. From time to time they fight, of course, but when the chips are down they forget their differences and all pull together against the common foe.

Whilst researching for the book I read a surprising article which claimed that over seventy per cent of mothers would admit to having a favourite amongst their children. I really don't think that I do but this made me wonder what it might feel like to know that you were the favourite child and how that would look to your siblings. This led me neatly into the nature versus nurture chestnut and before I knew it I had the makings of a novel. I must say, though, that the personalities of the Bliss children bear absolutely no resemblance to my actual children and that child number three is not my favourite!

I would like to thank Victoria Pepe at Amazon Publishing for sharing my vision for the book so completely, and to Celine Kelly for helping me get there.

READING GROUP QUESTIONS

Do you think parents really do have favourites? If so, how might that affect the lives of the children as adults?

Miriam has to give up on her dreams to support her family. Was it fair of Dorothy to expect her to do that?

By asking for the letter to Clare to be destroyed, Dorothy is choosing to take her secret to her grave. Do you think that was the right thing to do?

Sebastian responds differently from his sisters to the news about Clare's paternity. Do you have any sympathy with his point of view?

Anna chooses to keep her mother's secret even though it causes trouble with her siblings. What would you have done?

Questions of nature versus nurture crop up throughout the book. How much do you think our upbringing rather than our genes shapes who we become?